Praise for the works of Catherine Maiorisi

Blood of the Innocents

Catherine Maiorisi knows how to write a police procedural. Her intricately woven plots captivate audiences, leaving them nearly hanging off the edge of their seats. Her storylines are more than simple whodunits. They're gripping narratives that explore deeper societal issues, making them relevant and relatable. *Blood of the Innocents* is an excellent example of this. Maiorisi crafts the story around the topic of transgender visibility and acceptance, making it not only compelling but timely.

-*Women Using Words*

Love Among the Ruins

Maiorisi intertwines Callie's personal healing with the exploration of a new place, with a wonderful cast of characters who add depth to the overall narrative. It's an authentic story about loss, healing, vulnerability, and love. It shows the resilience of the human spirit in the most breathtaking and heartfelt ways. I highly recommend grabbing a copy and immersing yourself in Callie and Dana's journey.

-Audiobook Review, *The Lesbian Review*

Legacy in the Blood

Some people are just born to write mystery stories and I believe that Maiorisi is one of those people. Whether it is another Chiara Corelli Mystery book, or the start to a new mystery series, I just hope Maiorisi keeps writing mysteries. We don't have a lot of current sapphic mystery writers and Maiorisi is a great one. If you are a mystery fan, I would highly recommend this whole series. If you are a fan of this series, you will not want to miss this 4th book that was through the POV of P.J. Parker, Chiara's detective partner. It was great to have P.J. star in her own book and I hope we get more of her POV in the future.

-Lex Kent's Reviews, *goodreads*

A Message in Blood

This is a dark and intense book that shows some of the worst sides of humanity—but it also shows good winning over evil. The characters feel real, and the mystery is filled with twists and turns—I never saw the end coming. If you enjoy a well-written dark mystery, I would recommend checking out *A Message in Blood*.

-KRL News & Reviews

Matters of the Heart

I'm a sucker for a slow-burning romance, and this one nicely hit that spot. As is made clear in the introduction, it's Maiorisi's first attempt at a full-length romance—previously she has been known for murder mysteries. If she wants to continue in this genre, she's off to a great start.

-Rainbow Book Reviews

A Matter of Blood

This is an excellent mystery and whodunit... I literally can't wait for the next one to see where Ms. Maiorisi takes us with both the crime-fighting team and the prospective romance.

-Lesbian Reading Room

The Blood Runs Cold

Love page-turner thrillers? Pick these books up—then try to keep up with Chiara. It'll be a breathtaking ride.

-Kings River Life Magazine

The Disappearance of Lindy James

This is not your typical Catherine Maiorisi book. The writing is solid with exceptional moments when describing the inner workings of Lindy's mind as she loses touch with reality. The storyline is intensely interesting as Quincy and Lindy's lives diverge...I could not put this book down.

-Della B., NetGalley

Behind the Veil

Other Bella Books by Catherine Maiorisi

The Disappearance of Lindy James
Matters of the Heart
No One But You
Ready for Love
Taking a Chance on Love
Love Among the Ruins

The Chiara Corelli Mystery Series
A Matter of Blood
A Message in Blood
The Blood Runs Cold
Legacy in the Blood
Blood of the Innocents

About the Author

Catherine Maiorisi lives in New York City with her wife, Sherry. Catherine is passionate about writing. And when she's not writing she's reading or cooking. Italian is her favorite but she's always on the lookout for good recipes in any cuisine.

Behind the Veil is Catherine's sixth romance. Her other romances are *Matters of the Heart, No One But You, Ready for Love, Taking a Chance on Love, and Love Among the Ruins,* winner of the 2024 Goldie for Best Romance: Long.

Catherine is also the author of the NYPD Detective Chiara Corelli Mystery series—*A Matter of Blood* (2019 Lambda Literary Award Finalist), *The Blood Runs Cold* (2020 Goldie and Lambda Literary Award Finalist), *A Message in Blood, Legacy in the Blood,* and *Blood of the Innocents.*

The Disappearance of Lindy James, Catherine's first general fiction book, won the 2022 Goldie for Best General Fiction.

Catherine also writes mystery and romance short stories.

She is a member of Sisters in Crime, Mystery Writers of America, and The Author's Guild.

Behind the Veil

Catherine Maiorisi

BELLA
BOOKS

Bella Books, Inc.
P.O. Box 10543
Tallahassee, FL 32302

First Edition - 2026

Editor: Medora MacDougall
Cover Designer: SJ Hardy

ISBN: 978-1-64247-705-4

Acknowledgements

Writing a book is a solitary undertaking. But the truth is, without the wonderful support team behind me, you wouldn't be holding this copy of *Behind the Veil*.

To Sherry, my wife, my first reader, and my biggest cheerleader, in ways big and small, you give me the gift of time to write. Thank you.

To Medora MacDougall, my editor, your wonderful insights, gentle encouragement, fast turnaround, and multiple readings, help me produce the best story I can. You are a dream to work with. *Behind the Veil* is a better book because of you. And I thank you.

To Jessica and Linda Hill and all the amazing women at Bella Books, it's a pleasure to work with you. Thank you for all you do.

To my readers, thank you for buying my books. I hope you enjoy *Behind the Veil* and will take the time to review it and recommend it to your friends and on social media.

CHAPTER ONE

Ariana

December 2022

"Ariana, Ariana, Ariana," the crowd chants. Wrapped in the love, overwhelmed by the roar, and brimming with adrenaline-spiked energy, I bow from the waist for the twentieth time and wave my arm to include the band. I fucking love these people. All seventy-two thousand of them. As I did the previous nineteen times, I speak the words in my heart into the microphone.

"Thank you, Houston. I love you." I swipe at the sweat dripping into my eyes and bow again, then raise my hands asking for silence. "Thank you, Houston, I love you all so much." I repeat it until the crowd quiets. I stand, arms spread wide. "What a wonderful ending to our gloriously successful six-month world tour. We"—I gesture to my bandmates—"are truly grateful for all the love and support we've received from you and fans all over the world. As you know, this is our last concert for a while and we're looking forward to three months of rest and then some time in the recording studio. We've earned it, don't you think?"

The crowd roars again. I truly love them. I love connecting with them through the music. Touring for so long in so many countries has been exhausting, but we've been successful beyond all expectations, and we're all looking forward to winding down after tonight. I raise my arms again and after a few minutes the crowd quiets.

"How about showing some love for Girls Breaking Out, the best band ever, starting with Gloria West on drums." The crowd roars as Gloria does a double stroke roll, stands, raises her arms, then bows. I signal for silence, then one at a time I introduce the others—Maggie Fortuna on keyboard, Nellie Garcia on bass, Erica James on fiddle, and Torie Stella on lead guitar. They each do a signature riff and bow as the crowd roars its appreciation. When the cheering for Torie ends, I throw kisses to the band. "Thank you, my friends. Even after living with you in a bus for months, I still love you all."

I turn back to the crowd. "Our live on-tour album will be dropping in a couple of months so keep your eyes and ears open for it. And now, one last song for all of you here in Houston and our fans all over the world."

Gloria hits the drums. Although we're exhausted, we give one hundred percent as usual. The crowd roars in appreciation. The girls leave their instruments and join me at the front of the stage and, holding hands, the six of us bow again and again. Then we wave to the roaring crowd and run into the wings.

Kim, our manager and my sister and best friend, hands me a towel, and I pull her into our after-performance group hug. "Love you all," we say, one after another. Kim smiles. "You guys were wonderful, giving everything to the very end of your spectacular tour. Go home, have a wonderful Christmas and a happy New Year, rest up, and write. I'll see you all in three months."

Micki, the head of our security team, joins us. "We're leaving from the side exit in twenty."

Normally the band stops to talk to the crowd waiting at the stage entrance to see us off, but we're all too wiped out tonight. Besides I want to avoid Tiffany, the woman I hooked up with last night. I don't hook up frequently and whenever I do, I'm up front about the no-strings, quickie arrangement, but some, like Tiffany, become clingy and want it to mean more.

We break and go gather our belongings. Kim follows me to my dressing room where she's already packed my things. I change out of my wet shirt and bra, then slip into my leather jacket. Kim and I hug. She kisses my forehead. "You were great tonight as usual. Are you sure you don't want to hang out here with me for a couple of days, then drive back to Austin together?"

I squeeze her shoulder. "As much as I'd love some alone time with you, I'm tired and so is my security team. If I stay, they have to stay. We're all ready to be home."

Kim smiles. "Sorry, just being selfish. After you leave, I'll tie things up here, meet with a few people, and go to my hotel downtown."

Arm in arm, Kim and I walk to the side exit so I can make a quick getaway to the van that will take the six of us from the arena to the airport hotel where we'll spend the night and, then, in the morning, catch our various flights. I can't wait to get home. According to Graciela, my cook and caretaker, the house is ready, stocked with everything I requested. I'm looking forward to a good long stretch of downtime there, relaxing, seeing friends, reading, and writing songs. I'll enjoy being alone for the first time in many months, but I have no doubt I'll be happy to see my bandmates in three months when they move into the sprawling guest house I had built on my property for them, their families, and occasional guests. It's always exciting to sift through the songs we've each written, select which to include in the album, and begin rehearsing and recording.

As we head out the door, I'm blinded by a flash. I stumble back into Kim's arms. What the fuck? How the hell did a photographer know we're using the side door? Micki lunges and grabs the photographer. Frankie and Dawn rush to hold her while Micki takes her camera and removes its memory card. "Where's your press pass?"

The photographer glares as Micki pockets the memory card. "You owe me for that."

"You're lucky I'm not having you arrested." She shoves the camera at the young woman, then waves a couple of our other security guards over. "Get her out of here and turn her over to house security. Tell them she was back here without credentials."

"You okay?" Kim asks.

"Yes, just surprised."

She hugs me tight and kisses my forehead. "I'll see you in Austin in a few days."

Micki escorts me to the van where Chioma and Evie, the two guards who will ride to the hotel with the six of us, are waiting with huge grins. "Great concert to end the tour," Evie says. She hugs me. Chioma, the quiet one, nods and high-fives me. I can't help smiling. It's great to be alive, great to be me. I raise my face to the sky, enjoying the splat of the cold December rain against my still warm face.

I turn to the group. "I call dibs on the front seat."

This is my band. Though I am the main attraction, I rarely pull rank but whenever I do, I endure a lot of good-natured teasing. Tonight is no different. "Sure, Your Highness." Nellie punches my shoulder and laughs.

Evie slides the van door open, Chioma gets behind the wheel. Her steady silence will leave me free to gaze at the sky, watch the rain, revel in the love of our fans, and savor the happiness and joy I'm feeling.

I climb into the front passenger seat and fasten my seat belt. We're all high from the concert, nothing else, and the van is filled with laughter and teasing for the first ten minutes, then one by one they drift off to sleep. Right before I drift off, I remember I told Chioma to leave before Kim's assistant brought me my favorite guitar, the one I use at every performance. My last thought before dozing is, Kim will take care of it for me. She always does.

I wake to the sound of blaring horns, screeching brakes, and Chioma cursing as she swerves, trying to avoid the semi headed straight for us. The earlier laughter is replaced by terrified screams. We're helpless. I feel the impact, hear the crunching metal and the shrieks, feel the van being pushed, then turning over and over. My seat belt snaps open and I'm bouncing off the seats and the ceiling, and, oh God, my friends. And then the van begins sliding on its side. The sound of metal screeching on concrete is horrendous but then it's eerily quiet and dark. I can't see anything except the sparks. I shout their names. "Gloria? Maggie? Nellie? Erica? Torie? Chioma? Evie?" No one responds. The pain is incredible. I feel as if every bone in my body is shattered. The stink of gasoline is overwhelming. Then there's a loud *whoosh*. And I'm being burned alive.

CHAPTER TWO

Ariana

January–July 2023

I wake to excruciating pain. I try opening my eyes but it's impossible. I try to sit up, but my arms are tied down and the movement lights a fire in my body. I scream at the burning pain shooting through every nerve. Gasping for breath, I force my body to relax, trying to ease the pain. My breathing calms, my heartbeat slows, and I become aware of the coolness of the air, a constant beeping, and an antiseptic smell. A hospital? Why? I search my memory for a clue, but what comes to mind is being on stage, singing to an adoring crowd. Wait. Someone is talking. Whispering actually. A woman. I can barely make out what she's saying.

"Hey, Ari, remember me, your friendly photographer?"

Photographer? When I don't respond, the voice gets louder. "Your asshole security guard stole my memory card, so you owe me. Just one picture of you in the hospital should cover the cost."

A slight pressure, warmth on my hand, then it's being crushed. Pain radiates up my arm and through my body. I scream.

She removes her hand. "Oh, shit. It's been more than a month. I didn't know you were still so bad. Sorry, it's so dim in here I didn't see the bandages on your hands. I thought maybe if I helped you sit up you could wave or something and I could get a really good shot. I guess that's not going to work." I drift, but her voice wakes me again. I open my eyes but the brightness is painful so I quickly close them again. "Geez, in the light I can see your whole body is bandaged. What a scoop! Pictures of you looking like a mummy will go for a ton of money."

"Who the fuck are you?" I recognize Kim's voice. "Give me that fucking camera." The bed rocks. Every cell in my body screams. I scream. There are grunts and curses and the rocking stops.

"You can't take my camera." The bitch sounds offended.

"I just did," Kim says. "There will be no pictures and no stories about this. DO. YOU. UNDERSTAND?" I never knew shouting could trigger pain. "Wait a minute. You're the sneak from the stadium. How the hell did you get in here?" It sounds like they're scuffling again.

Kim is scary when she's in protective mode. She always has been, even back when we were ten years old. What's going on? I try my eyes again, but they don't like the light and the lids come down.

"There haven't been any pictures or stories about Ariana's injuries since right after the accident. The public has a right to know how she's doing, to see she survived. It will be good for her career. You're her manager, you must know that any publicity is good publicity."

"Are you trying to con me? Or are you trying to make yourself feel better about doing something so sleazy?" Kim's voice is razor-sharp. "You must have missed me asking the media and the public to respect Ariana's privacy. There haven't been any recent stories or pictures because she needs time to deal with the accident and focus on healing. Updates will be issued when appropriate."

Accident? It sounds like they're scuffling again.

"You fucking sleazebag. We're still not sure Ari is going to live and all you're thinking about is making money off her suffering." Kim chokes up. "If you had any decency at all you wouldn't be trying to exploit her when she's helpless. Be assured, as long as I'm around neither you nor any of the other vultures like you will ever take advantage of her."

Thank you, Kim. But wait, I might not live? Judging by my pain, I'm definitely dying.

"Give me my camera or I'll sue."

"Be my guest," Kim says. If voices could kill, the photographer would be dead. "Now get the hell out of here and leave Ariana and those of us who care about her in peace."

"I'm not going anywhere without my camera."

"You got it back after the concert but not this time. Wait a minute. How did you know Ariana was here?"

"I'm not stupid." She sounds angry. "I followed you."

Something starts to chime.

"We'll see how stupid you are. If one word about Ari's accident, her condition, or the hospital she's in gets out, I'll know it came from you and I'll squash you like an insect. I'll track you down and not only will I sue the pants off you, but I'll also make sure you never sell another picture, get another job, rent an apartment, or live in peace. If you've read anything about me, you know Ariana is my sister and I'm incredibly protective of her, but you may not know I always mean what I say. And I always follow through."

The only sound is heavy breathing, but I can't tell whose it is.

"Judging by your pallor, you've heard what I'm capable of when it comes to protecting her." Was that the door opening? "About time, Gwen. Where the fuck were you when this woman got in? Get her out of here. And after she's gone, I want to know how the hell she got past you."

Suddenly there are several male voices, and the woman is screaming again. A weight falls on my legs. It seems as if a herd of wild horses is trampling me. The pain is excruciating. The men are cursing, Kim is screaming at them to get that bitch out of here and have her arrested. The door slams, but the screaming doesn't stop. I feel the vibration throughout my body. It's me. I'm screaming. It would be better to die than to endure this pain.

"Dammit, give her something for the pain." Kim sounds panicky. There's a rush of air nearby and then I sink back into merciful darkness.

The next time I wake, I open my eyes. A woman is peering down at me. I blink, trying to clear my vision.

"Oh, you're awake. Good morning, Anna." The woman standing over me smiles. "I'm Millie, your nurse. I'll get the doctor."

Anna? I'm Ariana. Ariana Calandre.

"Oh, thank God, you're awake?" Kim's voice. Kim leans over me, tears streaming down her face. "Ari, thank God. Um, Anna."

Anna again? I try to smile, but it hurts. Damn.

Kim leans in close to my ear. "You're here under the name you use when you want to be undercover so we can control the media coverage. Everyone here thinks your name is Anna. Blink if you understand."

I blink. I open my mouth to speak, but there's no sound. I try again. My throat feels like I'm swallowing shards of glass, but I push a word out. "What?" Despite the effort it's barely a whisper and sounds like rocks grinding against each other. Oh, shit. My voice. I gasp for air. I can't breathe.

"Nurse, I think she's having an anxiety attack," Kim screams.

"Look at me," someone commands. The nurse? Tilly? Lilly? I open my eyes and gaze at her, still gasping. "That's it. Now try to inhale for four seconds and breathe out for six seconds. Good. Do it again. Now look at my hand, now this glass, the call button, and Kim. That's it, keep breathing." She takes me through this a few times before I'm able to breathe easily.

And so is Kim, I assume, since the color has returned to her face. "Here's the doctor."

A woman wearing a white coat, in her late fifties or early sixties, with dark hair, red glasses, and a big smile leans over me. "Hello, Anna. I'm Dr. Rawlings. Welcome back."

I move my eyes to Kim. Back? Where have I been? And as she often does, she reads my mind. "Your van was hit head-on by a semi. You were in an induced coma on a respirator for a month and have been heavily sedated for the last several weeks."

"Girls?" I push the word out despite the pain. I have to know about my friends.

Kim's gaze shifts to the doctor. Is she asking permission? She closes her eyes for a second. "They're all…" Her voice breaks. "You're the only one who survived."

Sobbing sends shards of glass through my body and the tears sting as they drip over my face, but I welcome the pain. My friends, my bodyguards. All dead. Why not me? The nurse hovers over me, and then I sink into blackness again.

A few days later or maybe a week—or weeks, since I'm unable to keep track of time—I ask Kim about my injuries.

"The left side of your face is burned, and your face also has several deep lacerations. The left side of your body has extensive burns, plus you have a broken pelvis, two broken ribs, a broken shoulder, a broken leg, two broken wrists, and a great deal of internal bruising. It's a miracle you're alive."

Not a miracle, a curse. I have nothing to live for. I can barely talk, forget singing. Singing is, was, my life. I'm in constant pain. Death would be a relief. Why didn't I die with my friends?

I stare at the shadow of myself in the mirror. The large sacklike dress I'm wearing is light so it doesn't rub too much, but it makes me look like a witch. I'm hunched in a wheelchair, emaciated, weak, in constant pain, red, raw skin on my left arm, patchy hair, my voice gone, one side of my face red and raw, the other scarred. I'm a monster. Even the staff flinches when they see me. And they don't even know who I really am.

Was. Tears threaten. Thirty-five and I look and feel the way I imagine an eighty-year-old feels. I can't bear the shock and distaste on people's faces. I can't bear the pity. Kim is watching me as I react to the horror show that is me.

"Kim, I don't want anybody to see my face. Buy me a mask—" It's painful to speak, but I try to grind out the words even though my throat feels like it's filled with glass and hot rocks and acid. I reach for my notepad and pencil and finish the sentence. *or a veil or something to cover me.*

"Ari, honey, Mom and Dad and the sibs saw you a couple of days after the accident. They love you and understand you're still healing. And the doctors and nurses need to be able to treat your facial burns and wounds."

I write a note. *I don't care. I don't want anybody to see how I look now. I'll give the doctors, nurses and therapists access for medical care, but that's it. Please, Kim, do what I ask.* I pause before adding: *Otherwise, no visitors but you.*

Tears fill her eyes. She leans toward me but knows not to touch. "I'm so sorry you have to deal with so much pain. It's not fair."

I know she worries about my mental state, so I don't say what I'm thinking. It's fair that I suffer. But it's not fair that I'm alive and they're dead.

"Mom and Dad and the rest of the family have been patiently waiting for you to feel well enough for them to visit again. I think you'd feel better if you at least let Mom and Dad come for a few minutes."

No. Absolutely no visitors unless I'm covered up. I draw lines under the words to ensure she understands. Kim is my best friend, adopted sister, and manager and she's always there for me. I know I'm hurting her, but I can't face anyone, even our mom and dad, who rescued ten-year-old me from hell. We sit quietly for a long time afterward, and when she leaves I hand her a note reminding her to bring a veil when she comes tomorrow.

Later, lying in bed wide awake, I wonder how Kim will handle the publicity when I appear wearing a dark veil, then I realize I can't go there, I can't be that person in the public eye again.

I'm disappointed when she arrives empty-handed the next day. And, of course, she knows it and explains before she's even said hello. "I looked online but there weren't any hats with veils that would prevent people from seeing you, so I found someone to make one. It should be ready tomorrow."

I ask the question that's been on my mind since last night. *What have you told my fans and the media about my situation?*

Kim chews her lip. "In the days right after the accident there were pictures of you being put in the ambulance and lots of pictures of the wrecked van plus stories about you being seriously injured but the only survivor. I put out a release confirming you were seriously injured and asking everyone to respect your privacy while you mourn the death of your friends and take the time you need to heal. Since then, I've put out short updates periodically in order to control the conversation and prevent a media frenzy."

I hold back the tears. As usual, Kim is looking out for me. *Thank you, Kimmy,* I write.

I should have had faith. The next day when she arrives she pulls two floppy hats out of a bag. "No one will see your face when you wear this one"—she hands me a hat with a heavy black veil—"but neither will you be able to see anyone. With this one"—she hands me a hat with a lighter black gauzy veil—"your face will be visible but shadowy, vague, and you will see others the same way. Which would you prefer?"

I try them both on, then have her try them on so I can see how each will protect me. *I want both, but for now I'll wear this one.* I put on the hat with the dark veil and that's the last time anyone in the hospital, other than the doctors and nurses tending to my facial wounds, have to pretend not to recoil. I wear the lighter veil when Kim and I are alone in my room so we can kind of see each other. And though I know it upsets Mom, I wear the darker one when the family visits.

* * *

It's July, more than seven months since the accident, and this morning we're meeting with Dr. Rawlings to discuss my progress. I've found that the veil makes many people uncomfortable, so I'm not surprised that she stares at the notes in front of her instead of looking at me.

"Anna, I'm projecting you'll be ready to leave in six to eight weeks. I suggest you start looking for a full-time live-in aide." I nod, but I have no intention of having a stranger hovering over me, just as I won't be talking to a therapist. What is there to say? They're all dead. I'm alive, but my life went up in flames with them.

Dr. Rawlings continues, "By the time you leave, all the skin grafts and bones should be healed, and you should be able to take care of your personal needs and switch between a walker and the wheelchair. If you continue with outpatient therapy, you'll eventually walk unassisted."

I watch Kim watching me. Of course, with the veil she doesn't know my eyes are on her, not the doctor. Because no matter what Dr. Rawlings says, I don't intend to have an aide or do physical therapy or talk to a psychiatrist.

Dr. Rawlings taps her papers into an orderly pile, then stands. "We'll meet again in four weeks to assess your progress."

Kim wheels me to my room. I'm pretty sure she knows I'm thinking about ending my misery. I just need to figure out how to do it. Maybe I can't kill myself, but neither can I go back to my previous life. I've been trying to get Kim to understand my need to be alone. We've been going round and round for days, but she refuses to help me. I refuse to stop pressuring her. I can't.

I grab my pad and pencil and write a note. *Please, Kim, I can't go back to Austin. I need to be somewhere no one knows who I am, somewhere I can be alone and quiet. I need time to get used to...my new life.*

"You won't always be like this, Ari. It's a long process, but the doctors assure me you will heal."

Right. I'll be a healed monster instead of a raw, unhealed monster. I don't dare say aloud what I'm thinking, or she'll decide it's not safe for me to be alone. As painful as it is to speak, I force myself to verbalize, hoping if she hears my voice she'll get it. "I'm begging you, Kimmie. Please find me a place where I can be alone and get used to my new self."

"You're depressed. You won't see anybody but me, and Mom and Dad occasionally. You barely talk, you don't read, you don't watch TV, you don't even listen to music. What will you do by yourself? How will you take care of yourself?" She starts to cry. "I have no idea what you're thinking. I'm afraid you'll hurt yourself. I can't lose you, Ari. Come home with me. You need to be surrounded by people who love you. I'll make sure you have privacy. Or go home to your own house with an aide where I can see you every day and Mom and the rest of the family are available to help if you need anything."

"I can't." I'm crying now. "I can't deal with people seeing me, pitying me. Please, Kim. I swear I won't hurt myself." We were always so touchy-feely, and normally, Kim would have wrapped me in her arms to comfort me. But I'm still raw and touch is still painful, so we just look at each other and cry. "If you don't help me, I swear I'll disappear, and you'll never see me again."

Kim wipes her tears and blows her nose. "If I do, you have to promise not to hurt yourself and to call me every single day."

"I promise."

She reaches for my hand and gently kisses my knuckles. "Okay."

I love her. She taught me to trust and love and helped me become who I am. Who I used to be, anyway. She became my role model when we were ten years old and I've always tried to emulate her: her kindness; her motto of a promise made is a promise kept; her valuing family; her loving, giving nature; her honesty; and her work ethic. "Thank you, Kimmy." I smile through my tears, pull her hand under the veil so I can kiss it.

CHAPTER THREE

Ariana

July–September 2023

Once she's committed to the idea, Kim gets to work. Within a week she shows me a few possibilities. I sift through them, view the videos, and select what appears to be the perfect place, an isolated, run-down farmhouse near a small town called Sharon Springs, the kind of rural town where people tend to mind their own business. The house has three bedrooms and three bathrooms upstairs and another three bedrooms, two bathrooms, a large living room, a dining room, and a huge old kitchen on the main floor, eighteen acres with a barn, a shed, and a bunkhouse. It's much too large for just one person, but otherwise it's perfect.

"This is exactly what I want, Kim, so please purchase it."

Brian, Kim's husband, handles my investments and finances, and he sets up a trust and purchases the house. To protect my identity, the trust will rent the house to Anna Solander, the name I will continue to use, probably for the rest of my life.

After the sale is finalized, Kim hires a cleaning service to scrub the house from top to bottom, an architect to draw up specs to make the downstairs where I will live wheelchair accessible, a contractor to do the renovations, and a painter to paint all the rooms. She doesn't bother me with any of it, knowing that approving specs and selecting paint colors are beyond me. My only request is no mirrors anywhere in the house.

Every other week, usually when she's in Austin with her family, she drives to Sharon Springs to oversee the work. When the house is ready, she has everything in my Austin house packed up and moved there. Last week she spent two days at the farmhouse directing the placement of furniture and unpacking everything. Anything not used is being stored in one of the upstairs bedrooms. She also opened an account for me at the general store and put in place a no-contact system for me to email my weekly food order and have it delivered and left on the table on my porch. Kim being Kim, she installed a state-of-the-art security system with cameras that show the outside of the house from all angles and an intercom that allows me to talk from inside the house with anyone who comes to the front door.

Today, I'm being discharged from the rehabilitation center and for the first time in almost a year, I'm reentering the world. But as Anna Solander, not Ariana Calandre. Kim insists on driving me to the house. We agree she will stay for two weeks to help me settle before, against her better judgment and her love for me, leaving me alone. Other than the promised daily check-in call with her and a monthly telephone conversation with our mom, I won't need to see or talk to anyone.

The day I leave rehab is sunny and warm, but as much as I'd longed to be outside in the sunlight, I might as well be in a tent since no skin is exposed to the air. I shudder at the sight of the luxury van Kim rented. It's fitting that the nurses settle me into the passenger seat, the same seat I was in for my last ride. I close my eyes and memories of the laughter rush in, followed immediately by the other memories, the screams, the sound of crunching metal, the smell of gasoline, the flames. My eyes pop open. Maybe refusing the tranquilizers offered was a mistake. I'm shaking so hard even my teeth are chattering. Kim slides behind the wheel. Her hand darts out to soothe me as she's done all our lives, but she catches herself.

"You don't have to do this, Ari. If I charter a plane it's a short drive to the airport here, an hour flight, and another short drive from the airport in Austin to your house." She sniffs, trying to hold back the tears. "I'll take care of you."

I'm terrified and I'm tempted, but I say the words I need to say to get her to take me to my isolated farmhouse, far from my old life and everyone I know and love. "It's my first time in a car so I think it's natural to be nervous. I'd like to go to Sharon Springs."

Kim dabs her eyes with a tissue. "You're the boss, kiddo, but do us both a favor and take these." She hands me the tranquilizers and a bottle of water. I don't argue.

Even medicated the drive is difficult. The van is comfortable as vans go, but I'm tense. I hear the sound of grating metal in my head, smell smoke, see flames in the flickering sunlight, and imagine oncoming cars are swerving into us. Every bump and crack in the road reverberates through my fragile body. I'm sweating and in physical and mental pain. The drive is also taking a toll on Kim. She senses what I'm feeling. She's worried and her gaze constantly shifts from the road to me. We stop frequently so I can rest and use the bathroom, and the five-hour trip from Houston takes seven hours. At each stop, I stand and walk a little on my walker, but though the large hat with the thick veil protects me, I'm anxious I'll be recognized. I'm not sure why Kim's patience surprises me because she's always been patient with me, even times when I've been off the wall.

Almost seven hours later, we reach Sharon Springs and Kim points out the general store, the library, the town hall, and other small shops, but I can only think about getting out of this vehicle. As we leave the town behind, she announces my house is about fifteen minutes from here. Finally, she turns from the quiet two-lane country highway onto a nondescript, dusty break in the trees. She stops the car and swivels to me. "We're here. This is your driveway."

Nothing but trees in any direction. I take a deep breath and try to hide my fear. I remind myself I wanted isolation. As Kim always does, she gave me what I wanted. I'll get used to it. I'll have to since this is where I plan to live for the rest of my life.

Kim knows me so well. She sees or senses my fear and puts her hand gently on my knee. "You'll be all right, Ari. There's too much property to make installing a fence and a locked gate feasible, but the house is alarmed and the area is safe. I've met with the sheriff and explained that you're a recluse and will be living here alone. You'll have her on speed dial. And, you know, sweetie, if you don't like being here, we'll do something else. Give it a couple of weeks and then decide."

I touch her face. "I'd hug you if I could, Kimmy. Thank you for always taking care of me. It's scary, but it's what I want."

She starts the car. "Let's get you into the house."

Kim has outdone herself. The house is at the end of a very long, potholed driveway that would convince someone who accidently turned onto it from the highway that they'd made a wrong turn. But the rutted driveway also is the final assault on my body. I close my eyes and clench my jaw to keep from crying out as Kim slowly drives the van through the minefield.

When the van finally stops, I take a breath, and open my eyes. I hold back tears as I stare at the house. It was empty for a few years before I bought it and it looks horrible. I glance at Kim. She smiles. "Don't worry, it's comfy inside. Remember we made updating the interior the priority so it could be ready on time."

I nod. Kim would never let me live in a dump.

I'd told her I didn't want a ramp to the porch because once I was in the house I expected to remain there and also so anyone who approached wouldn't know I was disabled. But now as I gaze at the six rickety steps up to the porch I wonder if I'd made another mistake. Before the accident I probably wouldn't have noticed the steps, but now I might as well be contemplating climbing Mt. Everest.

"While I unload, you sit and relax." Kim pops the rear door and begins to move the suitcases and boxes with my new clothing and personal things like the notebooks I write my ideas for songs and other important thoughts, photo albums, address book, contact lists, and mementos to the porch. My eyes widen when she walks by with my favorite guitar, the first really good guitar I'd ever owned. I had scrimped and saved to buy it and soon after I started playing it the group took off. I'd always considered it my lucky charm, the one I'd forgotten to take with me the night of the last concert. The tears I've been forcing back escape. I rub my fingers on my knees, knowing the calluses on the tips are gone. Kim knows how important that guitar is to me, and I know she brought it out of love, so I won't give her grief. She hopes I'll play again, but I know better.

Finally, she drags a weird-looking thing to the porch. I watch as she unfolds it and arranges it on the steps. It's not until she turns with a shit-eating grin that I realize she's brought a portable ramp. She runs to the van, brings my wheelchair around, and opens my door. "May I escort you into your new home?"

The tears come again. It seems my emotions are readily accessible today. She holds out her hand and helps me into the wheelchair. The ground is rough, and it takes some effort, but she pushes me to the ramp and hands me my walker. After three attempts I make it to my feet. Placing a hand on my back to steady me, she escorts me up the ramp to the porch. She gives me a minute to steady myself, then brings the wheelchair up the ramp and helps me sit. She unlocks the door and pushes me inside.

I'd seen pictures of the original kitchen, and I knew she was doing some updating, but I never imagined the total remodel I'm looking at. The walls are now a pale yellow, the floors natural wide-plank wood, and the alcove with three small side windows now has a cushioned bench and one large window opening the space to the outside. A huge refrigerator, a freezer, a Viking range similar to the one in my kitchen in Austin, a beautiful wooden table and six chairs, a cooking island, wooden cabinets, and a padded rocking chair in the corner near a small desk, complete the space. I used to love to cook, but I have no appetite and cooking anything elaborate is beyond me now. But there's no takeout option here, so I imagine my meals will probably be limited to grilled cheese and canned soup. I would take bets that Kim has stocked my refrigerator and the cabinets with my favorite foods and snacks.

The entire ground floor has been remodeled to accommodate my wheelchair and Kim rolls me through the rooms—dining room, living room, guest bedroom, guest bathroom, then the bedroom which she's converted to what she calls the den, a room that looks suspiciously like the music room where I compose, rehearse, and work in my Austin house. It has a large desk, leather executive chair, an easy chair, a love seat, my entertainment center plus all my music, a large TV, huge speakers, and the recording center with all the equipment I use when developing music.

I don't comment or criticize, but I understand what she's done. It's painful to think about the past so I'm silent as she rolls me into the master bedroom and then the ensuite bathroom with a roll-in shower, a jacuzzi, and a high toilet, all fitted with grab bars. The beds are made and the bathrooms have been set up. As I requested, there are no mirrors. I should have known Kim would never let me live in a dilapidated old farmhouse. Every room is freshly painted, and all the wood floors are freshly scraped and finished. It's beautiful and feels warm and welcoming.

She rolls me into the living room and helps me into a super-cushioned recliner like the one in the hospital. It's comfortable and with the press of a lever it will push me to a standing position.

"Relax. I won't unpack until tomorrow, but I'll carry everything in from the porch and then I'll make us some dinner." She studies me for a moment, taking in the tension in my body, the tightness of my jaw, and the whiteness of my knuckles grasping the recliner. "Do you want your pain medication?"

My body is throbbing. I'm tempted, but I fear getting addicted so I avoid the drugs until I can't tolerate the pain. "No, thanks."

"Okay, let me know when you're ready." She heads out.

Overcome with sadness at being so useless, I lean back, hoping against hope Kim won't notice I'm near tears again. But in my heart I know that will never happen. I close my eyes, so I don't have to watch her carrying the heavy boxes and suitcases, but I do notice her walk past with the guitar, which I assume will go into the music room where she hopes I'll pick it up and play again. I must doze because when I open my eyes, I smell lasagna baking. How did she do that so quickly?

Kim is sitting on the couch near me. "Hey, sleepy girl. Can I tempt you with some lasagna?"

She knows I'd never say no to her lasagna. "Yes."

"Wheelchair or walker? The table will accommodate either."

"Wheelchair. I know you did all the work today, but I'm exhausted." The recliner makes it easy to stand and once again I bless Kim's thoughtfulness. There's no way I could do it on my own right now. She helps me swivel into the chair.

I force myself to eat a small portion, mainly as a way of thanking her for taking such good care of me. "How did you cook the sauce and make the lasagna so quickly?"

Kim laughs. "I made it when I was here unpacking things last week. There are several small portions in the freezer that you can just pop in the oven when you're hungry."

I don't sleep much the first night of my new life. I've spent nearly ten months in the hospital. There's always noise—the shuffle of feet, the muffled laughter and conversations of doctors, nurses, aides, and cleaners, and the constant checking and poking of my body. Someone is always nearby. This bed is strange but comfortable, and the only noises are the creaks of the old house and the wind moaning through the trees. Kim is here but just for a few weeks.

I try to imagine being alone with nothing but my thoughts. My heart races. I remind myself of how much I craved time alone in my former life but that leads me to thoughts about how much less this life is and how lonely my aloneness will be. The tears don't surprise me this time. I must have dozed at some point because I'm roused, not by the rattle of breakfast trays, but by the sunshine streaming in through the window.

I reach for the bell Kim left on the night table, then catch myself. The hospital didn't allow me to get out of bed unassisted, but if I don't show Kim that I can take care of myself during the two weeks she's here, she won't leave. Inch by inch I pull myself to the edge of the bed. I'm covered in sweat but triumphant when my feet hit the floor. I sit for a few moments, then transfer to the wheelchair. I grab the hat with the gauzy veil, take a deep breath, and eye the bathroom door. It seems farther away than I remember. Slowly and painfully, I roll myself into the bathroom. I rest for a few seconds to catch my breath.

Though my arms are rubbery, the toilet is high, and I use the grab bars to steady myself as I swing on and off. My toothbrush, comb, the moisturizer I use on my face for the burns and scars, and a washcloth and towel are on the sink. Thank you, Kim. And the sink is low enough so I can wash my face, brush my teeth, and run a comb through my hair. I put on my hat and pull the veil down, then doggedly make my way to the kitchen. I'm exhausted, but when I see Kim's huge grin, I'm proud. I knew this was the right thing to do. "Good morning."

"Good morning." She sips her coffee. "Ready for some coffee?"

I'm tempted to try to serve myself, but my arms feel boneless and I'm not sure I can lift the pot to pour a cup. Besides, I do have two weeks to prove myself, so I nod. "And a fried egg on a roll, please."

Her expression tells me how happy she is that I'm asking for food. Now I just have to eat the damn thing.

Each day thereafter is pretty much the same. I work hard to prove I'm capable of taking care of myself, washing, dressing, even cooking some simple things. I want her to feel comfortable leaving me alone. I spend a lot of time dozing in my recliner in the living room while she works on her computer, but I also sit on the porch with Kim enjoying the fresh air, the sunlight, and the comfortable silence between us.

The two weeks we negotiated have flown. I've enjoyed having Kim here, but I'm ready to move on with my new life. I'm relieved, and terrified, that she's leaving today.

She loads her suitcase and computer bag in the van and comes back to the porch.

I gird myself for a battle, but I've thought a lot about this. "Take the ramp with you."

Kim frowns. "Why? You'll need it to get on and off the porch."

I laugh. "I'm not going anywhere, Kim. I can't go up or down in my wheelchair and even if I could manage with the walker, there's no place to walk so I'll probably sit on the porch sometimes, but I'll never go off it." What I don't tell her is I'm scared that if anyone sees it they'll know I'm disabled and an easy target. "Please, Kim, I'll feel better, safer, without it." I can see she's horrified, so I attempt to appease her. "You can bring it back the next time you visit in case I feel like going out."

She opens her mouth to protest, I assume, but closes it. She shakes her head. "I wish you'd just come home with me." She chokes out the words.

I feel her agony. I'm petrified. But I know I can't go home. "This is my home now, Kimmy." I struggle but the sobs escape.

She moves toward me and I back away. "No. I can't."

She swallows. "You're sure?"

I don't know whether she's asking about the ramp or my home or touching me, but I nod. "Yes. I'll be fine."

"Okay." Against her will she loads the ramp into the van. "I'll talk to you tomorrow, right?"

"Definitely."

"You know I'll be worried the minute I leave so I hope you won't fight me on this." She hands me one of those alarm things old people wear so they can summon help if they fall. "Please? I can't leave you alone unless you promise to always keep this on you."

I get that this is as hard for her as it is for me. It's a small price to pay for her comfort. I hang it around my neck. We say our tearful goodbyes and I wish I could hug her for her sake and mine. But I roll into the house, lock the door, then sit in my wheelchair in the kitchen, looking at the screen of the security system she'd had installed, and watch her get in her car and drive away.

The only sound is my breathing. The tears come of their own accord. Today is the first day of the rest of my life. I'm alone. It's the price of being comfortable. I will get used to it.

CHAPTER FOUR

Lee

January 2024

"I really am Lee Wilton. Could you repeat that again?"

The woman standing in the doorway glares at me. "For the third time, I purchased this house seven weeks ago, December first to be exact, from a woman named Lee Wilton. She said her husband was being discharged from the Army and she and her daughters were moving with him to California to be near his family."

"She didn't leave a forwarding address?"

"No. She did not." Clearly the woman thinks I'm an idiot.

I blink, trying to absorb the information. "Do you happen to remember the name of her attorney?"

The woman closes the door without answering.

"Thank you," I speak to the door, my door. "What the hell is going on?" I turn toward my rented car.

"Hey." I start at the voice and turn. The woman is standing on the porch.

"I'm sorry. She was a real bitch, and it's obvious she did something bad to you." She stares into space for a second. "Rippletoe. Her attorney's name is Jonah Rippletoe. I thought it was strange that he had the same name as that lawyer who represents all the Austin big shots, but his office is in a bad section downtown. Thomas or Thompson Street, I think." *You might say she did something bad to me. She sold my house and stole my daughters and I have no idea where she is.*

"Thank you." I stumble to my car, drive a block or two, then pull over. I'd suspected Gina was using again and having an affair, but as much as I wanted to be there for her, to help her get off drugs again, I couldn't do much from Jordan where I was stationed. And then I had an emergency. The maternal grandmother of my two adopted daughters who was caring for them until I completed my current enlistment, died suddenly, and I became fully responsible for them. When I flew home to make arrangements, Gina made it clear she didn't want five-year-old Mara and four-year-old Tessa in our lives, and I'd had to beg her to take them for the nine weeks between Leslie's death and my discharge. I knew then that I'd file for divorce when I got back. But I hadn't shared that decision with Gina, and everything had seemed normal, or at least the same, when we'd Zoomed yesterday. The girls were thrilled I was coming home. Even Gina seemed happy about it.

I close my eyes and try to center myself. Getting the girls is my top priority, so I need to be calm when I speak to Gina. I pull out my phone and initiate the call. It rings, but then a message comes on. "This is not a working number. Please hang up and dial again."

I disconnect and stare at the screen. I check my phone. It's Gina's number, the number I've been calling since we met seven years ago, the number I'd called yesterday. I feel lightheaded. This can't be happening. I try again and get the same message.

I look through my contacts and call Gina's closest friend, Amelia. "I got back to Austin an hour ago and I'm anxious to see the girls, but Gina's phone is disconnected. Do you have her new number?"

"Damn," Amelia said. "I had a weird conversation with her a couple of weeks ago, but she didn't say anything about changing her cell number. Let me put you on hold and call her." While I wait, I try to figure out where she'd go. Not to her family, for sure. "Sorry, Lee. I got the same message. Did you try the house?"

I clear my throat, not sure why I'm embarrassed. "I went there first. It seems she sold the house seven weeks ago."

"Whoa! I thought the house was yours. How could she sell it?"

"Good question. You didn't know?"

"Absolutely not. That's a crime and I would never…you know, even if it wasn't a crime, I wouldn't have let her do this to you. I mean I knew she was doing drugs and having affairs, but this is beyond the pale. What are you going to do?"

My head is spinning. I'd sensed the affairs and the drugs. How could I not have sensed her plan to take the girls and run?

"I'm worried because she's disappeared with the girls and, you know, she isn't crazy about having them around. Hopefully, she left them with Carley and Tammy or the sitters. If she contacts you, tell her I don't give a shit about the house. I just want my daughters."

"I would feel the same way, Lee." Amelia has kids so she gets it. "I'll call our friends to see if anyone knows where she is. I'll also contact a few of the women she was sleeping with, maybe one of them will know something."

A few? "Thanks, Amelia." My heart racing, I call Carley. She and Tammy are my oldest friends in Austin, and Gina knows they adore the girls.

"Lee, you're home. How are you?" My heart clenches when Carley doesn't mention the girls. I'm so anxious that I just blurt out the question. "Have you seen Gina and the girls?"

She probably hears the panic in my voice because she responds immediately. "Not since your last leave when you all came over for dinner. What's going on?"

I tell Carley the story.

"Shit, Lee. What can Tammy and I do to help?"

"I'm not sure, Carl, but I'll call you later." Before I end the call she invites me to stay with them.

I go through my contacts and call our other mutual friends. No one has seen Gina or spoken to her in weeks. And no one has any idea she isn't still living in my house. Neither Liana nor Caroline, the two nursing students I hired as live-in sitters to care for the girls because I didn't trust Gina, answers their phone. I leave a message for each, explaining what's happening, and ask for an immediate call back.

My last hope is Jonah Rippletoe, the attorney who represented her in the sale of the house.

I stare at Rippletoe's office building. Between what appears to be a boarded-up storefront window and a garage door is an entrance with a camera focused on it. The run-down building in a run-down section of town doesn't surprise me. Gina needed an attorney who didn't know her and wouldn't ask too many questions. From the look of things, Rippletoe probably fits the bill.

I ring the bell, look into the camera, and am buzzed in. A paper sign directs me up two worn dusty flights to a door with another paper sign taped to it, Offices of Jonah Rippletoe, Attorney at Law. The door is ajar. A man I assume is Rippletoe eyes me, then stands as I walk to the chair facing his desk. Rather than the old decrepit man I expect, I'm looking at a man in his forties, with a shadow beard and long black hair tied back in a ponytail, wearing a clean pressed black suit and a white turtleneck. He smiles. "How may I help you, Ms.?"

"My name is Lee Wilton." I watch his face for signs of recognition. He frowns. "I had a client with that name recently. Are you related?"

I gaze at him, trying to assess whether he's being honest. "Actually, she was pretending to be me."

His eyebrows shoot up. "How do I know you're not pretending to be her?"

I need to get this guy on my side. His eyes become the proverbial saucers when I reach into my backpack for my identification. He must expect a gun because he kind of collapses in his chair.

"I was discharged from the Army yesterday." I hand him my discharge papers, my military picture ID, and my driver's license. "If you still don't believe me, we can do a FaceTime call with my commanding officer or a police officer I know in town."

He carefully examines everything, looking from the photos to my face, then leans back. "My surroundings have probably led you to assume I'm a less than honest lawyer, but I assure you I'm a reputable attorney with a reputable firm. I do pro bono and low fee work out of here one day a week for people who can't afford a lawyer." He hands me a business card. "I'm the managing partner of that firm and this is my payback work. You can call and confirm that."

He meets my eyes. "I had no reason to doubt the woman who claimed to be you. She had all the proper documents including the deed for the house, a picture driver's license, and a bank account in your name. Her signature matched the one the bank had on file. Do you know her?"

There's that tickle of embarrassment again. "She's my wife. She seems to have disappeared, and she's taken my two daughters with her." I place the picture of the four of us taken on my last leave on his desk.

He studies the picture. "That's her. You said *your* children. Aren't they hers too?"

I reach for the picture and slide it back into my wallet. "I became their legal guardian after my best friend and her husband were killed in an accident six months ago, and then I adopted them. Gina was supposed to file second parent adoption papers once my adoption went through, but I doubt she did."

He taps his fingers on the desk. "If she didn't adopt them, you can file a kidnapping charge. If she did, I'm not sure what options are available. I'd have to do some research." He eyes me. "Why don't you meet me in my other office tomorrow morning to discuss how to handle this? And don't worry about fees. I'd like to track her down. Give me her real name, her social security number if you know it, and anything else you think might be helpful."

He seems believable, but I plan to check his credentials at the other firm. "That would be great, but I'd like to know the telephone number and bank account she was using."

"Sure." He walks to the file cabinet and pulls out a folder labelled Wilton Sale, thumbs through it, and provides the information I requested.

"The house must have sold for a pretty large amount. So why did you take her on as a client in this office rather than uptown, where I guess fees are higher?"

He flushes. "You're not the only one she scammed. She told me she and the father of her children weren't married and he had been killed in Syria and she wasn't getting any benefits. The house was her only asset. She promised if I did the paperwork as soon as she got the money for the sale, she would contribute five percent to my fund to help people with no resources. Of course, once she got the check she stopped answering my calls and never sent the money." He gets up to refile the folder.

In the two hours I sit in my car watching Rippletoe's building only one shabby man enters. He leaves a half hour later, looking a little more energetic. In the meantime, I try Liana and Caroline again, but neither answers, so I call the friends I didn't reach before. But no one has seen or heard from Gina in weeks, and no one has any idea where she is. Or at least they aren't telling me.

Finally, I've called everyone I can think of and now, in the silence of the car, I face the reality that Gina has disappeared with my daughters. But why? She had absolutely no interest in them and wanted them out of our lives. An image of their happy faces when I told them I was coming home to be with them forever pops into my mind and all the emotion I've been suppressing bursts out and I break down. Sobbing, I wonder whether they have their favorite stuffed animals and books, whether she's feeding them, whether her drug-clouded brain remembered their car seats? And was she strapping them in? I almost vomit at the thought she's probably driving while high. I'd sensed she was back on drugs. I'd sensed she was cheating on me. How did I miss the fact that she was stealing my identity and selling my house? How did I miss the fact that she was planning to steal my daughters?

When I run out of tears I realize I'm exhausted. I need food, a drink, a bath, and the privacy to allow myself to experience the gut-wrenching loss of Mara and Tessa. Since I'm not ready to deal with my friends' anger when I'm struggling with my own feelings, I make a reservation for the night at a hotel. When I call Carley to let her know I won't be coming to stay with them tonight, she reminds me that I'd left my truck parked at their farm. At least Gina didn't sell that too.

The garage door of Rippletoe's building opens, I wipe my eyes, start my rental car, and follow the BMW that emerges to a large beautifully landscaped house in a fancy neighborhood, with a discreet sign indicating it is the law offices of Rippletoe, Rippletoe and Morgan. Which Rippletoe is he? I drive to the hotel.

My phone rings while I'm eating dinner in my room. It's Liana. "Lee, hi, how are Mara and Tessa?"

"I was going to ask you that question."

"What?" She sounds shocked. "Aren't they in California with you and Gina?"

"I'm here in Austin. I was discharged yesterday and came home today to find Gina has sold my house and disappeared with the girls. You had no idea?"

"Absolutely not. She told us you'd sold the house and wanted her and girls to meet you in San Francisco. We had no reason to doubt her, so we help her pack up the house, said goodbye to the girls and moved in with friends. I'm so sorry, Lee. I know how important the girls are to you. It's weird that Gina took them. She barely noticed they were there."

"If you see or hear from Gina, please call me. Thanks for taking such good care of them."

By the time I arrive at eleven a.m., Jonah, as he's asked me to call him, has already determined that Gina hadn't filed the paperwork to adopt the girls, that she'd had the money from the sale deposited into a checking account in my name in a different bank than the one we'd always used, and that she'd moved the money to an account in a brokerage firm in her name and then it had disappeared.

He sits back in his luxurious leather chair and clasps his hands. "I believe we can make a case for kidnapping, for the theft of the house, plus forgery and several other crimes. If you'll allow me, I'll put our private investigator on tracking her. All I need is your signature and a copy of that photo of her and the children. I've asked a detective I know to come here so we can file charges."

I stand. "I appreciate your effort, Jonah, but I really don't have the money to pay"—I wave my hand, taking in the office—"what I expect are your fees."

"Sit, please, Lee. I meant what I said about this being on me. Your wife thought she was dealing with an attorney who was just barely making a living by serving poor clients. She not only cheated that poor attorney but all the clients he could serve with the money she promised to pay. I would like nothing more than to find her and send her to jail. As you can see, I'm not that poor attorney. Let me do this."

I take a minute to decide. I need to find my daughters as quickly as possible. Jonah is offering resources at no cost. It's a no-brainer, as they say. "Thank you. I accept your very generous offer."

I spend the next several hours meeting with Nancy Lavelle, the firm's private investigator, and Detective Karin Sharp. I know they need the information to do their jobs, but their questions fan the flame of my fears for the girls and twice I'm so overcome with emotion that I leave the room, walk around the block, and when the tears have stopped flowing, return.

Finally, when I've provided them with every bit of information I can remember about Gina and the girls, Detective Sharp and I go to the police station to file kidnapping and theft charges and activate an AMBER Alert for Mara and Tessa.

"Hopefully, the work we've done this morning and the steps we've taken will help us find the girls. But it may take a while." As we reach the door of the station house, Detective Sharp touches my arm. "I don't mean to be presumptuous, Lee, but you're already stressed and exhausted and I encourage you to take care of yourself. Take a break before going back to Jonah's office to deal with your finances. Have a cup of coffee and something to eat, then take a nap or a long walk."

I nod my agreement, though I have no intention of stopping. But then I slide behind the wheel and I barely have the energy to start the car. I sit with my head on my arms on the steering wheel and let the tears come again. The tapping on my window jerks me awake. Detective Sharp looks worried. She makes a motion indicating I should lower the window. "Get out of the car." She sounds angry and I wonder whether sleeping in the parking lot of a police station is illegal. "Come with me."

I follow her to a small restaurant across the street. "Let's have lunch."

I'm sheepish, but I realize she's right. We each order a sandwich and coffee and talk about our experiences in the military. We say goodbye and I drive to a park and walk for an hour.

Food and exercise do help, and I'm feeling more energetic when I return to Jonah's office and do what he and Detective Sharp recommended—move all my financial accounts, banks, mutual funds, and insurance to new institutions and new accounts so Gina can't get access. Gina has always resented any money I spent on the girls. Luckily their money, the money awarded them from the accident that killed their parents, is locked up in trust funds so she couldn't touch it, and I'd never told her about the mutual fund accounts I'd opened for them with the monthly support payments I was receiving—so that money was safe too.

I stop to thank Jonah before I leave. He stands. "I almost forgot. The house was supposed to be delivered empty to the new owners, but after they moved in, I got a call that they'd found a locked room in the basement filled with boxes, furniture, and who knows what else. I assumed Lee, er, Gina, had forgotten it. I asked them to give me some time to contact Gina so she could move it out. If you're interested in going through what she left, I'll call now and arrange a time for you to go to the house."

I nod. He speaks with the new owner, then turns to me. "Is ten a.m. tomorrow okay for you, Lee?"

"Fine." He makes the appointment and hangs up. "One more thing," he says, as I get ready to leave. "Should I file for divorce?"

I've been so focused on getting the girls back that I forgot she was totally screwing me. "Doesn't she have to sign?"

Jonah considers the question. "There are ways to get it done without her."

"Then, if it's not too much work, I'd appreciate it."

Once she realizes I'm not going to contest the sale of the house, Janet Minor, the new owner, is friendly and sympathetic. She walks me down to the basement and leaves me to it.

After going through some of the boxes, I realize Gina has left all my clothing plus the things that were important to me—photograph albums of family and friends, my vinyl record collection, my music center equipment, the amp and other equipment I'd used when I performed before I'd enlisted, all my important papers like my birth certificate, diplomas, military papers, and the girls' birth certificates and adoption papers, my desk, boxes of my music, my books, and many other important or memory-laden items. I was relieved to see she'd also left the boxes filled with the things I'd kept for Mara and Tessa when I cleared out the apartment they'd lived in with their parents and their grandmother's house. The only thing missing was the house folder with the deed and insurance papers and my banking records.

I go upstairs to talk to Janet. "I'm going to have everything moved to a storage unit, hopefully later today, if that's okay?"

"Sure, I'll be here. I guess it wasn't just junk?"

"No. Far from it. I'd like to think Gina was being thoughtful by packing it up and leaving it, but I'm sure it was easier and cheaper than having to dispose of it. Thank you for not tossing it."

I leave, sign up for a storage unit, and then arrange for a moving company to transfer everything. They can't do it until tomorrow, so I call Janet to arrange a time in the morning, then let Jonah know what's happening.

I spend the night in the hotel again, then arrive at the house to oversee the loading of everything onto the truck and the unloading at the storage unit. That done, I lock the unit, drop off my rental car, and take an Uber out to Carley's farm to pick up my truck. I'd forgotten that when Carley offered to keep the truck in her barn I'd stored my guitar, my camping gear, and camping clothing in it to get it out of the way in the house. Carley and Tammy insist I stay with them a few nights, and I agree so I can regroup. As is their way, they offer love and support when I share my plan to limit my search for Gina to Texas because as far as I know she had lived her whole life here and I assumed if she was high she'd probably stick to the familiar. As I lay out a route, gather supplies, and ready myself emotionally to be on the road for a while, I speak to all our mutual friends, Jonah Rippletoe, Detective Sharp, and PI Nancy Lavelle to let them know I'll be traveling but can be contacted on my cell phone if they have news of Gina and the girls. On my way out of town I stop at the storage unit. I take the girls' birth certificates, adoption papers and medical records, a thermometer, several outfits and underwear for each of them, some sweaters, a couple of toys, a few favorite books, and two pictures, one of them with their mom, dad, and me and a recent one of them with me. I have all the information on the new financial accounts I'd setup but I also take my birth certificate and discharge papers, some of my shirts, T-shirts, pants, shorts, underwear, sweaters, plus sandals and boots. I already have my guitar and I add the amp, favorite CDs and the CD player, and a few favorite books. On the way out, I grab several hats. I load the truck, check to be sure I have everything, then lock the storage unit.

CHAPTER FIVE

Ariana

April 2024

The last seven-plus months have been long and lonely. Other than the daily call with Kim and the monthly call with Mom and Dad, I've had no contact with the outside world.

I've spent most days and nights in the special power lift recliner in the living room, dozing between nightmares about Gloria, Maggie, Nellie, Erica, and Torie pleading for me to help them as they burn alive or yelling at me for not having the decency to go to their funerals. Kim says she told their families the truth, that I couldn't because I was in an induced coma, and they understood. She encourages me to call them on a day I feel good. But I can't. I have so much pain of my own that the thought of dealing with their pain is overwhelming, so I've written them notes expressing my love for my friends, my sorrow, my understanding of their loss. I don't burden them with my wish that I had died too. I don't receive mail here, don't even have a mailbox, and if I did I'd have no way to get to it, so I gave the notes to Kim to mail on her last visit.

Kim believes I'm trying to punish myself for being alive. Maybe. My monthly call with Mom and Dad, Kim's morning phone call, and her periodic visits are the only pleasures I allow myself, no books, no music, no television, no radio. I barely eat. I barely walk. I sleep a lot, and when I'm awake I spend a lot of time trying to imagine the next fifty years of my life as more of the same, sitting alone in this chair, doing nothing, filled with regrets about promising not to hurt myself. Kim would drive here to check on me every few days if I let her, but I only allow her to visit one or two days every couple of months.

I don't admit it, but even though I deny her, I look forward to her visits. I'm grateful she controls herself and never pushes. But it drives her crazy that I wear the hat and veil the whole time she's here so she can't really see me. She tolerates it because I won't let her visit if she doesn't. Even though she saw me at my worst in the hospital, I don't ever want to see disgust or, worse, pity or fear in her eyes. But she loves me and she comes whenever I allow and spends the time taking care of me, cleaning the house and cooking, filling the freezer with meals I can microwave. Of course, she knows I barely eat so she's tailored the size of the meals to me.

This visit has been up and down. As much as I try to hide what I'm feeling, she noticed that when she's not engaging me, I sink into a stupor. And that I've lost more weight. She insists I need more stimulation and has tried to get me to listen to music or watch a TV program. She hasn't voiced it, but I get that she thinks the more depressed I am, the more likely I am to kill myself. It would mean breaking my promise to her, but the idea of dying is even more appealing than before. And on this visit, for the first time, she's been subtly pressuring me to go home to Austin with her. I try to rally, to show her I'm fine, but I worry if I continue to spiral down, she'll forcibly move me to her house or, worse, an institution.

Now that she's leaving, she makes me promise, as usual, to heat and eat at least one meal a day. I never break a promise. But she can't resist encouraging me to try to eat three.

I'm shocked when she opens her arms and moves close to hug me. I put my hands up and back away. "No. No touching."

She's distraught. She backs away. "I'm so sorry, Ari. I forgot. Do you still hurt?"

The truth is I ache all over, but I don't know if my skin is still sensitive because there's no one to touch me. But I don't deserve the comfort of a hug, even from Kim, the best friend I love. And, truthfully, I'm afraid I'll fall apart if I let her hug me. I try to soothe her. "Maybe another time."

She nods. "Okay, honey. Talk to you tomorrow and see you next time." As always, she bounces back to her loving, cheerful self.

Sitting in my wheelchair, I gaze at the camera and watch her get into her car. She glances at the house, then quickly dabs her eyes with a tissue. Maybe she's learned to put on a show for me and she's not as cheerful as I imagined. Leaving me alone like this hasn't gotten any easier for her. Nor has it for me. After she leaves, the house feels cavernous and empty like my life, my depression worsens, and my loneliness becomes almost unbearable.

I feel a soft breeze on my face and turn toward the window. Did Kim leave it open on purpose? Or did she forget to close it? She's rarely devious, so I think she forgot. An open window is not a big deal for her. But for me, it means being exposed to the world outside the prison I've been sentenced to. Wait. That's too dramatic. I'm here through choice, my choice, no one else's. If Kim had her way, I'd be living in her house in Austin or in mine, if she hasn't already sold it.

I roll to the window, intending to close it, but something about the softness and the fragrance of the early-morning spring breeze wafting in through the kitchen windows brings back memories of happier times, times when I lived in a world filled with the warmth of friends, times when music filled me and my life, times when I wasn't a weak, scarred monster, times when I wasn't so painfully lonely. But that was then, and now is now. I reach for the handle. It's a struggle, but I persist and slowly close the window, sealing myself in again.

Everyone said I was lucky to be alive, but was I? Ariana Calandre died in the flames, leaving Anna Solander in her place. The accident robbed me of five close friends and my ability to sing and play the guitar. It left my face and body horribly scarred and stole my spirit. It took my vitality and my will to live. At thirty-five I move like an old woman and can only walk a few feet with the walker, so I almost always use the wheelchair. I catch myself spiraling into self-pity and, knowing how that will turn out, I pull myself back to the beauty of the day and the comfort of remembering happy times with my good friends. My mind drifts to our last concert, the love, the joy, the happiness, and suddenly I'm sobbing. I haven't cried in a long time, and it hurts. I doze in my wheelchair in front of the window with the sun warming me, and when I wake, the pain I feel isn't just physical, it's also emotional, the feeling of utter hopelessness. I roll into the living room, switch to my recliner, and for the next three days I drift in and out, memories of fun times with Maggie, Torie, Nellie, Erica, and Gloria mixing with dreams where I jump out of the recliner and like so many times in our lives the six of us laugh and tease as they play their instruments and we dance, clap, and sing. I only rouse to speak to Kim every morning and use the bathroom.

When I answer Kim's call on the fourth morning, I notice it's the first day of April. A little over sixteen months since the accident, seven months since I left the hospital. For the first time in four days, I feel hungry, and I go into the kitchen to get something to eat. Since the huge storm several nights, or is it weeks, ago took down a lot of trees near the house, including one whose branches are blocking the window, the kitchen is dark and dreary, and I feel entombed. It suits my mood. Despite, or maybe because of the happy memories and dreams, I've never felt this hopeless and alone. Kim and Brian will be vacationing in Greece for two weeks, so there will be no daily phone call, just email. This might be a good time to kill myself.

CHAPTER SIX

Lee

April 2024

It's dawn and I'm sitting in a coffee shop so generic I might be in any one of the scores of small towns and cities I'd driven through in the three months I've been searching for Gina, Mara, and Tessa. I'm exhausted and depressed and hopeless after the most recent AMBER Alert lead, like the many previous tips, petered out. I've driven all over Texas, checking out leads to five foot, four inch dark-haired, dark-eyed women reputed to look exactly like Gina, some with, and others without, two little girls in tow. The police in Houston had even arrested a look-alike who turned out to be a wealthy and powerful attorney, not pleased to spend two days in jail. Detective Sharp and Jonah's PI hadn't had any luck either, though they'd tracked down numerous tips which turned out to be bogus.

Jonah tried to cheer me up during our telephone conversation late last night but failed miserably by following his thoughts to their logical end. "The good news is that neither Gina nor the girls have been found which probably means she hasn't abandoned them." He hesitated. "The bad news is she may have buried the bodies."

"No, Jonah. Gina is an addict and she might drop the girls off at the movies and forget to pick them up, or she might even leave them someplace because she can't deal with them, but she'd never physically harm them."

I guess he heard the exhaustion and defeat in my voice because he offered advice, which he rarely does. "Find a place to rest and regroup for a while, Lee. The only thing chasing supposed sightings has accomplished is to wear you down. The team is actively working on finding them and I recommend you sit tight someplace until we turn up something concrete."

I rejected the idea out of hand last night, but today I'm having second thoughts. Spending endless days alone driving across Texas pursuing reported sightings has been frustrating and has left me feeling aimless and rootless. When I left the Army I planned to take a month or so to figure out what to do next, but that got lost in the panic to find my daughters. If I found them today, I would have no idea what to do, where to go. So I'm thinking that taking time to figure out my life and make a plan for when we're back together is a good idea.

I kind of like Sharon Springs, the small town I've been camping near for a week or so. They have a great library and I'd taken out several books when I arrived, something I only do in places I intend to stay for more than a day or two. This morning, as I packed my camping gear, I decided to follow up on the job posting for a handyman I'd seen in the general store a few days ago. If I get the job I'll stay. Otherwise I'll return the books and move on.

Being on the road is lonely for someone like me. I'm a people person. When I was in college and performing in small local venues, I spent a lot of time with other students and musicians. And in the Army I was always surrounded by friends and colleagues and when at home mainly by friends. Now I'm feeling hopeless, and I don't have the energy to call friends or even my mom in whatever time zone she and my dad, the General, are stationed at the moment. So except for an occasional conversation with someone in a restaurant, I only speak to people to inquire after Gina and the girls or to place an order.

I force myself to eat the eggs I ordered, knowing I need to feed my body if I'm going to continue. I pay my bill, drive to the general store, and check the bulletin board in the rear. The job is still posted, but there's no telephone number or address. I wait for the owner to finish with a customer, then step up. "I'm interested in that handyman job you have posted. Is it still open?"

He gazes at me as if evaluating whether I'm worthy. "Do you live around here, Mister...?"

I don't correct him. Maybe it's the pants, shirt, boots, and Stetson, or my five foot ten inches, or the way I carry myself after twenty plus years in the Army, or my military haircut, but this happens all the time. "Lee Wilton. No. I'll stay if I get the job. Otherwise I'll move on."

"Well, Mr. Wilton, the woman, Anna Solander, is a recluse. She was in an accident and badly scarred, so she doesn't allow anyone to see her. Some say she's a monster. I don't know about that but something about her spooked the two guys I sent out there. That's why the job is still available. If you think you can handle somebody like that, I'll give you the information and you and she can decide."

"Where is she and what kind of place does she have?"

"She's about fifteen minutes out of town in a big old farmhouse with a lot of acres, but she doesn't farm or anything. She doesn't have a car, so I imagine she doesn't get out much. The house was empty for a couple of years before she rented it, so it's pretty run-down."

It sounds to me like just what I'm looking for. If she's got a lot of acres, maybe I can camp on her property. "If you feel comfortable giving me directions, I'd like to check it out."

He writes the information on a piece of paper. "Here you go. If she hires you, ask her to let me know so I can remove the advert."

"Will do." I leave the store, set my GPS, and head out into the countryside. This Anna sounds kind of creepy, but if she wants privacy that means I'll have privacy too. And uninterrupted time is what I need to get my head together and figure out a plan.

CHAPTER SEVEN

Ariana

April 2024

The slamming of a car door jerks me awake. I raise myself out of the recliner and tumble into the wheelchair. I rub my arm over my eyes and catch a whiff of myself. I reek. When was the last time I bathed? My stomach rumbles. Have I eaten recently? Since Kim is in Greece we've been checking in through a daily email, so there's no phone call to signal the start of a new day. I roll into the kitchen. A glance at the calendar confirms the weekly food delivery isn't until tomorrow, so it must be someone else. I start to sweat. I never have visitors.

My gaze goes to the camera scanning the front of the house. A lanky, slender man exits a truck, slaps his Stetson on, marches to the porch, and vaults up the steps. I feel a pang of jealousy, followed by a burst of anger. I was once agile like that, able to strut and sing for hours under hot lights, and after, indulge in hours of sex, then run five miles the next morning. A stab of loss takes my breath away, but I catch myself before I tumble into the void of another pity party.

I look at the camera again. Maybe this stranger is lost. Cursing the intrusion, I roll to the camera and speak into the microphone. "Can I help you?" My voice is rusty from lack of use, and it sounds like a growl, an angry growl. It seems I no longer have a filter, because I sound as angry as I feel.

He steps back with a look of surprise on his face. His head swivels, looking for the source of the voice. Then he looks straight at the camera and tips his hat. "I'm sorry to disturb you, Ms. Solander. I'm Lee Wilton and I'm here about the job you posted at the feed store."

"What job?"

"You wanted someone to do some outside work?" He takes a breath. "If you've filled the job, I'll leave."

Kim has been after me to get the outside of the house painted, but that's not it. Then I remember. I raise my eyes to the large window in the alcove in the kitchen, now blocked by the branches of a tree downed by a horrible storm. At night the branches scraping against the alcove window sound like someone trying to get in. It makes me anxious. I'd forgotten I'd emailed and asked Mr. Stone to post the notice for a handyman again. The last two who showed up decided they didn't want the job after talking to me.

"It's not much of a job, just cleaning up the property, doing some outside repairs, painting the house, and other things as they come up." I cringe. Because I haven't spoken to Kim since she left for Greece, my voice is rough and creaky. I sound like I'm ninety-three. I clear my throat. "The pay I posted includes breakfast and lunch, if you're interested." I can pay much more, of course, but I'd asked Mr. Stone, the owner of the general store, what would be a fair wage.

"It sounds perfect." He moves closer to the door as if that will allow him to see me.

"What did they tell you about me in town?"

He stuffs his hands in his pockets and looks away. "That you're a recluse, that you'd been in accident of some sort, and that you don't let anybody see you."

I nod. "Can you live with that, Mr. Wilton? Not seeing the person you're talking to?"

He rolls back on his heels and stares at the camera. "I prefer to look people in the eye, but I wouldn't consciously do anything to make you uncomfortable."

"We would have minimal contact."

"To be honest, I usually enjoy engaging with people, but right now I'm dealing with some losses and I need some private time and space to regroup. In fact, if I could pitch a tent on your property, it would be the perfect job for me. And I'd take less money if you include dinner."

I study the handsome man rocking on his feet. Probably late thirties, early forties with short dark hair, sad blue eyes, high cheekbones, full lips, good posture, and taller than me but probably average for a man. If he's really looking for privacy, this will work just fine.

"Okay, let's give it a try. I'll include three meals and a place to pitch your tent at the same rate. Just be sure your tent is far enough away from the house to give us both privacy."

"Thanks. That's very generous of you." He extends his hand, then realizes I'm still in the house. He looks uncomfortable. "Sorry, I'll get used to it."

"When can you start?"

He smiles and seems to relax. The smile softens the angles of his face, and he almost looks pretty. "Now is good for me. What do you want me to do first?"

"We had a big storm that uprooted a lot of trees. Cut them up and put them out by the woodpile. If you don't find the tools you need in the shed, I'll authorize you to purchase them at the general store. Do you need breakfast?"

"No thanks, ma'am. I'll move my truck around back and then get started."

"Please call me Anna. You'll eat your meals at the table out there on the porch. I'll place your lunch on the table and ring a bell when it's ready."

"Sounds good. And please call me Lee." He bounds down the stairs and heads for his truck.

Something about him, the way he holds himself, his walk, his energy, I'm not sure what catches my eye, but I realize I've made a terrible mistake. I grab the microphone again. "Lee."

He turns slowly, his gaze on the camera.

"I'm sorry I mistook you for a man."

She grins. "Happens all the time."

I smile, but of course she can't see it. The rarely used muscles involved tighten, a mildly painful reminder of my isolation. I watch Lee saunter to her truck and, without a backward glance, get in and drive to the field behind the house. I stare at the camera monitoring that side of the house, watch her jump down, stretch, and head back. To divert my thoughts from what I can't do, I think about what I have to do. Have coffee and a slice of toast, shower, and figure out what to make for lunch and dinner.

As I sip my coffee, my traitorous mind wanders to Lee. She looks butch, just my type, but that doesn't mean she's a lesbian. Lots of country women look masculine because they do men's work on their farms and ranches but they're not gay. In any case, it doesn't matter to me, since I'll never enjoy the love and attention of a woman again. But I'm not dead and there's no harm in looking. I put my cup down. Where did that come from? The first woman other than Kim I've seen in months and suddenly I'm a hot and bothered lesbian?

On second thought, I have been dead. Or feeling like I died in that accident. Or wishing I'd died. My reaction to Lee is the first positive feeling or thought I've had in ages. Despite my best efforts to pretend otherwise, I am alive but instead of being filled with love, friends, and laughter, my life is, and will continue to be, filled with despair, pain, and loneliness.

Overwhelmed by my thoughts and feelings, my eyelids feel heavy and it's a struggle to keep my eyes open. I roll into the living room and shift to my recliner.

CHAPTER EIGHT

Lee

April 2024

Anna is quicker than most to realize her mistake. Is it my voice, my ass, my walk, or something else that reveals I'm not a man?

I'd been told she was a nasty old bitch, rigid and demanding, that she doesn't allow anyone in the house, that the hired help has to eat outside like a dog. The disembodied voice was weak and raspy, as if it hadn't been used in a while, so she might be old. Though she sounded angry, I hadn't encountered her nasty side, if she has one. I shrug. I'd successfully worked with plenty of nasty, condescending people in the service and I'd give Anna the benefit of the doubt. Old people and those in pain were often short-tempered.

I was curious, though. Anna must really look horrible if she feels she has to hide behind a camera. I like to look people in the eye when I talk to them. Speaking to someone whose face I can't see makes me uncomfortable, but I'd adjusted in Afghanistan and Iraq, where many of the women I'd interacted with wore garments that covered their entire face and body and left just a mesh screen for them to see through. The hell. If Anna needs to hide behind a camera to protect herself from the curious gazes of strangers, so be it. I'm sympathetic and I'll respect her choice.

In any case, Anna isn't the only one who wants privacy. I'm hoping being in one place, doing physical labor, and spending lots of time reading and playing my guitar will reenergize me.

I park in the field behind the house. Sitting in the truck with little exercise day after day and sleeping in the tent has taken its toll on my body. My lower back hurts and my neck and shoulders are tense, I really need to move, which is why I said I'd start right away. I'll put up my tent and settle in later. I stand, do some stretches, then grab my hat. I take a few minutes to check out the buildings on the property. The barn looks to be in decent condition though it needs some work, and the bunkhouse is moldy, smelly, dusty, and filled with cobwebs but seems solid. The shed looks fairly new, and, like the barn and the bunkhouse, it's wired for electricity, so I turn on the light. It's dusty, but the tools are neatly arranged on the wall.

Had Anna used these tools before whatever caused her to hide? Or did she have a husband or an adult child who left? Or passed away? I retrieve the axe, then examine the saw. Unless there are outlets outside the house, Anna will have to buy a generator. I grab the ladder and the saw and go to the side of the house where the branches of a downed tree are blocking a picture window. Relieved to find an outlet that looks new, I plug in, climb the ladder, and start cutting the branches in front of the window. As the first branch falls away, I realize I'm looking into the kitchen. I immediately turn off the saw and climb down to avoid catching Anna off guard. I'm not sure what to make of that beautiful, modern kitchen in what appears to be a dilapidated house. Is Anna a chef? I walk to the front door and ring the bell. It takes her a few minutes to come to the camera.

"What?" She sounds really annoyed. Well, she'd be more annoyed and probably think I was spying on her if she unexpectedly saw me looking at her through the window.

"Anna, I've started clearing the branches blocking the window on that side of the house." I point. "And I want to let you know that I can see into your kitchen so you should probably stay out of there for a while."

She doesn't say anything for a minute, but I can hear her breathing. "Thank you, Lee. I appreciate the warning." Her voice is still rough, but it's softer. No anger this time.

I wait a few seconds, but she doesn't add anything, so I return to the window and work quickly to clear the branches and the stump of the tree, then head to the other side of the house.

After so many months on the road worrying about Mara and Tessa, it feels good to throw myself into the hard, sweaty work and feel the warmth of the sun on my back. I lose track of the time until the ringing of a bell penetrates my consciousness. I stop to figure out what it is. Then I remember Anna said she'd ring a bell for lunch. I put down the saw and stretch my fingers to ease the tension from gripping it. Then I remove my hat, wipe my face with the bandana I'd tied around my neck, and pull out my phone. Not lunch time, but I've been working for two hours without stopping. No wonder my tank top is soaked with sweat. I gaze at the house. Maybe Anna needs help. I walk quickly to the porch.

CHAPTER NINE

Ariana

I'm wakened by the doorbell. Damn. Now what? I shift to the wheelchair again, put on my floppy hat with the dark veil and roll to the kitchen. Agitated, I pull the hat and veil off. What was I thinking? I can see them, but they can't see me. It's Lee again. "What?" Once again, Lee gets my nasty voice.

"Anna, I've started clearing the branches blocking the window on that side of the house. And I want to let you know that I can see into your kitchen so you should probably stay out of there for a while."

I swallow. She's considerate and respects my need for privacy. "Thank you, Lee. I appreciate the warning." I feel bad for being so bitchy.

While she's working on that side of the house, I shower, wash my hair, and change clothes. I feel better. The sound of the saw has shifted to the other side of the house, but still I put on the hat and veil before going into the kitchen to make coffee. The branches have been cleared from the window and the sun is streaming in. I roll to the window. The branches are in a neat pile and Lee is gone. I remove the hat and veil. My usual breakfast is a half slice of dry toast, but I have a sudden desire for a fried egg on a roll. I defrost a roll and toast it, then add the fried egg and catsup. My tastebuds are awake this morning and this sandwich is the first thing I've enjoyed eating in I don't know how long. I open my computer while I'm eating and email Kim. I mention hiring a woman, Lee Wilton, knowing she'll want to check her out, and drop the fact that I'm enjoying an egg sandwich for breakfast. The fact that I'm enjoying something will make her happy.

After I clean up, I sit in the rocker in the living room near the windows overlooking the front yard where Lee is sawing the fallen trees into fireplace-sized logs. I tell myself I'm overseeing the work, but if I'm honest, I'm envious of Lee's lithe athletic body and her ease with the physical labor. I long for the days when I could count on my body, when I didn't have to worry about toppling over or being immobilized by pain. As the morning wears on and the logs pile up, Lee strips down to a tank top and I realize I'm staring at her muscular back and arms, the curve of her hips, the rise and fall of her breasts. It's good to know I can still appreciate a good-looking woman. Unfortunately, it isn't like before. Now I can look but not touch. Suddenly my heart is racing, my skin prickles, and the blood pulses through my body. It takes me a few seconds to recognize what I'm feeling. I'm in a rage. I turn away from the window and drag myself up onto the walker. I need to think about something else. If I'm not careful, I'll spiral into depression again. Or kill Lee out of jealousy.

It takes a while for me to calm down and recognize that Lee is not the problem. It's me. I've become a shell. A nonperson. I can't hold back the tears, and after a good cry, I remember I'm expected to feed Lee. I wash my face and begin to prep for lunch and dinner when it occurs to me that Lee has been working in the hot sun for two hours without stopping. That can't be good. I pour a large glass of lemonade, then put a bottle of water, a bar of soap, and a towel in my lap. I open the door, grab the lemonade, roll outside, and place everything on the porch table. I feel the sun on my arms and realize this is the first time I've been outside since Kim's last visit. Wanting to feel the sun on my face, I look up, but of course the hat and veil keep me in the dark. I'd love to sit out here, but I don't want Lee to see me. I ring the bell, roll back into the house, and close the door. Using my walker, I struggle to my feet and head for the refrigerator to see if I have anything for lunch. Lee appears almost immediately. Hat in hand, drying her dripping face with the kerchief she's worn around her neck, she looks up at the camera. "Do you need something, Anna?"

I walk back and speak into the microphone. "No. You must be thirsty working in this heat. The lemonade on the table is for you, but I have iced tea if you'd rather?"

"Lemonade is great." Lee drinks, then glances at the camera. "Doing physical labor after spending months on the road feels good, but I got so involved I didn't pay attention to how warm it got. If it's okay with you, I'll sit here for a short break."

"It's fine. You don't have to do it all today."

Lee sits. "I'll keep going till lunch, then I'll do something less taxing."

"Speaking of lunch, the only things I have on such short notice are either an egg salad or tuna fish sandwich. Which would you prefer?"

"Tuna."

Before I can turn away, she continues, "I noticed an old garden patch out back. Do you intend to put in a vegetable garden?"

"Just a second." A groan escapes as I lower myself into my wheelchair again and roll close to the microphone. "Sorry, I was on my walker, and I get tired if I stand too long."

"Oh, I didn't mean—"

"It's okay. I like the vegetable garden idea, but I can't...it's not something I can do. Would you—"

"I'd enjoy it."

I hesitate. "Maybe we should give it a few days, see how you like being here before you spend time putting in a garden that I can't maintain."

"You've had trouble keeping help?"

My laugh sounds harsh even to me. "More like trouble getting. Most people aren't comfortable conversing with a disembodied voice. Like the Wizard of Oz, I spook people." I stare at Lee's back, the damp short black hair curled behind her ears, the sweaty tank top, a hint of a tattoo peeking out, the tanned unblemished skin of her neck, and the muscular arms. This time it's not rage but an almost forgotten feeling that stirs in my belly. Treacherous body.

Lee stands but doesn't turn to look at the camera. "Well, I'm not spooked so far. I'll get back to work now."

"The water, bar of soap, and towel on the table are for you."

Lee pivots, places the glass on the table, and grabs the water. "I'll take the soap and towel later when I'm ready to wash up. Thanks for the lemonade. See you for lunch." She walks around to the front of the house without a backward glance.

I open the door, grab the glass, and quickly lock myself in again. I envy Lee's freedom, being out in the sun, feeling the air, working her body, not having to plan every move. I smile, remembering how much I enjoyed the outdoors, riding my horses, walking the trails on my property, swimming in my pool. I took my body, my life for granted. We all did. At least none of us was into drugs or alcohol. We got high on performing. And if we desired sex, there were plenty of women willing and able. Who could have imagined what I've been reduced to? What would the girls think? I shake my head. Nope, not going there right now.

I make tuna salad and defrost two rolls, then consider the options for our dinner. I like the sound of that. Cooking for one is no fun and eating alone is the pits. It's only been a few hours, but I have a good feeling about Lee. She seems fit and able to do the job, and she doesn't seem at all thrown by my desire to not be looked at.

And speaking of being looked at, Lee is not at all hard to look at. Damn, my brain goes there again. In fact, she arouses feelings I thought had gone up in the flames that took everything from me. While it's nice to know I'm not totally devoid of those feelings, I remind myself I can never act on them. Even Lee, as nice as she seems, would flinch at making love to a cripple with a scarred face and body and a damaged mind. I gasp, surprised where my thoughts have taken me. Maybe I need to reconsider hiring her. Maybe she's too dangerous to the balance I've achieved in my new life. I'll give it a day or two.

CHAPTER TEN

Lee

At the sound of the lunch bell, I gather the tools and put them in the shed. Using the bar of soap and the towel Anna provided, I wash my hands, face, and upper body at the spigot at the back of the house, then retrieve the book I'm reading from my truck. My lunch is on the table when I get to the porch.

I sit in the chair with my back to the house, place my hat on the floor, unfold the napkin, and take a bite of the sandwich. Tuna with a tangy dressing on a baguette. It's delicious. I sip the lemonade, eat a forkful of potato salad, then relax with my legs stretched in front of me. Immersed in my novel, I eat slowly.

"Do you want another sandwich?" The gravelly voice jolts me out of the book.

"No thanks. It was delicious, but one is enough. I could use a little more lemonade if you don't mind."

"Just a second." The screen door squeaks. "Here. Turn but don't look up."

Keeping my eyes low, I swivel and take the glass, noting the long, slender fingers wrapped around it. Lovely hand and young skin. Maybe Anna isn't an old lady after all.

"Why don't you take the rest of the afternoon to set up your tent and settle in? I'll ring the bell for dinner about six."

"That would be great. Thanks." I head to the back of the property. Anna is prickly, but she's also kind and considerate. If no one has worked here before me, who could have started the stories about her being a monster? It's probably just small town gossip to explain why she stays hidden. When I turned to get the second glass of lemonade, my gaze went a little higher than it should have, and I caught a glimpse of the dark veil she was wearing. I'm curious, but I'll never ask. She'll tell me what she wants me to know and that will have to be enough.

I assess the property, then drive my truck close to the spot where I'll set up my tent. I clear the area, put down the ground mats, erect the tent, and then place my clothing, guitar, and the camping lanterns inside. I leave my cooking gear and the other things in the truck. Once the tent is ready, I gather some large rocks, make a fire ring, and place my lounge chair in front of it. When I'm finished, I sit in the chair and read until I hear the bell.

CHAPTER ELEVEN

Ariana

I like having Lee here. She makes me feel safe. I've solved the problem of her attractiveness by only speaking to her when necessary. She seems okay with my rules and limitations and is content to let me control our interactions. Though I'm sure she's as curious about me as I am about the losses she mentioned and why she was on the road for months, I appreciate that she doesn't ask questions or offer information about herself, so I don't feel any pressure to relate to her. We've fallen into an easy rhythm, with contact limited to minimal exchanges about meals or the work I've asked her to do. She's self-sufficient and seems happy to go back to her tent at night. Any thoughts of sending her away have disappeared.

I've taken to eating my meals with her. Of course, she doesn't know that since she's on the porch and I'm in the kitchen watching her on the security screen. I feel less lonely and after the first week I realized that for the first time since Kim left me here, I'm eating three meals a day. They're tiny compared to what I serve Lee, but it's still a meal. I'm sure Kim would be thrilled if I told her, but I haven't. Nor have I mentioned eating with Lee.

Lee sits with her back to the camera, totally unaware of being watched as she eats and slowly turns the pages of whatever book she's currently reading. Am I stalking her? I don't think so. I'm just enjoying the illusion of having company, of sitting down to a meal with someone, of not being so alone.

Lee's habit of reading while she's eating reminds me of me in my old life, always with my head in a book. My friends teased me mercilessly about being the only big singing star living vicariously. I enjoyed nonfiction and many genres of fiction, and I loved to discuss what I was reading with anyone who would engage. I'm jealous of Lee's ability to concentrate, to lose herself in another world, something that is beyond me now. I haven't read a book since the accident. Remembering the pleasure and feeling the loss hits me like a gut punch. For the first time since Lee arrived, I experience the emptiness of my life. Suddenly I'm sobbing. I quickly roll into the living room, afraid Lee will hear me.

It's almost as if I was living in a state of suspended animation before Lee arrived ten days ago. I thought she was dangerous because she awakened my body, but I now understand she's dangerous because she's awakened my mind. Even with our limited connection, she's touched parts of me that I thought were dead and I'm happier than I've been since I woke up after the accident. And yet, I'm desolate. There's no future with her. She'll be gone and I'll still be here alone. I dry my tears, but I'm in too deep now so maybe I'll take whatever pleasure, the little happiness I can, while she's here. I wash my face, return to the table and gaze at the camera. As usual she's slowly reading while eating lunch. I wonder if it's an older book, something I've read.

"Anna, I'm done. Thanks for another delicious lunch." I jump at her voice. She always lets me know when it's safe for me to go outside to clear the table. She stands, grabs her hat, and walks off the porch.

I wait a few minutes, then roll out, load her glass, dish, and napkin in the basket on my lap, then eye the book on the table. This is the first time she's left a book behind. Based on the flashes of the jacket I've seen I believe this is the one she's been immersed in for a few days. I look in the direction Lee walked and she's not in sight. I pull the book close. *The Paying Guests* by Sarah Waters. I've read some of her books but not this one. I turn it over and read the jacket copy. Intrigued, I open to chapter one and read the first three pages. I'm immediately pulled into the story. I close the book, check for Lee again, and take it inside with me. I load our dishes in the dishwasher, stir my sauce, and finish making the meatballs for dinner. I like cooking for someone, even if we only eat together remotely. What is it about Lee that makes me comfortable? Is she a lesbian? She looks like she could be, and she is reading Sarah

Waters. But I remind myself, looking butch doesn't mean she's a lesbian. And neither does reading a lesbian author.

Hours later, I ring the bell for dinner. I can see Lee's truck parked in the back field but not her tent. As she saunters across the yard, I place her book, the plate of spaghetti, meatballs, and the garlic bread on the table, then step inside the screen door and close it.

Lee sits at the table, then glances at the camera. "Wow, this looks fantastic. You're spoiling me with meals like this."

"Would you like a glass of wine? I have Chianti."

"Wine would be perfect."

I smile to myself, pleased that I remembered Kim's stash of wine. I pour her a glass, roll to the screen door, and open it. I touch her shoulder. "Here's the wine."

She doesn't turn, just reaches back for the glass. She takes a forkful of spaghetti. "Mmm, this is good. Are you eating, too?"

"I'll eat later." I don't know why I lie since I plan to eat with her as usual.

She opens *The Paying Guests*. "Are you enjoying the book?"

I stiffen. "Have you been spying on me?"

Lee laughs. "I assure you I've been working my ass off all afternoon chopping logs into firewood, but there are a couple of long blond hairs sticking out that weren't there before and they definitely aren't mine."

I let out a breath. "Sorry. I'm paranoid—"

"You don't have to apologize. I'm sure your need for privacy makes most people determined to see what you're hiding, but I'm happy to be here on your terms."

I smile. "Is it okay if I join you and talk while you're eating?" Shocked to hear the words come out of my mouth I clamp my lips together. This isn't good. I'm getting too relaxed around Lee. I consider saying I've changed my mind, but that would be rude. I'll allow myself to engage just this one time.

"More than okay."

I get a glass of lemonade and roll to the screen door. "I am enjoying it, the book, I mean." She jumps at my voice right behind her instead of over the mic, but she doesn't turn to look. Between the screen door and my veil, she won't see anything even if she forgets, so I relax. "I used to read a great deal. But since the accident, I've found it difficult to concentrate so I haven't even tried."

This is another lie. It may be true that I couldn't concentrate, but the truth is I haven't attempted to read because I've been punishing myself for being alive.

"It's the first book I've had the opportunity to look at in a long time and it pulled me right in and held my attention." I hesitate, not wanting to reveal too much. "What do you like about it?"

"The characters, the period. Waters is a fantastic writer. She paints a picture of the changes in society in the early 1920s resulting from the First World War and the claustrophobia of being a woman and a lesbian at that time. I only have about ten pages left to go so why don't I finish it after dinner and leave it with you?"

"You don't have to do that."

"I'm not heartless. You're already invested, and I insist you read it. It's not due at the library until next week, and I'll be starting another book later. By the way, the meatballs are spectacular."

"Thank you." I sit behind the screen door sipping my lemonade as Lee eats. "You belong to the library. Are you from around here?"

"No. But the first thing I do when I decide to stay a while in a new town is join the library."

"Will you be here long?"

"I'll leave eventually. But I expect to stay a few months, at least until the garden I'm going to plant for you yields all its vegetables and I turn it over to get it ready for next year."

"That would be wonderful. Just so you know, Lee, I'm smiling." Suddenly I feel exposed and anxious. I'm freaking out because I'm enjoying talking to Lee. "I'll eat dinner now and let you finish your book. Let me know if you'd like more of anything. There's plenty." I close the door and, breathing heavily, I stare at the camera for a few minutes. What the hell am I'm doing?

A half hour later, Lee speaks. I look at the screen. She's standing, facing the camera.

"I'm leaving now, Anna, and the book is on the table. Good night."

I wait until Lee is on her way back to her tent before going outside to get the book and bring in the dishes, then I sit at the kitchen table eating and reading. It's been a long time since I was able to lose myself in anything, forget the scars and the pain and my loneliness. The strumming of a guitar interrupts my thoughts. I look up at the alcove window. I've taken to opening it in the morning to bring some of outside in. It's getting dark, but I can see Lee's light and it makes me feel safe. Strange, I hadn't realized I didn't feel safe before.

The lovely voice floating gently on the evening breeze from Lee's tent draws me closer to the window. It's the first music I've heard since the night of the accident, and my first instinct is to close the window and go into my bedroom where I won't hear it. I'm flooded with regrets and the pain of all I've lost, the people I've lost, but then an image of Torie and me playing our guitars and harmonizing, not on stage, but for our own pleasure in the bus during our last tour, pops up, and I can't help but smile at the happy memory, the first in a long time. I can't resist the beauty of Lee's voice and her music. I feel the ice in my heart melting as I remain in my wheelchair in front of the window listening. I don't recognize any of the songs, but they're filled with sadness, longing, and regret.

I stare toward Lee's tent long after the music stops and her light goes out, wondering whether she'd written the songs. I close the window, put the dinner dishes in the washer, and roll into the bedroom. While I get ready for bed, I realize that tonight is the first time I've felt comfortable leaving the window open after dark. I lay in bed with Lee's voice in my head and the tears flow. I'm not sure whether I'm crying for the voice I've lost, for the songs I'll never sing, because the music is gone from my life, or because of the pain Lee's songs express. Perhaps it's all of the above.

I'm curious about the source of Lee's pain. What has she lost? Who is she longing for? I won't ask, of course, because I'm not ready to answer her questions about me. But I feel for her.

The next morning, I'm awakened by the sound of the saw and remember that Lee plans to repair the barn door today. I'm sleeping soundly since she arrived and this morning for the first time since I moved here, I slept late. As I'm dressing, I decide not to mention hearing her sing or how much her songs moved me or the impact of hearing music again. I'm afraid if I say anything, she'll stop singing. And as unsettling as it is, I crave more.

I jump as someone bangs on the door. I hear the screen door opening and closing. "Delivery."

I put on my hat, lower the veil, drop into my wheelchair, and go out to the kitchen. The redheaded delivery boy is on the porch, grinning. I speak into the microphone. "You're not supposed to come in." I strain my voice, trying for volume. "Just leave everything on the porch as usual." I feel a panic attack coming on.

I focus on breathing until I feel in control. I take another deep breath and bang on the door, hoping if he's still there he'll hear me and go away. I rotate the camera. Tears sting my eyes. He's done it again. The van is gone, but my groceries are strewn around the front yard, making it necessary to go up and down the six steps, steps that are treacherous to get up and down with the walker, multiple times to get everything into the house. Kim was right. I should have a ramp.

Once I wouldn't have noticed six steps but doing them one time is difficult now and doing them multiple times without falling is almost impossible. And getting up can take hours. I don't understand why, but this is the third time he's done it in the last couple of months. Several weeks ago, I fell going up the steps and it took me an hour to get to my feet and another hour to drag the boxes up the steps and into the kitchen. I couldn't eat that day and lay awake all night angry and anxious. The old people's "I can't get up" alarm that Kim made me promise to wear would be helpful right now, but I only wear it when Kim is here. The truth is I'd rather suffer than have a stranger see me so debilitated.

I consider calling Mr. Stone, the owner of the store, and asking him to send someone to pick up the groceries for me, but I'm afraid to draw attention to myself. How pathetic. Resigned, I hold my walker on my lap, open the door, and roll onto the porch. I place the walker next to the wheelchair, set the brakes, and edge forward. I don't have the strength or control to lower myself to the porch, and I drop, hard. The pain shoots through my body. Panting, I rest, then ease myself over to the first step, dragging my walker with me. Dropping from one step to another is agony, but finally I'm on the bottom step. I rest for a minute, trying to catch my breath, then I try to stand. It takes multiple attempts to get to my feet. I'm soaked with sweat but triumphant. Holding onto the walker I lean over, grab the smallest carton, and drag it toward the steps. It's not until the saw goes silent that I remember Lee.

I'm shocked when she dashes past me and runs down the driveway yelling. I can't make out the words, but I'm thrilled when she pulls the redheaded delivery boy out of the bushes and throws him against a tree. She towers over him, one arm holding him in place, the other raised as if to strike him. Her voice is hard and angry, and the boy sounds as if he's pleading. Finally, using both hands, Lee pulls him away from the tree and throws him into the bushes. Hands on her hips, she keeps her eyes on the van as it bumps down the driveway toward the road. When it's out of sight she starts back toward the house. I bend over the carton.

"Leave it, Anna. I'll carry everything into the kitchen. You can go into another room." She hurries toward me. As she gets closer, her eyes widen. She's seeing me for the first time, taking in the hat and veil and the long baggy dress. She stops far enough away so I feel comfortable.

I straighten, turn, and place my foot on the bottom step but lose my balance as I try to pull myself up. Arms flailing, I fall back, screaming. Suddenly strong arms encircle my waist from behind.

"I've got you, Anna." I shiver at the intimacy of her warm breath close to my ear and the gentleness of her voice as she reassures me. She seems to misinterpret my reaction as fear and tightens her hold. "Don't worry, I can't see your face. Let me help you up to the porch."

Shaking, I lean back into the comfort of the strong embrace. Kim's hug before I left the arena the night of the accident is the last body-to-body contact I've had with anyone. Now despite the fear and anxiety leading to this moment, I savor Lee's voice in my ear, the warmth of her breath on my face, the soft pressure of her breasts against my back, her arms around my waist, and the earthy smell of her sweat. She doesn't say anything, just holds me tightly from behind, until I stop shaking, then she asks softly, "Ready to go up?"

I nod and we start up. Lee continues to embrace me from behind as she half carries, half walks me up step by step. On the porch, she turns me to face her but respectful as always, her gaze is over my shoulder. She holds me a few seconds before gently easing me down to the wheelchair and dropping her arms. I immediately feel the loss. She goes down the steps.

"How did you know, Lee?"

She answers without turning. "I just happened to look up when he drove in. I recognized the delivery van, so I relaxed and got out my water bottle to drink and rest a bit. I saw him head down the driveway, but I was puzzled that he left the van behind the trees and walked back toward the house, so I kept my eye on him. When he trained binoculars on the house and started taking pictures with his phone, I lost it. I hope you don't mind that I roughed him up, took his phone, and told him not to come back."

I feel a prickle of anxiety. What if he recognized me? "I don't mind. Um, did you look at the pictures he took?"

"I did. At that distance you were just a tiny blob. I'm not sure what he thought he was doing, but they're useless. Do you want to see them?"

Do I? It would be better to be sure. "Yes."

Lee hands me the camera, and I flip through the photos. She was right. With the veil and long baggy dress, there's no way anyone could tell I'm Ariana Calandre. I relax and hand the phone to Lee.

"He's supposed to leave the groceries on the table out here and today isn't the first time he's spread them out on the ground. The last time I fell trying to get them up the stairs. And this morning he was rattling the screen door so I thought he was coming in the house, although he knows he shouldn't. I'll send an email to complain later."

"Why don't I pick up the groceries from now on? And I'll register a complaint in person this afternoon if that's okay?"

I choke up at the feeling of being taken care of, of being cared for. "Thank you. That would be fine, but let Mr. Stone know that once you leave, I'll need delivery again." I tense. I'm getting too dependent on Lee, too close to her. I'll be devastated when she leaves.

Lee must sense my emotions because she nods and doesn't look at me. "Are you going to relax in the sun or go into the living room while I carry the groceries into the kitchen?"

She's already seen me so there's no need to hide. "I think I'll just enjoy some time out here." Lee's eyes widen. I've surprised her. And myself. I feel the need to explain. "The veil and the hat are enough to protect me…my privacy. Besides, I trust you, Lee." I smile, but of course she can't see it.

Her grin surprises me. "Wow. That's great. Can I bring you lemonade or iced tea when I come out?"

"If you can wait a little longer for breakfast, I'd like a glass of cold water." I might as well do this relaxing in the sunshine thing right. "Thank you for rescuing me, Lee. I—" My voice breaks, I take a couple of deep breaths. "It's nice not to feel so alone."

Lee clears her throat. "I'm glad. I'm happy to have your company as well."

She goes down the steps, gathers some of the groceries, and carries them into the house, then comes out to pick up the rest. I hear her moving around the kitchen and then, soothed by the warmth of the sun, the rustle of the wind, the sound of the birds, and the earthy fragrance of the trees and greenery, I doze. Her voice startles me and for a moment I'm on my deck in Austin. Then I open my eyes. And remember.

"Everything is in, Anna. Your water is on the table. Ring the bell whenever breakfast is ready. No hurry." She walks down the steps. "See you later," she tosses out.

I sit in the quiet and enjoy being outdoors. With Lee nearby, I'm relaxed and not afraid. When I hear the saw start, I glance around, though I know Lee and I are alone, then I raise my veil and lift my face to the sun. Such a simple thing but it's been a long time. After a few minutes I feel anxious at being exposed, so I lower the veil and sit until my heart steadies, then I go into the kitchen to put the groceries away. I can't help but smile when I see that Lee has put all the perishables away, saving me several trips between the table and the refrigerator and freezer. I put the remaining groceries in the cabinets, then move on to breakfast. I break four eggs in a bowl, add cinnamon, vanilla, and six slices of bread. While the bread is soaking, I make a pot of coffee, throw bacon in a frying pan, set the table, and then lay the bread on the griddle.

The smells of the perking coffee, sizzling bacon, and frying french toast awaken a hunger I haven't felt in a very long time. Did sitting outside in the sunlight rouse my senses? Or did being embraced by Lee? I ring the bell. As I wait, I resolve to sit outside and read when Lee gets back from town later.

CHAPTER TWELVE

Lee

Seeing Anna in person for the first time is shocking. I'm not sure what I was expecting, but the big floppy hat with a heavy veil covering her face, a baggy, long-sleeved dress hanging on her frame wasn't it. Even her feet are hidden by socks. I can't see enough of her to tell her age, but she's tall, maybe a little shorter than my own five-ten, and thin. She felt so fragile I just wanted to cocoon her in my arms forever and keep her safe. But with my face buried in her luxurious blond hair I couldn't help breathing in her scent. And when she shivered in my arms, I felt, as much as I'd like to deny it, turned on.

That shocked me. I mean, how does one feel attracted to someone who has mainly been a disembodied voice? Now that we're engaging about the book, I'm enjoying her intelligent and thoughtful analysis and reacting to who she is, not what she looks like. So far I like what I know of her. But maybe I need to go out and get laid rather than lusting after my crippled, scarred, reclusive landlady. I realize that based on her voice, the blondness of her hair, the youthfulness of the skin on her hands, her gentleness and kindness, I've formed a picture of her in my mind that doesn't include crippled, scarred, or reclusive. I need to take care to not fall for someone who is not available. Maybe it's just the mystery of her that I find attractive.

What is Anna's story?

The more I know, the more I want to know, but I remind myself that I'd resolved to let her share what she wants, when she's ready. Or not. She is vulnerable, physically and emotionally. If she had been alone this morning, she might have broken a bone or injured her head and died out there without anyone knowing. As long as I'm here, I'll get as close as she can tolerate and protect her from little shits like the delivery boy. I put the fear of my fists in him, but just thinking about what he did throws me into a rage.

When I left her on the porch, it occurred to me that, to my knowledge, she'd hadn't been outside at all since I arrived. On my way to finish the job at the barn I turned and saw her body relax. I imagined she was purring with contentment. How much better would she feel if she could turn her face to the sun without that heavy veil? How horrible could she look? I shake my head and walk away, thinking of the questions I couldn't ask and the questions I couldn't answer.

After lunch, I drive into town. As I walk through the door of the general store, conversation slowly grinds to a halt and all eyes track my progress to the rear, where the proprietor stands behind a counter. All eyes except those of the red-haired boy, who hightails it to the back room when he spots me.

As I approach, the proprietor crosses his arms over his chest, his expression not hostile but not friendly either. "Can I help you, sir?"

Without correcting him, I lean on the counter and speak softly. "You may not remember that you gave me the information about the job at Ms. Solander's place, but I've been working there for a couple of weeks, and I've come to lodge a complaint on her behalf."

He frowns. "Something wrong with the groceries?"

"No, something is seriously wrong with the grocery delivery boy. I'll be picking up her groceries from now on."

He scans the store and, not seeing what he's looking for, he walks to the door of the back room. "Thomas, come out here, immediately." His tone of voice leaves no question that he is to be obeyed.

The white-faced boy sidles into the room. The man turns to me. "What's wrong with the delivery boy?" His voice is no less commanding with me.

"He"—I point at the boy—"seems to believe that a disabled woman living alone is fair game to torment."

The boy turns to run, but the man grabs him by the collar and pulls him back. "You will listen to this, Thomas." He tips his head in my direction. "Continue, please."

"Ms. Solander uses a wheelchair and occasionally a walker. She never leaves the house and steps are extremely difficult and dangerous for her. Today and several other times that I'm aware of, Thomas scattered the groceries on the path rather than placing them on the table on the porch as arranged with you. In order to bring her groceries inside, Ms. Solander has to go up and down six rickety steps multiple times. During one of these instances several weeks ago, she fell and lay there for hours struggling to stand and then drag the groceries up the steps and into the house. Today, I was working on the side of the house, so I didn't hear him rattle the screen door and make sounds like he was entering the house, something that terrified Ms. Solander, who, as I believe you know, doesn't wish to be seen by anyone."

"Did you do that, Thomas?"

The boy looks down, his eyes brimming with tears. Feeling sorry for himself apparently. "Yessir."

I continue, wanting the man to understand how despicable his son's behavior is. "I saw him arrive and assumed he would leave the groceries as usual on the table. But when he sped down the driveway at high speed, he got my attention. I watched him park the truck behind some trees, then, using binoculars, observe Ms. Solander make her way down the steps, which, as I said, is difficult and dangerous for her, and attempt to pick up her groceries to get them in the house. He was taking pictures of her with his phone, when I grabbed him, threw him against the tree, and threatened his life if he ever showed his face again." I put the phone I'd taken from the boy on the counter. "I've deleted all the pictures I could find, but he may have some on his computer."

"Thomas, you're an embarrassment to me and your mother." He pushes the boy toward the back room. "I'll deal with you later. I'm so sorry, um, I don't remember your name. I'm Elton Stone."

"Lee, Lee Wilton. And it's Ms."

He studies me for a few seconds. "My mistake, Ms. Wilton, please excuse me. And please let Ms. Solander know I'll make sure my son learns a lesson from this. Let me give you my cell phone number. If you can't get into town to pick up her groceries, call me and I'll deliver them myself. Also, I won't charge her for this week's groceries."

"Thank you, Mr. Stone. I'll pass that on."

"I'd be pleased if you called me Elton."

CHAPTER THIRTEEN

Ariana

The feelings from our encounter—Lee's breath in my ear, the heady scent of her sweat, the softness of her breasts on my back, the heat everywhere our bodies touched, the strength and safety of her arms holding me close—linger throughout the day, making me happy and anxious. I didn't know how much I missed being touched. All my nerve endings are buzzing with the pleasure of it. It's unsettling, though, because my body is reacting as if it was a sexual contact. And it wants more.

I've let myself go too far. First reading and discussing books, then listening to her music, and now feeling aroused by her touch. A touch, I'm sure Lee saw as just a kindness she would do for anyone and not at all sexual or pleasurable in any way. I take a deep breath. I've forgotten how it feels to be alive. When she leaves I'll sink back into the grinding unfeeling loneliness of my life before she came. But at this point I can't, don't want to, send her away. I'll enjoy what I can now. Future pain be damned.

I cook and read and at dinner we resume discussing *The Paying Guests*. I let myself feel the pleasure of the give and take of our discussion and the connection. I'm sad because I'm almost done with the book.

"Thank you for another delicious dinner and another engaging conversation, Anna." Lee stacks her dishes and stands. "I'm going to the library tomorrow. Do you have any idea what you would like to read next?"

I choke up at her kindness. "I'm not up on current books, but it seems we have similar taste so something you've read you think I'd enjoy or something that looks interesting to you at the library."

She smiles. "Okay. Good night, Anna."

I put our dishes in the dishwasher and sit at the table sipping my wine and reading. Then I close the book, shut the lights in the kitchen, and sit in front of the window enjoying the night air. A little while later the music starts. Tonight, my fourth night of listening, she mixes what I believe are her own songs with covers of older artists like Joan Baez and Judy Collins. And then she sings two of mine. I'm honored. She has a beautiful voice and her rendition is gorgeous. The music washes over me and fills the dry empty spaces inside me with beauty.

As my breathing evens, my heart slowly opens, like a flower facing the morning sun. The feelings of loss and pain dredged up the first time I heard her music are replaced by happy memories of singing with my girls in rehearsal, concerts, and, occasionally, spontaneously because, like Lee, music was how we expressed our feelings. Kim is right. I've been punishing myself for being alive by depriving myself of music and books and other simple pleasures.

Now that I'm letting pleasure in, I feel almost like my old self. At least on the inside. And for the first time since the accident it occurs to me that if I had been the one to die I would have wanted Erica, Torie, Maggie, Gloria, and Nellie to live the best lives they could without me. In fact, thinking about my five loving friends, I'm sure they'd be outraged to see me choose to curl up and wait to die rather than enjoy, to the extent possible, the life I have, even if it's different than the one I had. Or maybe I'm just trying to make myself feel less guilty about letting in the pleasure.

CHAPTER FOURTEEN

Lee

The next morning, I look up at the sound of a vehicle coming up the driveway and seeing the grocery van, I run to make sure Thomas isn't here to exact some revenge. It is Thomas, but he isn't alone. His father pushes him toward the porch.

"Morning, Elton." I extend my arm to keep them from getting closer than necessary, then call out, "Ms. Solander, you have visitors."

Elton looks around. "Nice spread, but kind of isolated."

I shove my hands into my back pockets. "She likes it that way, but it doesn't mean she should be tormented and abused."

Anna appears, a shadow in a floppy hat in a wheelchair behind the screen door.

"Who is it, Lee?"

"It's Mr. Stone from the grocery store and his son, Thomas, the delivery boy."

Stone clears his throat. "Ms. Solander, I'm sorry to meet under these circumstances. I'm here because Thomas has something to say to you." He pushes the boy forward.

Thomas stands with his head hanging. "I'm sorry for trying to scare you and for putting you in danger by not leaving the groceries on the porch like I'm supposed to."

Anna had been resigned and frightened when it happened, but now as the horrid boy spouts meaningless words of apology, she abruptly stands, fists clenched, and leans toward the screen door. It's hard to tell with her baggy dress but I think her chest is heaving and I get the impression she wants to incinerate him. A human response to retaliate, to hurt him like he'd hurt her.

"Are you really sorry, Thomas, or are you just trying to get yourself out of trouble?"

His head jerks up at the rage underneath the words. His eyes wide, he glances at his dad but gets no help. He shifts uneasily, then clears his throat. "I don't know." He speaks so softly I wonder how she can hear him.

"That's honest, at least. Mr. Stone and Lee, please take a seat at the table while I chat with Thomas."

Anna takes a long minute to study the boy. He's frightened. Good. But hopefully she remembers he's just a boy. Destroying him won't help either of them. I take a breath. This could be a teaching moment. If Anna helps him understand the impact of his actions and gets him to take responsibility for his lack of consideration for another human being, she can change him.

"Thomas, did you watch me crawl up and down the stairs with the groceries the first time you didn't leave them on the porch?"

He rocks on his heels as if getting ready to run. "Yes, ma'am."

"Did you enjoy seeing me fall the second time you did it? Did you watch me struggle to stand and then in pain drag the groceries up the steps to the porch? Did you think it was funny? Was that why you did it again and brought binoculars with you the third time?"

He nods.

"I didn't hear you, Thomas." She raises her voice, making no attempt to hide her anger.

"Yes, ma'am." His voice is a whisper.

"What was funny about it, Thomas? Seeing me fall? Or watching me drag myself up and down the steps?"

He shrugs.

"Please answer me, Thomas. I don't think you understand the impact of your actions. You hurt me physically and emotionally. The first time, I didn't eat anything all day or sleep that night because I was so frightened you'd come back. And the second time, the pain and bruises from falling and struggling to get up, then lifting the things you carelessly scattered on the ground and crawling up the steps to get them into the house, lasted two weeks. Did it make you feel powerful?"

He swipes at the tears running down his face. "No, ma'am."

"Then what did you feel, Thomas? Help me understand why you did it three times."

He wipes his nose on his sleeve. "I guess I wanted to see what you look like."

"What have you heard about me?"

He looks at his dad.

"It's a simple question, Thomas. Why do you think I hide in here instead of sitting out in the sunshine?"

"I heard you was old and really ugly and crippled, like a monster."

"Would it surprise you to know that I'm probably younger than your mom and dad, maybe even younger than Lee and that I don't let people see me because it upsets them and that upsets me?"

"Yes, ma'am, it would."

"Have you ever burned your hand on a hot stove or splashed bacon grease on your face while cooking breakfast?"

"Yes, ma'am."

"It hurts doesn't it, especially the hot grease? And if it's really a bad burn it can be painful and raw for a long time and leave a scar. Try to imagine having many of your bones broken, then gasoline splash on half your body and burst into flames. Believe me, burning alive is agony while it's happening and agony while the doctors try to fix you after. And it leaves awful scars. I wouldn't wish it on anyone, even someone as thoughtless and sadistic as you who intentionally harmed me so you could enjoy seeing me struggle in pain. Think about it, Thomas. Which one of us is the monster?"

"I'm sorry. Really sorry." A sob escapes. "I didn't think about your pain or how you got that way." He swipes his arm over his face.

"Your lack of compassion and empathy for another human being is a huge problem, Thomas. If you can't be a better person, you're doomed to be the monster." Anna stares at him for a minute. "Is that what you want, Thomas. To be a monster?"

"No, ma'am."

He's sobbing, so it's clear he got the message.

"I'm satisfied, Mr. Stone. Thank you for giving me the opportunity to…educate Thomas."

"No, thank you for being so frank, Ms. Solander. Thomas has lost his driving privileges and the privilege of spending time with his friends for the entire summer. I'd like him to suffer as much as possible for his meanness. Perhaps he could assist Lee with some of the work around here? I'd be happy to drop him off every morning."

"It's nice of you to offer, Mr. Stone. But I'd want to know what Thomas thinks about that before committing. Are you willing to help Lee, Thomas?"

"I don't know." He looks down at his feet. "I'll try if you let me."

"Then I'll discuss it with Lee and email your dad later."

As father and son drive away, I grapple with the horror of Anna's story, the agony of broken bones and gasoline burns. At the same time, I'm buoyed by the generosity and kindness in her attempt to save the boy who tormented her. Because it was forgiveness to expose herself and her feelings to educate the boy, to make him understand the pain he caused, to force him to see her as a human being and not the monster in his head. I'm not sure I could show that kind of grace toward someone who intentionally tried to harm me. I can't even find it in my heart to forgive the driver who killed my best friends, Ella and Jeff, orphaning Mara and Tessa. I take a deep breath and turn to face Anna, who is back in her wheelchair and just a shadow behind the screen door. "Are you okay, Anna?"

"Yes. Just tired. Do you think I went overboard?"

"No. I think you were perfect. The little shit needed to be confronted with his actions."

Anna's laugh is a surprise. A welcome surprise. And a sound I want to hear more often.

She rolls onto the porch. "I think I'll sit outside for a while and enjoy the sun and the fresh air."

I turn to go back to work but think better of it. "It sounds like you've had a horrendous time of it. I'm sorry."

"Thanks, Lee."

CHAPTER FIFTEEN

Ariana

That night, I wake just before four a.m. to thunder, lightning, huge gusts of wind, and unrelenting rain that seems to come from all directions. Worried about Lee, I get out of bed, pull on my robe, grab my walker, and go to the kitchen window. I stare into the darkness, but I can't see anything. I turn the porch light on, hoping she sees it and comes to the door, then I put on a pot of coffee.

I sit at the table. I can't let Lee stay outside in this storm. I try her cell phone, but either she can't hear it over the roaring wind or service is out. I don't know what to do. But I can't go outside to find her. Would she hear the bell over this wind? It's worth a try. I stand at the screen door, ringing the bell, then in a flash of lightning I see her truck. I grab my hat, pull the veil down, and lean out the door, ringing the bell as hard as I can. The light in the cab of the truck goes on, and Lee jumps out and dashes onto the porch. I push the screen door open. "Come in."

"Are you sure?"

"Yes. I'm wearing my veil but try to avoid looking at me just in case."

Lee closes the door but continues to face it. "Do you have a towel? I'm dripping all over the floor."

I grab a set of my sweats and several towels from the linen closet and hand them to Lee. "I'm going into the other room. Dry yourself off and change into the sweats. The pants will be a little short, but you'll be dry. Sit at the table and call me when you're ready."

When Lee calls me, she's in the laundry room off the kitchen. "I hope you don't mind I'm washing the clothing I was wearing."

"Not at all."

She sits at the table, and I pour coffee for both of us, then sit in a chair behind her. "Did you lose everything? Your guitar?"

"I sensed it was going to be bad, so I moved everything into the truck except me. Then when the tent got soaked and the mud moved in, I got in the truck and moved close to the house to avoid flying objects. How do you know I have a guitar?"

"I hear you playing and singing sometimes. You have a lovely voice and are quite good on the guitar."

Lee flushes. "I hope I haven't bothered you."

"Not at all. I've enjoyed listening."

"Do you sing or play an instrument?"

"I used to sing and play the piano and the guitar but not since the accident."

"I don't think a singer can ever stop singing."

I ignore the comment, not wanting to explain, not ready to share. The last thing I want is for Lee to start nosing around. "Are you curious about me?"

"I am. But I figure you'll tell me anything you want me to know."

"Thank you. Is there anything you're dying to know?"

"Nope. I'm happy." She yawns. "Well, maybe. What kinds of music do you like?"

I consider whether that is something I can share without giving away too much. "Yours is the only music I've heard since the accident."

"Really?" Lee's eyes widen. She glances around the room. "You don't have a radio or a music center to play CDs or records?" She catches herself. "Sorry. I don't mean to pry."

I don't tell her about the equipment in the music room, but I take pity on her. "Yes, really. I have eclectic taste. I love classical including opera, and folk, bluegrass, pop, rock, and country, but as I said, yours is the only music I've heard since the accident." I can feel the sadness leaking in. It's time to change the subject. "You know, when I was lying in bed listening to the storm, I realized that instead of having you pitch a tent I should have told you to move into the bunkhouse out back. I've never been out there and I'm not sure what shape it's in, but I was told it was solid."

"I looked in the day I arrived. It's dirty and smells moldy because of the mattresses and stuffed chair, but with a good cleaning it might be habitable and better than my late tent. You wouldn't mind?"

"It's far enough from the house so we'd both have our privacy. Check it out when it stops raining and if you like it, take some time to make it livable, then settle in. I have whatever cleaning supplies you'll need."

"Okay, I'll see if I can clean it up." Lee yawns again.

"The storm doesn't seem ready to abate and even if it does there's no need for you to sleep in your truck. You can sleep in the guest bedroom. The sheets are clean. Come on." I show her to the bedroom Kim uses when she visits, then go into my bedroom. Having Lee so close is comforting and yet my body throbs with unfamiliar feelings. I lie awake a long time.

When I open my eyes a couple of hours later the rain has ended and the sun is shining. The guest bedroom door is open, the bed is neatly made, and my sweats are folded on the chair. Lee is not in the house. I wash and dress, then make breakfast. When I ring the bell, I notice the table and chairs on the porch are still wet. I hesitate. I was comfortable with her in the house last night and as long as I wear the veil, I'm protected, so I invite her to join me in the kitchen.

She sits facing the windows, as I usually do. She's always so careful to avoid looking at me that if I wasn't afraid I'd scare her away if she accidently saw my face, I would remove my veil and have breakfast with her. Instead, I place the biscuits and butter and jam in front of her, put the hash browns on a plate, add three eggs over, as she prefers, and serve her. I sit behind her drinking a cup of coffee.

As she eats, Lee describes the state of the bunkhouse. "It will take some work, but I can clean it up. Mice and mold have gotten into the mattresses, the linens, and the easy chair, so I'll burn them, if that's all right with you."

"Do what you have to do. I want you to be comfortable."

After breakfast I stand on the porch and watch Lee carry cleaning supplies to the bunkhouse, happy I'd thought of it. It hadn't been used since I bought the property, but I remembered Kim saying that this had been a working farm and several ranch hands had lived there until the owner died and the house was sold. Hopefully, with some elbow grease it will be livable, at least as livable as a tent.

When I ring the lunch bell, Lee sits at the table on the porch and as soon as she hears me sit behind her she goes into high gear.

"The bunkhouse is in really good shape. All it needed was airing, and a good cleaning to get rid of the cobwebs and dust and the smell. I swept and dusted then washed the walls, windows, and floors. It has electricity, and after a little tinkering with the water heater, hot and cold running water, a small kitchen, bathroom with a shower, a bedroom, and a small living room."

I laugh. "Whoa, you're really hyped about this."

"It's solid and it'll be really comfortable when I'm done. It even has built-in bookcases. Have you seen it?"

"Other than retrieving the groceries Thomas spread around, I haven't been off the porch since I arrived here months ago. I've never walked on the property, and I doubt I could walk there by myself."

"I can take you after lunch if you like."

"I…maybe."

"I'll drive to one of the big stores on the highway later to get a mattress and sheets, towels, an easy chair, and a lamp so I have a place to sit and read."

"You know, Lee, when I moved here I was in no shape to make decisions, so my sister had all the furnishings and linens from my house in Austin packed and moved here. I understand that three of the bedrooms upstairs are furnished and everything not needed in the bedrooms or down here is stored in the fourth. I would guess I have everything you need up there, so before you go shopping go up and look around. If there's anything you can use, have Thomas help you carry it out when he gets here tomorrow."

"That's great. My tent is ruined, so I was planning to sleep in my truck for the next couple of days, but maybe I'll be able to move in tonight."

"Forget your truck. You'll sleep in the guest bedroom until the bunkhouse is ready."

I expect Lee to object, but after a moment of silence, she says, "Thank you."

"What do you have planned for Thomas other than helping you furnish your nest?"

"Nest. That's exactly how it feels. A place of my own to sleep and read and listen to music, and to relax. It's been a while since I've had a home."

The sadness I've only heard in Lee's songs surfaces and my heart goes out to her. Did she lose more than her home? A husband? A wife? A child? Lee stares into space, then her shoulders straighten. Clearly, whatever caused the sadness has been slotted back into its hidden space. "I thought justice would be served by having Thomas turn the earth to prepare the garden for planting since it will allow you to be somewhat self-sufficient and need fewer deliveries."

After lunch I walk out on the porch and stand next to Lee. Without looking at me, she puts an arm around my waist, takes my hand and half carries, half walks me down the steps and over the rocky ground, stopping just beyond the house. This is the first time I've been out here where I can see the bunkhouse, the barn, the shed, and the land beyond. We start walking, but even though she's bearing much of my weight, I'm fading fast. Lee must sense my exhaustion because we stop. She points to the garden and the stakes with pieces of cloth hanging from them. "If it's okay with you, I'd like to make the garden larger than the former owner's so we can include a bigger variety of vegetables."

I squeeze her arm. "That would be wonderful."

"It's no problem. Besides, Thomas is going to do all the work and I'll reap the benefits in the fabulous meals you'll prepare. But we may have too much to eat. Do you know how to can vegetables?"

I laugh. "It's not something I've ever done, and I haven't looked at the Internet in a long time, but I imagine there are articles on how to do it. Have you ever done it?"

"I have. I could teach you."

"I'd like that." I cling to Lee's arm. "I'm tired. I need to go back while I can still stand."

We move slowly, with Lee taking most of my weight. I'm dreading the stairs, but she surprises me and carries me up the steps, into the kitchen, then helps me into my wheelchair. I fan myself. "You did most of the work, but that's the most I've walked since I left the hospital. I'm tired, but I enjoyed being outside and seeing the garden. Thanks."

"I'm happy to do it as often as you feel up to it." Lee touches my shoulder. "I'm going upstairs to see what you have that I can use."

Being in her arms, her casual hand on my shoulder, put my body on high alert. Does she feel anything? Or is it just me? I wheel myself out to the porch. My life has changed since Lee showed up. I've changed. I laughed for the second time in just a few days. The last time I laughed before that was in the van the night of the accident. We were all still high on the adrenaline rush from the performance, teasing each other, giggling, and laughing. I remember that night, remember my friends, my band, I hear our laughter, feel the love we had for each other, and I feel happy. I hear Lee moving things upstairs. I don't know how, but she's made me feel again.

Flushed and smiling, Lee joins me in the kitchen. "You're right, Anna, everything I need is up there. If you don't mind, I'll drive into town and pick up the things I need to paint the rooms. If I take care of that today, Thomas can help me move everything in tomorrow."

"That sounds good."

"Okay. But before I go let's discuss what to plant and how much of each so while I'm in town I can let Elton know what we'll need when we start planting. Are you up to that now?"

"Yes."

We sit side by side at the kitchen table, decide which vegetables to include and what percent of the garden they would occupy. We quibble about what to include but easily agree on broccoli, cauliflower, several types of lettuce, tomatoes, peppers, garlic, onions, and potatoes among others, but Lee votes to exclude turnips because she ate too many in the Army—an interesting bit of new information—and I insist we exclude yellow squash, which I hate. Lee sketches a map of the plot as a guide for planting and makes a list of what is needed to plant the garden and deal with canning its output.

She leans back. "You know, if we get some hens, we can have fresh eggs."

The idea that we're in this together warms me, but as much as I'd like us to be here together permanently, Lee will move on in a few months.

"Who will take care of the chickens when you leave?" It comes out harsher than I intend, and I feel Lee tense.

"You're right, Anna. I guess the idea of having a place of my own lulled me, and I forgot I'll leave eventually. I'm sorry." She stands. "Unless you need me to do something, I'm going to run into town now."

I don't want her to feel bad. "I didn't mean to lash out, Lee. I love having you here and I love the idea of having chickens, but I won't be able to take care of them when you leave and I'm alone again." My traitorous voice breaks, revealing the pain I feel. I take a deep breath and force a smile, but of course she can't see it behind the veil. I extend an olive branch. "The idea of fresh eggs is tempting, though, so let me think about it."

"It's up to you, Anna. Unless you need something, I'll go into town now."

"I'm good. Since the painting of the bunkhouse constitutes improving my property, be sure to charge everything you need to my account along with the gardening stuff."

I roll my wheelchair into the sunlight on the porch and watch the truck's taillights as Lee heads down the driveway. I semidoze, while I replay our conversation. There's no reason we can't enjoy the chickens while Lee is here. And depending on how Thomas works out, I can pay him to care for them, or, if not that, we can give them away before Lee goes. The sound of a motor wakes me. I panic when I realize I'm on the porch, that I slept out here while I was alone. I'm about to go in when I recognize Lee's truck. I relax.

She waves and drives around to the back of the house. I hope it's because it will be easier to unload everything closer to the bunkhouse and not because she's avoiding me. When she doesn't return, I go inside to prep dinner—baked pork chops, sauerkraut, mashed potatoes, and roasted carrots. I'm not much of a meat eater so I'll only have a few bites of a chop, but Lee works hard and she's a meat and potatoes gal, so I accommodate her.

CHAPTER SIXTEEN

Lee

As soon as I return from town with everything I need to paint, I spread the drop cloths and get started. I'm applying the roller to a bedroom wall when I have a fantasy of bringing Mara and Tessa here. It's the first positive thought about finding them I've had since I realized they were gone. I imagine reading to them in the bunkhouse, and them running around the yard, helping in the garden, and collecting eggs from the hens. I think they'd love it here.

But does Anna like children? Would she let the three of us stay here, at least until I figure out my life? Not likely. Children are curious and would want to see what she's hiding. Anna would hate having them around. Besides, she has no idea Mara and Tessa even exist. I snort. Do I expect her to feed and watch them while I do odd jobs around the place? I move the roller and continue painting while I consider whether to tell her why I'm on the road.

She seems relaxed today. The more time we spend together, the more present she seems. Judging by her body language yesterday, she was just as surprised as I was to hear the short burst of what, no doubt, was a laugh. Maybe knowing she can trust me to not try to see behind the veil frees her to let down her guard.

Discussing books with her I've learned she's curious, intelligent, and witty. And she's kind and generous, not only sharing her belongings but also providing fabulous meals and letting me live rent free. I really care about her. I lower the roller. It's true. I can't deny it. I like her as a person, as a friend, but holding friends doesn't turn me on. It's ridiculous. I don't even know what she looks like. How can I be attracted to her? Maybe it's that I'm lonely and the time we spend together is the highlight of my day, every day. I shake my head and get back to work. But my brain is still thinking of Anna. Is her face so hideous that she feels people can't deal with it? Do I care about her looks?

I stand back and admire the bedroom, then clean up and start on the living room walls. Several hours later I dry my hands and walk from the entryway to the living room, through the kitchen into the bedroom and then to the bathroom. I'm pleased. The white brightens the rooms and makes them seem larger.

Tomorrow I'll arrange all the furniture Anna has graciously provided to make me comfortable. Once everything is in place, I'll add some splashes of color to make it feel homey. But first Thomas and I, if he shows up as planned, will move the two bunk beds into the barn to make room for the queen bed. I'd been able to push the bunks into the center of the room so I could paint, but they are too heavy for me to carry to the barn by myself.

Losing my house and living out of my truck while driving around looking for the girls left me feeling unsettled. Making the bunkhouse mine and imagining the girls here with me, makes me feel rooted again. And, I realize, I'm happy here, happy spending time with Anna, which was probably why I suggested we get chickens. As if we're a couple. No doubt I overstepped. But Anna seems to have forgiven Thomas or at least she's giving him a chance at redemption, so hopefully she won't hold it against me.

CHAPTER SEVENTEEN

Ariana

Lee seemed understanding about my less-than-nice response to her suggestion about getting chickens when I apologized at dinner last night. We talked a little about what having chickens would entail and other than building a coop for them and feeding them, they won't involve a lot of work, so we agreed to get a few and not worry about what happens to them until she's ready to leave. With the air cleared, she was whistling when she went back to finish painting last night. She must have worked late, because I was asleep when she went to bed in the guest bedroom.

Now while we eat breakfast she's outlining what she hopes to accomplish today and seems confident she'll be able to start sleeping in the bunkhouse tonight. I like having her close. I don't say it, but I'm sad she's moving to the bunkhouse.

We both look up at the sound of the truck coming up the driveway. Lee stands and puts her plate in the sink. "That's probably Elton dropping Thomas off. I'll meet with him on the porch and let you know when we'll be traipsing through the house with furniture and things from upstairs."

"Okay." I have mixed feelings about having Thomas in my house, touching my things, gossiping about how I live. But he's a teenage boy.

Will he even notice the luxuriousness of the inside versus the peeling, run-down, outside of the house?

The truck drives away and I hear Lee on the porch talking to Thomas. "I hope you appreciate Ms. Solander's kindness. Unlike most people, she's allowing you to redeem yourself rather than trying to hurt you like you hurt her."

"I know," Thomas mumbles.

"When we go inside, remember the house is her sanctuary, her safe place. You've already hurt her enough, so keep your eyes to yourself while we're in the house. If I see you gawking or hear that you've been gossiping around town about anything you see or hear on this property, I will drag you back to your dad and makes sure he understands what a piece of shit you are. Do you understand?"

"Yes, ma'am."

Wow. Lee really gets me. I know I'm getting too close to her, but I can't think of anyone other than Kim who is so protective of me. Is it any wonder that I'm so invested in having her here? Just by sharing her easygoing, kind self, Lee has given me music and books. And she's changed my attitude toward my life and living. In the few weeks she's been here things between us have shifted from strictly employer and employee to more like friends or at least friendly strangers. I trust her. Does she realize how much she's improved my life? Does she know she brought me back into the world? I wish I could ask her to stay. She seems to enjoy my company, but she hasn't seen my face or my body and she has no idea who I am. I'm not so far gone that I believe she could be romantically interested in me. In fact, if she saw, if she knew, she'd probably politely back away as fast as she could.

"Anna, is it okay if we start moving things out in five minutes?" Lee is standing at the screen door. I'd been so deep in thought I hadn't heard her.

"Sure. Give me a couple of minutes." I swing my wheelchair around and go into my bedroom. Last night I dreamed Thomas pulled off my veil to see my face, screamed in horror, then pointed and laughed. I believe everyone deserves a second chance, but I feel uneasy. I sit on the bed and listen to them laughing and chatting as they carry the furniture down the stairs. I feel excluded.

And suddenly I'm filled with rage. Instead of punishing Thomas for torturing me, I've invited him here and now he's with Lee in a way that I can't be. They are back quickly, and I realize Lee must be staging the move, first taking everything out to the porch and then carrying it out to the bunkhouse. I'd love to help carry things and witness her pleasure as everything is put into place, but I don't have the strength or stability to walk down the few steps by myself or walk on the uneven ground, so forget carrying anything. I'd only be a distraction.

As if I'd scratched the scab off a wound, the pain of everything I've lost takes my breath away. I'm useless. My life is a waste. Why didn't I die along with everyone else? I double over and bury my face in the bedding to smother the sobs tearing through me.

The sound of the screen door slamming wakes me. The room is dim. Someone is coming. I panic, then realize I'm still wearing my hat and the veil is covering my face. I'm stiff and unable to stand.

"Anna, Anna, are you okay?" Lee sounds worried.

"I'm fine, Lee. I'm in my bedroom, but I can't seem to get up. Can you come in and give me a hand?"

"Sure. Do you mind if I turn the lamp on?"

How long have I been asleep? Even wearing my veil, I blink at the sudden brightness. Lee looks worried.

"It's been hours since we last talked. I assumed you didn't feel well enough to make lunch, so I came in and grabbed some sandwich stuff from the refrigerator, but it's way past our usual dinner time. I was afraid you'd fallen." She extends her arms. "Just grab on and I'll pull you up." Once I'm upright, Lee swings me into the wheelchair.

"Thanks, I don't usually have trouble getting out of bed, but I couldn't roll into the right position. What time is it?"

"Seven thirty. After we moved everything to the bunkhouse, I spent some time arranging it while Thomas started digging up the garden. When I got back from driving him to town, the house was dark and I decided you were late getting started, so I did some stuff in the bunkhouse. Then I got worried."

"Sorry. I guess all the work you two did made me tired and I fell asleep. Are you okay with another sandwich or an omelet for dinner?"

"I could put something together if you're too tired."

"No, I'm fine. Come have a beer in the kitchen while I make us omelets."

We sit side by side at the table, facing the windows, and chat while we eat. It feels companionable, like family, like we're in a relationship. There's no question that Lee makes me feel safe, that I enjoy her company, that I'm slowly letting her closer. I side-eye her, the only person since the accident, other than Kim, I trust enough to allow into the house, to sit with me for a meal. And the only one since the accident to cause my body to come alive, to remember being sexual. Of course, other than the nurses, Dr. Rawlings, and Kim, she's the only woman I've seen since the night of the accident.

Lee clears her throat. "I sense you're upset. Did I invade your privacy by stomping up and down the stairs, taking so many of your things, things from your, uh, former life?"

"No, it's nothing you did." I hesitate, not sure how much to share but I don't want Lee to feel responsible. I take a sip of water. "Hearing you and Thomas run up and down the stairs carrying heavy things out to the bunkhouse made me feel, no, made me see how helpless I am. I wasn't always like this. I'm only in my thirties and it frightens me that I may live the rest of my life trapped alone inside this house." If I say anything else, I'll cry so I take a bite of my omelet and wait for Lee's response.

"You're not helpless. You cook and clean and just yesterday you walked outside."

"But let's face it, I can't even go down the front steps without your help. And there's no way I can walk even as far as we did yesterday by myself. Frame it as you will, I'm a prisoner in this house." *And that will be even more true when you leave.*

Lee clears her throat. "I hear what you're saying, but it won't be like this forever."

"I hope you're right." I'm feeling exposed and need to change the subject. "Tell me how the bunkhouse looks." She's animated, eyes sparkling, arms moving, as she describes the furniture she took from upstairs and where it fits. I'm mesmerized. Through the haze of the veil my eyes are riveted to her face. I'm fascinated by her lips as she speaks. They look so soft. I fantasize kissing her and the blood rushes through my body, flooding my neck and face. Luckily, the veil covers me so she can't see. But I know. It's hard not to lean over, touch her cheek, and pull her lips to mine.

Always sensitive to me, Lee stops speaking. "Are you all right, Anna?"

"Sure," I croak. I clear my throat. "I'm fine, just tired."

Since I'm wearing my veil, she turns to me. "Let me clean up before I head out."

I need to touch her, to feel her skin, so I place my hand on hers. I'm sure her palm and fingertips are callused, but the top is as soft and warm as I imagined. My heart races as the warmth travels up my arm and through my body. I've touched Kim's hand occasionally on one of her weekend visits, but it doesn't feel like this.

"Thank you. Go figure, you did all the work and I'm tired." I turn the wheelchair. "Good night, Lee. Sweet dreams in your new nest."

She laughs. "Sweet dreams to you too, Anna." She stands and clears the table as I roll toward the bedroom. I don't look back, but I wonder if she's watching me. I grab my book from the living room. I doubt I'll sleep much tonight.

CHAPTER EIGHTEEN

Lee

As I read in my easy chair in my cozy nest, my mind wanders to Anna again. I'm surprised she trusts me enough to share her feelings about her life and reveal her age. And touch me. A first. It was electric. I was aware of feeling connected to her, but her touch confirms what I'm avoiding thinking about. I'm attracted to her. And I sense she's attracted to me too. It's hopeless of course. Even if I could have a relationship with someone whose face I never saw, she's so hung up on her looks I doubt she'd ever go there. But what do I have to offer? I have no job and my priority is finding Mara and Tessa and building a life with them. When I leave, our connection will break and it will be painful for both of us. Despite knowing all that, I still can't seem to stop thinking about her. The more I think, the more I'm convinced life shouldn't be so hard for Anna. Being able to walk out on her property would eliminate the feeling of being trapped and, perhaps, strengthen her legs, which get little exercise in the limited open space of the first floor of her house.

The next morning I walk to the back of the property and assess the pile of lumber I noticed when I first arrived. It's more than enough to implement the plan I'd sketched last night and still have enough wood to build a small coop for the chickens we intend to get. Looking forward to surprising Anna, I join her for breakfast. We chat until Thomas arrives. I meet him outside. "Before you go back to turning the soil in the garden, I need you to help me move some wood from the rear of the property closer to the bunkhouse." As I lead him to the lumber, I tell him my plan.

Thomas is flagging. It's obvious he hasn't done much manual labor. He straightens as we drop our load on the pile near the bunkhouse. Anna rings the bell for lunch. "What's that?"

I laugh. "That's Anna calling us for lunch."

He flushes and shuffles his feet. "Do you think she'll want me to eat too?"

"Of course." I touch his arm. "Come on, let's wash up."

He doesn't look convinced, but he follows me to the back of the house and then to the porch. His eyes widen seeing two plates with sandwiches and two glasses of lemonade. I point to the chair facing away from the house. "Sit. If you hear Anna's voice, don't turn to look at her. Okay?"

He nods. We sit.

"Is lemonade all right, Thomas?" He jumps, hearing the voice behind him. "I also have tea."

"Yes, ma'am. Lemonade is fine."

"Okay. Enjoy your lunch. Lee, let me know if either of you need anything else."

"Sure, Anna." I should have realized Anna wouldn't be joining us and we wouldn't be having our usual lunchtime book discussion. I feel a pang of loss. Thomas and I don't have much to say to each other, so we eat quickly. I let Anna know we're finished, and we head back. It takes us the rest of the afternoon to move all the lumber.

Thomas dozes as I drive him home. I smile. Redeeming oneself is hard. He's going to be sore as hell tomorrow. Back at the bunkhouse, I take a shower, put on clean clothes, and, anticipating our usual discussion, happily respond to the dinner bell. I sit at the place set for me. "I really missed talking with you at lunch."

Anna hands me a beer. "I missed it too. I don't feel comfortable talking with Thomas here, so we'll be limited to dinner discussions for now."

I chew a bite of the stew Anna prepared. "As usual this is delicious, Anna."

"Thanks. What are your thoughts about the chapters we read last night?"

The next morning, Thomas is back to turning the soil in the garden, albeit wearing gloves and taking lots of breaks to rest. I retrieve the saw from the shed and begin to cut the boards to the size I need. It takes two days to cut everything, and another four days to build a boardwalk from the house to the bunkhouse, around the garden, and back to the house. Hands on hips, I survey my work. I've taken pains to make the walkway level so Anna can walk unassisted from the house to the bunkhouse, around the garden, and, when necessary, stop to rest on one of the crude benches I've built along the way. I glance at the house, excited to show her what I've done, then frown. She'll still need assistance to get down the steps from the house to the path. After dinner, I measure the height of the porch, then with some help from YouTube videos, I work late into the night to construct a ramp sloped so she can get up and down by herself on the walker. I also build another segment of boardwalk to connect the ramp to the walkway.

When Thomas arrives the next morning, he helps me move the ramp and the connecting piece into place before going back to digging up the garden. I'm adding the railings on both sides of the ramp when Anna appears behind the screen door.

"What are you doing?"

"Just finishing a ramp so you can walk off the porch by yourself. Come on, try it." Anna is tentative, but she grabs her walker and slowly walks down the ramp. At the bottom, she turns to me.

"Wow, I did it." Her gaze goes to the walkway. "What's that?"

"I built a boardwalk so you can get some exercise without having to deal with roots and stones and holes in the ground."

"Is that all the hammering I've been hearing?" Anna's hands flutter. She must be nervous. "How far does it go?"

"Let's check it out."

"You think I can do it?"

"I do. The boardwalk is solid and there are benches along the way so you can rest. If you need it, I'll get the wheelchair to take you back. I bet if you start walking every day, you'll get stronger. Come on."

CHAPTER NINETEEN

Ariana

With Lee at my side, I inch along to the first bench a little way beyond the house, then ease myself down. I'm surprised, yet not surprised, that Lee has built the bench high enough so sitting is easy and standing will be just as easy later. I'm out of breath, but it's the longest I've walked since the night of the accident. I tense when I notice Thomas digging in the garden. He glances up, then quickly lowers his eyes. Good. Lee's talk with him seems to have stuck.

I close my eyes, feeling the gentle morning breeze, breathing in the scent of pine and freshly turned earth, and hearing the glorious songs of birds. This feels different than sitting on the porch. Out here, I feel born again into a world soaked with sun and song and possibilities. I inhale deeply, then, aware of Lee sitting beside me, I open my eyes and survey what she built for me. The boardwalk goes from the house to the bunkhouse, around the garden, and back to the house. My eyes fill as I turn to Lee.

"I don't know what to say, except thank you. I hope someday I'll be able to walk beyond this bench." I stand unassisted. "But this is as far as I can go now. I need to go back."

"If you walk every day, you'll walk the entire path. I'm sure of it," Lee says.

With her beside me I creep toward the house. "I'm slower than a sloth."

Lee laughs. "A sloth. Really?"

"I believe sloths are the slowest mammal on earth." I laugh. "But don't ask how I know that bit of trivia or why it popped into my mind."

Probably sensing my fatigue, Lee stays with me right to my bedroom door, though it seems to take forever. "You did great, Anna, rest now. I'll see you later."

As soon as I hear the front door close, I collapse on the bed. Exhausted physically and emotionally. Overwhelmed with feelings. Something inside of me breaks free, my body shakes with sobs. For the second time in just a few days, I'm letting the pain of the losses out. I didn't know how frozen I was, how I'd steeled myself to face the life I'd been left with. Other than Kim and the girls, no one has ever done anything so nice, been so thoughtful, so caring, without wanting something from me.

I'm confused when I wake. I lie there, unable to name what I'm feeling. It takes me a few minutes to recognize it. Hope. I feel hopeful. And determined. I can do this. It might take some time, but I will walk around the entire beautiful path Lee has built for me. I glance at the clock. I've slept for over an hour, but it's still early for lunch, so I pick up the copy of *Ammonite* Lee passed on to me. Another wonderful gift from her: a renewed interest in reading and discussing books, giving me something outside of myself to think about, dragging me back into the world. We'd agreed to start discussing it at dinner tonight. Because I often get lost in the world of the book I'm reading, I've learned to set an alarm on my phone to ensure I have enough time to make our meals.

At the sound of the alarm, I close the book, pull myself up, and head to the kitchen. As I slice the bread for sandwiches, I think about how much pleasure I get from preparing and cooking meals for us, another gift from Lee, just from her being here. And since I started sharing meals with her, my appetite has returned, and I feel as if I've regained some of the weight I lost after the accident. I reach for the leftover roast beef and stop. Before Lee came, I spent my days dozing in the living room, lost in the past, mourning my friends and my life, basically waiting to die. She brought hope.

My life will be empty when she leaves. Which she will. After all, there is nothing to keep her here. I shake off the sadness and remind myself to enjoy her company while she's here. There will be plenty of time to mourn later. And maybe by the time I'm alone again I'll be stronger, ready to face who I am now, and able to live a better life than the one I had before she arrived on the scene. I mix a tangy dressing and make four and a half sandwiches, two for each of the workers and half for me. Suddenly I'm starving. I add another half for me.

I place four sandwiches and two large glasses of lemonade on the table outside, then ring the bell. I'm sad. Depriving myself of Lee's company because Thomas is present hurts me, not him. I can deal with him as long as he doesn't look at me. I pull a chair to the screen door. "Lee, I'm going to eat lunch with you two so we can talk about our book while we eat. Is that okay?"

Lee smiles. "Great. Thomas, Anna and I read the same book, then discuss it at meals. Feel free to join the conversation."

Thomas is quiet. I assume it's because he's not sure how to relate to me, but he'll have to figure it out because I'm not ready to make it easier for him. As Lee and I discuss *Ammonite*, I recognize the idea of change, accepting it, adapting to it, and moving on with the life you're given is particularly appropriate for me, something I now see I need to do. While it's true my life has changed radically, my body, my spirit, is letting me know I'm still alive, still young, still want a life. But I have work to do to get there. And from what Lee intimates, she is also at a place of change and adapting in her life.

"You read books because you like them?" Thomas's incredulous question interrupts our discussion. We're so involved neither of us reacts.

Lucky for Thomas, Lee recovers before I do. "You don't like to read?"

"I hate it." He flushes. "It's all gibberish to me." With his eyes on his plate, he continues, "If I don't read and write a report about *To Kill a Mockingbird* this summer, I'll have to repeat the tenth grade." The last sentence is barely audible.

I can't see his face, but I can feel his feelings. Thomas is ashamed. He feels hopeless. I know what hopeless feels like. Maybe hurting me was his way of trying to feel powerful, to deflect his pain. Surprising myself, I feel my heart go out to him. And before I know it, I'm offering to help. "Maybe if the three of us read the book together and discuss it over lunch, you'll be able to understand the words. What do you think, Lee?"

"Great idea."

Thomas looks at Lee, then gazes at the screen door for a few seconds before he catches himself and lowers his eyes. "You would do that for me after what I did, Ms. Solander?" He sounds near tears.

"I would, Thomas." Strange. Moments ago, I wanted him to suffer, but suddenly I want to help him. "Are you having problems with other subjects?"

He shifts in his chair, then looks at the floor. "Yeah. Social studies. I have to take a test at the end of the summer. My teacher gave me a list of things to study."

"We can do that, too," Lee says. "Bring your books and the list tomorrow, and we'll figure out how to approach it. I'll call the library to see whether they have copies of *Mockingbird* for me and Anna. If not, we'll get them at the bookstore."

After lunch they go back to work, and as I do the dishes I think about my response to Thomas. The preaccident me would definitely have jumped in to offer help to someone so obviously suffering. The posthospital me, lost in my own world of pain, would not. The response of the post-Lee me, the one at lunch today, came from the gut. Maybe I'm still me under the veil.

CHAPTER TWENTY

Lee

On day ten of walking the boardwalk twice a day, Anna makes it to the bunkhouse. She's thrilled at her progress, and after she rests on the bench outside, I invite her in to see the finished product. She is suitably amazed at how comfortable and attractive I've made it. She laughs, something that is happening more often lately, and I love hearing it. "Now I can visualize you sitting in your easy chair reading."

I warm at the thought that she thinks about me when we're not together. I find myself thinking about her often as well. Too often.

I wait at the bottom of the ramp as Anna makes her way down for our after-breakfast walk. In the last several weeks, she has surpassed her goal of reaching the bunkhouse. She's now walking the entire path three times a day, once in the early morning, once at midday, and then again in the evening. Another change occurred recently. We've been sitting together for dinner, either inside or on the porch, depending on how hot it is. I've schooled myself to keep my eyes forward, and we always sit side by side so she can eat with me. Then we clean up together and do the evening walk. It's companionable.

After I acknowledged to myself that I was attracted to Anna, I tuned into her and sensed she felt the same. The intimacy we share while eating and walking, where we discuss everything and anything, seems to be as important to her as it is to me. Gina and I never had the kind of intimacy, connection, or challenging discussions that I have with Anna. Now I realize, other than sex, Gina and I had little in common, but because we were only together when I was on leave, I didn't notice. Or maybe I just didn't know what a real relationship could be.

Anna steps out of the house, but instead of reaching for her walker as usual, she takes my arm. "I'd like to ditch my walker this morning. Is it okay if I hang onto you instead?"

I've been waiting for her to suggest it. She's steady on her feet and hasn't needed the walker for a while. "Definitely. I think you're ready."

Anna is tentative as we start, but it doesn't take long for her to find her stride and get lost in the sounds of the birds singing as she does most mornings. Without the punctuation of the walker hitting the boardwalk, we settle into an easy pace and an easy silence. We round the bunkhouse, stop to admire the growth of the garden, and then continue. It takes a few minutes for me to realize Anna is softly singing. I can't place the song. "What's that you're singing?"

Anna stops and faces me. Since she's still wearing her big hat with the veil, I can't see her face, but her surprise and anger come through loud and clear.

"What are you talking about? I can't sing."

I didn't expect the anger. "Sorry to disappoint you, Anna, but not only *can* you, but you *were* singing. It was something like..." I hum what I'd heard.

Rather than respond, Anna starts walking. I'm not sure what's going on, so I don't question her. Why is singing such a touchy subject? Did it have something to do with the accident that crippled and burned her?

When we arrive at the porch, Anna grabs the railing and turns to me. "I'm sorry I was so sharp, Lee. I lost my voice after the accident, and I was shocked that I was singing. I didn't know I could. Maybe my vocal cords have loosened because I'm feeling so much better and so much more relaxed lately. But I need to process this and I don't want to talk about it right now."

"We don't have to talk about it ever unless you want to. I'll go pick up Thomas now. Do you need anything from town?"

"No, thank you."

CHAPTER TWENTY-ONE

Ariana

I sit at the table. Why did I lash out at Lee? I *had* been singing without realizing it. And my throat didn't hurt. No surprise that Lee didn't recognize the song because it hasn't been written yet. I've been composing it in my head for the last week or two. Realizing that I was writing a song was as shocking as hearing myself singing it. After the accident I had absolutely no interest in music, singing it, writing it, or listening to it. But, of course, listening to Lee play her guitar and sing sparked my interest and recently the words started coming.

Once Lee drives away, I sing a scale, then another. Not bad. A little gravelly. I couldn't sing when I was in the hospital, and assuming my vocal cords were permanently damaged, I haven't tried to sing since then. I sigh. What a waste. So sure my life was over, wallowing in self-pity, I gave up. And settled in to wait to die. But now, I'm physically stronger and finding my way emotionally. I've let Lee in and can't deny I have feelings for her. But how could I expect Lee to have feelings for me, a woman whose face she's never seen, a woman whose face is horribly scarred? I'm afraid to let her see the damage, but it will be better for both of us to do it sooner rather than later. She'll either stay or run.

I sing a few more scales, then sing what I have of the song through a few times. I stand and go to find my music notebook. I'd bet my last dollar that Kim brought it here, hoping I'd pick up my guitar and sing and compose again. Sure enough, the notebook is in the guitar case I haven't touched since the night of the accident. I write the lyrics and the chords down.

THEN YOU WERE THERE

Each day all I did was hide,
And at night I cried.
Day and night I was in pain.
Alone and lonely,
Death seemed easier than living this way.
And then you were there.
At the door. In my life.
Bringing hope.
Bringing peace.
Seeing me, really seeing me.
Under the hat,
Behind the veil.

At the sound of the truck pulling in, I rise, put the guitar back in the case, tuck in the notebook, and snap the latch. I shut the door to the music room as usual. Lee has never seen the inside of that room, and I'm not ready to reveal that part of myself.

As I walk to the kitchen, I hum the song. It's rough, but I like it, and later I'll tune my guitar and work to make it better. I sneeze. This is the first time I've been in the music room since the day I arrived. I'll dust it tomorrow. I sneeze again.

Despite feeling low energy and slightly headachy, the rest of the day goes as usual. I put the roast pork we're having for dinner in the slow cooker, take a break to read the book Lee and I are sharing, and then prepare sandwiches for lunch. Once we've eaten, the three of us read a chapter of *To Kill a Mockingbird* and discuss it for about an hour. We're nearing the end of the book, and Thomas is starting to understand and enjoy the story. He still struggles a bit, but more and more he is able to offer his own opinions on the text and answer the questions we ask to help him analyze what he's reading. At Lee's suggestion, rather than waiting until we finish the book and relying on his memory for his book report, he's been making notes as we go along about things he might want to include. Having the notes will make it easier to pull the report together when we're done. So each time we discuss some part of the story one of us asks Thomas if he thinks it's important. Within a couple of days, he's already made a note by the time we ask.

After lunch, Thomas goes back to weeding the garden while Lee accompanies me on my afternoon stroll around the boardwalk. And Lee being Lee, she doesn't bring up my singing again. I want to tell her, but revealing who I am will change everything. And though I trust Lee, I'm wary of being exposed. When we arrive at the house Lee waits for me to walk up to the porch, then goes to help Thomas with the weeding. Tomorrow, the two of them will start to paint the outside of the house.

I wash the lunch dishes, make a salad to go with the dinner, and bake a loaf of bread. As usual, Lee works with Thomas on his social studies assignment before she drives him home. But instead of just helping him answer the questions, Lee has him read the textbook aloud and explain what it means. Thomas seems to be glowing with all the attention and growing more and more self-confident as the days go by. I'm sitting on the porch reading when they head to Lee's truck so she can drive him home. As they walk past, I notice that not only has Thomas grown intellectually, he's also taller and all the digging and gardening has increased his muscles. He's sneezing as they walk by, though, and his face is flushed.

After dinner, Lee and I clean up, then take our evening walk. As usual we bounce from one topic to another. The only thing off the table is anything personal, neither our past lives nor our hopes for the future. We complete our laps and say good night. I'm exhausted and feel hot and headachy, but I'm excited. I've waited all day to get back to my song. I'd written a few songs while we were on tour and made a ton of notes for lyrics of songs I intended to compose after the break at the end of the tour. This is the first song I've written since several months before the accident. I sit in the music room with my guitar in my arms. My nose is dripping, my eyes are itchy, my fingertips ache, my voice is weak, but I'm so excited to be composing again I work late into the night rewriting the lyrics, testing different chords, and refining the melody. Finally, feeling woozy, nauseous, and overheated, I decide to go to bed. I'm walking from the bathroom to the bedroom when I get dizzy and black out.

CHAPTER TWENTY-TWO

Lee

When I arrive for breakfast the door is locked, the kitchen dark, and there's no sign of Anna. I knock, then call her name. I pull out my phone and select her name. No answer. Something is wrong. Thomas's dad called earlier to let me know that Thomas has the flu and won't come today. Is Anna sick too?

I run back to the bunkhouse and retrieve the key she gave me in case of an emergency. I open the screen door, knock again, then unlock the door and call out. "Anna, it's Lee. Are you all right?" No response.

"Anna, I'm coming in." I give her thirty seconds, then enter the dark house. The living room is empty. The door to Anna's bedroom is open, but I can't see in from this angle. "Anna, are you okay?"

My heart racing, I move into the doorway. The room is dim, and I almost trip on her, lying face down on the floor near the bed. I hesitate. It looks like she's wearing boxer shorts and a tank top but no hat or veil. I'm flummoxed. If I see what she takes such pains to hide, she might ask me to leave. That would be terrible, but I can't just leave her on the floor. I put the bedside lamp on. Her hat is on the nightstand. Maybe I can put the hat on and pull the veil down to cover her face before I move her. I take a deep breath and wish myself luck. I place the hat on her head. She's dead weight, and it's hard to lift her without exposing her face, but

I manage to raise her upper body so she's still facing down and pull the veil over her face. I lay her back down and tug on the veil to be sure it's covering her face and neck, then I turn her over. I rest for a minute or two before lifting her onto the bed. I grin, proud I managed to protect her privacy.

Her body is hot. She has a fever. I slip my hand under the veil and place it on her forehead. She's sweaty and burning up. I run to the bunkhouse and retrieve the kid's thermometer I'd taken from the boxes Gina abandoned in the basement of my house.

I carefully slip the thermometer under the veil and point it at her forehead. Geez. One hundred four degrees. Way too high. She must have caught the bug from Thomas, who didn't show any sign of being sick until late afternoon yesterday.

I take a bowl from the kitchen, add a handful of washcloths and warm water in the bathroom then go back to the bedroom. Anna's body, which is usually hidden under a baggy dress, looks frail and vulnerable. I can't help noticing the burn scars on her shoulder, arm, and leg, a contrast to the paleness and perfection of the surrounding skin. I wonder how bad her face is but turn my attention to the job at hand. I squeeze the water from a washcloth and even though the veil will get wet, I place the cloth on her forehead. I reach for another washcloth and sponge her neck, arms, and legs. Then I remove another two washcloths from the bowl and repeat the action, forehead, neck, arms, and legs. After about twenty minutes, I go into the bathroom for ibuprofen, into the kitchen for a glass of water and place them on the night table. She hasn't roused at all, so I don't expect her to be able to drink and swallow pills, but I want to be ready just in case. I watch her sleep for a few minutes, set the alarm on my phone to remind me to sponge her again in two hours, then go into the kitchen to see whether she has the makings of chicken soup.

Luckily her freezer is well stocked. I pull out a frozen chicken, then some fresh vegetables from the refrigerator. After eating toast and drinking a few cups of coffee I get to work making chicken soup. As I chop, I think about Anna. It seems to me she's heavier, not as fragile as she was the day I caught her to keep her from falling off the steps, but such a high fever is dangerous. I'm sure she wouldn't want me to involve anyone else, but if her fever doesn't start to come down in the next few hours, I'll take her to the nearest hospital. I'd rather deal with the consequences of her anger than have her die. No one has visited since I arrived, so if she has to go to the hospital, I'll have to search for insurance information and an emergency contact.

I hum as I prepare the soup and after a few minutes I realize it's the song Anna was singing last night when I returned to the house to get the book I'd left on the porch. The same song she was humming on our morning walk, only last night she was singing it in a rather raspy but good voice, changing lyrics, and trying out different arrangements. It was so beautiful I'd sat on the steps and listened for a while. Why was she upset that I heard her singing? Why was she so adamant that she couldn't sing when she sounded damned good to me?

Once the soup is bubbling on the stove, I retrieve my book from the table on the porch and settle in to care for Anna. After the third round of sponging, her fever drops a bit, and as the day goes on, it continues to drop. As usual, though, it rises again in the evening.

About midnight, as I finish the sponge bath, she rouses. Hopefully, she'll wake enough to drink and take the pills. "Anna, it's Lee. Can you open your eyes? You have a high fever, and you need to drink and take some ibuprofen."

She groans. "Lee?"

"Yes, can you put your arms around my neck so I can lift you enough for you to drink and swallow the pills?"

She moans but doesn't answer. "Anna, open your eyes. Put your arms around my neck." Her eyelids flutter but no response. I drag her to a sitting position, lean her forward, and place a pillow behind her. Keeping the veil in place, I hold the glass to her lips. "Drink."

It takes a few moments for her to react, but then she takes several sips of water. "What's wrong with me?"

"You have a high fever. Thomas has the flu. I think you must have caught it. I found you face down on the floor when I came for breakfast this morning."

Her hand goes to her face. "My veil? Did you see—"

"Don't worry. I put the hat and veil on you before I turned you over, so I didn't see your face."

"Thank you." Her voice is draggy. She's falling back to sleep.

"Can you swallow some pills?" I lift her hand and put a pill there.

"I think so." She puts the pill in her mouth and takes several sips of water to wash it down. I give her the second and she swallows it.

I'm able to get a little broth into her before she dozes off again. Every two hours, I sponge her and encourage her to drink some soup or water.

Anna is more alert after the four a.m. sponge bath, so I help her sit up, then I go into the kitchen and heat a cup of chicken soup. Her head turns to me when I set the soup on the night table.

"Thanks, Lee, but I don't have the energy to eat."

"You need to eat if you're going to regain your strength. I've been feeding you, so if it's all right, I can do it now."

Anna is silent for what seems like minutes but is probably only seconds. "Okay."

Relieved, I tuck the napkin in the top of her tank top, pick up the bowl and the spoon, and sit on the bed. I lift the veil slightly and put the spoon to her lips. After a brief hesitation, she opens her mouth, then swallows. "Yum, good."

I grin. "Is the temperature all right?"

"Perfect." When she's eaten all the soup, I put the empty bowl on the night table and help her take the pills.

"You need to rest."

"First I need to use the bathroom."

"Put your arms around my neck and I'll help you." I wait outside the bathroom until Anna calls to say she's ready to get back into bed, then I help her lie down and cover her. "I'll be napping in the living room. If you wake up first, call me. Don't try to get out of bed alone."

I stretch out on the couch. I shouldn't be enjoying taking care of Anna so much, but I am. I've gotten very attached to her. I love her strength, her intellect, her kindness, her caring, her warmth, and her generosity.

CHAPTER TWENTY-THREE

Ariana

The sun is streaming in through the window when I open my eyes again. The house is quiet. I'm positive Lee wouldn't leave knowing I'm too weak to get out of bed by myself. Maybe she's asleep in the living room. Waking every two hours to bathe me must have exhausted her.

Thinking of Lee reminds me of being vaguely aware from time to time of being touched gently. I felt delicious things I hadn't felt since before the accident, but I thought I was dreaming, remembering. And I'd been too out of it to connect the touch with someone seeing my scarred face and body. The last time I'd seen my face in the bathroom mirror in the hospital, it looked like a raw steak, like something out of a horror movie. It was then I'd asked Kim to have the mirror covered and buy me a hat with a veil. I haven't seen my face since. And neither has anyone else, including Kim.

Though I was attracted to Lee almost from the day we met, I've tried not to think about the possibility of anything beyond friendship because of the scarring. Unfortunately, I've failed miserably. I think about it constantly. I'm sure Lee cares for me. But that way? Might I have another chance at life? Stupid. How could Lee, or anyone, love someone whose face she's never seen? I doze again.

I wake as Lee enters my bedroom with a bowl and a stack of washcloths.

"Good morning." She smiles. "It's good to see you looking alert. How are you feeling?" She picks up the thermometer. "I want to check your temperature, but I'll have to put my hand under the veil. Is that all right?"

"Hey, you've had your way with me already, why ask now?" My voice is weak, but I hope the tone conveys that I'm not upset.

Lee grins. "I could lie and say I asked your permission, but the truth is you were so far out of it that I was on my own as to what was permissible. I hope you'll forgive me for invading your privacy."

"I'm still wearing clothing so I guess you were as honorable as I would expect."

"Ah, your temperature is almost normal."

I struggle to sit up, but I don't have the strength.

"Can I help?"

"Please, my arms are like wet spaghetti. What happened?"

Lee helps me sit up against the headboard. "You have the flu, which you probably caught from Thomas. When I found you on the floor yesterday morning you had a temperature of one hundred four degrees. The fever seems to have broken this morning, but you'll have to take it easy for a few days."

"Is Thomas okay?"

"His fever only lasted a few hours, and he's feeling better. But living out here without being exposed to people probably left you more vulnerable to the bug than a healthy teenager. You need to eat. I'm going to heat some soup for you." She leaves before I can object.

When she returns, I attempt to sit up straighter and somehow the brim of my hat catches between my shoulder and the headboard and is pulled off, taking the veil with it. I gasp. Lee stares. The blood drains from her face. She looks shocked. She averts her eyes, but I feel exposed. I burst into tears. "Now you know."

"Know what?"

"Know what I look like behind the veil and under my long dresses." I keep my eyes down. I don't want to see pity, or worse, disgust on her face. "Get out."

"What?"

"You heard me. Get out of here. Now!"

"You're too weak to be alone. Let me—"

"I. Said. Get. Out."

CHAPTER TWENTY-FOUR

Lee

I feel helpless, but I see that Anna is struggling to hold herself together, so I do what she asks. I leave her, but there's no way I'll leave her alone in the house when she's so weak and so distraught. I go into the living room and sink onto the sofa, elbows on my thighs, my head in my hands. I'm not sure how her hat was pulled off, but if only it had happened before I came back into the room. I was so careful. I was afraid of this, afraid that if I accidently saw her without her veil she would tell me to leave. A part of me is glad I saw her face, but I hurt for her, hurt that she believes she looks so ugly that she's been hiding behind that heavy veil, hurt that she's so alone and yet is so horrified I saw her that she's willing to send me away. I thought she trusted me, but clearly her fear of my reaction to her looks outweighs any trust we've built. Hopefully, when she calms down she'll let me explain that the shock on my face was not because I found her so horrible but because I found her so beautiful.

She's sobbing and it breaks my heart that I can't go in there and comfort her. I'm so attached to her, I care so much, I don't know what I'll do if she doesn't let me stay with her. My own tears are flowing and I'm getting a headache going round and round about what to do next. Should I go back and try to talk to her? Should I wait a while then go back? Or should I ignore her, just take her in my arms and comfort her? She'll need help getting out of bed. Maybe she'll call for me.

CHAPTER TWENTY-FIVE

Anna

I'm devastated. She's seen my face. And the look on hers is…

I burst into tears. Even though I knew this would happen if I showed myself, it still hurts because I trust Lee. All the good feelings, the good times, the connection, all my dreams of having Lee accept me, gone in an instant of carelessness. Even though I expected a strong reaction, I was surprised by the shock on her face, and I didn't wait to see it evolve to disgust and horror, I just went on the offensive and ordered her to leave. Why did I do that?

I feel hopeless and more alone than I've ever felt. I let myself feel the pain. I don't try to control the sobs. I cry myself to sleep.

My eyes pop open. Oh, my God, somebody is trying to break down the door, and I'm too weak to even get out of bed to hide. The tears come again.

CHAPTER TWENTY-SIX

Lee

I must doze because I'm jolted awake by screaming and banging. Anna? I turn toward her bedroom, then I realize the pounding is coming from the kitchen door. I dash to the kitchen.

"Ari, Ari, Ariana, are you okay?" It's a woman's voice, and she's frantic, screaming and pounding on the door.

I pull the door open and come face-to-face with a wild woman. I grab her as she tries to push past me. "Just a second, lady. Who the hell are you?"

"Who the hell are *you*?" She glares at me. I sense she's ready to take me on. "Where's Ariana?" She breathes fire in my face, or maybe I just imagine it because she is seriously scary.

"There's no Ariana here. You have the wrong house." I push her back so I can close the door.

The woman blinks. "Oh. I meant Anna. I'm Kim, her sister. We usually touch base every day, but she didn't answer her phone yesterday or this morning. She's never missed calling me before. I couldn't sleep last night. When she didn't answer again this morning, I was frantic and drove here from Austin to make sure she didn't...that she's all right."

I eye the woman. Her jeans and shirt, her haircut, her manicure, and the BMW parked in the driveway all scream money. Her agitation seems genuine. And Anna might have mentioned someone named Kim.

"Anna is sick. She's had the flu with a high fever, and she's basically been asleep for more than a day. I haven't heard her phone ring, though." I relax. "Come in. I'll see if she's awake."

Kim nearly knocks me over as she rushes past me and dashes to Anna's bedroom. I run after her, afraid she's going to hurt Anna. She stops in the doorway. Shock on her face, she gapes. "Ari?"

Anna is lying just as I'd left her, but now her face is pale and she's sobbing. Her eyes pop open. "Kim?"

"Oh, my God, you look beautiful."

"What?" She grabs her hat and pulls the veil down.

I can't control myself. "She's right. You're beautiful. Don't hide."

"I told you to get out." The same steely voice from Anna again. Kim jumps in before I can respond.

"What the fuck, Ari. You haven't called me for two days. And you haven't answered any of the dozens of texts and voice mails I've sent since yesterday. I drove like a bat out of hell to get here because I thought you'd…that something had happened to you. And here you are, looking like yourself."

"What do you mean, looking like myself?" Anna straightens.

"I mean, you look like yourself before the accident."

Anna's jaw drops. "I do?" She looks from Kim to me and back to Kim.

"You do," Kim says.

"Take that fucking hat off, please," Kim says. "And please tell me why you haven't called me or answered my calls?"

Anna slowly pulls the hat off.

I can't help grinning and I'm not surprised to find Kim doing the same when I glance at her.

Anna touches her face with her hand. "I'm so sorry to worry you, Kimmy. I think my phone is in the music room. I turned it off because I was working on a song, and you know how I am when I get into it."

Kim gasps. "You're composing?"

"Yes, and then I must have passed out because Lee found me on the floor yesterday morning. She's been caring for me, but I've been totally out of it until this morning. I'm still weak because of the fever, but as you can see, I'm alive. And confused."

"Confused about what?" Kim asked.

"Does my face really look all right?"

"Not just all right, almost like before."

Anna looks at me. "I need to talk to Kim privately, but please don't leave yet."

Kim swivels to me. "Walk out with me, Lee."

I follow her into the kitchen.

"What happened? Why is Ari upset with you?"

"A little while before you arrived, she accidently knocked her hat off and her face was exposed. I think she misinterpreted my shock at seeing her face, at seeing how beautiful she is, for something negative, because she ordered me to leave. She wouldn't let me explain, but as weak as she is there was no way I was going to leave her alone."

Kim touched my arm. "You're a good friend."

Not so good that Anna wants me to stay. "You need to get her to eat. I was going to make her some eggs and toast for breakfast. I was afraid she might throw them at me. She might be more receptive if you do it."

"It's understandable she's upset that you saw her. She's worn that damn veil since she saw herself in the mirror at the hospital, and even I haven't seen her face until this morning." She paced for a few seconds. "You're staying in the bunkhouse, right?" She didn't wait for my answer. "Why don't you hang out there for a while. I'll get her up and make breakfast and, hopefully, talk some sense into her. I'll come and get you as soon as she's calmed down."

"Sure." I start to leave but turn to speak to Kim. "Be careful, she's weak and will need help standing and walking. She won't like it but put her in the wheelchair."

"Thanks," Kim says. "I've got her."

I turn to the door.

"Wait. Doesn't she always use the wheelchair?"

"Not anymore." Now Kim is the one who looks shocked. I close the door behind me.

After taking a shower, I sit on the bench in front of the bunkhouse trying to understand the sadness I'm feeling. I don't want to leave. I care for Anna. I should be happy her friend is here for her, but instead I feel pushed aside. Why did Kim call her best friend Ariana instead of Anna? I'm missing something. I find myself humming Anna's song, the words playing over and over in my mind. Clearly Anna was writing about her pain and loneliness. Am I the person who gave her hope? Or am I kidding myself?

About an hour and a half later, Kim walks the boardwalk and sits next to me on the bench. She eyes me.

"Everything is okay. Ariana understands that it was her fault you saw her face and she also understands that she's not the monster she thought she was. She'd like you to come back to the house."

I breathe out, letting go of the tension. "Thanks." I stand, then ask one of the questions swirling in my head. "Why do you call her Ari or Ariana?"

"Fair question. But I'll let her answer it if you don't mind."

Anna is in the wheelchair at the kitchen table, a steaming cup of tea and an empty plate in front of her. She's so beautiful I can't help staring.

She blushes, then lowers her eyes. "I'm sorry for treating you so badly. You didn't deserve it. It was my fault the veil slipped off, but I felt exposed. I lashed out at you because for months I worried that if you saw my face you would leave." She looks up and meets my eyes. "I care about you, Lee. And seeing disgust or pity on your face would have destroyed me, so I told you to go." She shrugs and smiles softly. "I really want you to stay. I hope you want to."

I relax. Seeing her smile lifts my heart. "I *was* really shocked to see your face. A, because I didn't expect it. And B, because you are so beautiful. I'm not sure what I expected, but it wasn't that." I smile. "I wasn't going to leave you alone. I won't leave you until you're strong enough to be on your own and you tell me to go. And mean it."

Her smile brightens. She takes my hand. "Thank you."

My heart flip-flops. I sit next to her.

Kim glances at Anna. "Have you had breakfast, Lee? I can make you eggs if you'd like."

Less than two hours ago this woman was ready to kill me, now she's offering to feed me. I welcome the quick turnaround in her attitude. "I haven't eaten, but I can make something for myself."

"I promise not to poison you." Kim stands. "How do you like your eggs?"

"Over medium," Anna and I say at the same time. Our eyes lock and my heart stutters. Not used to being able to look at her, I avert my gaze. Could she really be attracted to me?

Kim's gaze bounces between us, then she puts two slices of bread in the toaster, drops some butter in a frying pan and adds three eggs. She hands me a cup of coffee.

I glance at Anna. She's watching with a sweet smile.

Kim butters my toast, slides the eggs onto a plate, and places both in front of me. I dig in with the two of them watching. When I finish, I sit back. "So who is going to tell me what's going on?"

Kim tips her head toward Anna. Her eyelids are drooping. I stand. "Come on, you need to rest, Anna. I can wait to hear what you have to say."

"Help me into bed. I'll explain before I doze off."

I roll the wheelchair into the bedroom. Anna insists on sitting up, so I shift her to the bed and place some pillows behind her. She clasps her hands in front of her, gazes at Kim, then looks at me. "My name is not Anna Solander. It's Ariana Calandre."

"The singer?"

She huffs out a sort of laugh. "The former singer."

"No wonder you look familiar." I should be awestruck, but I'm not. I don't see the mega star. I see the wonderful woman behind the veil. "I'm a fan of your music, but the accident must have happened while I was stationed in Jordan near the Syrian and Iraqi borders because I wasn't aware of it. And I didn't realize you weren't recording."

Kim clears her throat. "That's probably because we've been slowly releasing songs from the world tour she and the band finished right before the accident and that took the focus off the encouraging updates on her health we issued around the same time."

Anna—no, Ariana—yawns. "I really want to talk to you, but I need to sleep. Kim can fill you in."

I help her lie down. She takes my hand and kisses my palm. "Will you be here when I wake up?"

"I will." I squeeze her hand, then follow Kim out to the porch. We sit in matching rockers.

"So," I say.

"So," Kim says. "Let me start by apologizing for my treatment of you earlier. I'm not just Ari's manager. She and I have been best friends since we were ten years old. My parents adopted her, so she's also my sister. As you saw, I'm extremely protective of her. After the accident which left her scarred and in excruciating pain, she was grief-stricken at the loss of five of her closest friends and two bodyguards. She was inconsolable, depressed, seemed to have given up on life, and insisted she wanted to be alone. I fought her mainly because I feared she might hurt herself but also because I believed she needed to be close to those who loved her so she could heal. But she can be stubborn. She threatened to disappear and cut off all contact, which meant she would have no money and no place to live. So we compromised. If she promised not to kill herself and also promised to call me every single day, I would find her a place to live alone and wouldn't send bodyguards to watch her twenty-four seven. And she did call every day. Until yesterday. I was terrified. I thought she had either committed suicide or was hurt and alone. I was out of town and couldn't get a commercial or a charter flight to Austin until early this morning. When I got in, I picked up my car and drove directly here. I knew you were on the property, but I had no idea that you and she were so…close. I apologize for being so rude earlier, I thought you were a man who had broken in and was taking advantage of her."

"Thank you for the explanation. And, FYI, most people think I'm a man at first. Until she accidently unveiled herself, I had never seen Anna, um, Ariana, without her veil and I knew nothing about her past. And since she just started singing the night she got sick, I didn't have a clue that she's Ariana Calandre."

"Well, from what she says, it's thanks to you that she's almost back to herself." Kim gazes at me. "Just between us, what is her voice like?"

I think for a minute, trying to remember what Ariana Calandre sounds like. "Her voice is lower, maybe a little raspy, but she'd only just started singing again, so I think with use and practice, she might sound pretty much the same."

Tears fill Kim's eyes, but her smile is radiant. "Music is her life, you know. If she's able to sing and write again, she'll be okay." She leans back and starts to rock. "Tell me a little about yourself. You mentioned Jordan."

"Can you wait until Anna, I mean Ariana, is awake? I'd rather not share anything with you that she doesn't know."

"Sure." Kim's smile is, as they say, knowing. "Tell me then, how did that ramp"—she points—"and that wooden walkway come to be? Ari was adamant about not needing to leave the house."

I laugh. "When I started working for Anna she agreed to let me camp on her property as long as I was far enough away from the house that I didn't interfere with her privacy. Then one night we had a horrific rainstorm that basically washed my tent away and Anna suggested I clean out the bunkhouse and stay there. Once it was cleaned, painted, and refurnished, I invited Anna to come out and see how it looked. I basically had to carry her down the steps and she could only walk a few feet before she was exhausted, but she seemed to enjoy being outside. I remembered seeing the pile of wood in the back of the property and I decided to surprise her with a walkway. I thought it would bring her pleasure to be able to sit outside and I also thought if I could get her to walk every day, she would get stronger."

Kim looked skeptical. "Does she go outside much? And does she walk on it?"

"She does. Every day. Before she got sick she was walking the whole circuit three times a day. At first, she used the walker, then the cane, and just the other day she walked on her own with me nearby. She'll be weak from lying in bed, but I'm pretty sure she'll regain her strength quickly. And I bet before long she'll be jogging."

Kim leans over and takes my hand. "I was afraid I'd never see my best friend, the happy musician, Ari, again, but you brought her back to life. I don't know how to thank you, Lee." She sobs, then laughs. "Sorry, these tears are the melting fear and stress and worry that I've been carrying around since the accident. They're happy tears."

"I don't know what to say to that, Kim. I didn't do anything special. Maybe by the time I arrived she was ready to move on."

Kim shakes her head. "From what she told me, you gave her hope when she was hopeless. I see you care for her. And I know she cares for you. But whatever happens between you, I'm sure Ari is on the road back." She squeezes my hand, then lets it go. "I hope you'll be walking beside her."

"Wow. I'm overwhelmed. And happy you didn't kill me before we got a chance to know each other."

"I'm glad too." She pauses. "I hate burying the bodies."

I snort.

Kim grins. "I have some calls to make and contracts to review so I'm going in. I'll take care of lunch as well. Roasted chicken, roasted carrots, and mashed potatoes should be okay for Ari. And for us as well."

I push off the rocker. "I was planning to start painting the outside of the house yesterday, but her fever was so high, and she was so out of it, I didn't want to leave her in the house alone. But now that you're around to keep an eye on her, I think I'll paint for a few hours."

"You could take the day off and rest."

"I need to move. I'm not used to sitting around."

"I'll let you know when lunch is close to being ready so you can clean up and eat with us."

I salute and head to the bunkhouse to change into painting clothes.

CHAPTER TWENTY-SEVEN

Ariana

I open my eyes to delicious smells. I'm starving. I roll toward the edge of the bed before I remember I've been sick and I'm not supposed to stand by myself. I notice the bell on the night table and ring it, expecting Lee to come in and help me. I'm surprised to see Kim. And then it all floods back. Kim frantic with worry and her astonishment seeing me without my veil. I knew she wanted to ask a thousand questions, but Kim, being Kim, sat back and let me tell my story as I ate an egg, nibbled on toast, and sipped tea. Never one to contain her feelings, Kim's joy and wonder at my transformation was endearing and if I didn't already know she loved me, it was clear then. In tears, she helped me from the bed into the wheelchair and we shared our first hug since the night of the accident.

Now she's smiling. "I'm glad you woke up naturally. I couldn't decide whether you need sleep or food more and whether to wake you for lunch. How are you feeling?"

"Better." I grin. "Can you get me a sweatshirt and sweatpants, then help me out of bed? I'm starving."

"Lunch will be ready in fifteen minutes." Since she unpacked my things when I moved in, she knows where everything is. She pulls out a matched set of sweats, then a pair of socks. "Are these sweats okay?"

"Perfect."

"Are you ready for more solid food?"

"Oh, yeah. Bring it on." She and Lee seemed to have made a truce earlier, but I'm not sure how things stand between them. "Is Lee around? I usually make meals for her."

Kim doesn't seem to notice my concern. "She's been painting, but I let her know lunch will be ready in fifteen minutes."

Good. They're communicating. She helps me sit on the edge of the bed. I pull the sweatshirt over my head, she slips my pants over my feet, I stand, she pulls my pants up, and I swing into the wheelchair. She kneels and puts the socks on. Damn, the long baggy dresses are easier, and I thought I was done with the wheelchair. But I feel normal, so I'll put up with needing help getting into sweats and using the wheelchair temporarily. "Bathroom, please."

Kim wheels me in and helps me onto the toilet. She turns her back, and when I'm ready she helps me into the chair. "If you push me to the lower sink, I can wash myself."

"I'll be in the kitchen. Call when you're ready."

I'm thrilled when Lee comes to bring me to the kitchen. She's in clean clothing but still smells faintly of paint. Her smile is shy, like she's unsure how to treat me. I reach for her hand. "If I haven't said it before, thank you for taking care of me." I hope my smile shows my feelings. Or at least the feelings I'm ready to share with her right now.

She relaxes. "You would have done the same for me." She wheels the chair into the kitchen. "Are you ready to do the hard work necessary to get your strength back?"

"I'm ready as long as you're here to help me." I swivel so she sees my face when I answer, and it occurs to me that I'm barefaced, without a veil. Suddenly I'm sobbing. I've spent so much time hiding from the world, then fearing Lee's reaction to seeing my face, sure she would run the other way, yet dreaming she would love me despite the way I look. Now it feels like the most natural thing in the world. I'm so thankful.

"Hey, what's wrong?" Lee kneels and wraps me in her arms. I feel safe with her, have felt that way almost from the day we met, so I let the tears flow, let myself feel the relief. When finally, the tears stop, I take a deep breath and sit back.

Lee stands. My eyes meet Kim's. She smiles, as if she gets it. And I'm sure she does. "Without understanding what I was doing I sentenced myself to a life of deprivation, pain, and loneliness. I'm so grateful you showed up and that you're here now, Lee. I don't have the words yet to tell you what I feel, but I hope you'll stick around to get to know the woman behind the veil."

"Funny, I think I do know her, but I'll be here as long as you want me. How about you eat as much as you can of this fabulous lunch Kim prepared. And after we'll get you on your feet to walk a little with your walker. Okay?" She glances at Kim. Maybe they still have issues.

I settle in at the table. I can't help smiling when Lee sits next to me. Out of habit? Or wanting to be close? I hope the latter.

Kim places a dish with sliced chicken, roasted carrots, and mashed potatoes in front of me. I inhale.

"It smells heavenly and looks divine. You do Mom proud, Kimmy."

"I hoped it might tempt you," Kim says.

"I'm definitely tempted, and I'll try my best to eat most of it."

Lee is looking back and forth between us, and I realize she doesn't know our history. I turn to face her. "My birth family was, uh, sort of hit or miss around caring for me, so when we were around ten Kim dragged me home and I ate with her family every night. This was my favorite dinner. Eventually, I moved in with them, and then her parents adopted me, so we're sisters as well as friends and business partners."

Lee quickly looks away.

I'm hurt, then I realize she's being protective. I put my hand on her arm. "It's okay to look at me, Lee. I can see by your face and Kim's that I'm not as hideous as I was. In fact, I'd like you to buy me a mirror the next time you go into town so I can see for myself." I pick up my knife and fork and take a bit of chicken. I blush at the moan that comes out of me. I side-eye Lee and see that she's blushing as well. So she *is* interested. Maybe I'll do it a few more times. I raise my eyes to Kim, who seems to be studying her plate, but I know her too well, and that little smirk tells me she sees what I see. I try another bite and moan again, this time with intent.

Kim clears her throat. "I asked Lee about her background. You know, how she came to be here, that kind of thing. She didn't want to tell me anything you didn't know. So, Lee, when Ari hired you, I had someone check to make sure you weren't a serial killer or maybe a thief, but I'd like to hear your story from you."

CHAPTER TWENTY-EIGHT

Lee

"Sure." I clear my throat. "My dad, Jaime, is a retired general in the Army, and my mom, Kaye, a retired high school English teacher. I have three brothers all considerably older than me—Jimmy, seventeen years, Mark, fifteen years, and Eric, thirteen years. My parents and brothers are all graduates of The University of Texas in Austin. My dad and my brothers are all in the military. I grew up on military bases all over the world, but when I was sixteen, I came back to Texas and enrolled in the Cockrell School of Engineering at UT Austin, as expected. I joined the ROTC program, assuming when I graduated, I would become an officer in the Army." I pause to take a sip of coffee.

"But you know how life goes. I had always sung and played the guitar, and it was impossible to resist the phenomenal Austin music scene. At first the music was just for fun, to help me relax, but people seemed to like my singing and playing and some professional musicians who dropped in to jam after their gigs encouraged me to get serious. Near the end of my sophomore year, my career as a singer/songwriter was taking off. But I was caught between my family's expectation that I graduate college and enlist in the military and my desire to pursue the career I wanted. Then my three brothers happened to be passing through Austin at the same time and I invited them to a performance.

Afterward, we went out to dinner together and I confessed I was torn between music and the military.

"No one said a word. I cringed. But then Jimmy looked at each of the three of us and spoke to me. 'When I attended UT Austin, I was torn between a career as a drummer and the military.' He gazed into my eyes. 'Don't give up your dream, Lee. You can always join the military if music doesn't work out, but it's not easy to go the other way.' The other two were supportive as well. So I gave myself two years to see if I could make it."

Suddenly I feel self-conscious, but Anna and Kim seem rapt, so I continue my story. "After finals in December 2000 the end of my sophomore year, I took a leave of absence from UT. I was starting to be in demand when September 11, 2001, happened. Like every American, I was stunned. But I was also enraged. I couldn't pursue my personal interests while my brothers and my dad left their families to fight this enemy. I immediately enlisted." I notice Ariana's eyelids drooping. "Hey. I'm tired of talking. Can we pick this up tonight or tomorrow?"

Kim follows my gaze and nods. "I agree. We need a break. You okay with that, Ari?"

Ariana blinks. "Sure. I'm feeling sleepy, so it's probably a good time to stop. Lee, would you help me into bed?"

I check in with Kim, hoping she isn't upset that Ariana asked me, not her, but she's smiling, and I assume we're good.

CHAPTER TWENTY-NINE

Ariana

I wake to wonderful smells again. I'm sure it's Kim's lasagna. She doesn't know my appetite had roared to life before I got sick so she's making my favorites to tempt me to eat. Now that I'm starting to feel better, my body wants food, and the smells are waking me. I glance at the clock. Five thirty. I've slept for almost four hours. I sit up and for the first time I haven't had to struggle. I'm pleased my strength is coming back. Lee says my muscles will be weak from the fever, so I don't try to stand on my own. I wonder how long it will take to rebuild my strength so I can walk outside whenever I desire to watch Lee and Thomas work. Thomas. My hand goes to my face. I forgot about him. I ring the bell and Lee comes in.

She bows. "You called, milady?"

I laugh. "I'm able to sit up by myself, but you asked me to not stand unless you or Kim are with me. Can I try standing? And walking with the walker a bit?"

She's immediately all business. "Sure. Are you able to move to the edge of the bed and swing your legs over?"

I do as she asks, and I'm rewarded with a grin.

"Okay." She extends her hands. "Take my hands and try to stand on your own. I'll steady you if necessary."

I stand. She places the walker in front of me, follows me with the wheelchair, and waits outside the bathroom as I pee, brush my teeth, and wash my face. I almost make it to the kitchen before I'm exhausted. Lee helps me sink into the wheelchair and rolls me to the kitchen table, which is set for dinner. I feel so taken care of. It's wonderful to be with the two people in the world who love me. Whoa. Does Lee love me? As more than a friend? I watch her pour water for all of us and wine for her and Kim. Maybe. Do I love her? Maybe.

Kim turns from the stove. "Have a good nap?"

"I did." I sniff. "Is that what I think it is?"

Kim beams. "If you think it's lasagna, you're right. It needs another five to ten minutes. Does it appeal?" She pulls a loaf of Italian bread out of the oven, then joins us at the table.

"And Italian bread, too? Are you kidding?" I turn to Lee. "Kimmy makes the best lasagna."

Kim leans toward me. "You mentioned you've been singing and composing. So are you thinking of performing again?" She tries to keep the excitement out of her voice, but I feel it.

"I haven't had time to think it through, but I admit that while I was composing the new song and playing the guitar, it did cross my mind. My voice felt and sounded okay to me, but I don't know how it would sound to anyone else."

Lee clears her throat. "I heard you singing when I came back to get my book, and you sounded great to me, Ariana. In fact, I liked it so much I sat on the porch and listened for a while."

I stare at her. I had no idea.

Lee looks away. "Does that make me a perv?"

I burst out laughing. "I don't think it qualifies. I had no idea you were out there."

Kim's eyes light up. "Would you sing the new song for me after dinner?"

I swallow. I'm nervous. Suppose she hates my voice? On the other hand, suppose she likes it. I'm not sure I'm ready to go in front of an audience, but what Kim thinks is important to me. And I'm confident neither she nor Lee will judge me either way.

"I'll do it now while I still have energy. While Kim gets my guitar from the music room, why don't you get yours from the bunkhouse, Lee. You have a lovely voice and if my voice is decent, I think we'd sound good together, so maybe after I sing it, we could try a duet."

Lee flushes. "I'm not in the same class as you, Ariana."

Kim looks from one to the other of us. "No harm in trying, Lee."

A few minutes later we're tuning our guitars. I place my notebook on the table between us and explain the chords I jotted down the other night. I drink some water and start playing, and then I begin to sing.

"Alone and lonely, in pain,
I cried. And wished I'd died.
Death seemed easier than living this way.
And then you were there.
At the door. In my life.
Bringing brightness and hope.
Bringing peace.
Seeing me, really seeing me,
Under the hat,
Behind the veil,
Beneath the sadness and the pain,
You saw me. You saw me under the hat, behind the veil,
Despite the loss of all I used to be,
You saw me."

I pause to take another drink of water. My gaze goes to Kim. She has tears in her eyes, but she's glowing. I glance at Lee. She looks…in love. I clear my throat and pick up where I left off.

"You made life worth living again,
Because you were there.
At the door. In my life.
Bringing brightness,
Bringing hope.
Seeing me, really seeing me,
Under the hat,
Behind the veil,
Beneath the sadness and the pain,
You saw me. You saw me under the hat, behind the veil,
Despite the loss of all I used to be,
You saw me.
And life was worth living again."

I sing the whole thing through a second time. I don't look at them. I'm afraid the song is awful or, worse, my voice is. I wait for the judgment. Kim leaps up. She rounds the table, kneels next to the wheelchair, and kisses my forehead.

"Oh, my God, Ari, you sound wonderful. And you'll sound even better once you start doing your vocal exercises and singing more. By the way, that song is beautiful."

"I totally agree."

I search Lee's face. And I believe she means it.

"It's still rough." I take a deep breath. "Sing with me."

And we do it. At first we're tentative, then I shift so we're facing each other, and we click. Our voices meld and soar together. When we finish, Kim claps. "You two are dynamite together. Let's not overdo it today, but I'm going to want to hear more of the two of you together and separately. And Lee, just so you know, I'm interested in representing you. But now, I believe we have a lasagna to eat."

As Kim serves our dinner, Lee places her guitar in its case, then does the same for mine. I suck the tips of my fingers. It will take some time to build back the calluses.

Lee and I moan when we take our first bites and the three of us smile. We even moan in harmony. I'm so damned excited about singing with her. I wonder whether she feels the chemistry between us, then I feel her hand on my knee. It's hot, and flames shoot through me, warming every secret place. I want to swoon, but I take a deep breath and turn toward her.

Lee smiles. "I never dreamed I'd sing with you, Ariana, and I can't believe how great we sound together."

I watch and listen while Kim asks Lee about her experience performing. Was it just her on the guitar or did she have backup? What venues in Austin? Did she have a manager? Who did they know in common? And on and on. Kim is excited about the possibility of taking her on as a client. I love the idea. Maybe it means Lee won't move on. When she picks up her story tomorrow, I want to ask why she moves around so much.

Lee volunteers to clean up after we finish eating, and Kim and I sit at the table. She takes my hands. "So, Ari, not right now, but in the not too distant future, would you be interested in performing?"

I check in with myself. It's kind of scary but exciting. We're not talking about tomorrow, so I can always change my mind. "I need to strengthen my voice, write new music, and rehearse a lot before I even think about going before an audience. And it's been years since it was just me and my guitar on stage, so I couldn't do an arena, but I can see myself at a small venue."

Kim turns to Lee. "Would you be interested in performing with Ari in a small venue?"

Lee doesn't respond. She looks at me. "Would you want that, Ariana, the two of us performing together?"

God, the woman is so caring and thoughtful. "It would be fun, I think, but not right away. First we need to sing and play and write some songs together. If you're up for that."

"I am," she says to me, then looks at Kim. "And yes, I would love to."

"Good." Kim knows when to push and when to let things go. She changes the subject. "You left the decision about your house in Austin up to Brian and me, and we decided to keep it. Graciela has been looking after it. I checked in with her a couple of weeks ago and she says it's ready whenever you want to come back to Austin."

I feel uneasy at the thought. "Let's not get ahead of ourselves, Kim. Ask me in a couple of months."

"No rush, honey. Just bringing you up-to-date. And just so you know, Mom and Dad are desperate to see you. Brian and the kids really miss you too. Whenever you're ready for visitors they'd love to come up, even for just an afternoon."

"I miss them too." I swallow. "I'll think about it." They, especially the kids, must feel abandoned.

Kim grabs my hands. No guilt trip, just reminding me there are people who love me. I turn to Lee. "Kim and Brian, her husband, have two set of twins. The older two are identical girls and the other two are a girl and a boy." I laugh. "God, we're old, Kimmy."

"Hey, I started early, so we're not *that* old."

"How are they doing?" I look away to hide my guilty feelings.

"Jessie and Jackie will be juniors in September and are starting to think about college. Willow and Wylie will be freshmen. She's trying out for the tennis team, and we've talked Wylie out of football, so he's going for track."

Kim clears her throat. "On the business front, Brian says the individual songs we've released from the world tour are selling really, really well. And, though it's taken us nearly two years to produce it, he expects the full on-tour album to go to the top of the charts when it drops in October. Most of your investments are doing great, but he's doing some tuning to maximize returns."

I nod. I haven't allowed Kim to talk about the people I left behind or anything related to the music business, so this is her way of acknowledging I'm on the way back. Even though we talk every day, it's not been the same as before because of my need to shut out the world. Being here with her now, so relaxed and related, I let myself feel how much I've missed her, missed our closeness, and the fun we used to have. Which reminds me. "How long can you stay, Kim?"

She grins. "I think they can survive a week without me. Is that too long for you?"

"A week sounds wonderful." I hesitate but then push on. "I've been thinking about Thomas," I say.

Lee looks puzzled. "What about him?"

I address Kim. "Thomas is the teenaged delivery boy that Lee and I have taken under our wing. He's working with Lee this summer to pay for his sins, and Lee and I have been helping him with his schoolwork, so he won't be left back." I look at Lee. "I'm not ready for him to know who I am, so I don't want him to come until Kim leaves."

"Judging by the music he plays on his phone while he's working, he's a big Ariana Calandre fan. Since he's going back to school next week and he might be tempted to brag to his friends about knowing you, I agree it's a good idea to protect your identity from him."

"But I don't want him to feel that we dumped him, so after Kim leaves let's invite him to dinner with us and officially end things. Maybe we can give him some sort of certificate to acknowledge the hard work he's done. I'll only need to wear the veil and you'll only have to call me Anna for the time he's here. What do you think?"

"It's perfect. I've been planning to call him to see whether he needs help with his book report and when I do I'll say you're still sick, and he should wait for my call before coming back to work."

"Good idea. I'm fading. Can one of you help me into bed?"

Kim and Lee gaze at each other for a second, then Kim says, "I'll do it."

How have they gotten so close so fast?

CHAPTER THIRTY

Lee

Scary Kim has been replaced with funny, warm, and friendly Kim. Last night after Ariana went to sleep, she and I sat on the porch and talked for a long time. She's serious about signing me as a client even if Ariana and I decide not to perform together. I never thought I'd have another shot at a singing career. Though she focuses on Ariana, her most successful client, and the other artists she signs are mostly managed by people on her staff, she believes I'll be a breakout artist and plans to manage me herself. I'm overwhelmed but thrilled.

I've been painting this morning so no chitchat, but after lunch Ariana insists I pick up my story. "Let's sit outside." She grabs her walker and goes out. Kim and I follow. Once we are all settled, I begin.

"So the day after 9/11, I enlisted in the Army. I served multiple tours in Iraq, Afghanistan, and on bases in multiple Middle Eastern countries, most recently, Jordan. About five years ago, I married Gina, who I met on leave between tours." Ariana gasps. Scary Kim glares at me.

"We're divorced now," I hurry to explain. "The reasons for that will become clear as I tell my story. I was a colonel and aiming to serve twenty-five years before retiring, but about fifteen months ago, my best friend, Ella, and her husband, Jeff, both musicians, were driving home after a gig and were hit head-on by a drunk driver. Both died instantly."

I glance at Ariana, hoping I haven't upset her. She seems okay so I continue.

"Three years before the accident, when Mara, their first child, was born, they asked me if they could name me as her contingent legal guardian in case Ella's parents, who were in their early eighties, weren't available or couldn't do it. Thinking it was unlikely either or both Ella and Jeff would die, I agreed. And I agreed to the same terms in their updated will when Tessa was born a year later. Ella was adamant, and I totally agreed, that I spend time with the girls. And so when I was out of the country we Zoomed every week if possible, and when I was in Austin, to Gina's annoyance, I spent a lot of time with the girls, sometimes taking them on my own for the day and other times hanging out with Ella, Jeff, Mara, and Tessa.

"About ten days after the accident, Sarah Conklin, Ella and Jeff's attorney, tracked me down in Jordan. The good news was that Sarah had immediately filed suit against the driver, who turned out to be an extremely wealthy businessman whose business was about to go public. The case was clear-cut, and he was desperate to avoid any bad publicity, so he immediately offered an out-of-court settlement of ten million dollars, which, after consulting with me and Ella's mom, she accepted. Most of the money went into trusts for the girls, but a generous amount was set aside for living expenses until they come into the trust money. The bad news was that Ella's dad had passed away a few months before and Leslie, Ella's mom, was eighty-six and not in good health. However, given the settlement from the accident, there was money to hire a live-in nanny to care for the girls, and because she understood I was aiming for twenty-five years of service, Leslie agreed to raise the girls until I could take them. But she wanted to start the ball rolling to make the transition seamless. Sarah, the attorney, worried that the amount of money involved might bring unknown blood relatives out of the woodwork to challenge the will, so she suggested I adopt the girls for added protection. Leslie agreed, and I gave Sarah the go-ahead to initiate the adoption process.

"Five months later, Sarah called to let me know that adoption had been finalized and four-year-old Mara and three-year-old Tessa were officially my daughters. Three weeks after that, Leslie passed away. I was frantic. I wrangled a week's emergency leave and went to Austin to make arrangements. Gina was not thrilled. I begged her to take them until I could wrap up my assignment in Jordan and arrange my discharge. She reluctantly agreed but only because Liana and Caroline, the nannies

Leslie and I had hired, would be there to care for them. My heart was broken but I had to leave them. At least the nannies would provide continuity. I Zoomed with the girls as often as possible, some weeks daily, others two or three times, some just once, so they clung to me. They'd lost their parents and their grandmother, but I was their auntie and they loved me."

I take a breath and gaze at my audience of two. Ariana smiles. Kim nods, encouraging me to go on. But I need a break. I stand, stretch, walk around the porch, then pour myself a glass of lemonade from the pitcher on the table, and sit.

"So when I was discharged in January, I discovered that Gina had impersonated me, using a false driver's license and other forged documents, and had duped Jonah Rippletoe, managing partner of one of the most prestigious law firms in Austin, into representing her in the sale, seven weeks before, of the house I owned. I was stunned."

"I know Jonah," Kim said. "He's a straight arrow. How did she get him to sell a house you owned?"

"He does low cost and pro bono work for people who can't afford a lawyer. Anyway, he bought her sob story and believed her when she promised to donate a percent of the sale price to the fund he uses to support the low cost work. According to him all the documents looked legitimate, so he had no reason to doubt her. Apparently the house was on the market for a few months before they had a buyer. The inspection report was completed right before my emergency leave, and they closed the deal a week after I flew back to Jordan. I believe she agreed to take the girls so I would leave right away. She Zoomed with me until the day before I came home, I guess to keep me from being suspicious. She could have left the girls with friends of mine, but she disappeared with the money and the girls. She'd changed her phone number and none of her friends had any idea she was gone."

I blow out a breath and push on, anxious to finish this story. "Jonah took me on as a pro bono client and his investigators are actively searching for Mara and Tessa. He arranged my divorce and made sure I filed criminal charges, including kidnapping, against Gina. I left Austin after ten days and drove all over Texas following up leads on the girls with no luck. After so much time on the road, I was exhausted physically and emotionally and depressed, so Jonah recommended I find a place to stay and chill while his investigators continued to search. And that's why I took the job here." I meet Ariana's eyes, surprised to see them bright with tears. "And I found so much more than I expected."

No one speaks. My throat is dry, so I take more lemonade.

"That's horrible, Lee." Ariana reaches a hand toward me. "And still no word?"

I shake my head.

"Thanks for sharing with us, Lee, I know it wasn't easy," Kim says. "How old are the girls now?"

"Mara is five and Tessa is four. They must feel so abandoned. Even worse, Gina is back on drugs, so I'm sure they haven't been well cared for."

I'm on the edge of tears. Without a word, I walk off the porch and go to the bunkhouse. I need time to pull myself together.

CHAPTER THIRTY-ONE

Ariana

I watch Lee walk away, her back impossibly straight. I sense her sadness. How cruel of us to make her relive the horror of losing her daughters. But how would we know if she didn't tell us? My instinct is to rush to the bunkhouse, take her in my arms, and comfort her, but I don't. I understand her need for privacy. I will give her time.

"Should I go after her?" Kim dabs at her eyes. Lee's loss probably triggers the sadness she rarely shows. I reach for her hand and squeeze it. She squeezes back, understanding I'm there for her.

"I think she needs some time alone. Let's see if she returns for dinner."

"Speaking of which, I'd better figure out what to make." Kim stands and visibly shakes off the sadness. My Kimmy never wallows. Unlike me, she lets herself feel the feelings, then moves back to her cheerful, upbeat self.

I'm so deep in thought it doesn't register when she leaves. It occurs to me that most people deal with deep pain at some point in their lives. For me it's been the pain of losing my friends and the life I'd known. If I'm honest, I've been wallowing in it for the last year. Punishing myself for being alive. But choosing to be alone with myself was the right decision. The emotional pain of losing Maggie, Gloria, Nellie, Erica, and Torie will always be with me, but I no longer wish I had died with them. Instead, because of Lee I'm back in my life, looking forward to figuring out the future, with her, I hope. I came here to find the new me, and I have. I'm slowly regaining my life.

For Kim, it's the pain of having lost her first child, a boy, to cancer at age one. That pain lingers in the background, but her love for her four living children has dulled it and restored her joy.

For someone like Thomas, it's the pain of feeling stupid and hopeless but, hopefully, Lee and I have helped him dull that pain and feel proud and confident.

And for Lee it's the pain of losing her adopted daughters and being betrayed by someone she once loved. The loss is still fresh, so the pain is sharp. I wish I could mitigate her pain. I wish I could do something to help find her girls.

Thinking about the pain of loss leads me to thoughts of the families of the girls and I resolve to call them. It will be hard, but I know them and now that I'm stronger I feel able to face their pain. I don't know who my two guards left behind but I'm sure Kim knows and can give me contact information.

I doze and wake with a start, still in the chair on the porch. Her hands on the arms of my chair, Lee leans over me with a soft smile. "Hey, sleepyhead, time to get ready for dinner." I sniff. Paint. Burying oneself in work is one way of dealing with loss. I smile, happy to see her. "Hey." I hesitate to bring up her pain, but I can't pretend I don't have feelings about it. "I'm so sorry about Mara and Tessa. I wish I could do something to help you find them."

"Thanks." She straightens. "It was hard to talk about them, but you're letting me see who you are so it's only right I do the same."

I take the hands she offers, and she pulls me up. I reach for my walker and take a minute to ensure I'm steady before going in the house to wash up.

When I walk into the kitchen Kim is sharing the story of little Ricky's illness with Lee. I'm surprised. She rarely talks about him anymore and never with a relative stranger. I understand two things. Lee's story really moved her. And she likes Lee a lot. Not as much as I do, I'm sure. I smile at that thought.

"It's so nice to see you smiling again, Ari. Want to share?" Kim puts an arm around my shoulder.

Nope. Definitely not sharing. "It makes me happy to see my two favorite people getting close." Kim and Lee react exactly the same way, with raised eyebrows. I smile again.

Lee breaks the silence. "It's nice to know I've made it into the ranks of your favorite people because you happen to be at the top of my list right now."

Kim is fun to be with, and we laugh a lot while we eat the delicious dinner that she has, she says, thrown together. I share the story of how I started reading again, claiming Lee left the book on the table to seduce me into reading.

"I most certainly did not intend to seduce her. I left it on the table so I could read it at the next meal. The truth is, she practically pulled the book out of my hands. I had to fight her off so I could finish it."

Then we launch into discussing our favorite books. Kim stands. "I'll make coffee and clean up."

"I'll help," Lee says. I'm feeling relaxed. And content. I watch them, listen to their chatter, and then they fade into the background. I'm composing in my head. It's still new enough that I'm thrilled to feel the urge to get the melody and lyrics echoing in my head down. "I hate to interrupt, ladies, but I'd love to have my guitar and my notebook, so if one of you—"

"I'm on it." Lee grins and leaves the room.

I don't have to look at Kim to know she's beaming. She doesn't say a word, just moves behind me, wraps her arms around me. And kisses the top of my head. She steps back when Lee hands me my notebook, pencil, and eraser, then removes my guitar from its case and hands it to me. I tune the guitar while they go about cleaning up and putting out coffee, ice cream, and slices of the pound cake Kim baked earlier.

I jot down the few lines of the lyrics I have and note the chords.

I don't always say it, but I hope you know,
I'm so grateful you're in my life.
You shared your home and your family.
Made funny faces and filled my empty spaces,
Our friendship changed everything.
You brought me love and set me free,
To sing and play, to sing and just be me.
What would I be? Where would I be?
If you hadn't rescued me, if you hadn't rescued me.
My world is brighter because of you,
Life is hard but you smooth the way,
Fight my fears, dry my tears, and lift me up.

It's always been true, my world is brighter because of you.

They look expectant. I strum the guitar, then smile at Kim. I'm brimming with love. "This is for you, Kimmy." They're quiet while I work and rework the lyrics and the melody. Every now and then I glance at Kim and, as always, I see love. Finally, I'm satisfied it's as good as I can make it now and I place the guitar in my lap. Kim has seen me and the other members of the band compose and Lee composes her own songs, so they both understand composing is cyclical, a process of writing, refining, and improving, then doing it all over again.

I sip my coffee, but it's cold, and my ice cream and my cake are a soggy mess. I shrug. "I forgot to eat dessert."

Kim jumps up. "There's plenty where that came from."

I side-eye Lee. She smiles. "It's a good song, Ari. And it will be even better when you finish it."

"Want to sing it with me? After I've had my dessert?"

She doesn't pretend. "I would love to. I'll go get my guitar."

And so we have another songfest. We sing the new one and she suggests additional lyrics and changes, and we move on to the other new one, then some of hers she's written down for me and a few of my older recorded songs. Forty-five minutes later I'm exhausted, so I say good night and Lee helps me into bed.

I feel like Snow White waking up after a long sleep. Lee is my prince, the one who healed me without even the kiss that I've been dreaming about. The world is crystal clear and exquisitely beautiful without the veil. My heart is full. I smile as the murmur of their voices lulls me to sleep.

CHAPTER THIRTY-TWO

Lee

I was flooded with feelings when I woke this morning. Four days ago, I had no idea what Anna looked like, but I was attracted to her anyway. And I thought she had feelings for me too. Now not only have I seen her beautiful face, but I've learned she's the extremely famous, talented, wealthy, singer/songwriter Ariana Calandre, not Anna Solander.

I've always loved Ariana's music and often sang along with her recordings, but I never dreamed I'd get to sing with her for real. Now I want to sing with her forever. She's amazing. It's hard to believe Ariana feels what I thought Anna felt. That she cares for me. But our connection is even more intense now. And intimate. Our chemistry and the way our voices blend and complement each other is amazing. Kim was stunned and immediately jumped ahead to us performing together. I will be there for Ariana in any way I can, including performing in a small venue if she wishes.

On the one hand, I'm ecstatic about finding Ariana and thrilled to have the opportunity to perform again. On the other hand, I'm distraught. Despite the efforts of Detective Sharp, Jonah's investigator, and the FBI, who Sharp recently brought in to assist with the search for the girls, Gina has disappeared without a trace. Jonah reminded me she's an addict and will eventually make a mistake. And since I believe Gina would never physically hurt the girls, I'm trying to be patient. I know going back on the road to search for them is futile, but I don't know what to do.

I'm feeling unsettled by my contradictory feelings, elation and depression, and at a loss about what to do. Then I remember Ariana's request for a full-length mirror so she can see what her new self looks like. How unsettled *she* must feel hearing that she looks normal, beautiful, after imagining herself a monster. At least I can do something to make her feel better. After breakfast I'll drive to town.

Breakfast is ready a few minutes after I arrive, and the three of us sit down to eat. Kim looks across the table at Ariana and me. "It's great being here with the two of you." She looks at me. "I'm so happy I've met you, mainly because of what you've done for Ari." I feel the blood climbing up my neck as she continues, "But also because I think you're super talented and I hope when you're ready you'll sign with me."

She turns her gaze to Ariana. "I'm thrilled to have my friend, my sister, Ari, back, thrilled to see you doing so well, thrilled that you're singing and writing again. Whenever you're ready to record or perform at some level, I'm here for you as always." She wipes her eyes.

Ariana reaches across the table and takes her hand, then takes mine as well. "I'm happy to be back. I've enjoyed having you here as well." She looks at me. "It will take a while for my voice to strengthen so I can hear how I truly sound, but if you will sing and write with me, Lee, I promise to work every day. I want to take my time and decide about performing later."

I squeeze her hand. "I'd love to work with you."

She smiles and turns again to Kim. "What do my fans know about my absence?"

"Initially, of course there was intense pressure for details, but we kept it simple, saying you were in the hospital and your serious injuries made it impossible to attend the funerals for the girls. Later we said you asked for privacy to heal and time to mourn your friends. From time to time, usually to coincide with releasing a single from the tour, we've posted things to indicate you were slowly recovering from the shock and your injuries. We still get requests for interviews and there's an occasional article wondering when or if you'll ever come back. And, as you would expect, along the way the tabloids and gossip sites specializing in sensationalist garbage have written about you being in a vegetive state, hooked on pills, or even secretly dead. But have no fear, based on the sales of the singles and the continued sales of your earlier releases, your fan base is as big as ever and growing. Whenever you're ready to perform again, you'll, without a doubt, be right back on top."

Ariana nods. "Knowing you, you've already planned my comeback."

Kim laughs. "Guilty as charged. I'm thinking we record two songs, you alone and you and Lee, then do an unpublicized performance in a small venue that I leak to a couple of influential music people so they can hear you. If they respond positively, we release the recorded songs, you do an interview with one of the biggies, then we discuss whether you want to perform with a new band, do smaller venues with Lee, if she's willing, or just put out an album and appear on talk shows. How does that sound?"

Ariana blows out a breath. "Like I need to do some thinking. Like I'd better start writing and singing more." She laughs. "Overwhelming. But good." She stands and hugs Kim. "I'll do the dishes for a change."

"I'm going into town to buy a mirror." I turn to Ariana. "I thought I'd also get a mirrored medicine cabinet to fit that space in the bathroom."

"Wait." Kim stands. "I had already bought mirrors before Ari indicated she didn't want any in the house. Come upstairs with me."

We look around and then Kim remembers she had them put into the attic. Sure enough there are several full-length mirrors, several for over dressers, and a medicine chest for each of the bathrooms. I carry one of the full-lengths down and lean it against the wall in Ariana's bedroom.

Ariana stands at the door to her bedroom. She inhales. "I'd like some privacy, but could the two of you stay close in case I need support?"

"We'll be on the porch," Kim says.

Ariana hesitates, then walks into the room and closes the door.

We stare at the door for a second, then go outside to wait.

"Do you think she'll be okay?" Kim asks, pacing.

"If she sees what I see, she will be." She's no longer emaciated or as pale as she was when I arrived, and even with the light scarring on her face she is by no means the monster she imagined. I think she's beautiful.

"You're right. She looks so much like her old self." She stares at the door. "What's taking her so long? Should we go check on her?"

I control my anxiety. Ariana needs to take the time she needs to adjust. "I don't think we should. It's probably scary for her to look." I sit in a rocker. "Let's give her some time."

"You're right." Kim sinks into a chair. "I'm impatient. Seeing her without that damned hat and veil, with a smile, seemed like a miracle when I arrived. And then finding out she's composing and singing again was thrilling. Being me, I jumped ahead to performances before a full arena of screaming fans. But I love having her back. Period. I just need her to be herself as she's been this week. Whether she performs again is up to her." She glances at the door again. "Any word about your daughters?"

"Only that Gina seems to have disappeared without a trace. I'm trying to be optimistic, but it's hard." We sit in companionable silence for a few minutes and the question I've been wanting to ask Kim pops into my mind. I clear my throat. "Kim." She looks at me. "I've only known you a few days, but I'm having trouble imagining you not having a complete background check done on me after Ariana told you I was working for her."

Her lips quirk. "Very astute, Lee. There was no way I was going to have her be here alone with someone who might hurt her. I had an in-depth investigation done. I even spoke to Jonah Rippletoe, who, by the way, had only nice things to say about you."

"But why ask me to tell you and Ariana about myself?"

"Well, for one thing, I never told Ariana what I knew about you, and I thought she should know your history. And I wanted to hear your version."

"And did I pass muster?"

"With flying colors."

CHAPTER THIRTY-THREE

Ariana

I sit on the bed trembling. I don't think I can look. I've been so happy these last few days thinking I look normal. I'm ready to live again. I can't go back to hiding away from the world, wearing the floppy hat, the veil, the baggy clothing. But what if I still look horrible?

I wrap my arms around myself and rock trying to soothe my nerves. I hear Lee's voice saying I'm beautiful. And then I remember Kim's wide-eyed stare seeing my face for the first time since I began wearing the veil in the hospital and her huge smile when she said I looked like my old self. As much as she tries to protect me, she's never lied to me. I glance at the mirror. I may not be perfect, but two people I trust have had positive reactions to seeing my face. How bad can it be?

I stand and move to the side of the mirror, then close my eyes and shuffle in front of it. I take a deep breath and narrow my eyes, then I slowly open them. I stare. My face is pale, but it's my face, and other than the two barely visible scars, one running from my forehead to my upper lip on the right side and one on my chin, I look like myself. My heart is pumping, my breath is coming fast as I pull my hair aside to expose the burn scar. It's shiny but not as large as I remembered and hidden by my hair, which has grown back thicker, and is longer than it's been in years.

I strip and examine my body. I'm thinner than I was before the accident, but I've built some muscle and I look pretty good. The burn scar runs down my left shoulder, my arm, my torso, and leg, but only a part of each is scarred. Funny, I remembered my whole left side was burned. The trauma must have skewed my perception.

I sink down on to the bed and the tears flow. Happy tears. I've gotten so much stronger since Lee came. The flu set me back a little, but I know if I continue to walk, lift weights, eat well, and get some sun I'll bounce back.

I sit up. They're waiting for me. I dress, grab my walker, and go into the bathroom to wash my face.

When I step outside, they jump up and reflect my smile back at me. I hug Kim. She says, "Welcome back, honey."

Lee smiles. "I told you so."

"Thank you, Lee, for awakening me." I pull her into a hug. "So I guess your next project is to put all the mirrors in place." The three of us laugh. "But let's do our morning walk first."

I grab my walker and lead us down the ramp to the boardwalk. I raise my face to the sun, enjoying its warmth, then we do our first trip of the day around the boardwalk. I'm already stronger, and maybe tomorrow I'll try walking with the cane. I'm enjoying being outside so we sit on one of the benches Lee built and chat.

After a while Lee stands. "I'll go hang the mirrors, if that's all right with you, Ariana."

"And while you do that, I think I'll do some voice exercises."

Kim stands. "I have a few more days to fatten you up before I leave, so I'll go figure out lunch and dinner."

I feel a pang of loss at the thought of Kim leaving, but the stronger feeling is happiness at being alone with Lee again.

* * *

I wake up with the sun as usual and get out of bed, happy that my body is resilient again. Before I dress, I take a few seconds to look at myself in the full-length mirror Lee mounted in my bedroom. The image of what I looked like when I left the hospital is fading from my memory, yet I'm still thrilled to see this healthier, stronger version of myself again. I dress, grab my cane and go into the bathroom. I study my face up close in the mirrored medicine chest. The skin of the area that was burned is not pretty, but as Lee promised, my hair covers it, and I'm sure makeup will cover the other scars. I don't doubt for a second that Kim packed my makeup when she brought me here, hoping I would want to use it, so I search the cabinets until I find the familiar bag. Some things have dried up, but the foundation seems okay. I apply a light coat, then lean in to examine my face in the mirror. Yes! The other scars aren't visible. I reach for the lipstick and stop. I applied the makeup without thinking about it. Like a lot of things lately, today is the first time I've used any since the night of the accident. I smile, put on lipstick, and walk to the kitchen.

Kim is going home today. She smiles at me across the breakfast table. "I'm a lot happier today than when I arrived a week ago. Not only are you just about fully recuperated from the flu, but I'm overjoyed to hear you singing, showing your beautiful face, and walking with just a cane. And, oh, wearing makeup. Not for me, I guess."

I blush. Before I can answer, Lee knocks and walks in. "Good morning." She places the bowl of eggs she's gathered on the counter.

"Good morning." Kim stares at the eggs. "Damn it, Ari. I've been so focused on you I haven't noticed that the eggs Lee brings in nearly every day are fresh. Why do I not know you have chickens?"

I blush and lock eyes with Lee. "Blame it on Lee, she suggested it." I look at Kim. "And, um, it didn't seem important enough to mention."

"Ariana Calandre, you should be ashamed." Kim puts her hands on her hips. Uh-oh, she's pissed. "I wasn't going to say anything about you failing to mention you've been living a secret happy life while I've spent every single day worrying, imagining you locked in this house, alone, depressed, and possibly suicidal."

Up to now, she hasn't chastised me for keeping her in the dark because she was thrilled about the me she found when she arrived. But, it seems, the secret cache of chickens is the last straw. Now I can't look at her. "I'm sorry. I'm not sure why I didn't tell you."

Kim pulls me into her arms, forgiving as always. I owe her the truth.

"I did share bits and pieces. I told you about hiring Lee because I knew you'd vet her, but I should have told you that connecting to her was bringing me back to life, that I was slowly resurrecting the me I'd buried in pain and guilt and self-pity. I was afraid you'd be suspicious of Lee, that you'd insist on sending her away or worse, sending Micki and my bodyguards to protect me, and she'd leave."

Kim tightens her arms. "I know I'm overprotective, sweetheart, and you're right. My first instinct would have been to rush here and take control. But I hope you know your happiness is the only thing I care about, and I like to think that once we talked, I would have backed off."

I do know that about Kim. "I'm sorry. You know I trust you with my life. I was feeling happy and hopeful and alive again and I should have shared that with you. But a part of me wanted it to be just us in our little bubble. Another part of me knew I'd be devastated when she left, and I didn't want you to be on the rollercoaster of my feelings again." I look her in the eye. "Forgive me?"

"Yes." She kisses my forehead. "How can I stay mad when the end result is you're you again?" She turns to Lee who has been watching our exchange. "Okay, our family drama is over now. Grab a cup of coffee and I'll get breakfast." She goes to the stove, ladles pancake batter onto the griddle, cracks eight eggs into a bowl, whisks them, then pours them into the waiting frying pan.

Lee picks up her guitar and walks it to the music room. We plan to work together after Kim is on the road. She returns quickly and pours coffee for herself.

I hold my cup up and she tops me off.

"When are you leaving, Kim?" Lee asks.

"After breakfast."

We've had such a great time this visit, I really am torn between wanting Kim to stay and wanting her to go. "Let's take a final walk before you leave."

Kim laughs. "I'd love to."

When we finish eating the pancakes and scrambled eggs, we sip our coffee and chat. Kim meets my eyes across the table. "Have you given any thought to"—she grins—"the proof-of-life visit with Mom and Dad, maybe just an afternoon?"

I blow out a breath. "Just the two of them and you? And Brian too, for a few hours?"

She nods. I see the small smile quirking her lips at my including Brian.

I glance at Lee. "This is all so new I'd like a few weeks to adjust before they come. Would that be all right?"

"Whatever you need, sweetheart. They'll be ecstatic. Would three weeks or a month be enough time?"

"What do you think, Lee?"

She takes my hand. "As Kim said, whatever you need, sweetheart."

"Okay, so we have a date." I stand and grab my cane.

"I'll clean up while you ladies walk," Lee says, clearing the table.

Considerate as usual, Lee is giving me private time with Kim before she leaves. Kim and I go outside and down the ramp. I put my arm through hers and we begin the first of several walks I'll take during the day. "I've loved having you here this week, Kimmy."

She pulls my arm closer. "It's been wonderful. I can't tell you how happy I am to have you back, Ari. I feel like a weight has been lifted off my chest. Keep up the walking and the weights and make sure you're eating." She's silent for a moment. "I really like Lee and I'm thrilled that you're so connected. No matter what happens between you I'll sign her when she's ready." She stops walking and turns to me. "I hope you know that other than wanting you to live a full and happy life, I have no agenda. Whether you perform or record again is up to you, but I hope you'll at least continue to compose and sing for your own pleasure."

"As I said, I need to think about just how much I want to put myself out there, but I'm totally clear that I'll continue to write and sing. And if Lee is willing, some of it will be with her." We're close to the house now, and Lee is in one of the rocking chairs on the porch.

Kim laughs. "In my humble opinion, Lee is so smitten that she's up for whatever you want. And I believe you want her. Yes?"

She lets go of me as we approach the ramp and I punch her arm. "Yes." I know I can't hide my feelings from her. Besides, I'm so happy to be feeling again, I really don't want to hide them.

Lee and I remain on the porch while Kim goes in the house to use the bathroom and get her things. She comes out carrying her huge handbag and a bottle of water. "Did you put my suitcase and computer bag in the car?"

"I did," Lee says. "I figured I'd save you a trip since no way could anyone carry that huge handbag of yours plus the suitcase and computer case in one trip."

We laugh.

Kim hugs Lee. "Thank you. Keep me up-to-date with what's happening with your girls."

"I will," Lee says.

Kim turns to me and pulls me in for a hug. "You know I'm going to make a pest of myself now."

I laugh. "Yes. But now I'm looking forward to our daily phone call and your next visit with Mom, Dad, and Brian. Give my love to the kids."

Kim climbs into her car, dries her eyes with a tissue, and drives away. I know her tears are happy tears this time. And so are mine.

CHAPTER THIRTY-FOUR

Lee

Things have changed so quickly.

Seven days ago, I hadn't seen Ariana's face and body. Seven days ago, I thought she was Anna Solander. I knew I was attracted to Anna, but I had no hope of anything happening. Now the sparks are flying between us. And I have high hopes, because I'm sure Ariana feels the electricity too.

Seven days ago, I hadn't met Kim and I hadn't thought about singing professionally in years. Now I'm composing and singing duets with Ariana. Now I can sign a contract with Kim whenever I'm ready.

Now my life has changed dramatically. And it's about to change even further.

Ariana feels she's getting her life back. I feel like I'm getting a new life, one with, I'm hoping, a worthy mate this time. When I find the girls, my life will be complete.

Which reminds me, I'd better have the children conversation with Ariana before I get much further into her. It's probably already too late, though.

* * *

Now that Kim is gone and it's just me and Ariana, I'm anxious. It's weird because we've been alone for months and I was fine. But now the veil between us has, literally and figuratively, been lifted. The more I know her, the more time I spend with her, the more attracted I am. I might be teetering on the brink of love, something that I see now I never felt for Gina.

What do I do with these feelings? I sense Ariana is attracted to me. But is that because I'm the only woman she's seen since she left the hospital? Will she feel different when she moves back into her glamorous world and is surrounded by many attractive women? I fear she'll ultimately think I want something from her. I've already benefited from our connection. Kim's offer to sign me is no small thing. She's a very big deal in the music world. As is Ariana.

It's true we make beautiful music together. Is that enough? It will have to be. In the meantime, maybe I can suss out how Ariana feels about children now that she's no longer hiding, at least from her friends. The girls and I come as a package. Whatever she feels, whatever I want, doesn't matter if she doesn't accept my total devotion to finding them. Or is not open to raising them with me.

Ariana touches my hand and as usual a shock runs through me. Once again I wonder if she feels it. "Are you in the mood to sing with me?"

"Always." I don't know how I got so lucky. I'm ecstatic that the fabulous Ariana Calandre wants to sing and write music with me. We go to the music room, do a vocal warmup, then tune our guitars.

"I'm feeling happy and sad at the same time," Ariana said. "Do you know what I mean?"

"I do." It's what I feel a lot lately. Happy to be and sing with her, sad about not having Mara and Tessa with me.

She plays a chord. "Want to write a song about those feelings?"

"Yes."

"Give me a line."

I think for a few seconds. "My heart is full because I found you."

Ariana nods and smiles. "But how is it possible to feel so sad too?"

Not great, but we can work with it. We continue adding lines, repeating lines, singing them together until we have a draft of a song. Then Ariana sings one of her hit songs, nods at me, and I take over, then pass it back to her. It's fun, and we work on new songs with breaks for old ones for about an hour before Ariana puts her hand up. "Let's stop now before I strain my voice and my fingers start to bleed. We can pick up tomorrow."

We put our guitars away, then sit on the porch rocking in the sun. I have a thousand questions for Ariana, so I ask one. "What is it like touring for months at a time?"

Ariana stops rocking, and I'm afraid I've brought up bad memories, but then she starts moving again. "It's audience appreciation and adoration on steroids, exhausting, but wonderful. Nellie, Maggie, Torie, Gloria, Erica, and I adored every minute. We were always joyful performing together, but there was something special about touring, being in close quarters for so long, totally focused on the music." She closes her eyes, smiles sadly, and blows out a breath as if trying to distance herself from the feelings. "Our last tour was no exception. We all felt like goddesses on the stage. I've never done drugs so I really can't compare, but I can't imagine a better high." She pauses. "Are you wondering whether you'll like touring when you sign? Would you take Mara and Tessa with you?"

"I've had a fantasy or two." I grin. "Once I get the girls back, they'll need time to feel anchored and safe, so I wouldn't leave them. But if I eventually do tour, I'd want them with me. Do you think it could work?"

"Some stars do it. Gloria brought her wife and two sons along when they were little, but once they started school and Jen went back to work, they decided it was better for them to stay home." Ariana swallows. "Anyway, being on a bus for days is not the best thing for kids, so it requires careful planning. Having a tutor/nanny along is a must as is limiting the number of performances and the distance between them." Ariana hesitates then continues, "Are you feeling more positive about finding Mara and Tessa?"

"I'm feeling more positive about everything these days. Jonah says they've been sending wanted posters to police stations around the country, so I'm hopeful Gina will realize she's being hunted and dump the girls to save herself."

Ariana seems interested and sympathetic, so I risk asking about the girls. "When I find them, I'll need to get a job and find a place to live. Would you be all right with us staying here until I figure things out?"

She doesn't hesitate. "Not only would I be all right with it, I'd demand it. I love children, and I can't wait to meet Mara and Tessa." She looks into my eyes, and we stare at each other for a few seconds.

"Thank you." I'm thrilled to hear she loves children. And knowing we can stay here relieves some anxiety about the future.

We rock in companionable silence for a few moments. "You know, Lee, signing with Kim would solve the job problem. I'm sure she'd be open to booking small venues in Austin while you record an album. You could have the girls with you in the studio and, if you wanted, even when you perform. And I have a big empty house in Austin you could live in. You and the girls and a nanny, if you hire one, would be welcome, whether I stay here or go there."

I force the tears prickling my eyes back. "Thank you." I'm overwhelmed so it comes out as a whisper.

Ariana places her hand on mine. "It's my pleasure, Lee. I'll never be able to repay what you've done for me." She pats my hand. "And who knows, maybe we'll be performing together."

We sit quietly enjoying the sunshine, birdsong, and the fragrance of pine and wildflowers wafting on the gentle wind. I doze and when I open my eyes Ariana is asleep. I'd avoided staring at her when I was taking care of her last week because I was trying to respect her wishes. But now she's no longer hiding, and I take the opportunity to really look at her. Her face is peaceful. I'd imagined she was scarred behind the veil, but it didn't matter because I knew she was a beautiful, caring person. I'm happy for her, happy she's confident enough to consider putting herself out there again. I resist the sudden urge to kiss her and go into the kitchen to make our lunch.

CHAPTER THIRTY-FIVE

Ariana

I wake feeling happy, but I don't open my eyes. What if getting the flu was just a happy dream and Lee didn't see my face and I'm not able to write and sing again? What if I'm still living in the aftermath of the accident, in pain, alone, and lonely?

I feel the sun on my face, a soft breeze ruffles my hair, birds are chirping, and someone is singing nearby. Am I really awake? I slowly open my eyes. I'm outside, which I never was before Lee arrived, and she is singing in the kitchen. Not a dream. I stretch, stiff from sleeping in the rocker. Something smells good. Lee must be making lunch.

I hear a car coming up the driveway just as Lee appears on the porch. "Someone is coming. Either put this on"—she offers me my big, slouchy hat with the veil—"or go in the house."

I do both. For the first time in more than a week I put on the hat and veil, then go into the kitchen and stand behind the screen door. The veil blurs my vision, and I want to rip it off. I'm done hiding, but I'm not ready to be known yet, so I resign myself to wearing it until our visitor leaves.

The car stops, and Thomas and his dad, Elton, step out and greet Lee. I step away from the screen so they can't see me, but I can see and hear them.

"Good afternoon, Lee. Sorry for the intrusion. I know Ms. Solander is still sick, but I wanted to come by and thank you both for what you did for Thomas."

"She's feeling a little better. Let me ask if she feels well enough to speak to you." Lee comes in the kitchen and closes the door. "Are you up for it now that they're here?"

I take a deep breath, hold it, then blow it out slowly. "Might as well. Invite them to sit at the table and I'll sit behind the screen door as usual."

After Elton and Thomas settle at the table on the porch, I greet them, keeping my voice low since Thomas is a huge Ariana fan. "Good afternoon, Elton, Thomas."

Elton speaks to the screen door. "Good afternoon, Ms. Solander, I apologize for dropping in unannounced, but Thomas and I were out meeting with some of our distributors, and since we were driving by, I took a chance and stopped to thank you." He smiles at Thomas. "When I asked you to allow Thomas to work for you, I meant it as a punishment for his cruelty. At best I hoped he'd learn that actions have consequences. I never expected you would teach him about kindness, humanity, and forgiveness by example and make him a better person. And I certainly never expected that you and Lee would teach him to be a confident student and get him interested in learning. You two succeeded where his teachers failed, and instead of being left back he was just promoted with honors. You two have profoundly changed his life and his future. From the bottom of my heart, I thank you both." He nods at Thomas.

"Uh, yeah, thank you. When I came here to work after, after I was so horrible, I thought you would be nasty and mean and try to hurt me the way I hurt you. I never expected you to be so nice to me. I didn't expect you would help me with my schoolwork and encourage me to think about issues and about the person I want to be, about my power to hurt or help others. I just want to say thank you. I feel happy. Dad says I'm more confident. And I'm looking forward to school this year." He places a manila envelope on the table. "I brought you a copy of my book report. At first my teacher didn't think I wrote it, but then I showed her my notes and Dad vouched for me."

I'm stunned. I see Lee is grinning, but she doesn't comment. I guess they're talking to me. I lean forward. "I'll admit, Thomas, when you first started coming here, I was still upset about your thoughtlessness and cruelty and a part of me wanted revenge. But when eating lunch with you and Lee, even if I was always behind this screen door, I realized you were angry, angry at being thought stupid, angry at feeling stupid, and angry at feeling helpless to change it, so you lashed out to hurt me." I stop to consider how much I want to reveal. "I understood you because I was feeling angry too, about the accident, about the losses I suffered, and the lonely life I was leading because of it. Once I recognized that we were feeling the same hopelessness, the desire to punish you evaporated. Helping you learn to study, analyzing and discussing the book with you helped me as much as it helped you. I think we're even. I'm not sure where I or Lee will be in a couple of months but call me if you need help. Your dad has my cell."

"Um, do you still need me to help Lee?"

Perfect. "Thanks, Thomas, we're fine. Focus on your studies and try to enjoy school this year."

Elton stood. "We can start delivering again if you wish."

"Thank you. But as long as Lee is here, she can continue to pick up my order."

"Are you thinking of leaving, Lee?" Elton asks.

"Eventually, but I'm not sure when. I'll give you some notice before I do."

Elton turns to the screen door. "Thank you again, Ms. Solander. Please let me know if you need anything, anything at all."

"Thank you, Elton. And good luck in school, Thomas." I watch Lee walk them to the car and chat for a few seconds, then they get in and drive away. I whip off the hat and veil and step onto the porch.

"That was intense. You see, Lee, you not only changed my life, but you also changed Thomas's life."

"Yeah, yeah, yeah. How about lunch?"

CHAPTER THIRTY-SIX

Lee

I had already set the table and prepared a big salad, so I ladle out two cups of the potato leek soup I'd cooked earlier, pour us both lemonade, then join Ariana at the table.

Her eyes widen. "Wow, you've been hiding your culinary talents. The soup smells wonderful." She reaches for the salad bowl and fills her plate. "Artichokes, chickpeas, tomatoes, olives, and is that arugula? What a gorgeous salad."

I'm pleased to see her healthy appetite. "I haven't been hiding anything. You cooked for us, and then Kim took over when she was here."

Ariana's smile brightens the already sundrenched room. "Right. Maybe we can share the cooking going forward."

"While you were sleeping, I checked the list of things you hired me to do, and I've completed everything, except picking the last of the vegetables in the garden. I'm not sure how we go from here. Maybe it's time for me to leave."

Ariana frowns and puts down her spoon. She leans her elbows on the table, places her chin on her clasped hands, and glares at me.

"Are you kidding? It's time for us to focus on our music, to write songs and sing together." She shifts her gaze to the window. "Unless you've changed your mind about signing with Kim and about...."

She blows out a breath, then continues while staring out the window. "Anyway, I thought you were interested in working with Kim while you look for the girls?"

I've hurt her. She thinks I'm not interested in her. And that couldn't be farther from the truth.

"I just don't know where I fit in here if I'm not working for you, and I certainly don't want to take your money while not doing the job you hired me for. I don't want to leave, but I'm not a charity case. I don't know what to do." Can she hear the pain in my voice? "Shit. I sound pathetic."

"You sound fine to me. I want you to stay. As my guest. No pay, but you won't have any expenses." She faces me. "I need you to stay. I need you to inspire me to write, to encourage me to sing, to cheer me on to walk and run and eat, and to just be with me. I love being with you. I can't be alone again. Please don't go." Tears fill her eyes. Her voice breaks.

Talk about making yourself vulnerable. How can I refuse? I don't want to refuse. I want her and I want to be with her. I reach for her hand. "I'll stay as long as you want me to, but if I get a call about Mara and Tessa, I'll go for them."

She smiles. "As long as you bring them back here, I'm fine with those terms. And if you need money to—"

"I have my Army pension and their allowance, so I'm good." We lock eyes for a moment, and my desire to lean in and kiss her is almost overwhelming. But the well-being of the girls is my priority and, after my mistake with Gina, I won't jump into a relationship again without really knowing the other person. Ariana and I have a lot to learn about each other before we become more than friends, but I know somehow that we'll be all right.

I smile. "So one of my jobs is to make sure you eat properly?" I take a fork full of salad and raise it to her mouth. With her eyes on mine, she leans in and takes the fork into her mouth. Whoa, I hadn't intended to feed her. I pulled the fork back and watched her chew slowly, eyes closed, moaning softly. Jeez. Those moans vibrate through my body. I look away, afraid I'll come right there at the table.

CHAPTER THIRTY-SEVEN

Ariana

It's amazing how quickly we settle into an easy working relationship. Walking, though now jogging, two to three laps around the boardwalk three times a day. Cooking breakfast, lunch, and dinner together, doing vocal exercises, enjoying joint writing and singing sessions several times a day, and spending hours strolling around the property. Making ourselves vulnerable, we share our pasts and our fears and dreams for the future. The only thing we don't talk about is our desire for each other, but it's obvious in the gentle touches and the tender looks we share, especially when we're making music together. I don't think I've ever been so intimate with or felt so close to anyone. Yet the thought of voicing my feelings makes me nervous.

Other than our daily telephone call, which she insists we stick to, Kim has left us alone for six weeks. This morning she calls while we were finishing breakfast. After chatting a few minutes, she clears her throat. "I'd like to visit for a few days to see how things are coming along. And if you're still okay with Mom, Dad, and Brian visiting, we'll come in two cars so they can leave after a few hours. Are you and Lee ready for company?"

I look at Lee sitting across the table from me. She lifts an eyebrow and I mute the phone. "She wants to bring Mom and Dad for a short visit, but she'll stay longer to check in with us."

"It's your call," Lee says.

I unmute the phone. "You're not coming to pressure us, are you?"

"Of course, I am." Kim laughs. "But I would call it gently herding you in the right direction, not pressure. The iPhone recordings you're sending are great, but I want to hear you and Lee in person and discuss next steps. You're the boss, so no is always an option."

Lee smiles as our eyes meet. And as usual my heart leaps and I heat up. I'm happy with her, with our life as it is, and I'm not sure I'm ready for the real world to intrude.

"It's okay if you're not ready, but it's not just business for me. I miss you and so do Mom and Dad."

Suddenly I'm filled with guilt. It's been wonderful diving into my music, focusing on my physical and emotional health, learning who I am now, and getting to know Lee, but I've taken Kim and all she does for me for granted. When I allow myself to think about her, I miss her too. And, I realize I want to see Mom and Dad.

"Okay, give us three days to finish the songs we're working on, then come for however long feels good to you."

Lee gives me a thumbs-up. The fact that Kim and Lee know—and like—each other is a wonderful bonus. In the past, Kim has mostly not been happy with the women I've been with. Not just the occasional one-night stand on tour but the two who lasted a year or so. In both cases, she saw, long before I did, that they were with me for what I could give them—for Rachel it was the trappings of fame and fortune, and for Sarah the possibility of a recording contract. Kim did approve of Morgan when we got together about five years ago. We were happy, I thought, for fourteen months, but she was an accountant, not a performer, and living in the spotlight was not for her, so we broke up. I wonder if Lee understands what living in the spotlight means for her and the girls, especially if she becomes as huge a success as Kim expects. Maybe we can discuss it when Kim is here.

Kim and I settle on the dates of her visit, and then she asks, "Do you want me to bring anything from Austin?"

I think for a second. "Mexican food. A lot of it." She knows what I like so I'm sure I'll be happy. "Lee, do you like Mexican food?"

"I love it, all of it, so whatever Kim brings is fine with me."

"You got it, kiddies. I can't wait to see you both." Kim laughs, then hangs up.

I look at Lee. "Let's see if we can wrap up the two songs we're working on before they get here." After breakfast we clean up, then head into the music room. We work all day polishing our newest songs before breaking for dinner and a walk. Rather than go back to the music room, we sit on the porch reading and chatting.

"Ariana." I hear my name and struggle to open my eyes. Lee is standing over me. "Time to go to bed."

"Oh, sorry. I just dozed off."

Lee laughs. "You've been asleep for almost an hour. I didn't want to wake you, but I couldn't leave you out here. I'm ready to head to bed."

I blink. "Okay, thanks for a great day. See you in the morning." I go into the house, lock the door, shut off the porch and kitchen lights, then get into bed.

I'm sleeping soundly these days, so I wake refreshed and ready for another day of work. Lee arrives and makes us breakfast, then we walk for an hour before heading into the music room.

We sit, as usual, facing each other, knees almost touching, and tune our guitars. We play our two new songs and are happy with them. We strum for a moment. "Do you have an idea for something new?" Lee asks.

I shake my head. "Not at the moment. Are you up to doing a run-through of all the songs we've written?"

Lee considers the question. "It would be great to see how they fit together. Let's do it without breaks or comments."

We've been working on the songs piecemeal, so playing them without interruption will give us a good feel for our sound and the message we're sending. "Good idea." We create a set list so we know the order of the songs, and then we start with the first song I wrote.

As we sing and play, I realize that without calling them that most of the songs we've written are love songs. As we sing the words and experience the emotions we've poured into each song, our eyes lock, and the smoldering feelings that are always there between us spark. By the time we sing the last notes of the last song, I'm breathless and burning for Lee. And judging by the flush on her neck and face, she is feeling the same. We're both on the edge of our chairs and breathing heavily. Our faces inches apart, gazing into each other's eyes, we slide to our knees. Even with our guitars between us we manage to make contact, but it's awkward and our lips touch only lightly. Lee moves her hands to my cheeks and tenderly kisses my forehead, my eyes, my nose, my burn scar, and then my lips again. I want more. I yank the guitar strap over my head and place my guitar on the rug behind me. Lee does the same. She wraps her arms around me and pulls me closer. Our lips meet. Hers are soft and hot. Gently, her tongue probes for entry. It's what I want so I pull her in. Heat shoots through me and settles in my crotch. I've been feeling versions of this without even touching Lee ever since that first morning I watched her work, muscles flexing, sweating in the sun. Now that we're kissing I never want to stop.

Our lips still connected, we fall over, and Lee covers my body with hers. She pulls back to look at me. "Is this okay?" She sounds as breathless as I feel.

"Don't you dare stop."

She grins and captures my lips again. Oh, my God, can she kiss. She's the greatest kisser I've ever had the pleasure of kissing, and her kisses send waves of heat through my body. I'm burning with lust. But what if I disappoint her?

"Bed," Lee breathes in my ear.

I'm yearning to feel her skin against mine, to touch every part of her. I open my mouth to say yes, but instead of words a huge sob erupts from somewhere deep inside me, unleashing a flow of convulsive gasps, whimpers, and tears from a reservoir of pain I didn't know I was still harboring.

Lee raises her head. Her eyes are glazed, and it takes a few seconds for her to register what's happening.

"Is it okay if I hold you?" Her voice is so gentle I'm surprised it penetrates the vibration of my uncontrolled sobs. I nod. She rolls off me, pulls me on top of her, and wraps her arms around me. She doesn't say anything or do anything except hold my trembling body tightly. I feel safe. Finally, my body settles, and the tears stop. I feel Lee's heart beating strong and steady, just like her.

"I'm sorry. I don't know where that came from."

"No matter where it came from, you feel what you feel." Lee uses her sleeve to dry my face. "Am I such a terrible kisser?"

I know she's trying to lighten the atmosphere, but I rush to assure her. "Quite the contrary, your kissing is the best I've ever experienced."

"Are you feeling better?"

My eyelids are heavy, my body is limp, and I'm fading. "Actually, I'm really wiped out."

Lee shifts so my head is on her shoulder. "Relax. I've got you."

When I open my eyes, I'm draped over Lee and her arms are around me. My mind fills with images of our intense make-out session, followed by my falling apart. Judging by the light in the window, we've been asleep for two to three hours and I've been semicushioned on Lee while she's been flat on her back on the floor. Even though the music room is carpeted, her body isn't going to be happy when she stands.

I watch her sleep. I take responsibility for the messiness of her short dark hair, but I had nothing to do with the long black eyelashes, high cheekbones, plump lips, strong chin, and lovely tanned skin. I'm enamored, well on the way to in love, so why the breakdown at the thought of sex, or rather, making love?

Until a few weeks ago, I hadn't felt anyone's body against mine for even a friendly hug since the night of the accident. Not since the night before it has anyone touched me sexually. And that was nothing more than a physical release quickie. It's been years since I've been skin to skin with someone I really care about. And even longer since I've made love with someone. Wanting Lee so much, just kissing her, feeling her weight on me, sparked every nerve in my body. Panicked, my overwhelmed brain reminded me of the physical and emotional damage I suffered in the accident and rushed all my insecurities to the forefront. Suppose I hate being touched? Suppose I'm not able to orgasm. Suppose Lee is disgusted by my burned and scarred body? Or, worse, suppose I don't know how to please Lee and she rejects me?

Now that I'm figuring this out, I'm confused. I want her so much. I dream of touching her and being touched, of being skin to skin with her, of making love to her. What if I can't?

Lee's eyes open. "What's going on in that lovely head of yours?" She runs her finger along my jaw. I shiver. "You don't have to tell me now. I'll wait until you're ready to talk."

I'm not surprised. Lee senses my discomfort, and though most women would be pissed to be stopped abruptly at the height of passion or lust, whatever we had going, she's ready, as usual, to put my needs first.

I turn away, ashamed.

She uses that finger to gently turn my head to face her. "Really, sweetheart. It's all right."

Sweetheart. There's no anger or pity in her voice or on her face, only kindness and, dare I say it, love. I swallow. I've trusted Lee with all of me up to now. Being evasive or dishonest will hurt both of us. "I feel totally inadequate. It's been too long and too much has happened. I don't know how to do this. Just kissing you took me to places I've never been and I'm afraid I don't know how to do that for you."

Lee laughed. "I was right there in those unknown places with you. I've never felt so turned on from just kissing before, and if we hadn't stopped I probably would have had an orgasm without going any further.

Obviously, we're not only electric together musically, but sexually as well. Still, you're not the only one with performance anxiety. After all, who am I to be making love to you, Ariana Calandre, the biggest music star in a generation?" She smiles. "How presumptuous of me to think I'm a good enough lover to make someone like you happy? I'm scared I'll disappoint you, but I'm attracted to the wonderful human being you are, and I want you so much that I'm willing to risk failing rather than live with regrets."

I stare at her. Is it possible she's as anxious as I am? Of course. Not only was her marriage unhappy, but she's also suffered her own trauma. The difference is she's brave and I'm a coward. I catch myself. It's not that I'm a coward. It's that I went from zero sexual stimulation to off-the-charts stimulation, and I wasn't prepared for it.

"I appreciate your sharing your insecurities with me, but from my perspective, you have nothing to worry about. It makes me realize that I'm making too much of my own lack of confidence. I think we went too fast. Maybe if we slowed down and I could stop us if I was feeling too much stimulation, we'd get where we both want to go."

Lee looks me in the eye. "Sounds like a plan to me. Why don't we have something to eat and hang out on the porch for a while?"

I roll off Lee. She moans as she struggles to get to her knees and that moan runs through my body. Despite the anxiety, my body seems ready to put the plan in action. Once she's on her feet, Lee extends a hand and pulls me up into her arms. "Are we okay?"

"We're good."

Lee kisses my forehead and takes my hand. We chat as we walk to the kitchen and decide to make one of our favorite pasta dishes.

We move around each other with ease, cooking the whole wheat fusilli, browning walnuts with red pepper flakes, blistering the broccoli, zesting a lemon, chopping mint, shredding pecorino cheese, then putting it all together. A simple but delicious dinner. Though we're focused on cooking, we manage to touch frequently, kiss, and gaze into each other's eyes often enough to stoke the embers of our passion.

After dinner we sit holding hands on the porch. Lee's thumb gently caresses my hand, warming my whole body. I lean in and touch my lips to Lee's. The kiss is tender, but one leads to another, and it doesn't take long for our passion to flare so we're seriously kissing. Once again, I'm desperate to feel her skin against mine. I pull away. "Bed." I manage to breathe the words out.

Lee raises her head. She gazes into my eyes. "Are you sure?"

"I want to be naked with you." I realize I should clarify. "But just kissing and a little touching until I feel ready for more. Is that okay?"

She stands and pulls me up into her strong embrace. She tips her head and we're kissing again, then break for air. Her breath hot in my ear, she mutters, "Perfect." Kissing my temple, my cheek, my neck, my collarbone, she shuffles us into the house. We stop to lock the front door, then kiss our way to my bedroom. She pulls back when I resist being lowered to my lovely king-sized bed.

"Clothes off." I'm breathless and a little anxious, but I know this is what I want. "I need to feel you all over me."

She grabs my hands as I begin to unbutton my shirt. "Let me."

All thoughts of my burned and scarred body are overridden by my need for her, the need to see her body, the need to kiss every inch of it, the need to give her pleasure. Just kissing and some touching, I remind myself.

She slowly unbuttons and removes my shirt, but her eyes slide down as she releases my breasts from my bra. I hold my breath as she leans down and kisses every inch of the burn scar on the left breast, while gently massaging the right with her large, callused hand.

She kisses her way down my stomach, unbuttons my jeans, and slides them and my soaking-wet panties down. She helps me step out of them and I stand there, naked and quivering, not from fear or anxiety but from anticipation and passion. She doesn't speak, but her eyes are soft and the love I see there says all I need to know.

I pull her T-shirt up, then drag it over her head. I follow it quickly with her sports bra, jeans, and boxer briefs, happy to note she's as wet as I am. I step back. Her muscled body is as magnificent as I imagined, but I'm surprised to see I'm not the only one with scars. I gently touch each of the pock marks on her leg and back, and the puckered skin on her side, then meet her eyes. She smiles. "Bullets and shrapnel, a souvenir of my last patrol in Afghanistan just before I transferred to Kuwait." Ah, hers are the result of her dedication to our country. I touch them again and when I look up this time, she wraps her arms around me and helps me onto the bed. I sigh when she stretches out on top of me and I feel her all over me for the first time, something I've dreamed of almost since the day she arrived. I'd expected the softness, the silkiness of her skin, but not the exotic scent, not just of her but of us together. Our mingled sweat and soap and shampoo smells jacked up by our arousal and maybe the heat of our bodies fill my head, stoking my need for her.

I trail my fingers from her neck, stop to tease the sides of her breasts, then continue down her back, over her buttocks, and back up to her neck. I raise my head to capture her lips. She's right there and her tongue immediately seeks entry. After minutes of lovely exploration, she pulls away. I moan but reconsider when her lips travel slowly from my chin to my toes and the soles of my feet. "Is this okay?"

"Yes." I almost shout. Every nerve ending in every part of my body is sparking, as if my body is proclaiming, "I'm alive, you've ignored my needs far too long."

Lee works her way back up and we're kissing again. When we part for air, she says, "I'd like to make love to you. If you're ready."

Am I? Ready? I feel like I am but what if I—I interrupt that thought. "I am."

She grins. "If it feels too intense, tell me and I'll stop." Another long, deep kiss and then she slides down and ravishes my breasts until I'm moaning and writhing from the exquisite pleasure. Eventually she starts down my body again, kisses every inch of me, stops to bury her nose in my pubic hair, then slips between my legs. She looks up. Our eyes meet. I nod. I moan as her tongue softly circles my clit. She replaces her tongue with a finger and her tongue shifts to licking me before she enters me with a finger, then another. I'm beside myself. The onslaught of feelings after not having been touched intimately in so long is overwhelming. I'm about to call time out, but Lee seems to sense my discomfit and focuses only on moving her fingers in and out in a steady rhythm that my body joins without my intervention. When I'm soaring, she adds her tongue and her thumb, and edges me higher and higher until I'm screaming her name. I seem to float as I come down, hit with wave after wave of pleasure. Lee holds on until I settle, then crawls up to hold me while I sob. Tears of relief. Happy tears.

I wake at one a.m., wrapped in Lee's arms. Her breathing tells me she's still asleep. We smell of sweat and sex. My body heats again as I remember how she took me apart. My mind fills with images of things I've dreamed of doing to her. I kiss her awake. She doesn't seem to mind my lips and hands on her. Quite the contrary. She tries to take control again, but I'm not having it. "My turn, sweetheart." I switch the bedside lamp on.

She gently touches my face. "I'm all yours. Do as you will."

And I do. And then she does. The sun is coming up when we drift off to sleep again.

CHAPTER THIRTY-EIGHT

Lee

Luxuriating in the remnants of a sensual dream so real the smell of sex lingers, I sniff. My eyes pop open. Not a dream. I'm on my back, Ariana is on top of me, her head on my chest, her beautiful blond hair draped over us both. I'm flooded with memories of making love to her. Of her making love to me. I don't think I've ever been so turned on.

I stare at her beautiful profile, and I'm filled with love and the need for her again. I never imagined I could feel like this.

What tricks the universe plays. If Gina hadn't sold my house and stolen my girls, I would have never met Ariana, have never found the love of my life. Remembering brings the pain of the loss, but now I am whole and hopeful about the future. I will find Mara and Tessa. We four will be a family. And Ariana and I will both have musical careers that suit our needs. I'm certain.

She stirs and looks up at me, her gorgeous blue eyes huge, as is her smile. "Wow. That wasn't a dream." She lifts her head and kisses me gently, at first, then more passionately. And then we're fighting for control, for who will give the other pleasure first.

CHAPTER THIRTY-NINE

Ariana

Except for breaks for meals and snacks, we spent the entire day in bed yesterday. This morning, we showered, ate breakfast, exercised, and revisited a couple of songs we'd agreed needed revisions. We're as ready as we can be, so we prep lunch before relaxing on the porch to wait for Kim, Mom, Dad, and Brian. They should be arriving any minute. We're both glowing, so it's kind of obvious that we did the deed. I know Kim will notice and chances are fifty-fifty that she won't make a big deal of it. The last thing I want is to discuss my sex life with Mom and Dad.

When we hear the cars coming up the driveway, I go in the house in case it's not them. I haven't used the camera in ages, but I turn it on and watch the two cars park side by side. Kim and Brian exit her car, both with huge grins. Mom and Dad sit for a few seconds then their doors open. I'm shaking. I haven't seen them without the veil since before the accident, or more accurately, since I woke up in the hospital. Mom reaches for Dad's hand, her eyes quickly scan the house, looking for me, I guess. I'm relieved that Lee painted the outside, so it no longer looks abandoned like it did when I arrived. I can tell Mom's nervous too. Kim leads them onto the porch and introduces Lee. I gather from their warm welcome that Kim shared Lee's role in my recovery with them. I take a deep breath.

"Mom, Dad, Brian," I say, stepping onto the porch, "I'm so happy to see you." I smile through my tears as Mom pulls me into a ferocious hug.

"Not as happy as we are to see you, Ari." She steps back to let Dad in and I see her tears, and though Dad is the strong silent type, he swipes at his eyes as he passes me to Brian, who lifts me and twirls me around.

"Damn, girl, I am so happy to finally see you again."

"My feelings exactly," Mom says, as she scrutinizes my face. I squirm expecting anger or recriminations, but she smiles. "You healed really well, honey. The last time I saw you without that veil you were so raw and red and in so much pain, and then you sounded so horrible during our monthly phone calls I was sure you were going to hurt yourself." She starts sobbing. I pull her into my arms and hold her tight until she's back in control.

"I'm so sorry I had to leave you and everyone, but I just needed time alone to adjust to, to things. And as you can see, it worked. I'm back to myself."

"Okay, unless you want to stand here reminiscing all day, I believe it's time for lunch." Kim pulls me into a hug. "Oh, Lord, I'm so happy to see you." She studies me for a second before gazing again at Lee. I recognize her gotcha smile. Happily, she steps back without commenting. "You look terrific, better than you have in a long time. Even before the accident you were never this relaxed. Or looked this happy." She kisses my forehead. "I have enough Mexican for lunch and dinner, so you decide when you want it."

"We prepared lunch," Lee and I say at the same time, then laugh.

She looks at me, then Lee, then back at me. "I see."

No doubt she sees how close and connected we are, but again she doesn't comment.

"Help me bring everything in from the car." She bounds down the ramp and opens the trunk. She hands Lee more bags than she can carry, so I go down to help. We put the food in the refrigerator and then, while Kim brings her suitcase and her computer to her room, I proudly show the others around the house, then take them back to the porch where Lee has set the table and set out pitchers of lemonade and iced tea.

Kim joins us and sips the lemonade Lee hands her and sighs. "It's great to be back. And to see the two of you looking so…happy." She's sending out waves of her own happy energy. "I'm not letting you off the hook today, but let's relax and talk. After lunch, though, I'm dragging you into the music room so they can hear how great you are together."

Kim brings me up to date on her four kids. Mom and Dad do the same for my brothers and sisters. Brian pulls me inside for a quick update on the business side of things and hands me a stack of reports. After he extracts a promise that I will read them and call him with questions, we rejoin the others on the porch.

We sit rocking and chatting about the family while they decompress from the drive from Austin. Kim breaks the silence.

"You know, Ari, when I'm not stressing about not being able to see you every day, this is a really nice place to relax."

I nod. "And to work. We've been really productive."

"Whispering sweet nothings in my ear will get you everything." She studies me for a second. "Did I say you look terrific? I see you're walking without assistance, gained back the weight you lost, built some more muscle, and have a great tan."

"Thank, Lee, the drill sergeant, for that."

She lifts her glass. "Good job, Lee."

Lee blushes. "My pleasure, I assure you."

"I'm sure it is." Kim's grin is evil.

I know Kim is anticipating hearing us sing the songs we've written since the last time she was here. I fan myself. I'm getting worked up remembering the last time Lee and I sang those songs in the music room. I desperately want Kim's honest opinion of what we've done, but I don't want Mom, Dad, or Brian involved in anything artistic, so I breathe in and out slowly until I come up with a solution. "Let's have lunch and afterward Lee and I will sing a couple of songs to show you what we've been up to. Then we can take a walk before you three drive back to Austin."

Kim gets it. "Sounds like a plan. Let's eat."

Lee and I move the chicken cutlets, mashed potatoes, and roasted broccoli from the oven to the table. I add the green salad from the refrigerator. Conversation flows. Lee and I clean up while they go out to the porch again. We get our guitars and select three numbers, one solo each and a duet. When we finish the duet there's stunned silence for a moment then they applaud.

Brian turns to Kim. "Wow, you weren't kidding. They're dynamite individually and especially together."

Kim grins but doesn't comment.

"That really was terrific," Mom says. "So are you planning to come back to Austin soon?"

"Not right away. Lee and I are productive here and I'm not sure that would be true at home."

"Will you be performing again, alone or with Lee?" Dad jumps in.

Lee places her hand on my thigh. I meet Kim's eyes across the table. I'm not sure how much she's shared with them, but I know what I tell them will not get out to the media. "I'm thinking about performing. And if I do, it will be in a small venue, not an arena. We're playing with the possibility of the two of us performing together somewhere in Austin, but nothing is definite yet."

Brian stands. "How about that walk around the property?" Forty-five minutes later after much hugging and kissing we wave as the car pulls away. I sigh and sink into one of the rockers.

"So how was that for you, honey?"

"Good. A lot easier than I expected. Thank you for making it happen, Kim, and for prepping Brian to keep to a reasonable schedule. I need a nap before we get to work, though."

"Understandable. Why don't we reconvene in two hours, hang out for a while, have an early dinner, then get to work?"

The three of us go our separate ways.

When we get back together, Kim entertains us with industry gossip and discusses a couple of stories she's planted, a rumor that I'm planning a comeback, and one about her having signed a hot new talent. "Since they're just rumors which I neither deny nor confirm, they don't commit either of you to anything but it's always good to get people thinking." She avoids any talk of contracts or performances by either me or Lee, though I'm sure after our concert she'll bring them up again.

The three of us are focused on getting to the music room, so we heat some of the Mexican food she's brought, eat, and clean up quickly.

Lee places glasses of water in easy reach, then we sit in our usual chairs facing each other and pick up our guitars. As we tune, Kim settles in the love seat facing us. I hand her a copy of the playlist Lee and I revised after our run-through this morning. She powers up her iPad so she can make notes. She and I have done this many times over the years and she knows to fade into the background and not comment.

Lee and I make eye contact, then launch into the first song, one of the ones we'd written the first time Kim was here. We've reworked it quite a bit, so it's almost new. Like many of our songs it's a duet. Immersed in the music, we quickly forget she's there and sing to and with each other in perfect harmony.

Aware that the last time we sang all the songs in one sitting we ended up on the floor and, ultimately, in bed making passionate love, we consciously avoid looking into each other's eyes. Despite that precaution, I'm surprised to find myself burning for Lee when we sing the last notes of the last song. And judging by her flush, Lee is feeling the same. We lock eyes for a moment. Kim clears her throat. I blink, remembering we're not alone. Lee's eyes widen and she breaks our connection. Kim ignores our flushed faces and focuses on business.

"That was pure gold, ladies. And Ari, your voice has a new depth. You sound better than ever." Kim meets my eyes, then Lee's. "I knew you were magic the first time I heard you sing together, but you've come so far beyond what you were then, I don't really have words yet. Congratulations. You have at least two fabulous albums there. If you're interested."

I take a slug of water. Am I ready? Is Lee? "What do you think, Lee? Ready to make a record or two?"

She shifts and places her guitar in its case. "We do sound fabulous together and assuming we can work around my needs related to Mara and Tessa, I'd be honored to record with you, Ariana. The question is, are you ready to return to your former life?"

I've given it a lot of thought. "I am. But I need to start slowly. Since I left the hospital, I've only seen seven faces and never more than five at one time. And only the two of you, Mom, Dad, and Brian have seen my face. If we can control my reentry, I'm ready."

Kim's smile is dazzling. It's clear she's thrilled. She bounds out of her chair and pulls me up into a hug. "You've made me the happiest woman in the world. Not because I'm your manager, but because I want you to be back in the world surrounded by the people who love you."

I tense and the blood drains from my face.

Kim pulls back and studies me. "What just happened?"

"Not all the people who love me. Maggie, Gloria, Torie, Erica, and Nellie will never be there again." I try but fail to blink back the tears.

Kim tightens her arms around me and kisses my forehead. "True, they won't be physically onstage with you, but they'll always be there in your heart and in your music."

I take a moment to pull myself back from the sadness that had settled on my shoulders like a shroud, then blow out a breath. "You're right. I always feel them with me when we sing."

Kim steps away. "Remember. I fully support whatever you decide about your career, and we'll go at whatever pace you need."

She turns to Lee. "And whatever pace suits you. This is about each of you doing what you love, not some rush to fame and fortune at great personal cost. You've already been there, done that, Ari. And, Lee, I understand your priorities.

"Which reminds me. I hope I haven't poked my nose in where it wasn't wanted, Lee, but I spoke to Jonah Rippletoe about an idea I had to help find your daughters. He thought it could help so I wanted to run it by you."

Lee sits up. "And?"

"With Ari's help, Micki, the head of her security, has built her firm into a security powerhouse with offices in many states. She's willing to use agents on the payroll and not on assignment to search for Gina and the girls. They would be able to operate under the radar and avoid tipping off Gina and the media."

We sit quietly while Lee considers the offer. "Why would she do this for me? We haven't even met."

"Actually, she'd be doing it for Ari, who is a partial owner of the business, and me, who also has an interest in it. But mainly I believe she's willing to do it because she has daughters of her own and understands what you're going through."

Lee nods. "And Jonah thought this was a good idea?"

"Yes. They are just one case among many for the police and he thought having professionals on the ground focused on searching for them would be more effective. He also feels the FBI isn't fully on board because there's no proof Gina crossed state lines."

"Okay, let's do it." Lee rubs her temples. "Please thank, um, Micki?" She appears to be close to tears.

I rub my eyes, flex my fingers, and bow at the waist to stretch my back. "I'm exhausted and I know you must be too, Lee. Why don't we take a break for an hour, maybe take a walk to unwind, then get together later to hammer out the details."

CHAPTER FORTY

Lee

My head is spinning. I'm overwhelmed. It's not just worrying about the girls, but also the kindness of strangers, signing with Kim, and what's happening between me and Ariana. I need time alone to process everything going on in my life, especially me and Ariana. So, on the pretext of giving Ariana some private time with Kim, I skip walking with them and come to the bunkhouse. I sink into my rocking chair, close my eyes and let the movement soothe me and slow my racing heart.

Each time we sing together it's as if we're making love, as if her voice is caressing my body, as if we're becoming one. I've never come close to feeling such an intense and intimate connection even when making love or, should I say, having sex with a former partner. I blush, remembering us performing for Kim earlier. If she hadn't cleared her throat, we would have embarrassed ourselves. How will we perform before an audience?

I don't think anyone present could miss the electricity between us. I know Kim sees and feels it, but she's our friend. We've worked hard on those songs and each of them has special meaning for one or both of us. When we do our first and maybe only performance, we'll only do a few of those songs and there will be a break and interruptions for applause. At least I hope there will be. And when we record, there will be many interruptions within songs and between songs. In any case, the tension between us will never be as intense as it was both times we sang the full set. Which is good because too much of both of us is exposed. Ariana will have a great deal of attention focused on her; no need to strip her bare.

However, there's no denying that whenever we sing, even a single song, our duet is unique and passionate. We feel it. And our audience will feel it.

After Kim leaves, Ariana and I need to talk about our feelings and the nature of our relationship. I'm almost positive we want the same thing.

I rock and think until a knock on the door startles me. "Come in."

Ariana enters and leans in for a passionate kiss. I'm ready to drag her down and make love again, but she steps back. "Down, girl. I promise I'll visit you out here tonight so we can have privacy." She grins and pulls me up. "Come on. Kim is anxious to get things rolling."

I take a deep breath, then stand. My life is about to change drastically.

CHAPTER FORTY-ONE

Ariana

Kim sensed how profound and intimate the experience of singing together was for us, so she waited for me to bring it up on our walk. She says it's obvious we're in love. I agree, but since we hadn't even kissed until a day and a half ago we haven't said it to each other, except through the music. She's right that we need to figure out what this means and how we want to handle it before we sing together in public. It's time to discuss whether this is more than incredible lust. I'm ready.

Lee is quiet when the three of us sit at the table on the porch. I'm sure she is as overwhelmed by her feelings as I am. In all my years of performing and singing with others, I've never felt what I feel with Lee. It's wonderful and a little scary.

"Ready to go?" Kim asks.

We both nod.

"The first document is my contract with you, Lee. It's my standard contract. It's straightforward, but you should have your own attorney look it over. I share a couple of clients with Lori Seaton, the attorney in charge of Jonah Rippletoe's highly regarded entertainment division, and I think she would be a good fit for you. Since you already have a relationship with Jonah, I suggest you give him a call and ask him to introduce you."

"Okay," Lee says.

Kim moves the contract to the side, and Lee and I do the same. "This document applies to both of you. It's a contract with Arikim Records for you two to record one of your duets together."

My head jerks up. "Arikim? What is that?"

Kim smiles. "It's our record company. Yours and mine."

I'm dumbfounded. And pissed. "You bought a fucking record company without telling me?"

"Whoa." Kim puts her hands up as if to hold me back. "Let me explain before you attack. About a month before the end of your tour, Ed Graf, the owner of Graf Records, you remember him, the guy who wouldn't even take my calls when we were getting started, the one who came begging after you took off? Anyway, he approached me looking for a partner. He'd had a couple of hits, thought he was in the big time, overextended on renovating his facility, and was in trouble financially. After I turned down the request to partner with him, he offered to sell me the company at a great price. I entered negotiations with the intention of bringing you in on the discussion when you got back to Austin after that last performance."

She sipped her iced tea. "After the accident you were in no condition to think about business, but Brian thought it was a good investment for both of us, so we bought it. You and I own it jointly. Thus, the name." She looked down. "I'm sorry. I'll buy you out if you want."

What an ass I am. Almost accusing Kim of overstepping when I damn well know she always does what's best for me. Of course, I didn't know. I haven't shown a speck of interest in the business side of things since my last quarterly review with Brian, which was months before the accident and definitely not while we were on tour or after the accident.

"No, Kim. I'm the one who needs to apologize. I'm the one who's refused to let you discuss business since the accident, even the last time you were here. I shouldn't have attacked you. It's just...A record company called Arikim, the name everyone used for us when we were kids, shocked me. And hearing that I own half of it made me feel out of control." I reach out and take both her hands. "Forgive me?"

She squeezes my hands. "Nothing to forgive, sweetheart. I shouldn't have sprung it on you like that. It's included in the reports Brian gave you, but I didn't stop to think that you haven't had time to read them."

There's my Kimmy, always forgiving. It's one of the reasons I've always loved her. "So we have our own record company?"

"We do. Before he ran out of money, Graf updated the whole facility and the equipment in all the studios is state of the art. You'll love it. And

I've negotiated some great distribution contracts, so the records I've put out for my other artists are doing really well. The good news for us is that when you failed to deliver either the edited live album or the new album on schedule I paid the penalties and got you released from your recording contract, so we're good to go with a new album on our label. Also, we're due to get the rights back on your earlier albums so we can rerelease anything we want."

"Sounds great. But let's get back to the contract for me and Lee."

"I took the liberty of splitting the royalties in the contract evenly between the two of you. I hope that's all right, Ari?"

"Definitely."

"So, Lee, this is also something your attorney needs to look at, though I doubt she'll object."

Lee looks like she's struggling. "Thank you both for everything. I'll speak to Jonah as soon as we finish."

Kim puts her hand on Lee's arm. "I know this is a lot, Lee, but contracts protect both of us, and I'm pretty sure Lori won't have a problem with either contract."

Kim puts the recording contract aside. "If you go ahead with a joint performance, we'll release the duet that day. If instead Lee debuts solo, then we'll figure out another release date to drum up interest in her. If that recording sells as well as I expect, I'm hoping you'll record several albums together."

"How will we record it if Ariana isn't ready to leave here?" Count on Lee to think of me and my comfort before her own well-being.

Kim shifts to face both of us, and the look on her face tells me she's in sales mode. "We're doing two things simultaneously. We're reintroducing you, Ari"—she tips her head to me—"and at the same time we're launching you, Lee." She gazes at Lee for a few seconds. "And while they mostly track together, there are some things that are only needed for Lee's launch. For your part, Ari, you will need to come to Austin for a day or so to record." She puts her hand up to forestall any protests.

"One of Arikim's recording studios is designed to deal with celebrities who want privacy. It's totally separate from the rest of the facility and has its own entrance, a small waiting area, the recording studio, and a luxury apartment with two bedrooms, a living room, and a kitchen. We'll use a vehicle not connected to you, me, or the business, and Micki has pulled herself, Frankie, and several other of your regular bodyguards from their current assignments to cover you full time from now on, so they'll transport you two from here to there. You can record one day, stay overnight, and finish up the next day without anyone but Freya, your favorite producer, seeing you. No one but Freya, your bodyguards, and the three of us will know you're in Austin."

I take a few minutes to think it over. I trust my bodyguards, and Freya is a friend as well as my producer. Staying in the apartment eliminates the risk of being seen at a hotel. It's another step back into my world. I glance at Lee. "What do you think?"

"If Micki is the owner of the security firm looking for Mara and Tessa, I assume she's trustworthy. I gather Freya is your producer, and while I don't know the other bodyguards I assume you both trust them." She raises her eyebrows, questioning.

"We do." I answer for Kim and myself since I know she wouldn't involve anyone she didn't trust.

Lee smiles. "Then it sounds like a solid plan to me."

"Okay, let's do it." The words echo in my head, which fills suddenly with sounds of crunching metal, the screams of my friends, and the acrid smell of gasoline.

"Ariana. Ari." I blink, hearing Kim call my name. She and Lee look worried. "What just happened? You look ready to pass out."

I swallow. My heart is racing. I'm afraid to admit I'm afraid. But these are the two people I most trust. Lee's hand on my knee helps me focus.

"I flashbacked to the accident. I'm petrified to get into a car. Even with the tranquilizers, I was terrified during the van ride here. And then I was sluggish for several days after. I won't take drugs and try to record. I'm really happy and relaxed here. What if riding in a car sets me back?"

There, it's out. Lee squeezes my knee. "You don't have to do this now, Ariana. Or at all."

Kim studies me for a second. "Lee is right, Ari. When, or if, is your decision. But I sense you're ready to ease back into your life, so maybe you won't be mad at me for spending a ton of your money on two armored, fireproof vehicles, an SUV and a van, that are probably safer than any car can be, even though I wasn't positive you'd ever be ready to leave here."

I should have known Kim would think of everything. "I don't care about the cost. Are they really safe?"

"Safe enough for the president of the United States, the pope, and many other heads of state."

I'm still anxious, but there are no guarantees in life. Kim, as always, anticipated my fear and took steps to make travel as safe as it can be. She knows me well. Though I'm not sure what it will look like, I am ready to get back to my life. The alternative to riding in a car is being isolated here for the rest of my life. I can't ask that of Lee and I don't want it for myself.

I take a deep breath. "Okay, I'll try, but I reserve the right to turn around if I freak out." I leap up and hug Kim. "You're the best. I'm not sure what I did to deserve you, but I'm grateful every single day that you're in my life. Thank you." I sit, take another deep breath, hold it, then slowly let it out. I repeat this several times until I relax.

Kim meets my eyes, checking in with me. We've always communicated silently. "Okay, now that I know you won't fire me for recklessly spending your hard-earned money on armored vehicles, I'm ready to move on."

She shifts her gaze to Lee. "You'll record with Ari as we've agreed, but you'll need to stay in Austin a few days after she leaves to record one of your solos, which we'll use as a teaser to attract an audience to your performance. And, on the business side, we need to get your contracts signed, so I'll reserve some time for you to meet with your attorney at the studio and then I'll introduce you to my staff. I've already involved them in the search for the venue, but they need to meet you and hear you sing so they're on board with the launch, for which they will be doing most of the work. I'll also schedule a photo shoot to get some publicity shots, and I'll arrange an interview with one of my contacts in the Austin music world so we can start to get your name out there."

She pauses. "I know it's a lot, Lee, but we don't have much time and I want to do this right. Unfortunately, Ari can't be with you, but I'll be there to support you through it all. What do you think?"

Lee looks overwhelmed. I take her hand and address Kim. "Have Graciela open my house. We can stay there instead of at the studio, and I'll stay until Lee is finished, then we'll come back here together." I squeeze Lee's hand. "It'll be no hardship to hang around my house for three or four days. It's private and comfortable. And it means I can be in the studio with you when you record your solo, and after the other events Kim has planned you'll come home to me, and we can relax together."

"If you think you'll be all right, I love the idea of you being in Austin with me." Lee looks at Kim. "It sounds scary, but I know it's all part of the game so I'm in."

Kim claps her hands. "So do we have a plan?" We both nod. "This next document contains my ideas about the performance, but I'm looking for input from you two." She gives us a few moments to scan the page. "The Up and Coming Music Hall, a relatively new venue in Austin, is perfect for the performance. It's a cabaret format with tables and a capacity of two hundred and fifty people. The dressing rooms are clean and comfortable, the stage is elevated, the sound and lighting systems are very good, and we can bring in our own security, which is a must as far as I'm concerned. Take a look."

She starts up a video tour of the venue on her iPad and slides it over to me and Lee. We watch it several times.

"It looks terrific. Talking about performing makes me anxious, but I'm ready, and I know once I'm on stage, I'll be fine. It's all the other stuff, having to ride in a car, the media vultures, and people grabbing at me, that feels overwhelming."

"That's why starting with the recording session we're going back to twenty-four seven security and why we're only doing one performance in a controlled environment. Once that's done, you can come back here or stay at your house in Austin. And how much exposure you feel comfortable with and how much access to give the media and the public is your call."

"Okay. When?"

"I've scheduled the venue for six weeks from tomorrow, but I can reschedule if it feels too soon."

I blow out a breath. Part of me wants to cocoon here just me and Lee forever, but I know that's not possible. It's time to restart my life. "It's fine."

Kim focuses on Lee. "I hope it's all right with you, but I've booked the performance in your name, as a solo performer. Ari won't be mentioned on their schedule or in their publicity."

"I'm good with that. I just hope we can fill the room."

"Let me worry about that." Kim smirks. "Ari, I thought you would remain in the wings while Lee opens with her two solos, then announces she has a special guest without mentioning your name. Lee will start the first duet and you will sing your first lines from the wings and then join Lee on stage. I'll invite some industry people like Katy Krick, the music blogger, and Gayle Fortin, the TV personality, who both have large social media followings. As soon as they recognize you, I'm sure they'll post a picture or a song. No doubt many in the audience will recognize your voice and post as well. When the first duet is over and the applause dies down, Lee, you'll introduce Ari, and the two of you will pick up with the next song. I foresee lots of phones pointing at you and, no doubt, the performance will go viral. Ari will be on her way back and you will be launched. Once the Internet is blowing up, I'll release the single, which I expect to hit the top of the charts. We'll tape the entire performance, and I'll probably release some video of the two of you singing together to intensify the excitement. And depending on how things go, we might put an edited video of the entire concert on sale. How does that sound?"

Lee huffs out a breath. "Wow. It sounds great to me, but what do I know? What do you think, Ariana?"

"Six weeks sounds perfect." I smile. "It gives me time to get used to the idea of performing and allows us about five weeks to relax, compose, and sing together."

Kim nods. "It also gives us time to get both recordings ready for release, print posters of Lee, and distribute flyers about the performance while we kick off a publicity campaign to introduce her. Let's take a break, then start putting the preliminary set list together."

CHAPTER FORTY-TWO

Lee

As I step outside to call Jonah about hiring Lori Seaton, my head is spinning from all the plans. He's pleasant as always but has no news of the girls. He whistles when I explain I'm signing as a singer with Kim Landers, and she recommended I hire Lori Seaton as my attorney. He agrees she's a good choice and after a brief wait while, I assume, he informs Lori about me, he brings her on the line, introduces us, and leaves us to it. We chat for a minute, and after I explain what I need and how quickly, she asks me to email the documents. Lori says Kim is always fair and honest, so she doesn't expect any issues, but she'll review the contracts and get back to me if she has any questions, otherwise she'll meet me at the studio and go over them with me before I sign.

Ariana is hungry so I go into the kitchen, pull out three beers and reheat some of the leftover Mexican food. We sit at our usual places at the table and fill our plates. For a minute the only sounds are yum, yum, delicious and a few moans.

"Everything go all right with Lori?" Kim asks.

I finish chewing before I answer. "Yes. She asked me to email her copies of the contracts, so I'll need you to send them to me after dinner."

"I need to amend your contract to include royalties on the video of the performance before I send it. I'm assuming the fifty-fifty split is okay, Ari."

Midbite, Ariana nods.

"Good. We need to move fast to get the recordings done. Are you two prepared to go into the studio the day after tomorrow?"

I turn to the side so I can see Ariana before answering, then we both say, "Yes."

"Great. While you finalize the set list, I'll change the contract and put everything in motion."

Ariana and I clear the dishes, put the remaining Mexican food in the refrigerator, and then go to the music room. We review the list, decide on my two solos, our duets, Ariana's solos, and finish with several duets. We select my encore, our joint encores, and a couple of Ariana's big hits as encores for her. Then we move on to choose the songs we think would be best to record for our duet and my solo. We list two others to give Kim options. Ariana trusts Kim's judgment implicitly. And so do I.

By the time Kim comes in, we're done. "I've emailed you the contracts, Lee. Now, which songs do you want to record?" She listens to each of the songs we've suggested and decides which would be best for our duet and which for my launch, then she sits back.

"Okay, day after tomorrow it is. Micki, Frankie, and a few other guards will drive up late afternoon tomorrow and stay overnight. The next morning they'll drive the two of you to Austin, and from that point either they or two of the other guards will be with you twenty-four seven. Okay?" She directs the question to Ariana.

She closes her eyes, then takes a deep breath. "Fine."

"Good. Freya will be in the studio when we arrive. She asked that you send her a recording of the songs along with the lyrics so she can start thinking about them. She estimates we can wrap both in two to three days if we push. Graciela will have the house ready for you and provide meals when you're there as usual. I've arranged for meals and snacks in the studio when you're working, so the only time you'll have to leave the premises is to go back and forth to your house." She turns to me. "Micki and Frankie would like to put their people up in the bunkhouse, so they asked that you move into the house. That means they can protect you both without splitting their focus."

I bristle. "I don't need protection. They should be in the house with Ariana. Besides there's only a double bed in the bunkhouse." I understand the need for Ariana to be protected but having guards around twenty-four seven means losing our privacy and the privacy of my nest. And that scares me. We've been so happy cocooned in our own little world. Can our still new relationship survive the intrusion of Ariana's other life?

"These are ex-military, and as one yourself you should know they can sleep anywhere. In fact, they'll be thrilled to have a bed to share." Kim laughed. "As for Ariana, there will always be two guards in the house. The bunkhouse is for those not on duty. You don't think you need protection now, but you'll understand once the record hits, so please trust me on this." She studies me for a second. "If giving up the bunkhouse feels onerous, we can always put up a tent."

Ariana grabs my hand. "I promise it will be okay. When we're on the road, the guards stick to me like glue, but when I'm at home Micki makes sure they don't intrude on my space. You can take one of the upstairs bedrooms so you have a place to go when you need to be alone. Believe me, it would be harder having them stay in the house."

I trust Ariana wants to preserve our happy space as much as I do. The good news is I'll be with Ariana all the time. The bad news is I'll be with Ariana all the time. At least my bedroom will be upstairs so I can take space if I need it. "I do trust you, Kim. I'll move my things into one of the upstairs bedrooms tomorrow morning."

"Oh, we'll have to get someone to feed the chickens." Ariana frowns. "I guess we can ask Thomas, but maybe it's time to give them away."

"No worries, as of the day after tomorrow, there will always be two guards on the property so you can instruct whoever is left here on how to care for them." Kim checks each of us out. "Anything else?"

We both shake our heads.

"Okay, are you ready to go review the playlist and record the songs for Freya?"

"We are," Ariana answers for both of us.

We work late, shuffling the songs on the list until we're all happy with it, then we make videos of us singing the songs we'll record, and Ariana sends Freya the videos and the music and lyrics we've written down.

When we stand, Ariana pulls me in for a kiss. "I hope you don't mind if I don't come to the bunkhouse with you tonight. I'm exhausted and I assume you are too, and we both know we won't sleep if we're together."

"I agree. I'm wiped." When I finally fall into bed, my body is thrumming with excitement. So many changes. Ariana and I are lovers. And I can't believe that—in six weeks—my career as a singer will be jumpstarted.

CHAPTER FORTY-THREE

Ariana

I'm exhausted. I think Lee and Kim are too. I don't think I've agonized so much over a set list since my first concert. It needs to showcase not just me but Lee as well. And what we came up with makes both of us look good. I really want Lee to succeed.

Poor baby, she's overwhelmed and excited at the same time. It's a lot to take in all at once. Usually you learn the ins and outs of the business as your career is growing, learning from your successes and your failures, but because of me, she's starting close to the top. I imagine it's scary.

My nerves are about the car and about emerging back into the world, not about performing. She's afraid she'll fail me, so she's stressing over the performance. But it's about having fun, giving ourselves to the audience, and as long as we enjoy ourselves on stage, we have nothing to worry about.

She panicked when Kim said she'd have to move in with me. But I like that she'll be living in the house. Somehow it seems more companionable than her having a separate space. But it will make things more difficult. I want to kiss her, to make love to her all the time, but we need to rest. I can't help but grin. In the greater scheme of things, struggling to find a balance between making love all day, composing, singing, and getting enough sleep is not a bad problem to have.

We're moving quickly. Kim is extremely goal-oriented. She always has been. When she knows what she wants, she makes a meticulous plan and goes for it. I've benefited so much from her focus since we became friends at ten years old. If not for her, I doubt I would have been so successful. She wants me to be happy and she knows music makes me happy. As long as I'm singing and writing and playing at a level I feel comfortable with, she'll be happy too. It's never been about the money for her. It's always been about getting me where I want to be. And along the way, we've both made enough money to never have to make a decision based solely on how much income it will generate. I'm proud of her. Not only is she a loyal friend and sister, a terrific mom, and a good, kind, caring human being, she's a brilliant businesswoman. Owning our own record company was a stroke of genius. Now we're not beholden to anyone except the fans. I'm glad she's taking Lee under her wing.

When Micki and Frankie arrive with six other bodyguards in the two armored vehicles, I think it's overkill, but I'm not on top of possible threats and I concede control to Micki and Kim. Micki is as organized and focused about my security as Kim is about my career. When she sees the look on my face, Micki explains that two guards will remain at the house when we leave. Not that they're expecting trouble here or in Austin, she assures me, but I haven't been seen in a while and if word gets out the paparazzi and some fans will be desperate to have a piece of me, so it's best to be prepared.

Micki keeps the meet and greet short and sweet, which I appreciate. Kim warned that Micki is enthralled with the new vehicles, so we're not surprised when she insists on explaining all the safety features to us. It does make me feel more secure about the drive, but my fear isn't just about dying, it's about the memories that being in the car will bring up, about the changes in my life once I leave the safety of this property, about entering the real world again. Having Lee beside me will make it easier, but it's still scary.

CHAPTER FORTY-FOUR

Lee

Today is the day. Micki leads us to the special armored fireproofed Lincoln Navigator and opens the door for Ariana. She tenses, then backs away with her hands up as if to protect herself.

"I can't." She's gasping for breath and shaking. She pales and starts to go down, but I catch her. I feel her heart racing, see the sweat on her forehead. I turn her away from the cars, and she tucks her head between my neck and my shoulder. She's wracked with sobs. "I can't."

Someone must have called Kim, because she's there, her arms around the two of us. I open my mouth to try to soothe Ariana, but Kim shakes her head, and I don't say anything. We stand in our three-way embrace, allowing Ariana the space to experience the profound physical and emotional pain called up by the cars, the memory of the crash. She stops convulsing, then the tears end, and she is quiet. She takes a deep breath, sniffs, then steps back. She looks embarrassed. She glances around, but it's just the three of us. As soon as I had Ariana in my arms, Micki pulled all the guards into the bunkhouse. To protect Ariana's privacy, I assume.

"I'm sorry. I didn't expect to, you know, fall apart." She avoids looking at us.

"No problem," Kim and I say at the same time.

Ariana laughs. "Maybe not for you two."

Kim touches Ariana's face, then lifts it so their eyes meet. "You don't have to do this, Ari. We can do it another day. Or never. Your comfort and happiness are what matter to me and, I'm sure, to Lee. You can stay here. Lee and I will go to Austin to record her solo and do the other things needed to launch her. You know she's a big talent and can do the performance solo. And if you never want to get in a car again, we'll build a recording studio on the property so you can record without leaving."

Ariana nods. She stares at the Lincolns for a few seconds. "I'd like to wash my face, drink some water, and think about it for a few minutes. Okay?"

"Whatever you need, sweetheart." Kim kisses Ariana's forehead.

Ariana goes in to wash up, then joins me and Kim on the porch, with a glass of ice water. She sits in the rocker and closes her eyes. About ten minutes later she opens them and moves to the table with us.

"I can't tell you how many times I wished I was dead in the months before Lee arrived. But I'm not the person I was then. I very much want to live. I made myself a prisoner out of guilt. I refuse to continue to live like prisoner out of fear." She takes my hand and kisses my knuckles. "I want to live my life with you, Lee, not watch you live your life from the sidelines." She turns to Kim. "I will go to Austin today. I will follow our plan. I can't promise I won't freak out again, so be patient." She stands. "I'm ready when you are."

Kim texts Micki, kisses us both, then gets in her own car for the drive back to Austin. I take Ariana's hand and walk her to the armored vehicle.

As Frankie helps her in, I walk to the other side. Micki puts a hand on my arm. "Lee, we'll do our best to protect you, but if the shit hits the fan, Ariana is our priority. As ex-military, Colonel, I'm assuming you have the skills to take care of yourself so if we run into trouble don't worry about Ariana, just look out for yourself and let us do our job. Are we clear?"

I shouldn't have been surprised she knew my rank. She's the one who checked me out for Kim, so of course she knows everything about me. I nod. "I can do that."

She studies me for a second. "I doubt it will ever be necessary, but should something happen, there's a Glock and four fifteen-round magazines under your seat."

I feel the blood drain from my face, but I nod again. She holds my gaze. "It's insurance. Other than one incident years ago, we deal with aggressive paparazzi and fans, so I doubt you'll ever need to use it."

I slide into the car and minutes later we're following Kim's car down the long driveway. Ariana and I are in the extremely comfortable captain's chairs in the Lincoln Navigator. Micki is driving, Frankie is next to her. The frosted glass divider is down so we could be four friends out for a drive. Four bodyguards are behind us in the second vehicle, and two guards remain at the house. It seems like overkill to me, but Kim assures me it's necessary. Even without a threat, Ariana could easily be overcome by a crowd of fans rushing her, and that would be a setback for her. And that was the reason starting today there would always be two guards at the house whether we're there or not and at least four with Ariana.

As we drive away from the safety of our quiet existence, of our private love, toward a new reality, I'm on edge. Will our love survive in the real world, or will Ariana recognize our differences and dump me? What if we don't sound as good together as we thought? What if I fuck up the recording session?

Ariana is staring at nothing, her face and her hands gripping the arms of her chair are colorless. This is incredibly difficult for her. I take her hand and she turns to me. I lean over and kiss her. "We're as safe as can be."

She smiles. It's not her usual room-blazing smile; it's vulnerable, soft. She's so brave confronting her demons. My heart opens to her.

She gazes at me. I'm not sure how she knows, but she does. "Don't worry, you'll be great." She strokes my hand with her thumb, calming me down, and I guess calming herself, because after a while, we both relax and semidoze in the comfort and quiet of the armored car.

An hour or so later we start seeing signs for Austin, and the closer we get the more tense Ariana becomes. Instead of gently stroking my hand she squeezes it in a painful death grip. To comfort her and ensure I'm still able to play my guitar when we arrive, I extract my hand from hers. She frowns, but when I release my seat belt, slide to the edge of my seat, and wrap my arms around her, she puts her head on my shoulder and relaxes. "Thank you."

"My pleasure." And it is. I enjoy the closeness. I rest my head on Ariana's. As usual whenever our bodies touch, they heat up, and right now with our combined heat I fear we might ignite. My body is telling me to make love to her. And my brain is reminding me we're not exactly in private. Listening to her breathing, I'm sure Ariana is feeling it too.

We both start at hearing Micki's voice. "Lee, we're moving into Austin traffic. Please put your seat belt on and sit back." I meet her eyes in the rearview mirror. "Sorry."

"It's my fault, Micki. I'm anxious and Lee's touch is comforting." Ariana sits back. "She's right, Lee. I want you to be safe, so put your seat belt on again."

I nod. Once the belt clicks in place, I reach for her hand again. I'm nervous about recording, about screwing it up, but she's recorded a million times so I'm curious. I speak softly so her bodyguards can't hear. "Are you nervous about recording or being back in Austin?"

She tenses, which changes the temperature between us, but tension isn't what I was going for. Just when I'm about to reassure her, she speaks in a whisper. "It's the memories of the band, my friends, making me sad. I've never recorded anything without the girls backing me up. I'm not sure I can do it without them."

I kiss her hand and hold it over my heart. "Kim sent me the video of your last concert together, and it's so clear how much you loved each other. I can't imagine they wouldn't want you to go on without them. Maybe you need to acknowledge their absence. Maybe before our song or after, you could say a few words about wishing they were with you and dedicate the song to them. I'm sure acknowledging them will make their family, friends, and fans happy."

She's silent again, then leans over and kisses my cheek. "I really like that idea. Thank you."

I notice Micki watching us in the rearview mirror. I don't think she's spying. She's extremely protective of Ariana, and she's still not sure about me. I'm happy when her eyes flick back to the road.

Talking about missing friends, an image of Mara and Tessa's mom, Ella, and me in the shabby recording studio we rented to make demo records for ourselves, flashes through my mind. We didn't know what we were doing and had limited money for studio rental, but we were sure the demos would launch both our careers. Unfortunately, it didn't work for either of us. Not too long after, I enlisted in the Army and thoughts of a singing career evaporated, and while Ella managed to create a solid career as a backup singer and cello player, the fame we dreamed of eluded her. She found true happiness with Jeff, though, and was ecstatic to be a mom. My happy memory of Ella morphs into the deep sadness that's been with me since I discovered Mara and Tessa were missing.

As usual, Ariana is tuned into me. "I sense you're sad now. Did I bring you down?"

"No. A memory of making a demo record with my friend Ella triggered thoughts of Mara and Tessa. I feel so helpless knowing they're out there with Gina, who's probably high most of the time."

"We're five minutes out, ladies," Micki's deep voice intrudes. "Please remain in the car until Frankie and I come to escort you into the studio."

Ariana blows out a breath. I assume she's relieved we made it. She squeezes my hand, then releases it, straightens her shoulders, runs a hand through her hair, and smooths her clothes. "Are you ready to do this, Lee?" Her smile is brilliant. I'm not sure whether encouraging her to dedicate the recording to her bandmates helped, but she seems to have worked through her anxiety. Or is that just her professional veneer? In any case, I'm here for her one hundred percent. But I'm still anxious.

Micki positions the armored car close to the doors of a large attractive building and the second vehicle pulls next to us, effectively creating a wall between us and anyone passing. As instructed, Ariana and I wait to be escorted. A few minutes later, Micki knocks on the window next to Ariana and opens her door. Frankie opens my door. They guide us into the facility. A guard follows with our guitars. Since this studio is for celebrities, I'm not surprised the heavy wooden door leads into a luxurious reception area, which is empty. Frankie stays with us as Micki heads into what I assume is the recording studio. When she returns, she leads us to a super-sumptuous lounge area surrounding a gleaming high tech recording studio.

Kim is already there and she and another woman, who I suspect is Freya, stand when we enter. Freya takes a second to look Ariana over before pulling her into a hug.

"Ari, I am so happy to see you. You look terrific." She steps away from Ariana. "And you must be Lee." The hug she gives me is briefer than Ariana's, but I still feel welcomed. "I love the songs you've written, and the two of you singing together is electric. I have no doubt that what we come up with is going to be wonderful." She rubs her hands together. "I'd like to get to work as soon as possible, but take some time to use the restroom, have something to drink or eat, and relax a bit. I'm ready whenever you are."

Fifteen minutes later, Ariana and I leave Micki in the lounge and sit facing each other tuning our guitars in the studio, which I've learned is called the live room. Kim is with us, but Freya is clearly in charge now. She chats with us about the song, then tells us what she hears, what she thinks the lyrics mean. We respond with our feelings. When she's satisfied she understands what the song means to us, she stands, fusses with the microphones, goes into the control room, asks us to sing a line or two, comes back, moves the mics, and repeats the sound check until she's happy.

"Okay, ladies, let's get started." She and Kim go into the control room. A minute later Freya asks us to sing the song through as we've rehearsed it.

When we finish, Freya and Kim talk, but we can't hear their conversation. Then Freya opens the mic. "You sound fabulous together. Now sing it again, please."

After the third time through, we begin to go through the song phrase by phrase, repeating everything multiple times. It's a grueling process and Ariana is the pro here. While I'm getting stressed, she's relaxing. After I screw up for the fourth time, she leans over and takes my hand. "Freya is a meanie."

"I can hear you, Ari," Freya's voice blasts over the sound system.

We both laugh. "Well, you are a mean taskmaster sometimes," Ari says, "but I love you anyway, because I know it's all about making the recording the best it can be." She turns to me.

"Remember what I said, Lee. We're magic when we sing together, but if it's not fun, why do it? This start and stop is part of the process. It doesn't mean either of us is doing anything wrong. Freya has high standards, and she pushes to get what she believes is possible and necessary. That's why a high percentage of the songs she produces go to the top of the charts. Just pretend we're back in the music room at the house, look at me, and sing. We've got this."

Her little speech does wonders for me. I relax. Freya seems happy with our work, and we move much faster. We break occasionally for ten minutes to drink water or to eat something, but other than that we work straight through to midnight. We're both exhausted by the time Freya is happy.

"Okay. I think we've got it. Let's get back together tomorrow morning at ten to listen with fresh ears and make any changes necessary before we start on Lee's solo."

CHAPTER FORTY-FIVE

Ariana

I forgot how exhausting recording is. I'm totally wiped, and Lee isn't much better. I'm almost sorry I decided to sleep at my house rather than the apartment in the studio, but I knew I would be more comfortable at home especially since we'll be here a couple of nights. We say good night to Kim and Freya. Dawn and Denise, who have relieved Micki and Frankie, drive us the twenty minutes to my house. The car behind us is filled with six bodyguards. The two guards at the gate to my property smile and wave us through. Dawn and Denise will be in the entry to the house until the morning, and the six others will be dispersed around the entrances to the house.

Lee's eyes get big as we go through the gate then drive up the long winding road to the house on the top of the hill. The lights are blazing in welcome. The tears surprise me. This is the first time I've been back since we left for the last leg of the tour. I never let myself think about what I was leaving behind when I went to Sharon Springs, but my life was, is, here.

Even though it's late, Graciela, my cook and the caretaker of the house, is standing in the entry hall when Dawn unlocks the door for us. Her smile is blinding. She steps forward with her arms open but waits for me to move to her, then she folds me into her. "Welcome home, Ari."

We cling together for almost a minute before separating, both of us with tears in our eyes.

"Graciela, this is Lee. Lee, Graciela runs this place so don't get on her bad side."

Graciela embraces Lee. "Welcome." She moves away. "Everything is ready for you. There's food and drinks in the kitchen if you want." She turns to Dawn. "The same for all of you in the guard room. Ari, do you and Lee need anything from me before I go to my cottage?"

I check in with Lee. She shakes her head. "We're good."

"Kim told me you need to be back at the studio by ten tomorrow, so I'll have coffee and breakfast by eight thirty. Okay?"

"Sounds good. Thanks, Graciela. Good night."

We move into the main living room and I'm struck by its beauty. I've forgotten. I'm pleased to see that Lee appears awestruck.

"Jeez, Ariana, I thought the Sharon Springs house was beautiful inside, but this place is gorgeous."

I can't help grinning. I'm so proud. "I worked very closely with the architect to design the house and the whole compound. I love the openness and the clean lines of the wood and glass construction she and I came up with. And I made sure the interior designer I hired got my vibe and she and I worked to bring the images I had in my head to life."

Lee spun around, taking in the whole room. "How did you ever leave?"

"I had no choice when we went on tour. And when I went to Sharon Springs I didn't let myself think about what I was leaving behind because I knew it would break me. But I'm back and it's still everything I dreamed it would be. I can't wait to show you the whole house, but I'm wiped so it will have to wait until the morning."

"I'm exhausted too, so I'm happy to wait."

Despite being tired, we're both too hyped to sleep, so we make tea, pile plates with some of the food Graciela put out and put the rest in the refrigerator. We take everything into the living room and sit on the sofa.

Lee sips her tea. "Why did you go to Sharon Springs instead of coming here after leaving the hospital?"

I chew the last bite of my taco and think about how to answer truthfully. "Mainly, I wanted to be alone, isolated, with no contact with anyone, and I knew that wouldn't be true if I was here. Second, with all the windows, I was afraid I'd see my reflection all the time and I never wanted to look at myself again. Third, I knew there would be too many reminders, too many memories of the girls here. It turned out the memories, their voices, their laughter, came with me to the Springs house." I move my plate to the coffee table in front of us. "Fourth, I thought I'd never play or sing again, and I wanted to find out who I was without music in my life. And fifth, I wanted to punish myself for being alive."

Lee takes my hand. "I would never have met you if you weren't in Sharon Springs, so I'm glad you made that choice."

I kiss her knuckles. "I am too." I don't want to bring her down, so I don't mention that we would never have met if her wife hadn't sold her house and kidnapped her daughters. "So how was today for you?"

"Besides sucking every bit of energy out of me, it was great."

We talk a bit about the experience of recording and our feelings about being in Austin again even though we haven't really stepped outside. We're quiet for a few minutes before Lee poses another question.

"I'm surprised at the level of security you have, Ariana. Kim said it was to keep fans from getting too close, but is there a threat I don't know about?"

I bristle. I don't want to think about this. Why is she bringing it up? And then I realize, I take the security for granted, but Lee is new to it, plus she doesn't know the history. I consider how much to say, then I realize she's ex-military and can handle it. Plus, I want no secrets between us, so I answer truthfully.

"There's no current threat. This is standard since an attempt to kill me after a concert in New York City about six years ago when the group was really taking off. We were coming out of a lesbian bar and a right-wing nut came at me with a knife. Micki was one of several guards we'd hired for the night. She jumped in front of me and was stabbed instead of me. Even with the knife in her, she managed to get the guy down with his hands behind his back and under control before the other three guards could help and the police arrived. Then she called her agency and requested additional backup. The six of us spent the night in the ER with her and eight other guards. When the police questioned the guy, they discovered he was involved with others in a plot to kill me. Kim immediately hired Micki as the head of security, moved her and her wife to Austin, and had her hire a full-time staff of seven which she now supplements with staff from the security firm she and her wife own.

"Anyway, the FBI eventually tracked down the group and they aren't an active threat anymore. But you know, sometimes even fans can be dangerous, crowding me, wanting to touch me, take a picture, take a lock of hair or a piece of clothing as a souvenir. Even when I was in the hospital as Anna Solander after the accident a would-be paparazzi found me and tried to take pictures, hoping to make money selling them.

Happily, Kim walked in, grabbed her camera, and after threatening to destroy her life if she breathed one word of what she'd seen, had her thrown out. Since the accident, Micki and her team obviously haven't traveled with me, but they constantly monitor social media and my fan mail for threats. I never resent—or take them for granted."

"If they're always with you, why weren't they hurt in the accident?"

Lee flinches at my quick intake of air, but I squeeze her hand, letting her know it's okay. If I'm going to return to my life, I need to be able to talk about the accident.

"We generally all traveled in a bus together, but this was the end of the tour, and we were just driving the twenty miles to the Houston airport from the arena. So we sent the bus on its way and rented two vans. The few times we'd rented vans before, we split up, three of us and four guards in each van. But that night we were all so high after the concert—high on the love of the fans, not drugs—that we wanted to hang together until we got to the hotel. So we all piled into one van with two guards. Micki and the other five guards in the second van should have been right behind us, but a group of fans surrounded the van, thinking I was with them. They were less than ten minutes behind us, but by the time they caught up with us our van was on its side, in flames. Micki and the others suffered burns on their hands, Kim told me, but they managed to pull all of us out of the wreckage and away from the van just before the fire engine arrived and put the fire out. I was the only one who survived."

"I'm sorry you lost so many people you cared about, Ariana. Thank you for explaining. I'm trying to understand, but I know it's not pleasant remembering."

"It's hard but getting easier." I pat the cushion next to me on the sofa. "Come sit closer and relax. Let's watch a movie to unwind."

CHAPTER FORTY-SIX

Lee

Recording is hard work. I don't think I ever quite took that in. I'm wiped out by doing one song today, and I'm not looking forward to doing it all again tomorrow. I can't imagine recording the two albums we already have lined up.

Telling myself that I wasn't on the same level as Ariana Calandre didn't help, but after Ariana reminded me that the music should be fun, I got past my imposter syndrome, and it got easier. But the process is grueling. Ariana didn't bat an eye, yet she was exhausted too. Hopefully, I'll get used to it.

And talk about getting used to things...I hadn't given a thought to just how wealthy Ariana is. The Springs house is really nice, but it looks like a shack next to this one. I've only seen the kitchen and the main living room, and they are stunning. And apparently her estate, or maybe compound is a better description, is huge and, besides her house, contains Graciela's cottage, a house for the bodyguards, a guest house, a stable, a pool and a pool house, and is surrounded by riding and hiking trails. It's overwhelming. I don't know how we'll work out the dissimilarity in our finances.

I feel awful about asking why her guards didn't die the night of the accident. Knowing how focused Micki is on keeping Ariana safe, I should have assumed there were guards in the van with her and the band. And since she was the sole survivor, I should have figured out that they died along with the members of the band. What an asshole. But Ariana seems to have come to terms with being alive when everyone else in the van died, and she seemed all right explaining it to me. I saw enough death in Iraq and Afghanistan to know there's no rhyme or reason why one person dies and the other standing next to them lives. As the clichés say, it's the luck of the draw or when it's your time it's your time.

Like Ella and Jeff. Thinking about them reminds me of the girls again and my failure to protect them. I start to slide into the melancholy that leads me into depression, but Ariana pats the sofa and says, "Come sit close to me. Let's unwind with a movie." Am I so obvious? Does she sense what I'm feeling? Or is it a coincidence that she pulled me back from the edge?

I'd never turn down sitting next to Ariana. We're both so tired, though, I doubt either of us will pursue more than a kiss, if that.

CHAPTER FORTY-SEVEN

Ariana

Someone clears their throat. I open my eyes and I'm staring at an ear. What? Oh. Lee. We were going to watch a movie, but I think she drifted off while we were talking, and I must have been right behind her. I lift my head off Lee's shoulder and gaze at Kim standing with her hands on her hips just a few feet away, grinning.

I groan and try to roll off Lee without disturbing her, but she turns her head and we're nose to nose. She flushes. "Good morning," I say, shifting to a sitting position. I run my hands through my hair and croak, "Is the coffee ready?"

Lee rolls off the sofa and notices Kim. She looks to me for a reaction.

"Relax, Lee, we're fully dressed. I think we dozed off before we even turned the TV on."

She rubs her hands over her face. "What time is it?"

"It's eight," Kim says. "You need to be in the studio in a couple of hours. Coffee is ready, and Graciela is waiting to make breakfast whenever you appear."

"I need a quick shower and change of clothes first."

"Me too," Lee says.

Kim settles in the easy chair. "I'll wait here."

I snort. "That's a good idea since neither of us invited you to join us."

Kim gives me the finger. I'm tempted to shower with Lee, but we really do need to focus on the music, so I lead her up the stairs to the nearest guest bathroom, kiss her, and then head into my own bathroom. I luxuriate in the wonders of the multiple showerheads in my shower.

Twenty minutes later the three of us are sitting around the kitchen table and Lee and I are drinking coffee and eating eggs, home fries, and toast. Graciela is at the sink washing pots and pans.

Kim waits for us to finish eating before she launches into business. "So, the recording sounds great, but Freya suggested adding in some background instruments to see how it sounds and I okayed it. Somehow she got musicians she trusts into the studio at seven this morning to play with what you've recorded. She asked that you get to the studio at eleven instead of ten, to be sure they're gone. When you arrive, the four of us will listen to the original and the one with backup and decide as a group which we prefer and whether we're good to go."

"Do you think they'll recognize my voice? I don't want to be outed before our performance."

"Freya doesn't think so. They've never recorded with you, and she told them you were two unknowns I'm grooming. Besides, you sound different in this recording—more emotional, more connected. I think we're good. Any questions, comments, feedback?"

I turn to Lee. She shrugs. "I'm good."

"There is one thing." I clear my throat. "I'd like to include a few words about the band and dedicate the recording to them."

Kim taps her fingers on the table. "Are you sure you're ready?"

I shrug. "I'd like to try. If I get too emotional, we can skip it and try again on the albums."

"I think it's a lovely idea." Kim brushes a tear from her eye. They were her friends too. "I'll speak to Freya." She takes a deep breath. "Lee, I spoke to Lori, your attorney, last night to iron out a minor point and she confirmed she'll be at the studio later today. I really shouldn't have gone this far without a signed contract, and all of us being there will speed things up. If you require any changes, we'll make them, and you and I will sign."

Lee leans forward and touches Kim's hand. "I'm following your lead on this, Kim. Having you and Ariana there to answer questions will make it easier for me, and I'll be glad to have a contract in place."

"Good. She'll be there about twelve. And I've invited her to be there when you meet my office staff tomorrow afternoon."

I feel bad that I can't be there for Lee tomorrow, but I'd let the cat out of the bag and be a distraction. I'm sure Kim will look after her, and having her attorney there will bolster her confidence.

Lee takes a deep breath. "That sounds good. The more support the better."

"I shared one of the songs you sent me and Freya with the team and they're hyped to meet you. They've come up with some ideas to get your name out there and promote the performance. And speaking of the performance, I need the names of people you'd like to invite as your guests. I'll have someone contact them or you can if you prefer, but I'd like to reserve the tables as soon as possible so we don't overbook." Kim gazes at me for a few seconds. "Ari, I'm assuming you want our family—Brian, my kids, Mom and Dad, our sisters, our brothers, and all their spouses and kids."

"Yes."

"What about the close family members of the band?"

"It will be hard, but I'd like them to be there if they're up to it. I spoke to them a few months ago, but it's time to see them in person."

"And your friends?" She hands me a list.

I scan it. "Yes."

"What about you, Lee?"

"Just my two best friends, Carley and Tammy."

Remembering her story about how supportive her brothers were when she was choosing between a military or singing career, I can't help myself. "Wouldn't you like your parents and your brothers to be there if they can make it?"

Lee frowns. "That would be nice, but I'm not sure where any of them are stationed these days." She rubs her forehead. "I suppose I could email them. That would be eight if they all can come."

"What about nieces and nephews?" Kim asks.

Lee grins. "You want to fill the venue? Fifteen adult nieces and nephews plus their spouses and kids. That's a lot of tickets to give away."

"Don't worry. This gig isn't about the box office, it's about an enthusiastic audience. We have room for all thirty-eight plus grandnieces and nephews, if they want to come."

Lee stares out the window. "If I'm not pushing it, I'd also like to include my attorney, Lori, and the people helping me look for the girls, Jonah Rippletoe, Nancy Lavelle, his private investigator, and Detective Karin Sharp."

"I'll reserve fifty or sixty for you in case they want to bring someone. We'll ask Lori to pass the invitation on to Jonah and the others but let me know when you hear from your family, Lee." She stands. "By the way, Ari, are you still planning to stay in Austin while Lee is taking care of business?"

"I am. We'll go back whenever Lee finishes and come back the day of the performance."

"Okay, I'm going to the studio to meet with Freya and the backup group. See you there. Oh, would it be all right for Brian, Jessie, and Jackie to drop by the studio this morning for a few minutes to say hello?"

Ready to frame a polite no, I stare at her for a second. She looks innocent, but it occurs to me that Kim rarely acts without intention. She almost always has a plan. I tap my fingers on my cup. But what? Ah, she's slowly introducing people back into my life. I'm godmother to Jackie and Jessie, her oldest twins, and we've always been close. Kim understands it's hard but necessary for me to reconnect with people, and this is her easing me back into my life.

The answer comes from my heart. "I would like that."

She nods. "Great, just for a few minutes, then I'll herd them out."

We watch her leave. "Are you really okay with them coming to the studio?" Lee asks.

I sigh. "On one hand, I'd much rather run back to Sharon Springs and anonymity. On the other hand, you've breathed life into me and awakened the musician and the performer. A huge part of me is anxious to be out there again. These are people I love, people I've been close to, so though I'm nervous I do want to see them. And each person I see makes it easier for me to just be me again. Seeing them now will reduce the pressure the night of the performance."

"Good. I look forward to meeting the twins. And I want to spend more time with the man who manages to love, work, and live with the dynamo that is Kim Landers."

I love the mischievous look in her eye. She is so beautiful I'm tempted to kiss her silly, but despite the hammering pulse in my lower body, we have unfinished business, both singing and personal. It's hard enough to fight these feelings when we're singing together without stoking them before we go into the studio. I stand to get some space and, hopefully, cool off. "Come on, I'll show you around the house."

Micki and Frankie escort us into the studio. Freya and Kim are waiting for us and the four of us sit down to listen to our recording. The first cut, just the two of us and our guitars, is wonderful. And the second cut, the two of us and our guitars backed up by the viola, cello, bass, keyboard, and drums weaving in and out of our voices, is stunning. No one speaks when the recording ends. Freya looks smug, Kim looks ready to burst, and Lee is awestruck. I'm beyond excited.

"In my opinion, we can't go wrong with either, but the one with the backup is awesome. Let's release that one."

Lee is shaking her head as if she can't believe what we've done. "Both are fabulous, so I'm going to leave it to the professionals to decide." She grins. "I take back all the bad thoughts I had about you, Freya. You're a genius."

"I agree," Freya says, still grinning.

I glance at Micki and Frankie standing nearby. "Okay, you two. What do you think about the recordings?"

It's not the first time I've asked their opinions about a recording or a performance, so they take a few seconds to confer. "Both versions are fabulous." Micki gives a thumbs-up.

Finally I turn to the marketing brain. "Kim?"

She nods. "I agree we can't go wrong with either. I'm thinking that the night of the performance we release the one with just you two because I'm guessing it will be one of the songs the audience members upload to the Internet. And a couple of days later we release the one with the backup. I'm thinking your fans will download the first immediately, and when they hear the second, they'll download that one too, so we double-dip."

I check in with Lee. "You okay with that plan?"

"More than okay. I love both versions."

I hesitate a split second, but I trust Kim's judgment. "Let's do it." I take a breath. "Do we have to rerecord anything or are we done?"

"I'm happy with what we've got, but Kim says you want to add some spoken words," Freya says.

"I want to acknowledge the band and dedicate the recording to them."

I shouldn't be surprised to see Freya's eyes fill, but I am. I forget how many hearts my goofy, loving friends touched. I'm not the only one who still mourns them.

"If you're ready, let's do it now so we can get this into production."

We do a few takes and end up with something reasonable.

"This recording is dedicated to my friends, my bandmates, Gloria West, Maggie Fortuna, Nellie Garcia, Erica James, and Torie Stella, each one a great musician in her own right and together the greatest band I could have wished for. I miss them every single day. I'm not sure why I'm here and they're not, but I have no doubt they're making music wherever they are. And when I'm making music I feel them in my heart and soul."

"Very nice, Ari. I think we've got it," Freya booms over the mic. "Are we ready to send these babies out into the world?"

I hesitate. This is it. My reentry into the world, to my old life. The surprise performance will please my fans, I'm sure. The release of these recordings will probably propel me right back to the top of the charts. Am I ready? Yes. I wished I'd died but I didn't, so I went to Sharon Springs to punish myself for living. And I did have six or so painful, hopeless, lonely, punishing months but then Lee gave me hope and a desire to live and I've become a better, healthier, happier version of the woman behind the veil. My gaze wanders to Lee, chatting with Kim in the lounge, and I move toward them. I'm definitely ready. I'm hoping I won't be alone this go-round, that Lee will be at my side performing and in life. "Let's do it. Let's ready both for release."

Freya grins. Kim turns and high-fives me. She knows I'm back. And Lee surprises me with a kiss on the cheek. "Thank you for the opportunity to sing with you. And the pleasure of being with you."

I grab her hands. "The pleasure is all mine, sweetheart," I breathe into her ear. She turns beet-red, so I know she gets the message. As we separate, I notice Micki touch her earpiece, then turn to the door of the studio lounge area. I follow her gaze. There they are. Brian, grinning like he won the lottery, the two girls, jittery and unsmiling. I freeze for a second. I haven't let myself think about them for fear I'd run back to Sharon Springs, but now all I want to do is hold them.

"Have my two favorite nieces forgotten what I look like? Come over and give me a hug." I open my arms. One of them, probably Jessie, the more outgoing twin, whoops as they throw themselves at me. I stagger at the weight, but Lee grabs me and keeps us from tumbling to the floor. "Oh, God, I've missed you two so much." And I feel it to my core, the lost time with these two precious girls. "You're almost as tall as me."

"Aunt Ari, we're so happy you're back." Jessie speaks for both of them, as usual.

Jackie bursts into tears. "We've been so worried." Seeing the quiet one so upset shreds my resolve to not cry. I didn't intend to hurt the people who love me, but holding these two underscores the fact that I did. Kim most of all. I tighten my embrace.

When the three of us are sniffling rather than sobbing, I speak. "I cherish you two and your brother and sister, and I shouldn't have missed so much of your lives. I'm so sorry I disappeared. But I'm back and I'm not leaving again. We have a lot of catching up to do, but right now

I'm focused on the upcoming performance. I'd love to spend some time together after that." I loosen my hold. "Let me say hello to your dad."

I turn and Brian wraps me in his arms. He's a six-foot-plus guy, and I always feel safe in his embrace. Today is no different.

His gaze shifts over my head. "Hey, Lee."

Lee steps next to us. "Hey, yourself."

Oops, I didn't introduce her. "Oh, sorry, Lee, I didn't mean to ignore you. This is Jackie and Jessie Landers."

Frankie comes in. "Lori Seaton is here. Where do you want her?"

"Give us a few minutes, then bring her to the apartment," Kim says. "Okay, my loves, time to go. We have business to conduct here."

Brian grabs Kim and kisses her passionately. "You're always so romantic," he teases.

"Yeah, yeah." Kim hugs her two daughters. "Shouldn't you two be in school?"

Jessie laughs. "Our mom gave us permission to miss morning classes."

"You guys have an awesome mom," Kim says.

"We do," Jessie says, hugging Kim.

After confirming I will get together with them sometime soon after the performance, the three of them hug and kiss me again and leave. I feel...happy.

After the door closes, Kim puts an arm over my shoulders. "Was that okay?"

"It was great seeing them." It's just me and Kim and Lee, so I speak freely. "I see now that I was too self-centered, too full of self-pity to think about how selfish I was being, isolating myself from everyone who loves me and focusing on my personal pain and the loss of my friends. I'm so sorry, Kim."

She tightens her hold on me. "You did what you had to do, Ari, and you came through it stronger than ever. It was painful for all of us to lose you and painful for me to see you so flattened and hopeless, but you're back now, so let's focus on that."

I kiss her cheek. "I love you, Kimmy. You're the best."

She slides her arm down and grips my hand. "Anything for my bestie."

Micki leads the way through the hall to the apartment. We'd decided earlier it was better if Lori doesn't see me, so I go into the bedroom while Kim and Lee wait for Frankie to bring her in.

I hear Kim introducing them, and then she comes into the bedroom to wait with me until they're done.

"It shouldn't take long. My contract is mostly industry standard, and the recording contract is very generous since the royalties are being split fifty-fifty."

She sits on the bed with me and looks me in the eye. "You and Lee are great together, as a couple and as musicians. She's going to need your support when she's launched and these recordings hit the charts, which I have no doubt they will."

I laugh. "I'm not sure I remember how to do this, so I'm going to need *your* support."

She hugs me. "Aww, it's like riding a bicycle; it'll all come back. But you always have my support. Don't forget we're easing you into it. After the performance, you'll go back to Sharon Springs and your anonymity. I'll handle the media and anything that comes up. But I don't want to lose the momentum for Lee, so I'll schedule some gigs for her following the performance and then again when you come back to record the first album."

"You should book as many performances as you can for Lee. Maybe I'll join her on stage occasionally just to draw the audiences until she's solid. And since I'll be here whenever she is, I'll let Graciela know to keep the house ready." I stop. "Wait. Weren't you supposed to move the furniture from the house to Sharon Springs? I just realized the house is fully furnished. What happened?"

She pats my hand. "I moved everything from the guest house except the living room furniture, which was worn so I bought a new set similar to the one in your house. The bedrooms and the kitchen were almost fully furnished from the guest house. I've already had the guest house repainted and refurnished."

I'm shocked. "Why didn't I notice?"

Kim laughs. "If I recall, you weren't thinking about furniture when you moved to Sharon Springs. I'm not sure you would have noticed an elephant living there with you. And now that you're back amongst us, your mind is on things other than furniture. In any case, the guesthouse is ready for guests. Since Lee's family is all from out of state, I thought she might want to have them stay there so they can spend some time together after the performance."

That's my Kimmy. Always taking care of everyone. "That's thoughtful of you. I'll discuss it with her."

We look up at the knock on the door. Kim opens it. Lee is beaming. I assume she's happy with the contracts. "Kim, Lori and I are done. She'd like us to sign now."

Kim walks out and Lee follows, but she flashes a thumbs-up before she shuts the door. Yes, I am definitely ready to make love to that woman again.

CHAPTER FORTY-EIGHT

Lee

I'm flying high after my meeting with Lori. She's down-to-earth, clearly knows her stuff, and explains everything in easy-to-understand language. She said I'm lucky to be represented by Kim. She's honest, her contracts are straightforward, and she takes good care of her clients. Even though she doesn't know the recording and the video contracts are for me singing with Ariana, Lori is amazed at the fifty-fifty royalty split. According to her, Kim must have a lot of faith in me, because that kind of split is unheard of for an unknown. I really like Lori, and I think she feels the same.

After Lori leaves, we take a short break, then Ariana, Kim, Freya, and I spend some time talking about the song I'm recording. I defer to the three of them on whether to record it with the backup group.

Kim doesn't hesitate. "You'll be singing it with just your guitar at the performance, and I'm sure that version will be posted on the Internet. But first impressions are important. As soon as we have the recording, my team will push it out to local radio stations and music influencers to generate interest before the performance. Going with the backup group will produce a more polished and professional record, which, I believe, will increase your airplay and garner more attention. And attention is what we're after." She gazes at me. "Lee?"

"Recording with a band makes me nervous since I've never done it, but I trust your judgment, Kim."

"Good." Kim grins. "Ariana, Freya? Any issues?"

"Go with the band," Ariana says.

"Since it was my idea, I think it's the only way to go." Freya stands. "Let's get to work."

Kim puts a hand up. "One thing before we break. Using the musicians on your duet amped up the track, and I think we'll see the same happen with Lee's song today. I'm thinking we should hire musicians to back you up during the performance. What do you all think?"

I expect Ariana to jump in with her opinion, but instead she defers to me. "What do you think, Lee?"

Intimidated, I hesitate. After all, Ariana, Kim, and Freya are the professionals. But then I realize Ariana respects my musical instincts and wants me to voice my opinion. And she's right, I do have a good ear and sometimes I'm too laid-back.

"I think we should do some of our duets as we rehearsed, because when it's just the two of us there's an intimacy that is harder to project when other musicians are involved. However, I like the idea of the backup band for some of our duets and some of the solos. You and I should spend some time in the next few days going over the whole list and deciding how to handle each, then we can score the ones that we want the band to play. We can send the band the scores so they can familiarize themselves with their parts, but we'll have to include some rehearsal time the day of the performance."

Kim does one of her silent communications with Ariana and then turns to Freya. "What do you think, Freya?"

Freya doesn't hesitate. "I agree. I've listened to the whole set list you sent me, so I have some opinions."

"Of course you do." Kim rubs her hands together. "I'll call the musicians and offer them the job."

Freya stood. "Ready to get started, Lee?"

"I am." I'm much more relaxed today working solo with Freya to get the song down. Ariana is in the booth with Freya and Kim and occasionally makes a suggestion, but for the most part it's me and Freya. It's grueling, but by eleven o'clock that night Freya is happy with the result and sends us home. Tomorrow, I'll record it with the backup group. And the following day I'll do the photo shoot to get pictures for press releases and for posters to publicize the performance, and then have the meet and greet with Kim's staff. The morning after that I'll do the interview Kim scheduled with Gayle Fortin, and then we'll drive back to Sharon Springs.

As she did last night, Graciela leaves food and drinks for us and the guards who are with us. Ariana and I relax in the living room while we eat and talk about the day. We snuggle and kiss, then go to bed and snuggle more.

CHAPTER FORTY-NINE

Ariana

What a pleasure to watch Lee record. She seems to have come into her own. Yesterday's nervousness is gone. She's poised and patient, at ease with Freya, and excited about the work. The session is hard, as they always are, but there are no holdups, and they finish at a reasonable time.

I was there to support her, but it quickly became clear she didn't need me. I'm happy to stay home tomorrow and relax rather than lurking in the studio trying to support her while hiding from the backup group. Lee seems comfortable with that, about dealing with Kim, Freya, and the musicians without me. In fact, I think she's looking forward to it.

I had plenty of time while she was recording today to fantasize about making love to her, so I have plans for us tonight. But I can see she's exhausted. Her next two days are going to be equally demanding, so I put my desires aside and let her rest.

I'm determined to not fall asleep on the sofa again tonight, so after a light late-night snack and a little time unwinding, I drag Lee up to what I now consider our bedroom and help her undress and get into bed. She's asleep almost as soon as I wrap my arms around her. And with the weight of her and her warmth, I'm right behind her.

CHAPTER FIFTY

Lee

Micki and Frankie are talking quietly in the front seat as we drive back to Sharon Springs. Ariana is asleep, either because she truly feels safe in the armored Lincoln or because she's totally exhausted or maybe a combination. I wish I could comfortably wrap my arms around her, but the captain's seats make it difficult to get close. We did start out holding hands and she's managed to pull my hand into her lap. Now she's tilting toward me and I've shifted as close as I can get so her head is on my shoulder. I estimate we're about an hour from home. Home. The word reverberates in my head. Yes, it's home. In truth, at this point any place with Ariana feels like home.

I'm tired, too, but my brain is swarming with so many thoughts I'm making myself dizzy.

Kim tells me my interview went well and assures me I didn't sound nervous. It was only about ten minutes, but Gayle Fortin is a hugely influential Austin music personality. Working from background material Kim provided, she asked about my enlisting after the 9/11 attack and its impact on my music career. Kim had already told her she heard me sing at the house of a mutual friend so there was no mention of Ariana. We talked about the upcoming performance and plans to record a full album. I guess because Kim and Ariana own the recording studio, Kim was able to bring a copy of my record, the one with the backup group, and I couldn't have been prouder when Gayle played it and practically swooned. She predicted a great future for me and promised to attend the performance. Ariana and I will watch the interview when it's aired later in the week.

What luck having my first recording session with Freya, one of the top music producers, and with Ariana, who even after being out of the public eye for more than a year is still the most successful performer in the business. I learned a lot. I'm high on how good we sound and how good our duet and my solo recording are. I'm not sure why I'm so lucky, but I'll take it.

It's not just luck, though. It's being represented by Kim. She's the one making these things happen. So hearing my agent/manager, who is widely acknowledged as the best in the business, tell Lori as we walk her out that she expects I will soon be a star in my own right makes me lightheaded. Kim knows her stuff, so I believe her.

The best thing about this brief foray into Ariana's world is learning more about her, the woman behind the fame. She listens to her advisers, doesn't inflict her stress on those surrounding her, is always professional, works almost fifteen hours with just short bathroom and snack breaks, and responds to each person with warmth, caring, and kindness. Those are the qualities that attracted me to the insecure, reclusive, and scarred, I thought, woman behind the veil. I'm amazed at how introspective and self-aware she is and how willing to share insights about herself with me and Kim. She's playful, funny, loving, and has a great sense of humor. She's generous to those who work for her and thinks of ways to make their lives easier, thus Graciela's cottage and the house for the bodyguards. Her wealth and lifestyle are beyond any I've ever imagined, but she's generous to a fault, I've learned by listening to her and Kim chat—giving to charity, investing in the dreams of others such as Graciela's catering company and Micki's security firm. Apparently, she has no connection with her birth family, parents, and two brothers and a sister, but she gave each a house, a car, and a monthly income, and her nieces and nephews have trust funds that will make them comfortable when they turn twenty-five.

We hit a bump, and despite the seat belt, she turns in her seat so she's semidraped over me. I can't imagine she's comfortable in that position, but still she manages to place one hand on my waist and the other on my breast. I take advantage of our closeness and bury my face in her luxurious hair, enjoying its softness, its scent, and the gentle sound of her breathing. As it always does when we touch, my temperature rises, my heart speeds up, and a drum beats in my groin. Images of making love flit through my mind and I fight the urge to kiss her.

"We're about fifteen minutes out," Micki says. Our eyes lock in the rearview mirror and she smiles softly. "Better start waking her now. You know how grouchy she is if she's woken too abruptly."

I nod. Micki's attitude toward me has changed in the last few days. It seems she's decided I'm good for Ariana. Was it seeing us sing together or just watching us interact? She's right about waking Ariana.

"Sweetheart, we're almost home. You have to wake up now."

She groans. "Nooo."

"Yes, unless you want to sleep in the car tonight."

She loosens her grip but doesn't move. "You're so comfy to sleep on."

She's talking but hasn't opened her eyes yet, so I jiggle her a bit to encourage her.

Her fingers move. I assume she's just realized her hand is holding onto my breast. My body reacts as if I've received an electric shock.

"You smell so good." She kisses my neck. I gasp. She managed to hit the right spot. Or maybe it's the wrong spot, considering we're in the back seat of an armored vehicle with her two bodyguards sitting right in front of us.

I'm not sure whether she can feel my body's reaction or her own body is reacting as well, but she slowly pulls away from me. "Sorry, Lee."

The smile in her eyes and the quirking of her lips tell me she's not sorry at all. "Well, I'm not, but…" I tip my head toward the front of the car.

She yawns and arches her back. "These seats are not the best for cuddling."

"I don't think ease of cuddling is a requirement for armored, fireproofed vehicles."

We turn into the driveway, and she stares out the side window as if there is more to see than the long, dusty, bumpy one-lane dirt path through the trees. It occurs to me that this is only the third time she's seen this part of her property. Hopefully, after our performance she'll get out more, but it will be very different being surrounded by bodyguards.

CHAPTER FIFTY-ONE

Ariana

I'm relieved that my first foray into the world went without a hitch. Though the seats make cuddling difficult, the car is comfortable, and knowing it is as safe as it can be made it possible to relax and enjoy the sights on the drive back from Austin. I napped for part of the trip and even managed to somehow cuddle with Lee. Waking to find my hand gripping her breast was a surprise and a turn-on. The heat from her body warmed both of us.

And since I'm much more aware of my surroundings than the first time I arrived, it was interesting to see the town of Sharon Springs and the area surrounding the Springs house. I'm surprised the house is so deep in the woods.

As much as I want to make love with Lee, I know she's exhausted and I guess I am too. Leaving here, my secure place, riding in a car, seeing people I hadn't seen since the accident, and recording without my band for the first time were draining. It doesn't help that I've barely seen Lee the last couple of days.

Before the accident I wouldn't have given any of this a passing thought and one day of recording wouldn't have registered, but even though my body is as strong as it ever was, maybe stronger, I still don't have the emotional stamina to deal with everyday life, everyday encounters with people, even people I love. I make a mental note to ask Kim to schedule extra time when we record the full album, but knowing her sensitivity to me, she probably noticed and will take care of it. I'm not totally back, but I'm confident I'll get there.

Now that the recordings are done, we have five weeks to rest, connect, and enjoy our last quiet time together. I have no doubt that it won't take long after our performance for my connection to the Sharon Springs house to be discovered, and even though the guards will keep intruders out, it will never have the same cocoon feeling. And though we'll be secure and private in my Austin house, the world will always be clamoring outside the gate wanting as much as it can get of each of us. Our choice, of course. That's the price of being a star as I am, and, I have no doubt, Lee will soon be.

We'll sleep again tonight. But who knows what we'll do in the morning and the afternoon and the evening.

CHAPTER FIFTY-TWO

Lee

We've been back from Austin three days, and Ariana and I have settled into an easy rhythm of making love often, jogging, composing, rehearsing, cooking and eating together. We take lots of quiet time for resting, reading, and ongoing discussions of books and everything and anything. Even with the constant worry about Tessa and Mara, I'm happy being here with Ariana. I'm so relaxed and in the moment that I'm not even nervous about our upcoming performance. We're still so hot and burning for each other, I fear we might incinerate during our performance. But I still haven't worked up the nerve to say the words "I love you." And neither has she. I don't know what's holding me back, because our bodies say it whenever we make love.

Since we got back, Ariana has been speedwalking on our walks, and this morning, she started running. Micki and the guards, as always, are scattered around the boardwalk watching us. Micki holds up her hand. "Ariana, if you want to run, follow me." Ariana looks at me. I nod, and we follow her to a path in the woods that one of the guards discovered while we were in Austin. Micki and the three other guards on duty run with us. I haven't run since I left the Army so I'm out of shape, but it still feels good. And it is thrilling to see Ariana run, even though she can't go far. She is exhilarated, breathing heavily, wheezing, and laughing, and it is impossible not to feel excited for her. With her hands on her knees and a blazing smile, she finally manages to speak. "Let's do this a couple of times a day. I need to build my stamina."

"Yes, ma'am." Micki mock salutes. "But more than once a day will do more harm than good. Be patient and you'll get there, so no more running today. We'll walk for a while, then go back for breakfast."

"Yes, ma'am." Ariana mimics Micki, then sticks her tongue out.

We are both revved, so Ariana quickly makes the strong coffee we love and mashes an avocado while I fry eggs to go on our avocado toasts. We sit next to each other at the table, knees touching, and eat as we sketch our rehearsal plan for the day. We put our dishes in the dishwasher and clean the kitchen, then go into the music room. We tune, focus on our fingering, and then run through the program we'll sing at our performance.

After the last song, we hold for a few seconds. I'm filled with love for Ariana and I want to tell her, but I can't find the words. Music will have to do. I strum my guitar and meet Ariana's eyes. "This one is for you."

The minute she recognized the chords of "The First Time Ever I Saw Your Face," her eyes fill, she reaches her hand out, and she caresses my cheek. As I sing the words that express my love, she leans toward me, mouthing some of the words. She chimes in with the last phrase—"your face, your face, your face"—and then sings the entire song to me, letting me know she feels the same. When she finishes, her face is flushed, and her eyes are sparkling. Her eyes lock onto mine. I lean over and brush her lips with mine. Without breaking eye contact, she pushes closer and presses our lips together. When I feel her tongue gently requesting entry, I close my eyes and give myself totally to the kiss. I open my eyes. Ariana's eyes are wide, and tears are rolling down her face.

"What's wrong?"

She smiles. "Everything is right." She gently touches my face.

I inhale. It's now or never. "I've been waiting for you to take the lead, because you've been dealing with so much. But I couldn't wait any longer. I'm in love with you, Ariana."

She's silent for a moment. "I'm in love with you too, Lee."

CHAPTER FIFTY-THREE

Ariana

Lee and I have had the freedom to touch and kiss whenever we have the impulse since the first time we made love but declaring our love for each other has increased our connection exponentially. Everything feels brighter. I can't remember ever being this happy or so in love. And running, doing weights, and taking long walks every day has increased my endurance and my strength. I'm feeling terrific. Which is good. Because. Today is the day. In a few hours we'll be performing together. I'm nervous and excited, but so is Lee and, it seems, everyone around us.

Kim arrived from Austin yesterday, a surprise visit to spend a little time with us before we both face our big moments. She can't seem to stop smiling this morning. Partly she's excited about tonight, but I think it's also because she's seen another shift in us.

Now we're gathered on the porch with the whole security team for a last-minute review of the logistics before we leave for the venue. The guards are used to seeing us holding hands and even kissing, but Kim's eyebrows go up at the public display of affection. I've always been very private, but with Lee I can't control my feelings. Kim smiles. She nods at Micki.

Micki addresses us. "We'll leave in an hour. Frankie and I will drive you with two other guards in one Lincoln. Dawn and Denise and the other four guards will follow us in the second Lincoln. When we get to the venue, six guards will go in first to ensure it's safe for you to enter. Dawn and Frankie will be stationed outside your dressing room. I'll meet with the additional security staff my firm has provided, the venue's security team, and the off-duty deputies I've hired for the evening from the sheriff's office. We'll vet the ticket purchasers as best we can, but guards will be posted in the back of the house, in front of the stage, and in the wings at the start of the performance, through intermission, until you take your final bows and are offstage." She turns to Kim. "You're up."

"Okay. I'm leaving right after we finish here to confirm that the lighting, recording, and sound equipment brought to the venue by our technical staff are all installed and ready to go. After you arrive at the venue, you two will have about an hour to rest until the backup band arrives. Once they set up, you'll rehearse for a few hours. After rehearsing and doing sound and lighting checks, you'll have a light dinner in your dressing room and relax."

She stops to drink some water. "I plan to introduce Lee."

I raise my eyebrows. This is highly unusual for Kim. She prefers to stay in the background.

"The three of us have been over this before, but it's important that Micki and her team know the plan. Ari will be in the wings as Lee sings her first two solos. At the end of the second solo, Lee will introduce her special guest, not mentioning Ari's name, and then sing the first lines of their duet. Ari will enter singing her part and sit next to Lee while they complete the song. The first set will be forty-five minutes, then a twenty-minute break followed by another thirty minutes, and about fifteen minutes for encores and applause. After the ticket holders leave, Ariana and Lee will mingle with their invited guests." She looks at Micki. "Anything else?"

"Yes. Frankie and Dawn will be backstage with Ari. I'll be in front of the stage with several others, watching the crowd. Guards will be stationed throughout the venue as well. We'll be searching bags as people arrive, especially those who bought tickets and are unknown to us. We should be okay."

"Everybody clear?" Kim asks. Everyone is silent. "Okay, you leave in an hour." The guards leave us. "Ari. I hope you're not mad that I've asked our invited guests to remain after the performance to meet with you and Lee. You need to move back into the world, and I thought you could begin by greeting people, mostly people you know, in limited numbers and in a controlled environment."

My breath hitches. Lee squeezes my hand. As usual, Kim is right. "All right."

Kim exhales. "Wow. No argument. And, as requested, Lee's friends and family are settled into the guest house. We brought them in through the rear entrance, so they have no idea it's on your property or who you are. Graciela is set to cater a late-night snack tonight and brunch and dinner for them and our family the day after tomorrow. If either of you wants to invite someone else, just let me know."

"Can I invite Jonah and his people?" Lee asks.

Kim makes a note. "I'll take care of it." She pulls me, then Lee, up and hugs each of us. "I can't wait to share you two with the world. I'm going inside to pee, then I'll be on my way."

"Shall we sit here and get some sun before we go?" Lee says.

Kim comes out with her bag and gets into her car. "See you there." She waves and drives out.

Her mention of friends and family in Austin pops into my mind. "Lee, did you pack enough clothing so we can stay for a week if we want to?"

"No, I was so focused on tonight that I didn't really think about it, but if my family is there I might want to hang out with them for a bit," Lee says.

We go inside, pack additional clothing, and place those bags next to the garment bags with the jeans, silk shirts, and boots we'd selected to wear for the performance tonight, and our guitars, to be loaded into the Lincoln. That done, we sit in the sun until Micki drives up. She opens the doors for us while Frankie loads our stuff.

Lee clasps my hand tightly and stares out the side window of the Lincoln as we speed toward the venue. She'd seemed happy earlier, so I wonder what's going on. "What's wrong, Lee?"

She turns and I see sadness, not nerves. "I was just thinking that Mara and Tessa are out there somewhere. Life would be perfect if they were with us."

I put my arm around her waist and pull her close. "After tonight, let's focus on finding them. Maybe we could do some interviews or an appeal even to get people to pay attention."

"You would do that? Go public?"

I kiss her temple. "I will do everything I can to make you happy, and I know finding them is the most important thing in your life right now."

She swivels and kisses me with such passion that my legs tremble. I pull away. "Hey, any more of that and I'll be too weak to sing."

She laughs, then elbows me. "Oh, then I have the pleasure of kissing you *and* the opportunity to take center stage tonight."

I know she's teasing. Lee isn't interested in stealing my thunder or taking my place. "You are always center stage for me."

"And you for me. You're going to knock them out tonight."

"I'm confident we'll knock them out—together and individually."

After Micki escorts us inside, Kim shows us around the venue and leads us to our dressing room. We'd decided to share. Our instruments and our clothing are waiting for us. There's water and snacks, just as I like it. I swallow the lump in my throat as memories of the band flood my brain. Happy memories. I feel the loss, but not the guilt. As if she can read my mind or maybe she feels the same, Kim puts her arm around me but doesn't comment. She kisses my forehead and leaves to make sure everything is perfect.

We rest for an hour, then there's a knock on the door and Kim walks in.

"The band is set up and ready to start rehearsing."

I pale. Weeks ago, when Kim broached the subject of bringing in backup for the performance tonight, I'd agreed because I knew it would enhance our performance. But now faced with the reality of standing in front of the total strangers replacing my friends, I feel like a traitor. The room spins. Lee is next to me in a second. She puts an arm around me. "We don't have to use the backup. Right, Kim?"

Kim chews her lip and stares at me. "We don't have to do anything you don't want, Ari, but if you're serious about coming back, backup is a step you need to take."

I know she's right. I breathe deeply like the therapist in the hospital taught me, and the room settles.

"It's not a betrayal," Kim says, reading my mind as usual. She takes both my hands and gazes at me. "They're just musicians, Ari, not replacements for your friends, our friends. And none of them are strangers. You've played with all of them at one time or another. What do you say?"

Lee squeezes me. She'll be with me. I can do this. I will do this. "Okay." I step away from Lee. "Do they know it's not just Lee?"

"They know there's someone in addition to Lee, but not that it's you. There will probably be a moment of shock with some gaping jaws, then a little gushing. I can talk to them before you meet them, if you'd like."

"I'll be all right. Do they have the music?"

"I gave them the arrangements for all the new songs plus the three standards of yours a couple of weeks ago."

"Let's do it."

Kim grins. Lee gives me a thumbs-up.

"Just so you know," Kim says. "I've confiscated everyone's phones, and no one is allowed to leave the premises until after the performance. Hopefully, no one will know you're here until you sing that first note. They'll get their phones back at the intermission when you two will already be trending on the Internet."

I hug Kim. "Thanks for thinking of everything."

She kisses my forehead. "I have to earn my keep."

Lee and I tune our guitars, then head out.

When we walk onto the stage, the musicians are in place, joking with the sound and lighting techs and others in the house. If jaws dropping made a sound, the room would be rocking right now. Instead, there is a stunned silence. Then the drummer stands and claps, and every single person in the room does the same, followed by whistling and cheering. My eyes fill. This kind of appreciation from colleagues is special. I struggle with a response and decide to keep it simple.

"Well, thank you all. I've missed you too, more than you'll ever know." I strum my guitar. "Are you ready to work?"

The cheer is heartwarming. And just like that everyone settles. Standing on the stage, looking out over the tables, I see the venue is larger than I expected, but an audience of two hundred fifty is still tiny compared to the many thousands in our performance spaces in the last few years. It reminds me of the places we played when we were starting out. I like it. Kim chose well.

I introduce Lee and suggest we sing one of our duets to give everyone a sense of our sound. Halfway through the song, the instruments join in, one by one, and by the time it's over, I know I'm fine with the backup. My gaze goes to Kim, sitting at a front table watching. She gives me a thumbs-up. I don't know how she pulled this group together because most of them are in bands, but somehow she managed to assemble a group that feels familiar and easy. I wave to the techs, walk back and hug each member of the band. And then I pick up my guitar, lock eyes with Lee, and we're off and running.

The applause from the crew and security people in the room when we finish rehearsing is unexpected but welcome. We spend some time running light and sound checks, then go back to our dressing room to rest before the performance.

CHAPTER FIFTY-FOUR

Lee

I'm in the wings listening to Kim introduce me as a breakout performer that everyone should keep their eye on. I turn to Ariana, who is standing next to me though she won't appear until I've sung my two solos.

"Does Kim really think anyone will remember me once you start singing?"

Ariana puts her arm around my waist and pulls me to her. "She does. And her introducing you is a sign to the music world that she believes what's she's saying. And so do I. Just wait and see, sweetheart, you'll be flying high."

I'm nervous, but her words and her voice in my ear are calming. And I know the minute I start playing I'll be fine. I'm excited to be the one to introduce Ariana back into the world of music and, as always, I'm thrilled to be singing with her.

"Come on out, Lee Wilton, show them what you have." The roar that follows Kim's final words, goes right to my head. Now I remember why I loved performing.

Ariana kisses me and smiles. "Go get 'em, tiger."

I walk on stage, wave, and wait for the applause and the shouts to quiet. "Thank you." I look into the audience, but of course with the lights I can't see anything. Kim told me my friends Carley and Tammy are seated in one of two front tables with my parents, my three brothers, their wives, and a few of my nieces and nephews. I was shocked that they'd flown in from all over the world. I know they're here for me because no one knows Ariana is performing tonight.

I strum a little to let the audience know I'm ready, then I go into my first song. It's silent for a second or two when I end, but then the audience comes alive with a roar. I'd forgotten the intoxication of having an audience on their feet cheering and whistling. Any doubts about performing again are gone.

"Thank you. Thank you." When they quiet, I sing my second solo. The response is even louder, if possible. I'm floating. I can't wait for Ariana to experience this again. Finally, I put my hand up to signal the audience to quiet down.

"Wow. What a great group. Tonight is special for me. I'll always remember it, not just because I'm making my debut as a performer but also because of how I got here and who made it possible." I bow in the direction I know she's sitting. "Thank you, Kim Landers." I wait for the applause and cheers to quiet down. "And to make this night as special for you as it is for me, I have a surprise guest who I'm sure will do just that."

CHAPTER FIFTY-FIVE

Ariana

This is it. I'm in the wings. Lee is introducing her surprise guest. Me. I'm trembling. I glance behind me. I can still make a run for it. Then I hear my cue. I position my guitar and take a deep breath.

It isn't the roar of seventy thousand fans and it's not my band behind me, but the minute I sing the first word and step onto the stage, I feel as if I've come home after a long journey through the desert without water. I hear the gasps as I'm recognized, then my name rolls through the house. Even with the blinding stage lights and tears blurring my vision, I sense the audience getting to its feet. Best of all, my voice is strong and as true as it's ever been. I'm back. I feel the love. And I give them everything I have. This is where I belong.

I cross the stage to Lee and we sing as if we're jamming together in the music room. The audience loves it. And so do I.

CHAPTER FIFTY-SIX

Lee

I play the chords, nod at the band, tip my head to Ariana, then sing the first verse of our duet. And right on cue Ariana steps on stage singing the second verse. The audience gasps as they recognize her voice, that gorgeous voice. Then they're on their feet screaming her name. Ariana stops playing and I do the same. I hold my hand up until they start to settle. "I knew you'd love her."

There are a few shouts, but then it is quiet. We face each other, lock eyes and sing the chorus together, then sing the other verses as we'd written them, two lovers speaking to each other through music. We finish, silence the strings, and smile at each other while the audience goes berserk again. Ariana is glowing. I place my guitar in its stand, wait a few minutes, then raise my hands to silence them again. "Ladies and gentlemen, if you haven't recognized that gorgeous voice or that gorgeous face, let me introduce my guest. I present the one and only Ariana Calandre."

Ariana puts her guitar on its stand, embraces me, then holding hands we take several bows together. She grins at me. "Come on. Let's show them what we can do."

We stand facing each other, guitars in hand, and wait for the band to begin. We sing the duets we'd written, interspersed with Ariana's two solos. And then the first half of the program is over, and we walk off the stage to thunderous applause.

We're drying off the sweat and drinking water when Kim bursts into the dressing room. "Oh, my Lord, you did it. You were better than ever. You should hear the talk out there. There were so many phones pointed at the stage during the entire performance the Internet is drowning in your music." She pulls us both into a hug.

Flying high, we're back on stage a few minutes later for the second half of the program. Ariana counts down, the band chimes in, and we start the next song on the set list, a duet.

As Ariana fluidly moves into her next solo, the crowd roars. She meets my eyes, puts her guitar in its stand, grabs the microphone, and suddenly she's strutting and posturing on the stage, like I'd seen on videos of her performances. Her stage persona is back. Up close, watching her back in her element, I love her more than ever. She was born to perform. Seeing her, it's hard to remember the gravelly-voiced, pained, lonely, withdrawn woman I met not so long ago. The audience is thrilled to have her back, but only Kim and I know how far she had to come to get here.

Out of breath but sparkling when she finishes, she bows. And bows over and over, soaking up the adoration. "Thank you. I missed you all so much." Lit from within she's even more gorgeous than usual. I want to drag her to our dressing room and make love to her. I can't see the audience behind the stage lights, but I'll bet many of them feel the same.

When the audience finally quiets, Ariana turns and kisses me smack on the lips. "And thank you." The audience loves it. I strum the chords for my solo until they calm down, then I speak.

"So how am I supposed to follow that performance?" I shout over the laughter and cheers. "Welcome back, Ariana. This one is for you, sweetheart." Instead of the song on the set list, I launch into a love song I'd written for her. I'd felt it was too personal to sing in public, but now I want the world to know I'm in love with Ariana. Tears fill her eyes as she realizes what's coming. After the first verse, one by one the instruments pick up the melody. The audience goes wild.

They love us. Whether we sing a solo or a duet, every song receives huge applause and cheers. And then we're at our final song, the one we recorded.

Ariana plays the first chord, I join her, just the two of singing together as we'd originally planned, and then we sing it again with the viola, cello, bass, keyboard, and drums. As we end, the audience is on its feet, banging on the tables, whistling, and chanting our names. We bow and Ariana points to the band. "Let's give these fabulous musicians a hand."

She introduces each one and they take several bows. The audience is still applauding so we sing another one of our duets. The cheering is deafening. I meet Ariana's eyes and she nods. I raise my hands and when the crowd quiets, I announce, "We'll each sing one more, then we're done." Ariana steps back as I sing my solo, then she confers with the band and sings one of her signature songs. And then we're done. The applause is thunderous.

As planned, when the audience settles Ariana stands in the spotlight. "Many of you know this is my first public appearance since my friends, the five women who helped me rise from a small town singer to the top of the charts internationally, and Chioma Achebe and Evie Durant, two of our bodyguards, were killed in an accident that left me severely injured."

She pauses. "Gloria West on drums, Maggie Fortuna on keyboard, Nellie Garcia on bass, Erica James on fiddle, and Torie Stella on lead guitar were top-notch musicians at the height of their careers, loving and giving human beings, and, together, the best band ever. I don't understand why the seven of them died and I didn't." She pauses again and takes several deep breaths. "It's taken me a long time to accept that it's all right for me to live. Though they can't be here with us, they live in my heart and my thoughts every single day. And tonight, they were with me on stage. I thank Kim Landers, my best friend, my sister, my manager, for always believing in me and always being there for me." She throws a kiss to where we know Kim is sitting. "I thank Lee Wilton"—hands in prayer position, Ariana turns to me and bows—"every single day for bringing me back into the world of the living and the world of music." She swivels to face the band. "I thank this great group of musicians for showing up and making Lee's debut and my first performance a success." She bows to them and then turns and bows to the audience. "And I thank you all for coming tonight. Lee and I enjoyed performing our music, and we hope you enjoyed it as well."

We stand there holding hands, enjoying the love from the audience, then the lights dim and we walk offstage. And kiss, a deep passionate kiss. I look into Ariana's eyes. "You were fabulous tonight. I love you. And the audience loved you."

She touches my cheek. "I love you too. Thank you for getting me here." She clings to me and sobs. I turn us so her back is to the backstage crew to protect her privacy.

"Let it out, sweetheart," I say.

She quickly regains control, wipes her eyes with the back of her hand, and leans back with a soft smile on her face. "Thank you again." She kisses me lightly. "Let's go."

The crew and the backstage bodyguards applaud as we walk to our dressing room. We grab the towels someone offers and flop on the sofa, grinning like fools while trying to cool down and decompress before going out to greet friends and family.

CHAPTER FIFTY-SEVEN

Lee

Ariana is glowing. And I'm feeling great. What an experience. Singing my two solos first allows me to hear the crowd cheering and chanting for me, just me, not because of Ariana, and gives me a lot of confidence. It makes it easier to accept the crowd's ecstatic reaction when Ariana joins me, for what it is, the shock at being there for her first appearance in almost two years and appreciation for the talent that she is. And professional that she is, she rises to the occasion and gives her all. Even though we've been singing together for months, something about being in front of an audience ups her game and even I am wowed.

We are toasting each other with glasses of water when Kim comes in. She closes the door and watches us for a minute before pulling a chair over to sit in front of us.

"You look so serious, Kim. Is everything all right?" Ariana says.

"Everything is wonderful. Tonight was even more successful than I'd hoped. You two were fabulous. The industry people are going crazy. Not just because you're back, Ari, and sounding better than ever, but also because they loved you, Lee, and they're betting the two of you, solo and together, are going to rock the charts. They want to say hello to both of you."

Ariana visibly tenses.

Kim joins us on the couch. "As usual, it's totally up to you, Ari. I can make excuses and send them out with the rest of the audience. But if you're going to continue to record and perform, you'll need to meet with them eventually. And it would be great for them to get to know Lee."

I put my arm around Ariana's shoulders. She pulls my other hand into her lap.

Kim puts a hand on Ariana's knee. "I know seeing and talking to so many people is a big step, but it won't all be on you. They're interested in Lee too. And I'll be there to run interference. I'll limit the questions to you and your music and Lee and her music." She grins. "And, since you made it perfectly clear on stage that you and Lee are in a relationship, that as well."

I kiss Ariana's temple. "You'll be fine. Better than fine."

Kim kneels in front of us and holds Ariana's gaze for a few seconds. Something seems to pass between them. Ariana straightens her shoulders and takes a couple of deep breaths. "Okay. But I'm depending on you two."

Kim stands. "I'll come get you after the paying audience has cleared out. You probably have another ten to fifteen minutes to relax."

Ariana grabs Kim's hand. "Kimmy, I've been thinking. Over the last few months I've had brief telephone conversations with the girls' families but seeing them in person for the first time is going to be emotional for me, and, I think, for them. Would it be possible for me to meet with them privately before we go out to greet everyone else?"

Kim kisses Ariana's hand. "Good idea. I'll need a few minutes to organize it but how about I bring the families back here one at a time."

"That will work." Ariana's smile is shaky.

Kim gazes into Ariana's eyes again. "Okay." She leaves us.

I know their connection is deep, but I'm curious. "What just happened between you and Kim?"

Ariana frowns. "I'm not sure how to explain it. But since we were kids, we connect like that. Somehow I feel her love, feel her strength, feel her courage, and it empowers me, reminds me that I, too, am strong and brave, that I can do whatever I set my mind to."

"I feel that kind of connection with you. I admire your strength and your courage, and your love emboldens me, makes me braver."

She laughs. "Says the woman who went to war, faced the enemy, and has the scars to prove it."

"That's what you do when you're in the military. You don't think about it. In everyday life, it's harder to take risks, to put yourself out there. Yet since being with you anything seems possible."

Ariana leans in and kisses me. "I feel the same with you. But my connection with Kim is primal, older. It's almost like we're blood sisters, maybe twins." Her lips quirk with a hint of a smile. "Kim was the only non-twin in her family before they adopted me. Our mom, Lily, is an identical twin, our dad, Tom, is a fraternal twin, our sisters are identical twins, and our brothers are also identical twins. Lily claims Kim was supposed to have an identical twin, but then at the last minute God foresaw that two of Kim would be too much for the world to handle so he created her as a singleton. However, rather than waste the brains, stubbornness, courage, kindness, intuition, and love that he'd set aside for her twin, God dumped them all into Kim, doubling the amount of those qualities in her and inadvertently guaranteeing she'd still be too much for the world to handle sometimes."

I laugh. "So that's how your mom accounts for her strength?" I remember my first impression of her. "She is kind of scary sometimes."

Ariana laughs. "That she is. You definitely want her on your side. And I know she considers you part of the family, so you can relax."

We both jump at the knock on the door. Kim sticks her head in. "I've got Maggie's family with me." Ariana tenses. She takes a deep breath and stands. The door open and a woman and a girl, maybe twelve years old, and an older man and woman enter, all look nervous.

"Lee Wilton, this is Connie, Maggie's wife, Angela, her daughter, and her parents, Mr. and Mrs. Fortuna." She hugs each of them. "Thank you for coming tonight. I'm so sorry about Maggie and sorry I couldn't be there for all of you after the accident. I miss her and the others so much." Her voice breaks and a tear escapes.

Tears fill Connie's eyes as she embraces Ariana. "Maggie and the others loved you and loved playing together. It's been hard for us to come to terms with it, and we understand you've had a hard time with your injuries and dealing with your feelings about it all. Recently, the five families have been meeting monthly, helping each other heal. It would be wonderful if you and Lee could join us at our next monthly meeting."

Ariana kisses her cheek. "We'd love to." She turns to Angela. "You've grown so much since I last saw you. Do you remember me, sweetheart?"

The girl wraps her arms around Ariana. "I remember, Aunt Ari. I miss my mom so much." She sobs and soon they're all sobbing.

Ariana wipes her eyes. "Are the boys here?"

"They're both on the high school basketball team and they have a game tonight." Connie smiles. "If they'd known you were here tonight I think they would have faked being sick."

Ariana steps away but holds on to Angela's hand. "She was so proud of you and your brothers, Angela. She missed you all while we were on tour."

Ariana smiles at Maggie's parents and then holds Connie's gaze. "We were all so happy after that last concert. I know Maggie was excited about coming home and sharing everything with all of you." She breaks down again.

Kim sticks her head in again. "Sorry to cut this short, but I have Gloria's family here." She locks eyes with Connie. "I'll escort you back to your table." A final hug, they leave and Gloria's parents, Jen, her wife, and two gangly boys shuffle in. Ariana hugs each of them, reminisces about the times Jen and the boys were on tour with them, shares a couple of funny stories about Gloria from the recent tour, and then the next group comes in.

By the time the last of the five families has left, Ariana looks wiped out. I hand her a bottle of water and hold her while we sit on the couch.

"I know that was difficult but seeing them privately was the right thing, Ariana." I kiss her temple. "Will you be okay seeing the rest of the crowd out there?"

"Kim will give us a few minutes, so I'll be ready."

CHAPTER FIFTY-EIGHT

Ariana

Though meeting with the families of five of my closest friends was emotionally draining, sharing the pain of the loss with them was also healing. And seeing them privately was the right decision.

I'm nervous about talking to so many people at once, but I calm down after Kim reminds me I've already done the hardest part. And then I'm laughing with Lee about the story our family tells to explain why Kim is such a powerhouse.

Despite the emotional meetings and my nerves, I'm still feeling the after-performance high and a glance at Lee confirms she is too. She catches my eye, grasps my hand, and kisses my knuckles. I take a deep breath as Kim leads us out for the meet and greet. As we enter the room, my eyes go to the tables with the industry people. It's clear Kim invited only those I consider friends. I should have trusted her. Everyone in the room stands, claps, and cheers, calling out both our names.

I relax and I feel Lee do the same. These are our people. I squeeze Lee's hand and we bow, several times. Finally, Kim puts her hands up and the crowd goes quiet. She has them trained. "Okay. I know you're all anxious to talk to Ariana and Lee, but we ask your patience for just a little longer. Please stay in your seats. They'll make their way around the room, and you'll all have plenty of time with them when they get to your table. In the meantime, relax and enjoy the food and drinks being delivered."

The duet we recorded is playing in the background as Kim leads us to the industry tables. Everyone stands but no one approaches us. Dragging Lee with me, I move to Annie Littlefield, the music critic for *The Austin Times* who boosted me when I first appeared on the scene and is now a good friend. She smiles. "Welcome back, Ari." She kisses my cheek. "I've missed you."

I embrace her. "It's good to be back." I introduce Lee.

Annie takes Lee's hand. "Congratulations, Lee. I see big things in your future."

Lee blushes. "Thank you."

As we move around the table, I greet each person and introduce Lee. All are excited about my return and thrilled to be among the first to hear me sing again and among the first to let the world know I'm back. But these are music industry people, and there's also an undercurrent of excitement about being among the first to know about Lee, a big talent whose career is about to take off.

We move on to my family and friends, hugging, kissing, chatting, and sharing some tears. Everyone is so warm and loving, I feel connected and alive. I've missed this, missed them, more than I knew. I tell Kim I'd like to say a few words and a few seconds later a technician hands me a mic. The crowd quiets.

"This has been an extraordinary night. For Lee, who made her debut. Isn't she wonderful?"

The crowd is on its feet cheering for Lee, who is blushing but loving it. She takes a few bows, then points to me.

"And extraordinary for me too. I was devastated physically and emotionally by the accident, by the loss of my wonderful friends and two of my wonderful bodyguards, and I chose to withdraw from the world." I choke back the tears and take a few seconds to gain control. "But you heard the lyrics. Lee came along. And just by being who she is, kind, considerate, loving, and gentle, she nudged me back to mental and physical health. I started writing "And Then You Came," one of the songs we sang earlier. And some time after that Lee and I...got together." I can't help smiling. "I'm so happy to be back. Thank you for your love and support. Thank you for coming tonight. I love you all." The applause and cheers are ear-shattering.

As I brush the tears from my eyes, I see lots of handkerchiefs and tissues being put to use in the audience. My gaze settles on Lee, who is standing with her family. I wave and throw her a kiss.

CHAPTER FIFTY-NINE

Lee

The applause is harder to handle when I'm not blinded by the stage lights and can see who is doing the clapping and cheering. I follow Ariana's lead and bow until Kim saves us. I spot my family near the front. I can't believe so many members of them have made the trip. All of them, even Dad, the general, are sporting huge smiles. I'm flooded with warmth at the love and support.

Kim leads us to the tables with the industry people. I'm nervous, afraid I'll be tongue-tied and come across like a dodo. Everyone stands as we approach but they wait for Ariana to come to them. Despite her earlier angst, she's confident, relaxed, related, and professional. She hugs each person, introduces me, and laughs and chats for a moment, answering questions about our songs and us. I answer questions about myself and my music and bask in the compliments, then she moves us to the next person. Gayle Fortin, who interviewed me, hugs us, and invites us to come by for a joint interview at our convenience. I'm not sure what to say, but Ariana thanks her and says Kim will call her. It occurs to me that they may be industry hotshots, but they're also Ariana's friends. Kim is easing Ariana out into the world, but she's doing it thoughtfully, in a way that makes Ariana feel safe. I'm so proud of Ariana and so proud to be with her.

Much to my surprise, I'm enjoying myself and I sense Ariana is too. Kim hovers protectively nearby but leaves us to it except for an occasional gentle push when we linger too long with one person. Faster than I thought possible, we move back to Ariana and Kim's family and her friends.

This is much more emotional, for both Ariana and the people she's seeing for the first time since the accident. I stand by in case she needs me, but despite the tears and the sobbing, hers and theirs, she seems present and in control. Letting out all these emotions, all the feelings she repressed, the survivor's guilt, the loneliness, the pain, must be cathartic. After a few minutes, Kim puts an arm over my shoulders. "She's okay. I'll watch out for her. Go greet your family."

"Thanks, Kim. Call me if she needs me."

I haven't seen my parents in more than a year and they greet me like a hero returning from the war. Mom and Dad sandwich me between them, my mom kissing me and crying and the general who is never emotional, looking a little teary and very proud, holds us both. My brothers, my sisters-in-law, and the youngsters of all ages crowd around us. Everyone is talking to me at once and I'm getting dizzy swiveling from one to the other.

Finally, Mom, the real commander in the family, takes charge. "All right, let's give Lee a chance to breathe." The group immediately falls back. "Good. We can do this in an orderly fashion. I'll go first." She pulls my hand to her heart. I can't remember how long it's been since I had physical contact with the general, but he grabs my other hand.

"So how did you meet Ariana? And where is Gina?" Mom is an Ariana fan, so of course she would lead off with that. But Mom and Dad were not too fond of Gina, so the second question is tinged with anger.

I tell them about Gina selling my house and kidnapping the girls. The collective gasp and angry murmurs stop me short. As a military family, we try to follow the rules, so of course they're shocked. "Anyway, the attorney she tricked into doing the sale is helping me search for her and the girls pro bono. I filed kidnapping and theft charges, and he took care of filing for divorce. But—"

Ariana's voice interrupts me. She's speaking to the crowd.

"I'll continue after we listen to Ariana."

I'll be damned if Ariana doesn't tell a bit of her story and my part in helping her back to health. When she finishes, I clap and cheer along with everyone else. She waves and throws me a kiss. My heart flip-flops.

I turn to my family. "That's a good summary of what happened and how I met Ariana. I'll provide more details when we get together on Sunday."

I know they have a thousand questions, but I'm exhausted. Just then Ariana picks up the mic again.

"I'm exhausted, and I'm sure Lee is too. Tomorrow is a rest day for us, but we hope all of you will come to a barbecue at our place Sunday so we can spend some quality time together. Come anytime starting at noon, and plan on spending the day around the pool, so bring your swimsuit. We'll be serving lunch and, for those who can stay, dinner." Hearing all the yeses, she turns to Kim. "We're going to leave now. Will you give Graciela a heads-up and give my address to those who don't have it?"

"Yes, ma'am." Kim throws a mock salute.

Ariana comes over and takes my hand. I introduce her to Mom and Dad. She flashes her million-dollar smile and hugs my mom, who is clearly thrilled. Then she steps back and opens her arms to the general. He hesitates but then walks into her hug.

"I'm dying to spend time with you, General and Mrs. Wilton"— she looks at the others standing around us—"and all you other Wiltons, because I want to hear all your stories about Lee. But I want to be with you when I can give you my full attention, so please be there on Sunday. And don't forget your swimsuits."

I look around. My mom and some of my nieces look like they're going to swoon. Even the general has succumbed to Ariana's charm.

A murmur of agreement passes through the group, and Mom officially accepts. I turn to Carley and Tammy, my best friends, who have been patiently waiting to speak to me. "Please come."

They hug me. "We'd love to," Carley says.

"Ready, Lee?" Ariana asks.

"Yes." I wave. "See you all Sunday."

Micki, Frankie, and two other bodyguards surround us. "Prepare yourselves. The word is out and the paparazzi are out there in force. I've radioed for additional guards. They'll be here in a minute. We've corralled the paparazzi to the right so try not to look in that direction. On the left there's a small crowd of fans, most of whom were at the performance. Do you want to sign autographs and take pictures?"

"I'd like to if you're up for it, Lee. The fans are what it's about."

She's as exhausted as I am, but she's right. "Sure."

Micki nods. "Okay, the guards will organize the fans in groups of four to meet with you for selfies and autographs. Try to be brief so you can fit in as many as possible. Let the guards know when you're ready to leave and we'll bring the cars around."

As we wait at the door for the additional security, Ariana grips my hand. "Welcome to our new normal, sweetheart." She leans in and gives me a quick kiss.

Micki briefs the guards, then the eight of them surround us. "Okay, let's go."

The flashes are blinding. Ariana squeezes my hand. "Look to the left at the fans."

The crowd cheers. Ariana raises our hands, our fingers intertwined, and offers a blinding smile. She glances at me. I feel her happiness and I'm smiling too.

When we're in front of the fans, Micki puts a hand up to quiet the crowd. "Okay, folks, Ariana and Lee want a minute with each of you. If you organize yourselves into groups of four and remain orderly, you'll be able to say hello and get selfies. If you push and shove and scream, we'll leave."

The crowd does as instructed, and surrounded by the eight guards we greet the fans in groups of four. The photos, the comments, and the autographs take more than just a minute but caught up in the fans' excitement, I love the interaction. A guard escorts two photographers over at a time and allows them to take pictures. We stay until we've met with everyone.

Finally, our cars pull up, we wave to the cheering crowd, and we get in. I'm in awe of Micki's ability to organize and control the crowd, not just the fans but the paparazzi. Ariana leans in and kisses me.

"That was great. Tomorrow those photos and selfies will be all over the Internet announcing your debut and my return. Kim will be thrilled." Ariana pauses. "Of course, she probably set it up."

CHAPTER SIXTY

Ariana

Some things never change. I'm as horny tonight as I ever was after singing to the huge arena crowds. I guess size doesn't matter, because I'm raring to go tonight. I side-eye Lee, trying to gauge whether she's feeling sexy too. As soon as we're in the car, I lean over and kiss her and I'm not sure whether I smell her arousal or mine. She responds immediately, but I sense she's holding back. Knowing her she's probably trying to protect me.

I whisper in her ear, "Have I ever told you how performing, feeling the love from the audience, always leaves me in a high state of arousal?" Lee heats up immediately, so I probe her ear with my tongue, then whisper, "What about you?"

Her eyes jump to the front of the car. Ah, she's inhibited. "Micki, please raise the privacy screen." Lee relaxes, but she's breathing fast. "My previous performances were so long ago I don't remember." She turns her head, her lips crush mine, and her tongue does exquisite things to my mouth and tongue.

When she pulls away, she grins. "But based on tonight's performance and our time with the fans, I can say, without a doubt, that feeling the love from fans leaves me in a high state of arousal as well."

We separate as the car stops at the front door to my house. I'm puzzled when Micki immediately opens my door and Frankie gets Lee's. "Aren't you going to clear the house?"

Micki smirks. "I know how you are after a performance, but I wasn't sure tonight until you had me raise the privacy screen. I called ahead and had Molly and Kelly clear it so you could go right in. It's all yours." She opens the door and stands aside.

I punch Micki's arm. "Thanks, wise guy." I drag Lee into the house and slam the door, but I can still hear Micki laughing. She really does know me. I like it.

Before I can comment, Lee has me against the door, her mouth crushing mine, her hands under my shirt. I'm wet and ready, but I'd rather make love on the bed instead of the hardwood floor. I push her away. "Bed."

She's disoriented for a moment, then she nods, takes my hand, and almost drags me upstairs to our bedroom. There will be no slow and sweet tonight, at least not for a while. We shed our clothing. Lee herds me to the bed, pushes me down, and stretches out on top of me. The heat as we go skin to skin is off the charts. I struggle to flip her under me, but even though I'm back to my former strength, Lee is stronger, and she pins me down. She kisses my forehead, my eyes, my nose, my chin, my jaw, then moves down my neck, to my shoulders, my chest, and my breasts. I writhe and moan as her hands cup and massage, her tongue licks, and her mouth closes around a nipple. Just when I think I'm going to come she moves down and down until she buries her face in my pubic hair. She inhales and makes a sound that's either a moan or a groan, then slides down to my feet. She massages my feet then kisses my toes. Oh. My. Lord. Pleasure shoots through my body. It's almost too much, then she's kissing and massaging my calves and thighs. She bats my hands away as I try to bring her up where I can kiss and touch her. She plants herself between my legs and licks and sucks my upper thighs. Her tongue lightly touches my clit, then she slides a finger inside me and another. She curls her fingers, finding the spot she knows so well, and sets a steady rhythm. My heart pounding, gasping for air, I climb higher and higher, until I scream her name and convulse with exquisite pleasure that seems to go on for days. Lee slides up and wraps me in her arms. When I open my eyes and lift my head, Lee gazes at me, love radiating from her. I'm overwhelmed with love for her. We're quiet for a few minutes, then I roll her over and begin my loving assault.

We both are so exhausted from the day and Lee is as boneless as I am after I make love to her, so we snuggle and fall asleep.

CHAPTER SIXTY-ONE

Lee

We wake our usual time this morning and make love. In contrast to last night, where we devoured each other, this morning is slow and gentle, more like worshiping each other. I've never felt this passionate about anyone before Ariana. Being with her is easy. And that's never been true before, especially with Gina. I force myself away from that thought, focus on Ariana, on how happy I am with her. And fulfilled in a way I never thought possible.

Ariana lifts her head off my chest. "Seems like there's some heavy thinking going on."

"I'm just thinking about how much I love you and how happy I am with you."

She kisses me lightly. "Funny. I was thinking the same about you. Even before the accident, I never dreamed I would have a love like ours." She kisses me more deeply. "There's nothing I'd like more than to stay in bed and make love, but I really need some exercise. How about we grab a light bite, then run, have breakfast, shower together, and get back into bed for the rest of the day."

"We could shower together now."

Ariana tickles me. "No way. We'll never make it downstairs if we start again. Let's get dressed."

By the time I'm dressed, Ariana is in the kitchen with a cup of coffee, two eggs frying, and two English muffins toasting. She hands me a cup. "I texted Graciela to say we'll need breakfast in about two hours, but this should hold us for now." She adds some avocado on each English muffin and tops it with a fried egg. "Want a sandwich?"

"Are you kidding. I'm starving. We used a lot of energy last night."

Ariana smirks and hands me the sandwich, but before I take a bite my cell phone rings. I freeze when I see the caller's name.

Ariana notices my reaction. "What's wrong?"

"It's Amelia, Gina's best friend." I'm terrified and my voice is wobbly.

"Maybe it's not bad news." Ariana moves behind me and wraps her arms around me. "Maybe she saw something about the performance or heard your recording played and is calling to congratulate you."

Her theory is much better than the scenario I imagine. I put the phone on speaker and accept the call. "Amelia." I try to sound normal. "What's up?"

"Lee?" I glance at Ariana and mouth, "Is she whispering?"

Ariana nods and tilts her head toward my phone.

"Gina is here with the girls. She wants to leave them with me. She's not high or anything, but she's nervous and rambling."

Ariana walks away and speaks to the guard out on the deck. "I'll be there in twenty minutes. Let her go, but please try to keep the girls with you." I hear a scuffle. "It's Lee, not the police."

"Let me talk to her." More scuffling, then Gina comes on the phone. "Lee? It's Gina. Please don't call the cops. I didn't mean to take them."

Frankie runs in and stops short. "Keep her talking," she mouths and points outside. I follow her to the armored car where Ariana, Micki, and two other guards are already seated. "Geez, Gina, how do you accidentally disappear for months with two little girls?" I bring up Amelia's contact information and show it to Frankie. She whispers to Micki, then keys it into the GPS.

Ariana points to my seat belt and I snap it into place. Micki steps on the gas. The other armored car with another four guards is right behind us. Micki puts the privacy panel up. I assume they're calling the police.

Gina's laugh is hollow. "I was high. And by the time I was able to think clearly, I knew I was in deep shit, and I couldn't figure out how to get them back to you. I'm sorry."

"I'll bet." I catch myself. If I antagonize her, she might run with the girls. "Are they all right?"

"They're great. I was lucky. I met Holly, a recovering addict who helped me get clean and took care of the three of us. But they miss you something terrible."

"Why bring them back now?"

The line goes dead. "Gina?"

My phone rings. "She's gone, Lee. She heard sirens and thought you called the police. We have the girls. She kissed them and ran out." Amelia's voice is shaky, but she sounds relieved.

"Are they okay?"

"They seem to be in good shape."

"Do they know I'm coming for them?"

"Not yet. Everything happened so quickly, I haven't been able to stop shaking."

The sirens are so loud I can't hear what Amelia is saying, then the call cuts off.

A minute later my phone rings. Amelia again. "Sorry, the police questioned us about Gina's car before going after her. I hope she doesn't do anything foolish." Amelia is crying. "Thank God she left the girls."

My girls are safe, my girls are safe. Tears run down my face, and the tension ebbs, leaving my body limp. I sit up, afraid for Gina. "Are you sure Gina wasn't high? Did you see the car she's driving?"

"I'm sure. We think it was a black Honda." She hesitates. "She did a horrible thing but still…"

As I listen to Amelia is sobbing, I squeeze my eyes closed and Ariana dabs at my face with a tissue. "We'll be there in less than ten minutes." I disconnect.

I call Detective Sharp and give her the information. "I'll check on the patrol cars, but black Hondas are pretty popular, so I don't have high hopes."

There's nothing to do now but breathe until we get there. I'm fluctuating between elation and anxiety. Will they remember me? Will they blame me for not being there?

Ariana grabs my hand and holds tight as we speed through Austin to the suburb where Amelia lives with her wife, Sandy.

When we stop, Micki turns to me. "I know you're anxious to see your daughters, but your ex could have put a gun to your friend's head to get you here. She may be holding everyone hostage, so we need to clear the house before you and Ariana go in."

I'm about to object when the front door opens, and Amelia and her wife, Sandy, each with a girl in her arms, walk onto the porch.

"Oh, my God, it's them."

Before anyone can stop me, I'm out of the car and running toward the porch. The girls see me and wiggle out of the arms holding them and run to me. Laughing and crying, I kneel and wrap them both in my arms. They're giggling and laughing.

Out of the corner of my eye, I see Micki speaking to Amelia and Sandy, then Micki and three other guards enter the house with Sandy.

Surrounded by four guards, Ariana kneels and wraps her arms around the three of us.

The girls are touching my face and kissing me. "You came," Mara says. "We always miss you, but today you came."

Amelia is gaping at Ariana. "Are you? You look like—"

Always polite, Ariana responds. "I'm Ariana, Lee's girlfriend."

"Really?"

"Really." Ariana's smile is dazzling. I expect Amelia will be a puddle soon.

Micki comes out. "All clear." She looks at Amelia. "Can we take this in the house?"

Amelia snaps out of her trance. "Yes, of course, Please come in."

We walk in, but Micki orders two of the guards to remain at the front door and two to stay with the cars. Micki and the three guards in the house do their best to fade into the background as Ariana and I sit on the sofa with Mara between us and Tessa on my other side. I place an arm over each of them and hold them close.

"This is my girlfriend, Ariana. We're going to talk to Amelia and Sandy for a few minutes, then we'll all go home together. Okay?" Two little heads nod. Ariana places a hand on Mara's leg.

"What happened?" I look at Amelia and Sandy.

"She rang the bell and walked in with the girls. We were dumbfounded. I lit into her about stealing your house and kidnapping the girls and now involving us in her crimes," Sandy says. "I think I made her nervous."

"And she got paranoid when she heard me on the phone with you. That's why she grabbed the phone." Amelia shrugs. "The sirens were the last straw. I was surprised. She seemed connected to the girls and even stopped to kiss them goodbye before dashing out."

"Did she tell you why she came today? She could have come here anytime."

"She said she heard an announcement on the radio that you were singing somewhere in Austin last night and she planned to leave them there while you were on stage, but they were all tired when they arrived in Austin so she checked into a motel. She dozed off and didn't wake up until the middle of the night. I guess she felt this was a safe place to leave them. Safe for them and safe for her."

"Was she strung out?" I couldn't help but wonder especially since the girls look like she managed to take care of them.

"She said she's clean. She seemed jittery, but I think she was nervous about seeing us after what she did and anxious about the police showing up." Amelia hesitates. "Other than being nervous, she seemed like her old self, confident and put together."

"We found those suitcases and that box on the porch after she left." Sandy tilts her head, indicating the three items. "She must have put them there before she rang the bell."

Before I can say anything, the guards carry the suitcases and the box outside. I stand. "By the way, where are your kids?"

Amelia laughs. "With my mom and dad. Today is our anniversary and they took the kids for the weekend to give us some time alone."

"Happy anniversary. I'm sure you didn't expect so much drama this morning. But thank you."

Ariana meets my eyes, and I tip my head understanding what she's about to do. She smiles at Amelia and Sandy. "Happy anniversary. Are you doing something special tonight?"

Sandy takes Amelia's hand. "Having time alone is special when you have three little ones, so we'll just hang out here and order takeout."

Ariana leans toward them. "I really appreciate you helping Lee get her daughters back. I'd love to treat you to a special anniversary dinner at my favorite Italian restaurant, if you'd let me."

Sandy looks uncomfortable. "You don't have to do that. What Gina did to the three of them was horrible. I don't know what I'd do if someone stole my kids. We don't need a reward or anything."

Ariana flashes her million-dollar smile. "I don't have to do it, but I really want to. It would make me happy. Just tell me what time."

"Hey, if it makes you happy, it makes me happy." Amelia grins. "Eight o'clock would be perfect." Sandy raises her eyebrows but doesn't comment.

"Okay. One more request. If you're free tomorrow, Lee and I are hosting a barbecue and pool party at our place, and we'd love to have you join us, with or without your children. Lee will text you the information after we leave. Just give your name at the gate."

Amelia blushes and turns to Sandy, who is grinning. "Thank you. We'd love to come, right, Amelia?"

"Yes, we'd love it." She looks like she might pass out.

Ariana turns to Micki. "Please make a reservation for them and give them the information."

Micki takes out her phone as she steps away.

The girls are hanging onto me for dear life, making it hard to stand. Ariana kneels in front of us and speaks softly. "We need to be safe in the car, so would one of you let me carry you and hold you on my lap so we can all have seat belts?" Ariana touches my arm. "Is that all right with you?"

I'm reluctant to let either of them go now that I have them, but I'm pleased Ariana is offering to share in their care. "Are you okay letting Ariana hold you, Mara?"

"Are you going to the Army again?" Mara asks.

"No." I hug them tighter. "I promise I won't leave you again."

"Okay."

Ariana opens her arms. "Come on, girlfriend." Mara giggles and leans into Ariana's arms. Ariana's smile is so sweet, if I wasn't already in love with her, I would have fallen right then. We say goodbye and leave. Two guards on the porch are going through the suitcases and the box. Four others escort us to the car. We slide in and buckle up.

Micki comes out of the house, stops to chat with the guards, then they carry everything to the cars. When everything is stowed, Micki gets into the driver's seat and turns. "Hi there, Mara and Tessa. I'm Micki and"—she points—"this is Frankie, we're both happy to see you." She looks at me. "We checked the suitcases and the box and there are no surprises in them." She grins. "And Amelia and Sandy are ecstatic about the anniversary dinner."

"Thanks, Micki." I reach over and pat Ariana's hand. "You made Amelia's day, probably her month."

"I hope it's all right. What they did is important, so the dinner for their anniversary seemed like a good idea. And Amelia is obviously a fan, so inviting them to come tomorrow seemed like the right thing to do. Give me your phone and I'll text them."

I hand her my phone. She types a long message, then gives the phone to me. I read the text: *Ariana and I would love for you to come to our house any time after noon Sunday, for lunch, dinner, and swimming. Kids welcome. The address follows.*

I smile. They'll be thrilled.

CHAPTER SIXTY-TWO

Ariana

When I woke this morning reveling in the feelings from last night's post-performance sex, sex which put any previous post-performance sex to shame because it wasn't just sex, it was world-shaking, passionate lovemaking, I didn't think the day could get any better.

And then Lee got the call. And seeing her relief having Mara and Tessa in her arms, seeing her love and her happiness, made me love her even more. The girls are adorable.

Poor things can't bear to be away from Lee. It's understandable. Happily, they seem to have accepted me into their little family bubble, so Lee and I walk with the girls between us, all four of us holding hands. Then we visit the swings I'd had installed when Kim's kids were young. After a lunch of tomato soup and grilled cheese, we take a golf cart and drive out to the stables where they pet the horses and the ponies. It's obvious they're exhausted, so we promise pony rides tomorrow. We spend the rest of the afternoon at the pool, trying to teach the girls to swim, but we do more splashing and laughing than swimming. We have plenty of time to do that.

Back at the house the girls have a simple dinner of chicken fingers and french fries, which Graciela promises her grandchildren love. They're both fighting sleep when we finish, so we decide to bathe them in the morning. But as we put on their pajamas, Mara says, "Holly always reads us a bedtime story. Will you read to us?" Diplomat that she is, she seems to include me in the request. Lee and I exchange a look, then she hugs the two of them. "We'd love to read to you. Choose a book." As soon as they've brushed their teeth, the girls make a beeline for the box of books and toys that Gina brought, and each picks out a book for us to read. They climb into our bed, giggling about how soft it is. I watch Lee read the book Mara picked. She is happy and relaxed, and her daughters are rapt and totally focused on her. I open Tessa's choice. And tear up at the inscription. "To Tessa, I wish you a wonderful life with Lee, your new mom. And I hope you never forget the happy times we had together. I love you so much. Auntie Holly."

I feel Holly's pain. I already feel myself falling for these two beautiful, resilient girls. I'm so thankful she was there for them.

After the girls fall asleep, I point out the inscription to Lee.

She smiles. "Yes, she wrote something similar in Mara's book. Knowing she cared for and about them helps me feel less guilty about not being there for them."

We decide to wash all their clothing, so we go to the bedroom next door and we each open a suitcase. I glance at Lee as she steps back quickly and stares into the suitcase. I move closer. There's an envelope with her name scrawled on it. "That's Gina's handwriting," Lee says.

I put my arms around her. "Open it. We have the girls, so how bad can it be?"

Lee removes two handwritten pages and reads the letter to me.

Dear Lee,

I'm truly sorry. I desperately needed money for drugs so I can almost justify pretending to be you, stealing your money and your house, but with the clarity I have now that I'm in recovery, I can't justify taking Mara and Tessa away from you. I'll never forgive myself so I don't expect you to forgive me, but I do need to make amends.

As I'm sure you see, the girls are in good health and good spirits. I wish I could take credit for that, but Holly is responsible. Holly is also a recovering addict. One morning about a week after I left Austin, we were in the car in the parking lot of a grocery store. I was high and the girls were crying because they were hungry. Holly spotted us and when she couldn't get my attention immediately recognized our situation. She got the girls to let her in the car, woke me, then drove us to her house. She left me in the car sleeping, took the girls inside, fed them, and put then down for a nap. Her next step was to dispose of the drugs she found in the car.

When I was relatively alert, Holly offered me a deal. I could stay with her, but I would have to attend daily NA meetings and commit to getting straight. Or I could leave. But the girls, who she thought were my nieces, would stay and she would take them to social services. I thought about it and agreed to try.

Holly is wonderful. She has a big heart and adores Mara and Tessa. She spent as much time as she could with them, made sure they ate well, got enough sleep, were clean and had clean clothes. And beyond the necessities, she played with them, sang to them, read to them, took them to the park, to the movies, and taught them about the world. For some reason, this beautiful soul sees goodness in me, and we've fallen in love.

Recently, Mara asked Holly when Auntie Lee was coming. Curious she asked, who is Auntie Lee? Mara told her about their parents' death, about you adopting them, and coming for them when you get out of the Army. Realizing the girls were not related to me, Holly pressured me for their story. When I confessed, she was shocked. Although she loves me, she said if I didn't immediately return them to you, she wouldn't have anything to do with me. That she would find you and bring the girls home.

A day or two later I heard you singing on the radio, and they announced you'd be performing in Austin. I drove to Austin intending to leave the girls at the venue, but I was exhausted from the drive and stressed about the possibility of being recognized and arrested, and I fell asleep in the motel. When I woke in the middle of the night, I realized I'd missed you and I didn't know where to find you. I lost all my contacts when I got rid of my phone and bought a burner, but I knew where Amelia and Sandy lived. I hoped Amelia would play intermediary so I could leave the girls and get away before you could call the police.

Just so you know, I didn't intend to kidnap the girls. I was high and in a rush to get out of Austin before you came home so I threw them in the car without considering what I was doing. And then when I sobered up, I had no idea how to get in touch with you. If I was thinking clearly at the time, I would have brought them to Carley and Tammy before I left town.

Also, the $10,000 cash in the other envelope is part of the money I got from the sale of the house. I was afraid that withdrawing all of it at one time would call attention to me. I'm not sure yet how to get the rest to you without exposing myself to arrest. I hate being a fugitive, but I'd rather die than go to jail. Maybe I can get the money to you through Amelia.

By the way, congratulations on the recording. You sound great.
Gina
P.S. Now that I'm not angry with you, I've grown fond of the girls. Who knew I liked children?

P.S.S. Holly is really attached to Mara and Tessa and this separation is painful for her. I hope if she ever appears, you'll let her see them.

Lee doesn't say anything. Finally, I ask, "What are you feeling?"

She looks up, tears in her eyes. "I'm thankful for the kindness of people like Holly. Without her the girls might have been scarred for life. Instead, they are healthy and happy. And I'm feeling bad for Gina."

"You feel bad for her?" I'm incredulous.

Lee shrugs. "It sounds like Holly gives her the support and love that I couldn't. If Gina had hurt Mara and Tessa, I would want her punished, but they seem fine. And, at this point, I don't really care about the house or the money. I don't want to send her to jail."

I wrap my arms around her. "You're incredible."

She shrugs again. "Listen, it takes two to make a relationship. I should never have married Gina. But I did, and, unfortunately, I couldn't be there for her, physically or emotionally. If I had been, she might not have started using again."

"Hey, don't blame yourself."

She smiles gently. "I'm just taking responsibility for my part in this. I'm going to think about it for a day or two, then talk to Jonah about whether I can withdraw the charges."

"You would let her go free? I mean she did commit forgery and theft, and, whether she meant to or not, she kidnapped your daughters and kept them for months."

"I know, I know. I need to think about it." Lee puts the letter aside and looks at the clothing in the suitcase. "We don't need to wash anything. It looks like everything is clean."

I check. The suitcase I'd opened contains the envelope with $10,000 cash and clean clothing. I hand the envelope to Lee. "This will be their bedroom once they adjust and aren't afraid to be separated from you, so let's put their things in this dresser."

Graciela brings our dinner to our bedroom so we can be there if the girls wake up, then we spend a quiet night snuggling and making out. We sleep with the girls between us, our hands clasped over them.

CHAPTER SIXTY-THREE

Lee

I wake up early, but Ariana is already out of bed. I want to be here when the girls wake up, so I lie there listening to them breathing. Poor things are probably stressed by the change in their lives and exhausted from everything we did yesterday. They seem all right, but who knows what harm being dragged away from everything and everyone they know has caused. I make some notes on my phone. 1. Find a therapist who works with children. 2. Call Liana and Caroline, their nannies, to see if they're available. It would be good for Mara and Tessa to have familiar faces around when they accompany me to the recording studio, interviews, meetings or any place where I can't give them my full attention.

The door opens and Ariana walks in with two cups of coffee. I get out of bed, and we sit on the sofa again, drinking our coffee. "We need to bathe the girls this morning." I realize I've assumed Ariana is interested. "Or I can do it myself if you don't want to be bothered."

She stares at me like I'm crazy. "Hey, I told you I love kids. I'm all in on co-parenting if you're willing to share them with me."

"I would love it."

"I spoke to Kim earlier and told her about the girls. She's excited for you and asked if she could come earlier to meet them. She gave me the name of her pediatrician in case we want to have a doctor check them. She also asked if we needed her to do anything."

"I was just thinking Mara and Tessa lost their parents, they lost their grandmother, and then I disappeared so they may have abandonment issues. Kim seems to know everyone so maybe she could refer a therapist who works with children."

Ariana laughs. "If she doesn't personally know one, I have no doubt she knows who to ask. I haven't found anything she can't get done, and I've known her since we were ten years old."

"She must have been a little dynamo. Planning, organizing, making things happen."

"She was." Ariana laughs again. "That's how I came to live with her family. She noticed the bruises I was hiding, then she noticed I never brought lunch to school, and she started bringing a sandwich and fruit for me every day. Little by little she got me to confess that my parents and sister and brothers abused me and withheld food most days. She confided in her parents, they spoke to me, then brought in the local authorities. My parents were given the choice of jail or giving up their rights to me, a no-brainer for them. I owe Kim my life. It took me five years in therapy to understand that I wasn't to blame, that I was a victim of a phenomenon called scapegoating where for some reason one individual in a family is blamed for all family problems." She smiles. "The good news is that as soon as they could, Mom and Dad Calandre adopted me. And Kim has never stopped advocating and caring for me."

"You two have done very well together so I'm sure she's been repaid a million times over. And I don't mean in dollars."

"Maybe, but the thing about Kim is that she never thinks in terms of being repaid. She is truly a good person. She does what she does because she wants to and because she can. But you never want to be on her bad side or hurt one of her people."

"Mama?" Mara sits up wild-eyed, thrashing.

I'm beside her in seconds and pull her into my arms. "It's Auntie Lee and Auntie Ariana, Mara. You're safe with us." I rock her until she calms down.

"Auntie Lee?" Tessa sits up and rubs her eyes. "I thought I dreamed you."

"No, honey, it's me." I pull her into my arms with Mara. "I've got you and I'm never leaving you again."

Ariana sits next to us and wraps her arms around the three of us.

"I'm hungry," Tessa says.

"Me too," I say. "What about you, Mara?"

She yawns. "Can we have pancakes?"

Not sure of our agenda today, I look at Ariana. "Graciela's catering team is setting up outside now. They'll start serving breakfast for us and your family in about twenty minutes. If you can't wait, I can make you some toast."

"I can wait," Tessa says.

"Me too," Mara says.

I stand. "Good. That gives us time for a quick bath before breakfast. Come on, you can brush your teeth while I fill the tub."

"Is it all right if I leave you guys for a couple of minutes to check in with Graciela to make sure they're no problems?"

"Of course." This is a big day for Ariana. She must be feeling overwhelmed at the idea of spending so much time with so many people, some of them strangers and some of them loved ones trying to make up for lost time. I kiss her deeply, trying to reassure her. Mara and Tessa watch for a second but don't seem particularly interested. I wonder if Gina and Holly were affectionate in front of them. I push the hair off Ariana's face. "You'll be fine."

We separate and I take the girls into the bathroom. I kneel next to the tub, letting them play before washing them. They giggle and splash water at each other, then they turn on me. Ariana comes in to see what's going on and they splash her too. When all four of us are drenched, Ariana washes Tessa and I wash Mara, then pull the plug. We wrap them in towels, dry them and ourselves. Ariana leaves me to dress them and heads outside.

CHAPTER SIXTY-FOUR

Ariana

I speak to Graciela and of course she has everything under control. I go back into the house. The girls are giggling and it sounds like they're splashing Lee. She's laughing. The minute I join them, they splash me. I'm soaked but full of joy, happy to be part of this small family. While we dry them and ourselves, Lee, always thoughtful, says, "Why don't you take some more time for yourself before people start arriving. We'll come find you when we're dressed."

"A good idea." I throw on dry shorts, a T-shirt, and sandals, put on light makeup, comb my hair, and go downstairs. Standing on the deck, I take a deep breath, turn my face to the sun, and listen to the birds. There's no time for a run now but maybe this evening we can have one of the guards drive the girls in the golf cart while we run.

I walk to the pool where the food stations are being set up, kick off my sandals, and sit on the edge with my feet in the water. My thoughts wander back to the girls. I don't know whether all children are so resilient, but Mara and Tessa inspire me. Their ability to adapt to new places and new people after what they've been through amazes me. Rather than focus on the bad things, they seem to be in the moment, letting the good feelings in.

I could learn a lot from them. I've been dreading today. I'll be exposed to lots of people, for a longer time than I have since the accident, and I'll have to engage. I've done well so far, but I'm afraid of sensory overload. Kim and Lee assured me I can take private time away from everyone when I need it, but maybe I can relax if I face each person or small group in the moment rather than lumping them into a massive crowd waiting to pounce.

"Good morning, Ms. Calandre. May I join you."

The deep voice jolts me into the present. "Good morning, General Wilton." He's in shorts, a T-shirt, and sandals but something about the way he carries himself makes me want to stand and salute. "Please do. Would you rather we switch to lounge chairs?"

"Poolside is good." He slips off his sandals, sits beside me, and dangles his feet in the water. He smiles. "It appears we're family now, so please call me Jaime."

"I will if you call me Ariana."

"Sure. Thank you for inviting us to the performance and for letting us all stay here. Until Kim dropped in to check on us last night we thought this was a fancy hotel."

"Are you comfortable?"

"We are. The staff is very helpful, and the food is wonderful." He clears his throat. "Before the younger members of the family out me, I'll admit I'd never heard your music before last night. And I'm embarrassed to say I didn't know Lee was so talented. I enjoyed the performance. You are fabulous, alone and together. I'm so proud of Lee. I'm told you've had a long and successful career, but since you are part of my family now, I'm hoping I'm not overstepping by saying I'm proud of you too. I'm happy you and Lee found each other." He drapes an arm over my shoulders.

I lean into him, moved by his openness. At least some of Lee's personality comes from him. "Thank you. It's probably obvious how happy Lee and I are, but I thank the universe every day for sending her to me."

"Ariana, Ariana." I turn toward the voices. It's Mara and Tessa dragging Lee to me. They come at me quickly, and Jaime and I catch them to keep them from tumbling into the pool. I grab Tessa and he grabs Mara. They giggle hysterically.

"Good morning, Dad."

His eyes widen. "Are these your daughters, Lee? When did you—?"

She doesn't wait for him to finish. "We got them back yesterday."

Noticing it's a strange man holding her, Mara's eyes widen and she struggles to get away. Lee takes her. "Don't be frightened, Mara. That's my dad and he would never hurt you."

She stares at him. "Is he my grandpa?"

Lee's eyes get big. "Uh, I…"

Jaime smiles and pats Mara's leg. "I'd love to be your grandpa, Mara. And yours too, Tessa, if you'll have me."

Lee is shocked. She was so worried about how her parents would feel about her having two adopted children that she never considered they would welcome them.

I jump in to give Lee time to catch her breath. "Are you alright with that Mara? Tessa?"

Tessa looks at Mara, who hesitates, then smiles. "Yes."

Tessa follows her sister's lead. "Yes. But can we eat? I'm starving."

I look toward the food stations. They're serving. "Why don't we all have breakfast together?" I stand with Tessa. "Coming, Jaime?"

Lee's eyes almost pop out hearing me use her dad's first name.

He gets up and opens his arms. Mara looks at Lee. She nods. "It's okay, but only if you want to." Mara swings into his arms, and we make our way to select our breakfast.

CHAPTER SIXTY-FIVE

Lee

I sit with the girls and help them with their milk and chocolate chip pancakes, while Ariana and my dad go fetch omelets, toast, and coffee for us. I can't believe that Ariana is on first name terms with my dad. I guess he's mellowed. Or maybe she charmed him.

Before they get back, my mom arrives with her breakfast. She hugs me from behind, then sits across the table. Since they're calling my dad grandpa, I introduced my mom to the girls as their grandma. She's surprised but looks pleased. She coos at the girls and then launches into a monologue about how wonderful it is to be staying here in Ariana's guest house, then raves about our performance, our solos and duets. She snorts and says she's not clueless like Dad and has always enjoyed Ariana's music. I'm not surprised when she jumps up and greets Ariana with a huge hug. And neither is Ariana, judging by her smile.

Ariana sits next to me and the four of us focus on the girls until Jimmy, my oldest brother, his wife, three children, and seven grandchildren surround us. I introduce Ariana and the girls, and after we chat a few minutes they move on to get something to eat. Not long after that, my brother Eric and his family stop by to meet Ariana and the girls then go in search of breakfast. When my brother Mark and his family approach a short while later, I realize this whole family meet and greet has been staged so as not to overwhelm Ariana. I smile as the last wave leaves us to finish our breakfast, and Ariana pokes me. "What's so funny?"

"Not funny. Mom, did you organize the family so Ariana wouldn't be freaked out?"

My mom laughs. "Well, we are a lot of people, and we can be loud so when Kim explained that meeting a lot of people at once might be too much for Ariana, Dad and I decided to bring them on in waves."

"Thank you." Ariana smiles at my parents. She seems to be enjoying getting to know them. We chat for a bit longer, then after Mom extracts our promise to join them for dinner tonight, she and Dad head to the pool.

Ariana places her hand on my thigh, and I cover it with mine. The girls are excited by the number of small children running around, but they aren't ready to leave me to join in the games. We finish our breakfast and stroll over to where the Calandre family is eating. Ariana introduces me and the girls to everyone. Although she told me that she and Kim are the only ones in her family who aren't twins, seeing them all together with Kim's two sets of twins is mind-boggling.

CHAPTER SIXTY-SIX

Ariana

I thought Lee's eyes would pop out of her head seeing my family for the first time. Knowing we are a family of twins is different than seeing the twins and their twin children and twin grandchildren all together.

"Damn, I've only had coffee," Lee mutters, "but I'm seeing double. And they all look like Kim."

I laugh as my mom pulls me into a crushing hug. "I really want to sit and chat, but General Kim has organized us into small groups, so we'll have to meet later on the sly." I laugh again. I love how she teases about Kim, the kid she admires the most. Other than me, of course.

I turn to Lee and the girls. "Mom, these beautiful girls are Lee's daughters, Mara and Tessa."

Mom kneels so she's eye level with the girls. "Hi, I'm Ariana's mom. I'm so happy to meet you."

Tessa leans into Lee, but Mara smiles. She looks up at Lee. "Is she my grandma, too?"

Before Lee responds, Mom says, "Yes. Call me grandma."

Kim clears her throat and we all gaze at her. "So, Mom, did you forget the plan again?"

"Oh, so sorry, Kimmy, I forgot." Her grin gives away how not sorry she is. "I'll take my seat and wait my turn. See you all later."

Kim shakes her head as Mom strolls away. I punch her arm. "You're just like her."

"Yeah, yeah." She meets my gaze. "Are you doing all right?"

I think for a second and realize I'm more than all right. My fear that large crowds of people would freak me out was unfounded, and I'm enjoying seeing everyone. I'm not sure whether the girls have inspired me or performing again has made me confident, but I feel like my old sociable self. "I'm terrific and I'm looking forward to talking to everyone."

"What about you and the girls, Lee?" Kim asks.

"Other than being stunned to see so many people who look like each other and you, I'm fine. And I think Mara and Tessa are good too."

"I'm thinking that sitting around while you two chat with people will be boring for them, so I've asked Jessie and Jackie to gather some of the young ones and see if Mara and Tessa can be lured into playing some games." Kim looks behind her, waves, then kneels. "Hi, I'm Kim, and these are my daughters Jackie and Jessie. Would you like to play some games with them or listen to their stories if they stay close to your Aunt Lee?"

Lee kneels. "Jackie and Jessie are fun. You can stay with me and Ariana if you want. Or you can try playing with them and stop if you don't like it. It's up to you."

"Okay. If you don't go far," Mara says. And Tessa follows her lead as usual.

Kim leads us to a large table, and Jackie and Jessie sit on the blanket set out next to it. A couple of little girls join the four of them on the blanket and it doesn't take long for them to be immersed in a story one of the twins is reading. "Listen I've organized everyone into small groups so you don't get mobbed. I've asked them to stay fifteen or twenty minutes and then move on. After you've seen everyone once, you can circulate freely. Okay?"

"Why am I not surprised? But I'm happy I can ease in to it."

We sit, and the first group joins us. I introduce Lee and we chat for fifteen minutes, then they leave, and the next group moves in. The groups shuffle in and out for about an hour and a half. It's not all family, though. Some of my high school friends are here with their spouses as well.

It's been pleasurable, not overwhelming, but neither of us is used to so much socializing and we go back to the house so the girls and we can take naps.

Once the girls doze off, Lee and I cuddle. I'm in that lovely, drifting place between being awake and asleep, and I recognize that I'm in my life and I'm happier than I was before because of the woman holding me. Life is good.

An hour later we're restoked and ready to go. We'd already touched base with everyone before our nap, so we're free to stroll or sit and socialize without any pressure. We spend some time with Lee's best friends, Carley and Tammy, who are fun and pleased that Mara remembers them. We chat at the pool with Amelia and Sandy while they keep an eye on their kids. They're appreciative of the anniversary dinner I'd arranged and seemed happy to be here. At some point all four of our parents join us, which is wonderful. They even make plans to get together for dinner next week. I get to know Lee's brothers and their wives a little, and though her great nieces and nephews are shy to start, they warm up to me after a while. My friends and my brothers and sisters are anxious to get to know Lee, and so they come by at various times during the day.

All in all, it's a wonderful day. I enjoy it more than I imagined. At nine we say good night. As the day goes on Mara and Tessa are more and more willing to detach from me and Lee, and under the watchful eyes of Jessie and Jackie, play near us, with the other children. They are exhausted. And so are we. But not too exhausted to make sweet tender love. Being surrounded by people who love us, family and friends, after being isolated so long, is extraordinary. Even though the events that brought us together were horrible, I am so grateful that Kim and my family never gave up on me, that I met Lee, that she saw behind the veil, and that we have each other. Now our little family is at the center of a large circle of love. I'm excited to see where life takes us next.

CHAPTER SIXTY-SEVEN

Ariana

Six Years Later

"Maaama." Twelve-year-old Mara stretches the word out because I'm not moving fast enough for her. "Should I take your dress and guitar downstairs?"

We're not sure why, but after living with us nine months or so, the girls started calling Lee Mommy and me Mama. The first time it happened we were stunned and locked eyes over their heads. When it happened again, we were so grateful for the love and trust it showed that we left the room and cried together.

I wrap my arms around her. "Auntie Micki will be up in a minute to bring my things and Mommy's to the car."

A show of affection is hit or miss these days, but Mara wraps her arms around my waist. "Yum, you smell good."

I kiss the top of her head. "Thanks, sweetie. Do you and Tessa have all your stuff together? And your guitars?"

"Yes." She's only a preteen, but she's already perfected the teen eye roll. "We brought our bags and guitars downstairs earlier."

After hearing us sing and play our guitars, Mara and Tessa asked for guitars so they could sing and play with us. It turned out, like their birth mother, Ella, both girls have lovely voices and, like both birth parents, they are talented musically, so we brought in professionals to train them. They are quite good and always look forward to jamming with Andrea, our lead guitarist, before our concerts. Lately they've been begging to perform with us. We haven't told them, but Lee and I have decided to bring them on stage tonight when Lee joins me for the final encore. It's the first time they'll be in front of such a huge audience.

Micki knocks and walks in. She picks up my garment bag, my suitcase, and my guitar. "We're ready to go when you and Lee are."

"Thanks, Micki. Come on, Mara, let's check on Mommy and Kimmie." I hold out my hand and she takes it. Yes, it's a good day.

We go into Kimmie's bedroom. Our two-year-old is a handful, but she has my genes so it's not surprising. She's bouncing on her bed, giggling and throwing herself at eleven-year-old Tessa, who's on the bed with her. Meggie, Kimmie's nanny, could have dressed her at lot faster than either of us, but we didn't get these early years with our older two, so we prefer to be hands-on moms, even though the frisky two-year-old can be exhausting. Kimmie won't come onstage, but she and Mara and Tessa are always with us no matter where or which of us is performing.

Lee straightens and smiles when she sees me and Mara. "Hey." She kisses me quickly, then hands Kimmie's shoes to Mara. "Please put these on her."

Mara rolls onto the bed and grabs Kimmie. Instead of pulling away, she puts her arms around her big sister's neck. "Mar."

Mara kisses her forehead. "Come on, sissy, let me put your shoes on so we can go bye-bye in the car." She tosses a shoe to Tessa. "You do one."

The little dynamo sits still for her sisters and in a minute she's dressed and out the door with them. We linger for a moment. "Good thing you didn't dress her; you wouldn't have any energy to sing this afternoon."

I brush the hair off her face. "I'm no dummy. I did that once and barely made it to the last song."

"Luckily I only have to sing the last song with you, so I have time to recuperate." Lee checks herself in the mirror. "With all the bouncing I was sure she was going to throw up on me."

"You look fine."

"Are you feeling good enough to do the entire concert alone?" She puts her hand on the bump that only we, our medical team, and Kim know is there. My hands cover hers. I'm three months pregnant, and this time I'm carrying Lee's babies. That's right. Plural. Two of the implanted eggs took. "Drag me on stage if you start to feel too tired. Your fans always love when we appear together."

I pull her arms around me and tuck my face into her neck. "This is my last concert for eighteen months or more, so I really want to be there, for myself and for my fans." I start kissing her neck, then catch myself and pull away. I'm always horny these days and I need the space to not think about making love. She laughs. "Maybe we'll have a few minutes privacy in the dressing room if you need me."

"Dream on. Between the kids, their nannies, Micki and the other guards, our assistants, and Kim, probably most of all Kim"—I laugh— "I'll be lucky to grab the solitary time I need to focus before performing."

Lee wiggles her eyebrows. "I'm really looking forward to tonight after the concert when the kids are asleep."

I punch her shoulder, then kiss her again. "Me too."

I stand on the stage soaking in the love from the audience. "Thank you, thank you. I love you all too." I put my hands together in prayer position and bow again and again.

As I swing up from a bow my gaze goes to the wings where the love of my life stands with our three children—Mara, Tessa, and baby Kimmie in her arms.

I run offstage, taking a minute before the encore. I meet Lee's eyes. She nods. "Mara and Tessa, would you like to sing the encore with Mama and me?"

Their eyes become saucers. Tessa recuperates first. "For real? On the stage in front of the audience?" She looks at Lee.

I wrap my arms around them. "If you feel ready and only if you want to."

Their brilliant smiles confirm they're ready and they want to be out there with us. "Yes," they scream, jumping up and down. I look up. Our assistants have brought their guitars.

"Okay, let's tune up."

Lee hands Kimmie to her godmother Kim. She picks up her guitar. The four of us have done this thousands of times, and when we're done I go back on stage.

I put my hands up and when the crowd quiets, I speak. "You've been so wonderful that I have a special treat for you." My fans know me. Usually "a special treat" means Lee sings a song or two with me, so they start to chant, "Lee. Lee. We want Lee."

I look back at the threesome in the wings and put my hand up again. "Not just Lee, though. This is a treat I've never shared before today. Please welcome Lee Wilton, Mara Calandre-Wilton and Tessa Calandre-Wilton."

The audience is on its feet, cheering and whistling as my three precious girls stride onto the stage. The three of them hold hands and bow several times, then Mara takes my hand, connecting the four of us. I feared the roar of the fifty thousand-plus people would be scary for them, but though they appear a little nervous, they smile as we wait for the audience to calm down.

Once the audience is quiet, I squeeze Mara's hand and drop it. She drops Tessa's hand, and Tessa drops Lee's hand. I strum the first few notes and the three of them follow, then I sing the first verse, and as we'd rehearsed, one by one, the three of them join in. From where I'm standing we sound terrific. And if the roar of the crowd is any indication, they agree. I turn to my girls. "Want to do one more?"

Of course, they do. It's in their blood, in our blood. After we finish, I turn and point. "Show some love for Mara Calandre-Wilton." I point again. "And how about some love for Tessa Calandre-Wilton." The look on Tessa's face is priceless. I point again. "And last but not least, show Lee Wilton how much you love her."

When Lee leads the girls off the stage, I turn to the audience. "You guys are wonderful, so here's one more for you." I nod at our band, then begin the real final song. I'm feeling tired, but I give it my all. After all it will be a while before I'm in front of an audience again.

This is it. I'm basking in the love from the audience. I've done many concerts since that first performance with Lee six years ago, but the rush never gets old.

"Thank you, thank you. I love you all too." As I always do, I put my hands together in prayer position and bow again and again, soaking in the love.

What can I say? I adore adoring fans. My hands go to the baby bump. Yet, their love pales in comparison to the love of my family.

Bella Books
Happy Endings Live Here
P.O. Box 10543
Tallahassee, FL 32302
Phone: (800) 729-4992
BellaBooks.com

More Titles from Bella Books

Jones – Gerri Hill
978-1-64247-598-2 | 260 pages | Mystery
One weekend getaway, six friends, and a deadly secret that will wash away everything they thought they knew.

Merry Weihnachten – E. J. Noyes
978-1-64247-610-1 | 292 pages | Romance
Christmas traditions aren't the only things getting mixed up when these two hearts collide beneath the mistletoe.

Sweet Home Alabarden Park – TJ O'Shea
978-1-64247-570-8 | 362 pages | Romance
She came to restore a royal estate—she never expected to rebuild her heart.

Dr. Margaret Morgan – Christy Hadfield
978-1-64247-628-6 | 286 pages | Romance
Facing the professor on campus everyone hates is terrifying—but falling for her might be even worse.

Overtime – Tracey Richardson
978-1-64247-630-9 | 278 pages | Romance
A charming romance about second chances, found family, and scoring the goal that matters most.

The Big Guilt – Renée J. Lukas
978-1-64247-657-6 | 206 pages | Romance
What if the one who got away became the one you can't have?